EYE
BROTHER
HORN

Bridget Pitt

CATALYST PRESS
EL PASO, TEXAS, USA

For further information, write info@catalystpress.org

In North America, this book is distributed by
Consortium Book Sales & Distribution, a division of Ingram.
Phone: 612/746-2600
cbsdinfo@ingramcontent.com
www.cbsd.com

In South Africa, Namibia, and Botswana,
this book is distributed by Protea Distribution.
For information, email orders@proteadistribution.co.za.

FIRST EDITION
10 9 8 7 6 5 4 3 2 1

ISBN 978-1-946395-76-4

Library of Congress Control Number: 2022944724

For Sicelo Mbatha

and Therese Boulle

EYE
BROTHER
HORN

Bridget Pitt

On its feet there were no toes, and its heel was so long as to penetrate the ground. It was mounted on an animal of great speed and carried a pole which spat fire and thunder and killed all animals it looked at.

A belief was prevalent among the tribes on the coast that white men were not human beings but a production of the sea, which they traversed in large shells, coming near the shores in stormy weather, their food being the tusks of elephants, which they would take from the beach if laid there for them, and placing beads in their room [place], which they obtained from the bottom of the sea.

Descriptions by indigenous people of the first white men in Zululand, as recorded in the Diary of Henry Francis Fynn, documenting his travels through the Natal region from 1824 to 1832. Published by Shuter and Shooter, South Africa 1950, pp 4 to 5

PART ONE
1862 TO 1864
BHEJANE

The rhino bursts from the reeds. Two tons of bone and muscle hurtle towards the women gathering grass for weaving. Their grass bundles fly up as they flee, screaming. As Nomsa races for the trees, her foot catches on a tussock. She stumbles, almost beneath the rhino's feet, and lies curled on her side. The other women fall silent, watching the rhino dip its massive head towards the infant still tied to Nomsa's back.

Two feet of curved black horn tapering to a sharp point— what child can survive this?

Three times it drives its horn towards the boy. Then, with a final squeal, it lumbers back into the reeds. The women run to the two figures lying on the ground, terrified to see what has become of the baby. Yet he is unharmed, save for a graze where the horn brushed his forehead. And a look of strangeness in his eye, as if he'd been lost in distant worlds.

The Reverend Whitaker calls it a miracle. His son was saved by Jesus, he tells everyone. If you come to Jesus, if you have faith in the Lord, you too can be saved.

Few people beyond his tiny congregation believe this explanation. They call the Reverend Whitaker *uMfundisi*, the Teacher, but credit little of what he says. They have their own theories, including witchcraft, ancestral intervention and good luck. But ever after, in that part of KwaMagwaza, the boy is spoken of as inkonyane likabhejane: the Rhino's child.

DANIEL

It's the first story Daniel remembers hearing about himself, and he asks his mother to tell it over and over. She always ends the story by saying, "No need to fear now, Danny. There are no more rhinos nearby. Cousin Roland shot the last one."

But Daniel is not afraid of a *rhino*. The rhino his mother showed him in her picture book is a small gray pig-like creature, which doesn't look frightening at all. What haunts his dreams—and fills him with an emotion too over-whelming to frame in any words—is something nameless and huge. It is a great dark curved thing, blotting out the sky. Beside that is an eye, a gleaming flash of intelligence rimmed with white and blood red. An eye that, through its single fleeting gaze into his own eye, forged some intrac-table bond.

This memory consumes him in sudden moments, making him tearful or enraged. He doesn't link it to the story of the rhinoceros. In that story he was with Nomsa, and Moses was there too, on Thuli's back. But this memory comes to him as a moment of stark isolation. As if there were a time in the world when the only things that existed were him and this formidable entity.

A time before Moses.

He has no way to express it—his voice is too small and he lacks the words to frame it. But one day he watches his mother sketching the dog, which is asleep on the doorstep. He stands beside her, mesmerized by the black line flowing from her pencil as it inscribes the shape of a nose, paws, two small bright eyes—and there is a dog lying on her page. It's a small gray dog—not big and brown like the one on the step—but with the same half-standing-up ears and stumpy tail, and whiskers sprouting from its muzzle.

"Nkosikazi, the women are here for the thatching," Dawid calls from outside.

After his mother goes out, Daniel traces the drawing with his finger. An idea steals up his spine and prickles his scalp. Perhaps he can pin the monster of his dreams onto this paper, just as his mother has captured the dog? He glances around the cluttered little room, checking for hidden observers. Baby Jesus is watching him from the picture on the wall, reaching out from his mother's arms. But Baby Jesus is his friend. More sinister is the double-barreled rifle hanging above the fireplace, fixing him with its cold dark eyes.

He takes the sketchbook and pencil and crouches on the floor beneath the table. He draws the curved thing

3

first beside the dog, scoring the paper nearly through to capture its black, curved pointiness. Then the gleaming eye, small and bright and set deep in dark folds. He stares at them, frightened to see them manifested in the world outside of him. How can he face their hunger alone? He bends over the page and inscribes a wavering circle between the two things. Inside the circle go two small dots and a smiling U. Two bunches of fingers for hands on either side. And there is Moses! Daniel is no longer alone with that memory, for Moses is *there*, right in the middle.

He hears the swish of his mother's skirts and the clopping of her shoes on the polished floor of the veranda. He rips the drawing from the sketchbook and thrusts it into the pocket of the shirt that was cut down to serve as a dress for him. He hurries outside, pushing past his mother, ignoring her calls as he jumps off the veranda and runs away, with the drawing singing in his pocket.

MOSES

Gogo wears long skirts made of old worn cotton that don't rustle or swish, and she moves unhurriedly and noiselessly on bare feet. Her lap is soft and warm and a good place to sleep, but now it is occupied by a dead chicken. Her hands dart at the bird on her knees, sending a flurry of small white feathers drifting across the dirt at her feet. The head of the chicken dangles loosely from its broken neck, its dead eyes fixed on Moses inquiringly as he tries to catch the feathers floating in the air.

"Yebo, mfana wami, yini le? What is it, my boy?" Gogo

asks without looking up, as Daniel runs up. He thrusts a crumpled paper under her nose.

Gogo looks at the paper, head tilted on one side, her hands busy with the feathers. She wrinkles up her eyes as if trying to make out an animal in the tall grass, smiles and nods.

"uBhejane," she declares. "That's the horn of ubhejane—and its eye. But I don't know what this spider is in between."

Moses cranes his neck to peer at the marks scrawled on the page. He sees a multi-spangled star between a moon and a pointy curved mountain.

"Yini ubhejani?" he asks.

Gogo laughs. "What's ubhejane? Isn't bhejane Dani's father?"

Daniel frowns. "uMfundisi is my father."

"A boy may have two fathers. Didn't ubhejane claim you when he spared your life? So then, you're the child of ubhejane, and uMfundisi is also your father."

"Is ubhejane also Moses' father?"

The laughter falls from Gogo's eyes.

"Moses' father is uMvelinqangi. The Lord of the Sky. And the River is your mother, Moses. You are a child of the sky and uMvelinqangi wanted to take you to live with him beyond the clouds. But the River hid you and brought you to uMfundisi to look after."

"Beyond the clouds..." Moses repeats softly, looking up. He lifts his hand to block the sun. "What is beyond the clouds?" He reaches out his other hand to touch the sky, his fingers silhouetted against the high wispy clouds dragged across the sky like sheep's wool when it catches on wire. When he's taller, he will reach it, he thinks. He could climb the pointy mountain in Daniel's picture.

"uMfundisi says Moses' mama and papa went to Jesus. So now his mama and papa are Kazi and uMfundisi, just like me!" Daniel snatches back his paper and crumples it in his pocket.

"Moses has many fathers and mothers here at uMzinyathi. But the River is a special mother. When you feel sad, Moses, sit by the river and you'll hear your mother sing to you..."

Gogo dips the bird back into the pot of water steaming on warm coals beside her. Her hands fly off again, showering their feet with damp feathers. The hen's head jerks with each handful she plucks, making the red comb jiggle against its beak. Moses thinks about his dead mother and father and wonders if a person is still a mother when they're dead.

DANIEL

Later Daniel asks his mother about ubhejane. Again she shows him the pig-like animal in her book. And for the first time he understands that the creature that grazed him with its horn was the dark thing of his dreams.

Ubhejane.

MOSES

When they turn six, they each get a "sailor suit"—white trousers and shirt with a blue and white striped collar that ties in the front. They came with the "Mission Society bundle," the source of all their clothes. The boys stand staring at their new sailor-suited selves in the looking-glass in their parents' bedroom. Moses is half-a-head higher and looks even taller in his sailor suit—the trousers are already too short. His face is neat and sharp, his eyes bright and black like the eyes of the robin that sits on the veranda rail waiting for scraps. Daniel is stocky with freckled cheeks and a snub nose, and round eyes the flickering brown of pebbles under water.

Daniel runs outside to show his sailor suit to Nomsa, but Moses is frozen by the stiff whiteness of his clothes. He sits silently on the veranda steps with buttoned lips and huge eyes, and when Kazi brings him blueberry pie, he shakes his head, imagining a purple stain from the blueberries erupting on that whiteness—especially after Daniel gets blueberry juice on his trousers. When uMfundisi scolds him for staining his clothes, Daniel throws his pie on the floor and stamps on it and has to sit in the corner.

"Give Dani my pie," Moses whispers to Nomsa. Later, when uMfundisi is not looking, she does.

Gogo gives Moses a set of nine animals that she molded from clay, baked hard in the fire, and painted with ink made from soot and oxblood. She brings them in a woven basket with a lid and names each one as he takes it out: indlovu, the elephant; ubhejane, the rhino; indlulamithi, the giraffe; ingonyama, the lion; idube, the zebra; ingwe, the leopard; impisi, the hyena; and inyathi the buffalo. She says that once these animals roamed the hills around the mission station, grazing, hunting or browsing in the very

7

place where the house is now, but white hunters chased them away so now they hide in the great Nkandla forest. "But if you keep very quiet at nighttime, you will still hear the roar of the lions."

Daniel wants to play with them, but Moses insists on keeping them in their basket. Daniel can be so loud, so boisterous, he is bound to set the animals galloping away. That night when Daniel is asleep, Moses takes out each animal and holds it before the lamp, imagining that the huge shadows cast on the wall are the living versions of the clay creatures, that the walls are trees, and that he lies on a bed of grass, surrounded by buffalos and elephants and rhinos. He holds his breath and tries to hear the roar of the lion. But all he can hear is the murmur of his parents in the front room, Daniel's soft breathing and the rustle of the straw mattress when he moves.

Cousin Roland shot the last rhino, Kazi said. Maybe he shot all the lions too.

He remembers Cousin Roland. Cousin Roland laughed a lot, his teeth leaping from his dark beard. His teeth were so square and so white—he would hold Daniel's fingers to his mouth, and say, Shall I bite your little fingers off? Just one little finger? You've got ten, you won't miss one. And everyone would laugh, as if it was a joke. But Moses dreamed of those square white teeth in the night, biting the heads off five baby sparrows, one by one.

Cousin Roland was too big and too loud for their small house. He seemed to stuff every corner of it with his presence. He carried Daniel on his shoulders which made him laugh, and tickled him which made him cry.

He didn't tickle or carry Moses—or threaten to bite off his fingers.

When he looked at Moses, he seemed to see right through him to the wall beyond so that Moses felt himself shrink to a tiny beetle under his gaze.

DANIEL

Their father says that they're now too big to sleep in their parents' room. They must sleep in a real iron bed in the storeroom, head to toe. The storeroom has two doors—one to the front room and one to the outside—and a window overlooking the trees growing down at the stream. The room smells of leather and tobacco and the fragrant imphepho bundles that their mother hangs to keep away flies. It's crammed with shelves holding jars, bottles, boxes and books, and with meal sacks and tin trunks filled with cloth for bargaining. An assegai spear and sword stand in the corner beside the tool chest. Hooks on the wall hold pieces of harness, rolls of dried tobacco leaves and an elephant tail.

Cousin Roland also shot the elephant that once owned that tail. uMfundisi says the elephant doesn't need its tail anymore because it's dead. But Daniel is disturbed by the theft of the tail and imagines the elephant's friends coming to fetch it, filling the room with their great trunks and tusks. He once left it out by the umsinsi tree for the elephant to fetch, but the elephant never came. Nomsa said he was a silly boy and hung the tail back on its hook.

On the wall by the bed, their mother paints a picture

of two boys—one brown and one pink—with white wings and yellow circles over their heads. She says that these are their "guardian angels," sent by God to keep them safe. uMfundisi says the brown angel is "unorthodox," which Daniel hears as "under a box," although it is clearly on the wall. Kazi says, "Show me where in the Bible it says that angels have white skins."

Daniel and Moses call their mother Kazi. It's from Inkosikazi, which is what most of the people call her. Daniel couldn't say it right when he was little, so he said Kazi and now that's her name. They call all the other women on the mission station Mama, except Gogo because she's so old.

At night the storeroom is steeped in menace, and Daniel doubts the angels' power to keep them safe. On their first night, he lies in bed looking at the boxes, meal sacks, and harnesses, transformed by the darkness into things sinister and strange. He can't see their angels and wonders if they have crept under a box after all.

He'd like to creep under a box too. The night is full of terrors—the abathakathi who ride on hyenas. Or the isidawane which carries children away in a basket in its head and feeds on their brains. And didn't Gogo say that uMvelinqangi wanted Moses to live with him beyond the clouds? So then, what was stopping him coming down and snatching Moses from his bed?

He hears the creak of the outside door opening and dives under the bedclothes.

"Vukani, abantwana bami, wake up."

It's Gogo. He opens his eyes to see Moses sitting up in

the stream of moonlight pouring through the door and sees that the angels are back on the wall.

"Thula uthi du...be very quiet, my boys," Gogo whispers. "We mustn't disturb Ma-mfundisi and uMfundisi. Come with me, I want to show you something."

They wind down the steep path through the thicket below the house. The trees loom over them in sinister shapes, but Daniel feels safe with the warm press of Gogo's hand. His feet move over the fallen leaves, gold and black in the moonlight. Somewhere far off a hyena whoops and is answered by another. A nightjar utters its evening prayer: *good-lord-deliver-us*. An eagle owl inquires, *Who? Who?*

At the edge of the stream, Gogo stops and points. Across the water stand two massive beasts with high curved horns and thunderous legs and sides nearly as big as the covered wagon in the shed by the kitchen. They move about slowly, eating leaves from small bushes, silent save for the rustle of the vegetation. One approaches the stream, dips its great head and drinks, meeting its reflection shimmering in the water. It raises its dark muzzle to look straight at them, scattering silver drops that fragment its reflection. The eye and the horn of Daniel's dreams convulse and arc across the river in a flash of recognition.

Bhejane, he whispers.

The leaves on the trees begin shivering as if shaken by an unseen hand. The air fills with a chorus of high voices, cascading like a fall of raindrops...*Inkonyane likabhejane, rhino's child....* He squeezes his eyes shut until the voices quieten. When he opens them, the creatures have gone.

"No rhino has been here for many seasons," Gogo says softly. "They came back to greet you boys—it's a gift."

"Our best birthday gift," says Moses.

In the morning, they go down to the place where the rhinos were. The place is empty now, but they find the massive footprints on the far bank. The tracks are imprinted with the wavy lines of the rhino's skin, flanked by three ovals formed by their toes. The spoor is nothing like the footprints of a human nor a dog nor a buck. It seems more like some kind of writing—a letter left by the rhino. Daniel places his own small foot on the print, feeling the energy of the rhino throbbing in the soil. He closes his eyes and imagines his body dissolving into dark bulky folds, two horns rising from his nose.

MOSES

Mvelinqangi made everything. That's what Gogo says. Mvelinqangi made the first human in the sky and lowered him to earth with a rope plaited from the intestines of an ox. The whole sky is his umuzi. The stars shine through holes in the ground of the sky that were created by the passing hooves of Mvelinqangi's cattle—the Milky Way is the entrance to the kraal. The earth is held up by four white oxen, and death came to the world because the chameleon was slower than the lizard.

In Gogo's stories, women give birth to crows and snakes; children cast out by jealous brothers grow up and come back as kings; a boy turns the assegais of his enemies to water; and another lives all his life on the back of a white ox. Gogo watches Moses as she tells the stories and asks him to repeat things she told him the day before.

Moses' favorite story is about Sithungusobendle (*she who gathers the fibers to make skirts for young girls*), who was stolen from her mother by the amajuba, the rock pigeons. They flew off with her to their land beyond the seas and made her their queen, but she never forgot her mother. Many years later she used her cunning to outwit the pigeons and escape with her children. When she came to the sea, she cried, "Sea, Sea, divide! I am uSthungusobendle!" And the seas at once divided. The king of the pigeons and his army were racing after her, but the seas closed behind her and the amajuba all drowned.

When Sithungusobendle came home she found only a mountain which was actually isiququmadevu, a great monster with smelly black whiskers that had consumed her entire village. She slit its stomach with her assegai and out came the fowls and the goats and the cattle and the dogs and at last all the people, and everyone was happy again.

Acting out this story becomes a favorite game. The best part is killing the isiququmadevu monster—which is the dung heap behind the stables—with Joseph's hay rake serving as its teeth. The boys plunge their wooden swords into the steaming pile again and again, pretending that the dung beetles scuttling out in alarm are the liberated villagers and animals. At night, the disemboweled monster grows back together and snaps at the heels of Moses' dreams with its sharp iron teeth and dung on its breath.

These stories unfold when they follow Gogo around as

13

she does her daily chores. They seem to haunt the places where they are first revealed. Mvelinqangi emerges from the billowing steam as Gogo stirs the sheets in the great copper pot in the outside kitchen. Mbadlanyana, who outwitted a cannibal by shrinking and hiding in his nostril, creeps out of the red earth when Gogo's hoe bites into the weeds of the cornfield. The isiququmadevu meets its end amongst the vegetable peels falling from her pail into the pigs' trough.

One afternoon when they're turning the soil to plant new beans, a small brown bird calls out with the sound like a clock whirring before it strikes. Gogo's eyes crinkle into a smile as though she is hearing the voice of a dear friend after a long absence. "Unomtsheketshe! The honey guide..." she exclaims. "Run quickly and fetch a bowl from the kitchen."

They follow the bird with Gogo talking to it all the while, saying, "Oh honey guide, who calls the women while they are digging, speak that I might hear you." The bird flies ahead, perches on a boulder or branch and calls to them until they catch up, then flies off again. At last, they come to a tree with a hole from which a thin thread of bees flies in and out. Gogo makes another hole on the opposite side of the tree with her knife. She croons her thanks to the bees and praises them for their industriousness and beauty. The bees crawl on her face and hand, as if getting to know her. She plunges her hand into the hole she made, pulls out a comb dripping with honey, and lays it in the white enamel bowl. "Don't collect honey yourself until you know how to talk to bees, for they'll surely sting you," she warns. Moses dips his finger into the golden liquid pooling in the bowl and licks it, his eyes widening at the warm woody sweetness.

Their mother doesn't know how to speak to honey birds, but she produces her own miracle by laying a hard white bean between two layers of damp cloth. A few days later, a pale root starts creeping out of the bean, followed by a curled tendril with two leaves. They plant it outside the kitchen and watch it grow. In a few weeks it's taller than Daniel, then taller than Moses. One night Moses dreams that the beanstalk grows all the way to the sky, like the one Jack climbed, and uMvelinqangi creeps down it and snatches him from his bed. In the morning he tells Daniel his dream. Daniel steals the big black kitchen scissors and cuts down the beanstalk. Everyone is cross, but Moses sleeps better that night.

They spend their mornings with Kazi, scratching letters and numbers onto their slates. Numbers come to Moses as something he has always known, a language he was talking before he was born. He counts everything—the pale ducklings flopping after the mother duck, the potatoes to be washed for dinner. Each night he tries to count the stars, kneeling on the blanket chest by the window and whispering numbers long after Daniel has fallen asleep. The numbers seem to float out from the stars, weaving among them, forming strange patterns and inscriptions in the black sky. He counts until his chest threatens to burst with the infinity of it, with the possibility of containing the infinity in a number.

In Kazi's world, the big bird with the red face and heavy

beak is a turkey buzzard. But in Gogo's world, it is insingizi, the rain bird, which you must never kill. For if you do, it will rain until the whole world is drowning. These two worlds live in Moses, side by side.

DANIEL

Daniel calls his father uMfundisi, like everyone else at the mission. uMfundisi knows all about God and reads from the Bible every Sunday after church. The words are too big to fit into Daniel's ears—each sentence rumbles at him like a wagon full of stern old men, frowning because he can't understand what they want. After reading, their father reminds the boys of the naughty things they've done to make Jesus sad, such as forgetting to close the gate of the hen coop or gathering too many eggs at once and dropping them.

That golden-headed baby Jesus in the picture on the wall looks far too happy to be bothered by a broken egg. But one day a new Jesus arrives in an ox wagon—a small wooden mannequin nailed to a high dark cross. This Jesus looks down from his cross with such stiff outrage that Daniel understands His sorrow to be a terrible thing. How shameful that their persistent naughtiness somehow caused Jesus to be transformed from the shiny-headed baby to this sad little man on the cross! He tries his best to be good, but even on his best days, Jesus seems unappeased.

It's all Satan's fault. uMfundisi says Satan is always trying to make you do bad things. Daniel and Moses play games of stuffing Satan into holes in tree trunks or burying him.

They make a mud Satan and poke it with the long white thorns of the acacia trees and roll it down the hill. They throw stones at tree trunks that are really Satan in disguise. Satan is good at hiding, but Moses always knows where to find him.

Their father tells them Bible stories. He especially likes the one about Moses, who was sent down the river in a basket by his parents. He says that Moses grew up to be a great leader who led his people out of slavery. He even made the sea dry up so that his people could cross it and reach the promised land. When Moses says that uSthungusobendle also made the sea dry up, their father winces, as if he'd been eating raisins and bitten on a stone. He says that Gogo's stories are just fairytales, made-up nonsense. But the stories of Moses are true, real things that happened, like everything else in the Bible. Nothing is more real or more true than the Bible.

"One day, Moses, I believe that you too will lead your people out of darkness and into the light of the Lord. That's why God told me to call you Moses. He has called you to be His servant, so you must always strive to be good."

Daniel wonders who Moses' people are, and whether he, like Sithungusobendle, will have to slit open the belly of a monster to get them. But he doesn't ask. Their father doesn't like stories that aren't Bible stories. Daniel also has a Bible story named after him, about a man who made friends with a lion, which he thinks sounds like more fun than leading your people out of darkness.

MOSES

On a crisp winter's day, the Reverend Whitaker takes Moses up to the top of the high hill alone. Moses trots beside him, trying to remember all his transgressions. Will uMfundisi cast him adrift in the hills, like Hansel and Gretel, because he's just too bad to keep?

From up here, the rolling hills look like risen loaves—pale gold now, but green and scattered with white flowers in summer. The forested kloofs and ravines intersecting the hills are densely green, even in winter, and are home to hundreds of chattering birds and monkeys.

His father tells him to kneel with him to pray. The stones hurt his knees, and he distracts himself by peeping past his folded hands at the buildings of the uMzinyathi Mission far below. So tiny, as if you could pick them up and put them in your pocket. The furniture is scattered outside the white-washed mud brick three-roomed house he shares with his parents and Daniel because the women are resurfacing the floor with water and cattle dung. Yesterday they woke to find that termites had built a small mound in the front room overnight. Dani is so lucky—look at him, sitting on the day bed right out there on the grass, as if the house had been turned inside out.

Beyond the house is the kitchen—a thatched roof on poles sheltering a woodpile, a mud brick fireplace, and a big copper boiler for the washings. Further up the slope is the "church"—a clearing of hardened mud with logs to sit on—under a tall ironwood tree. A small thatched roof shelters the wooden altar, the wooden Jesus, and uMfundisi* when he's preaching. There's also a big brass bell on high wooden poles. It calls people to morning and afternoon prayer, Sunday matins and evensong. Sometimes Joseph lets Moses ring it. It's very loud, but most people don't seem to hear it. uMfundisi catches them if they come to trade amadumbe tubers, mealies or thatching grass on a Sunday. He tells them that he can't trade on the Sabbath, but if they attend the church service, he'll trade with them on Monday.

"Amen!" his father says now.

Moses drops his head quickly and screws his eyes shut. "Amen," he shouts and leaps up, eager to get back to the floor-smearing party.

But his father just stands, staring out at the scattered hills around the mission. He shakes his head and clucks his tongue. Moses worries that his poor attention during the prayer was noted, but something else is disappointing his father.

"Moses, my boy, do you see those poor heathens toiling away in blind ignorance?" he asks, waving a hand to encompass the imizi of the Magwaza clan on the surrounding hills. Each homestead is a cluster of grass-woven domed homes around a cattle byre (empty now for the cattle are out grazing) and encircled by a stockade of thorn branches. Beyond the stockades, women are hoeing the weeds amongst the sorghum, mealies, and calabashes. The cries of the cattle herders, young boys not much older than he, are carried to them on the wind.

"How sad to think," uMfundisi* sighs, "that those poor

children will never know the love of God if we do not teach them..."

Moses frowns. "Doesn't God love all children?" he asks.

"Yes, but they cannot enter the kingdom of heaven if they know not how to pray for their sins. We are all sinners, Moses, but only those who repent and ask the Lord for forgiveness can be saved from the torment of Hell."

"But if God loves all children, why would he send them to Hell?"

"Lord Jesus can't save them from Satan, Moses, if they don't live a Christian life. That is why the Lord sends us out as missionaries, to save these lost souls. Now that's enough questions, son," he adds sternly as Moses opens his mouth to ask another. "It is not for us to question the ways of God."

His father tells him that if Moses grows to be a good Christian, he'll bring the Gospel to the Magwaza people, and they'll wear proper clothes and come every Sunday for service and won't do bad things like witchcraft and polygamy.

"Don't you want to save these poor children from savagery?" he asks.

"I don't want them to go to hell," Moses replies cautiously. He's not sure what savagery is or if he wants to save them from it. uMfundisi* bends down to peer at him, as if he can detect his uncertainty.

"There's a good boy. You were born a heathen, yet you have been baptized in the name of the Lord and are learning to be pure of heart. I know that Daniel is naughtier than you, but you have to be especially good, Moses, so that you grow up free of sin and save these poor children."

Moses stands with his hand in his father's, watching a group of Magwaza children who are splashing together in the stream. Their shrieks of delight float over the grass to the hilltop. They don't seem to miss God's love. Sometimes he envies them. They spend their Sundays—indeed every day—wandering after the cattle and making clay animals by the river instead of sitting in a stifling room learning about who begat who.

He fights the urge to pull his hand free and run down the hill to join them.

DANIEL

Dr. Galsworthy has fleshy cheeks and a bulbous nose as red as the raw-skinned haunches of the ox that was slaughtered in his honor. Beneath his nose hangs a great brown moustache, curving up into waxed tips like the horns of a buffalo. His belly strains against his waistcoat, his hands are lumpy sausages. Daniel and Moses run after his horse as he rides up to the house, past the severed head of the slaughtered ox that is lying on a tree stump by the cattle kraal. Daniel tries not to look at it, but he can hear it singing. *Is this why I was killed, for a man so red and so fat?*

Kazi says he has come to vaccinate people so that they don't get sick from smallpox. Daniel watches as Dr. Galsworthy clasps Moses' arm in his meaty paws and barks at him to keep still and take his medicine like a man, while he scratches his skin with a needle. Moses stands rigidly, making no sound but bearing a fixed expression of such terror that when Daniel finds himself in the dreadful grasp of Dr. Galsworthy, he roars and kicks until the doctor slaps him. He is so aggrieved that he hardly feels the scratching of the needle. The whole experience seems far worse than smallpox, which can't be so bad if it's only small. Bigpox would be another matter.

Dr. Galsworthy is to sleep in the children's bed so the boys are put to bed on a blanket on the floor of their parents' bedroom. They lie near the open doorway, watching the adults at dinner. Dr. Galsworthy eats his ox stew with greedy relish, sucking on his spoon and scattering drops of gravy all over his whiskers and the napkin straining to cover his stomach.

"We'd *never* be allowed to eat like that," Moses whispers.

"He looks like Albertina"—the pink and black sow—"if Albertina had whiskers."

"And boots…"

The boys explode into giggles. uMfundisi*, who is facing them, wags his finger sternly.

Dr. Galsworthy peers in their direction. "Is that those cheeky little whippersnappers? No doubt that little native boy is putting your son up to mischief. I'm surprised to see that you allow him to sleep in your bedroom. Surely, he should be out in the huts with his own kind?"

"Moses is our own kind," Kazi replies. "We're raising him as one of our family."

"How extraordinary!" the doctor declares. "Well-intended, perhaps, but a dangerous experiment, I'd say. We must beware of cultivating intimacy with the natives—

familiarity breeds contempt and all that. And I doubt his primitive mind can benefit much from education."

"Actually Moses is quicker at his lessons than Dan, particularly at numbers. His grasp of mathematics is quite unusual for one so young."

"But surely, Madam, civilization is not just a matter of parroting the times table? One may dress a chimpanzee in a sailor suit and teach him some clever tricks, but he remains a chimpanzee."

Kazi's cheeks take on a dangerous flush. "I trust you're not comparing Moses to a chimpanzee, Dr. Galsworthy? Even you must acknowledge that the Zulu are human beings."

"Perhaps, my dear madam, but of a lower order. New scientific evidence suggests that they have physiological constraints—the shape of their skulls and so forth—which render them childlike, susceptible to criminality and primitive sensuality. They can never reach the level of Europeans."

"Yet Englishmen are hanged daily for thievery, while I have never had to lock a door at uMzinyathi. You can send a Zulu man on a three-day journey with money for a purchase and he'll battle rivers and wild animals to return with the item and your change."

"Perhaps you've been spending too much time with them, my good lady. I do believe you might have forgotten how a civilized person conducts himself."

"If I have, my good sir, the present company has done little to remind me."

Dr. Galsworthy leans back in his chair, extracts his handkerchief and blows his nose forcefully, setting his moustache a-trembling as if it might fly off altogether.

"I beg you to dissuade your good wife from pursuing this project, Reverend. It seems to have quite bamboozled her thinking."

uMfundisi* coughs up a sickly chuckle. "Ah well, the boy is not the same as our biological son, of course, but he's a loveable little chap. We've no doubt that the good Lord's hand brought him here to give us this opportunity to raise a native child in a Christian home. By showing what can be achieved in a life guided by Jesus, Moses can only inspire his brethren to give up their heathen ways and follow his example."

"Well, Reverend, you may be better acquainted with the will of God than I, but I'm of the opinion that nothing good can come of this. If you teach your dog to speak, he'll soon be barking orders at you."

The adults lapse into a stiff silence, broken by the scrape of their spoons against their bowls, and Dr. Galsworthy's vigorous chewing.

In the adjoining bedroom, Daniel lifts his hands to form a bowl, lowers his face over it, and makes slurping noises. "Look at me, I'm Dr. Galspiggy," he whispers. But Moses doesn't giggle. He rolls away and lies facing the wall. Daniel falls into puzzled silence.

Stupid Galspiggy, he thinks.

MOSES

"What's a bio...biolil child?" Moses blurts out the next morning as they stand with their mother, watching Dr.

24

Galsworthy and the Reverend Whitaker riding off to take the vaccination to the king.

"A what?"

"Biolil child...uMfundisi* said I wasn't the same as your biolil child..."

"Oh...*biological* child.... Well, you're even better than a biological child. You're our surprise child, a gift!"

Kazi takes him inside to help sort her sewing basket. Few things please Moses more than the chance to arrange the buttons and beads according to color and size and to untangle and rewind all the thread. But he doesn't believe that uMfundisi* thinks that a surprise child is better than a biological one. He lines up the buttons, turning over the word in his mind. *Bio-lo-gi-cal.* The word sticks in his throat like the cod-liver oil Kazi makes him swallow when his stomach hurts.

Nkathazo arrives on a blustery day with two wives, five small children and two wet skinny dogs shivering in the rain. His wife says that many people have died in their village, and they've been accused of causing the deaths through witchcraft. uMfundisi* says he'll have to seek permission from the chief, but they can stay at the station for now if they help with farm work and attend the prayer services. The man keeps silent while the women talk, glaring at the Reverend Whitaker through hooded eyes as if he blames him for his troubles. Later Gogo tells uMfundisi* that Nkathazo was in the same regiment as her son. She says they should take the women and children, but turn him away because he's umthakathi and a troublemaker. uMfundisi* says that the people are dying because of smallpox, not witchcraft, and Christians don't believe in witchcraft, and we should leave it to God to judge him.

The women work hard at building their shelters and hoeing the fields while Nkathazo finds secretive sunny corners and dozes with his back against a tree or a wall. The boys watch him surreptitiously, daring each other to touch his foot when he's napping. One day, they peep around the wagon house wall, watching as he extracts a small snuff box from the hole in the lobe of his ear, takes a pinch, holds it to his nostrils and sniffs it up loudly, first one nostril and then the other. He sneezes three times, and, on the third sneeze, shoots out a long thin arm like a branch of the buffalo thorn, hooks Moses by the shoulder and pulls him roughly in front of him.

"You like spying on people, don't you, little dog?" Nkathazo sneers, pinching Moses' arm.

"No, sir."

"Don't you raise your eyes to me, boy. Don't you know how to speak to an adult? I've seen you sneaking around. Look at you, swaggering about in your trousers like a big iphumalimi boss. But you're just a dressed-up dog, the white man's cur. You don't even know your amadlozi. No family, no clan, no zithakazelo."

"Hayi wena, you rubbish you, leave my boy alone, or you'll feel my stick!"

Nkathazo pushes Moses roughly so that he falls in the dust. He raises his eyes to Gogo, who is standing with the yard broom upraised.

"Yes, mother of Hoshumoya...What does the big man say about his mother hiding with the Christians? I'm sure he'd like to know where you've been all this time."

"Hayi, suka wena. I don't talk to abathakathi!" Gogo shoots a ball of spit impressively at his feet.

But Nkathazo just smiles and lets his hooded eyes drop from Gogo's face to Moses. "Where did abelungu get that stray puppy? He looks a lot like uHoshumoya's oldest boy, don't you think?"

"This boy comes from the colony. Don't you stir up trouble! If I tell the missionaries to put you out, you're a dead man and you know it."

Gogo grasps Moses' hand and pulls him away. Daniel, who was hiding behind the wall, ducks around the side of the wagon house and joins them as they head towards the kitchen. Gogo is walking very fast so that Moses and Daniel have to run to keep up.

"Ubani uHoshumoya?" Moses asks.

"No one you need to worry about. Just stay out of uNkathazo's way. He's dangerous."

"I'm not scared of him," Moses retorts. "God will protect me from evil."

"The Christian God doesn't know about Zulu witchcraft."

She tells them to help her move logs from outside the kitchen to the pile by the stove.

But Moses just stands, glaring at the logs. "That umthakathi says I have no clan, no amadlozi, no zithakazelo..." he blurts out. "He says I'm a just a white man's dog."

"He's stupid. Everyone has ancestors, and you do have a clan. One day you'll find it or start a new clan. Like Nhlathu."

She tells them the story of Nhlathu who was born to a woman who'd been infertile. When he was born, the other wives were jealous and wanted to kill him, for their children were all crows. So, his mother hid him in the skin of a python, and he was lost for many years. But then he was discovered by a beautiful girl and together they founded a new great clan.

"Will I found a clan?" Daniel asks, squinting against the smoke curling from the kitchen fire.

Gogo laughs. "You have a clan already, Bhejane! You're a son of the great uThika clan."

"uThika" is how the people at the mission say Whitaker.

"That's not a real clan," Moses says. "It doesn't have izithakazelo."

"White people's clans don't have those things. But it's still a clan," says Gogo.

DANIEL

That evening Daniel asks Kazi why their family doesn't have izithakazelo.

"English people don't need these things. Zulu clans need praise songs like izithakazelo to help them remember their ancestors and family histories. But we write our history and don't need to remember it in a praise song."

She's allowed the boys to stay up to help her feed a suckling lamb whose mother died during lambing, but Moses has fallen asleep on the day bed.

Daniel sits holding a bottle of warm milk with a rag stuffed into it for the lamb to suck. When the bottle is empty, the lamb pushes against him with its hard head and kicks out its back legs. Kazi wipes Daniel's hands clean, lifts the big black Bible off the shelf and opens it on the last page.

"This is our family tree," she says, although the scrawled writing looks more like a nest of spiders than a tree. She shows him the names of his grandfathers and great-grandfathers and grandmothers and aunts and uncles written there. There is Great Uncle Robert and Cousin Roland, and there is his own name, with his birth date written next to it.

But Moses isn't there.

"Why isn't Moses here?"

His mother stares at the page as if waiting for it to explain itself.

"This is only biological family," she says at last, hesitantly, as if she doesn't trust the words. "But he is part of our family, all the same."

"Is Moses really my brother?"

"Yes, he is your true brother, your best brother and probably the only brother you will ever have."

"But he is not *biological*."

"It doesn't matter, Dan. He's your brother just the same. Don't forget that."

Later Daniel lies awake next to his sleeping brother, his best brother, his true brother, and thinks about the family tree: the little black lines joining all the names, the blank space where his living brother should be. The lines are holding them together. If Moses is not joined to them with

29

those black lines, he might be snatched away by anything, by uMvelinqangi, by Nkathazo, by Moses himself on the day he walks out to found his new clan.

When he's sure that Kazi is asleep, he lights a candle and creeps into the front room. He climbs on a stool to get the Bible down from its high shelf, staggering with the weight of it. He lays it on his father's desk, open to the last page where the family tree is drawn. With trembling fingers, he takes the pen that uMfundisi* uses to write his sermons, pushes open the lid of the inkpot, dips the pen, and brings it to the page. The pen hovers over the page, releasing a black drop that half obscures Great Uncle Robert. He brings it down and writes MOSES next to his own name. The letters are big and clumsy, the ink blobbing at the ends— he's never written with a pen before. He knows he'll be punished for this. But now Moses' name is there, he is part of the uThika clan. And no one can take his name away.

MOSES

The lightning comes in the night, but Moses is awake, listening to the thunder and watching the angels on the wall come and go in the lightning flashes. He kneels on the bed and stares at the lightning forking through the sky. His body vibrates with energy, as if the bolts were coursing through him.

"Come," he whispers to the lightning. "Come closer."

He murmurs a praise song for the lightning's beauty and ferocity. He is filled with an urge to touch it, although he has been told often enough how dangerous it is.

A deafening thunderclap shudders through the small house, reverberating in his chest. The door bursts open, and Kazi hurries in.

"Moses! Get away from the window, child," she cries. She looks wild in the blue light, her long dark hair loose on her shoulders instead of neatly pulled into a bun.

The mission bell sounds, ringing urgently. Kazi tells them to stay there and hurries out of the room. But Moses runs after her, and Daniel follows. Outside is a confusion of people tumbling half-dressed from the huts in response to the bell. The air is thick with the smell of burning and there is a blaze of light beyond the huts. As they run closer, Moses sees that the bell tower is blazing, the bell now fallen at its feet. The grass between the bell tower and the huge ironwood is burning and the tree is in flames, threatening the thatched shelter that serves as a church. The firelight flickers on the face of the wooden Jesus.

The adults form a line down to the well and pass buckets and pots of water to pour over the church roof and the burning logs. Moses stands holding Daniel's hand, feeling thrilled and appalled. Was it him? Was it his song that brought the lighting to his church?

When the fire is out, uMfundisi* gathers everyone in the shelter to pray. He stands beneath the blackened dripping thatch, raving about the power of a Lord who can "smite from the heavens and rent trees asunder." It was the Lord who rang the church bell, he cries, for who but the Lord brought the lightning strike that had caused it to ring? And who would ignore the call of a bell rung by the Lord's hand? And how merciful of the Lord to keep their church safe by causing the tree to burn instead. Moses wonders why the Lord saved the church, but didn't save their swing in the tree, which he liked better than the church. The church is a place of excruciating boredom, where you have to stand very still with ants running over your bare feet, listening to uMfundisi* rain down infinite words about the mysterious ways of God and the cunning of Satan.

Gogo comes to the house the next morning to tell uMfundisi* that Nkathazo brought the lightning to destroy the mission. She says no one will come to worship in their church now, because everyone knows that when lightning strikes a homestead, it is cursed. They need a Heaven Herd to protect it. uMfundisi* tells her not to believe in heathen superstitions—only God can cause lightning. And Nkathazo may be lazy and disobliging, but that doesn't make him a witch. And they certainly shall not have any witchdoctor performing rituals at God's mission.

"It wasn't Nkathazo, it was me," Moses tells Daniel later. "I called the lightning."

"uMfundisi* says only God can bring lightning."

"It was me," Moses repeats insistently. "I called it to come closer."

Daniel looks at him, uncertainly.

"Why?"

"I don't know...I just wanted to. To see what it would do."

"That's silly. You can't call lightning."

"I have powers," Moses whispers softly.

32

Daniel looks puzzled, then frightened, then angry.

"You're silly," he says, pushing Moses in the chest. "You can't call lightning. You're telling lies."

Moses just looks at him, his eyes dark with secrets, and walks away.

"I'll tell on you," Daniel calls into the emptiness that Moses has left behind him.

DANIEL

After the lightning, Gogo becomes more urgent in her conversations with Moses and draws him away to murmur stories to him. When Daniel asks what she said, Moses just shrugs. His face still has that tight, mysterious expression, and he never wants to play. Daniel takes to spying on them, trying to penetrate the secrets of their whisperings.

One hot afternoon, when hard white clouds are bumping the edges of a deep blue sky, Daniel sits scratching in the dirt behind the pigsty. He's half-heartedly making a kraal for the cattle he's made from river clay, but really he's listening to Gogo and Moses speaking in low voices behind the wall. He can't hear what they're saying, but after some time he hears a rhythmic tapping and the scuffling of feet in the sand.

"Nina, bantu bomfula," Gogo's voice roars out, sending a flock of starlings in the nearby umsinsi tree flapping up in a flurry of red-tipped wings.

"Nina, bantu bomfula," Moses echoes.

"Nina, bantu bomfula," Gogo says again. "You, people of the river with the power of the great rivers of KwaZulu, Nina bantu bomfula, you who sing with the voice of the mighty rivers, while others can only croak, you who were chosen to live by uMvelinqangi himself, you who run with the swiftness of the impala, while others crawl like the tortoise, you who know the secrets of the wizards from across the seas, you who were carried by the waters of the White Imfolozi to walk in two worlds—born of indoda yomfula, the man of the river."

Daniel peeps over the wall. Gogo, usually so small and quiet in her soft skirts, has expanded into a great twisting sinewy form. Her bare feet stamp the earth, raising clouds of red dust. Her skirts billow and swirl as she swings her body to and fro, her voice resounds through the still air. Moses is beating an upturned wooden slops pail, eyes closed, transported by some indefinable ecstasy. His high voice roars in concert with hers.

Daniel slides down, feeling lonely and afraid. What is this game of theirs? *Is this the start of Moses' new clan?* He creeps away, resolving to find Kazi. As he walks towards the house, he sees his father striding past, mumbling to himself as though rehearsing a sermon. He trots along beside him, but uMfundisi* barely glances at him.

"Moses is...(what *is* he doing?)...*dancing*," he announces.

His father breaks off his muttering and looks at him sharply.

"What did you say?"

"Moses is dancing..." he falters. He's not sure if he offered this to diminish it by uMfundisi's* inattention or to get Moses into trouble, but he's disconcerted by the alarm in his father's blue eyes. "With Gogo...by the pigsty."

uMfundisi* swings around and hurries towards the pigsty. Daniel runs after him, catching up as he comes around the corner and stands staring with horror as though Satan himself was cavorting on the pigsty wall.

Gogo glances up and freezes. Her skirts fall, folding her into their soft silence. Her voice swallows itself in her throat. Moses' eyes fly open. His hands flop onto the pail, like two dead mice.

"Agnes! What are you doing?"

Gogo casts down her eyes.

"It's just child's play, Mfundisi," she mumbles.

"Moses and Daniel, go inside now. Go inside at once to Kazi."

Moses walks away, his head down, eyes fixed to his feet. Daniel hurries after him.

"What was Gogo singing?"

"Nothing."

"Was it izithakazelo? Was it for your new clan?"

"No, you don't know anything. It was just child's play. Like Gogo said," Moses snaps and walks faster.

It hadn't sounded like child's play. It had sounded solemn and powerful, like the praise songs the men sang for the Chief when he visited the mission. Like a prayer, but not to any God Daniel could recognize.

Daniel follows Moses as he strides across the yard, up the veranda steps and through the front room, where Kazi is kneading the dough.

"What is it, little man?" she asks, but he marches past

into the storeroom. It is Daniel who runs to her for comfort. She strokes his head with her floury hands, as he stands sobbing, with his face buried in her skirts. uMfundisi* comes in behind him.

"Daniel, go to your room," his father says, quite gently. Kazi leads him into the storeroom, where Moses is sitting with his face to the wall.

"Just sit here and look at your picture books, boys...we'll go out for a walk by and by."

She goes out, closing the door behind her. Daniel creeps up to the door and puts his ear against the crack to hear his father's agitated voice.

"...he was drumming and she was dancing...both in a trance. And she was uttering these frightful incantations, I couldn't make them out at all...thought Agnes was our best convert but it seems her heathen ways have never left her... could undo all our good work with this mumbo-jumbo..."

Later uMfundisi* comes into the room and sends Daniel out. Daniel sits on the ground beneath the window, listening to their father's voice going on and on. He can't hear the words, but it's that awful quiet, sorrowful voice he uses to talk about how sad Jesus gets when the boys are naughty. Moses says nothing.

When their father leaves the room, Daniel climbs in through the window. Moses is still sitting staring at the wall.

"Let's play Christian soldiers," Daniel suggests, eyeing the wooden swords and shields with red crosses that their father had recently made for them. They had devised a game in which the potato bushes growing on the edge of the hill were Turk armies, each blue flower they knocked down with their swords another infidel slain.

Moses looks at him blankly. He gets up and walks to the chest. He opens the top drawer and takes out the basket of clay animals that Gogo gave him. Daniel feels a surge of excitement. He longs to play with the animals, but Moses has always refused in case they get broken. Moses takes the lid off the basket, lifts it high into the air and turns it upside down, letting the animals fall out onto the floor. He throws the basket down on top of the broken animals and walks out of the room. Daniel sees him through the window, running towards the river.

"Moses!" he calls, to the empty room. "Moses, come back..."

He kneels on the floor. All the animals have at least one broken leg, the rhino's horn has broken off, and the elephant's trunk is in three pieces. He picks up all the pieces and carefully packs them back in the basket.

In the following days, Moses avoids Gogo. He stays with Kazi or watches Joseph milking the cows or Dawid sawing planks for the new church. Daniel goes where he goes too, but sometimes he sits beside Gogo in the afternoons while she plaits reeds into baskets for storing seeds and maize. He watches her fingers moving nimbly over the reeds, trying not to remember how he told their father about the dancing. He half-wishes he could awaken the Gogo he'd seen with Moses, with her stamping feet and swirling skirts and deep–

throated roar. But she remains as tightly coiled in herself as the round baskets she is weaving.

Often she goes still, with her eyes focused on the distant hills and her head tilted, as if she is listening.

"If the men come for me, you and Moses must hide."

"What men?"

"Never mind. Just remember what I told you."

She gives him the string of white beads that she wears around her neck and asks him to give them to Moses. He decides to keep them until Moses is not so strange and angry, just in case he throws them down like he did the animals.

MOSES

The men come soon after that, one misty morning, when the Reverend is away visiting the mission at Eshowe. The boys are helping Kazi pick peas from the garden trellises. For Moses that means curling his fingers into the wiry green tendrils to feel their gentle tug and cramming his mouth with sweet peas when he thinks his mother's not looking. The world has been rubbed out by the mist slowly rising from the valleys, trailing shreds of cloud through the buildings and dark trees. Moses can hear the banging of Dawid's hammer as he creates the scaffold for the new church and Gogo's *kulukulukulu* as she feeds the chickens. But he can't see anything beyond a few feet, as if he, Daniel and Kazi were marooned on an island, far from the rest of the mission station.

A new sound breaks through the clouds, a muffled roar that coalesces into rhythmic chanting, the slap of bare feet on wet soil, the thud of spears against ox-skin shields. Kazi peers out into the mist, reaching halfway between the trellis and the basket, the peas forgotten in her hand. As the sound rolls over them, something emerges from the whiteness. At first, he thinks it's a multi-headed monster. Then he sees that it's men brandishing assegais and knobkerries. Their arms and legs are encircled by white fringes of animal hair that ripple with each stamp of their feet.

"It's the men!" Daniel shouts. "Gogo said we must hide if the men came. Run!"

He grabs Moses' hand and takes off through the mist. Moses runs after him, stubbing bare toes on sticks and stones. They head for the stream where they can hide in the bushes. But a dark shape looms in their path. Moses feels rough hands grasping his arm and pulling him half off his feet, smells the pungent mixture of sweat and tobacco. *Nkathazo.*

"Let me go," he yells. Daniel tries to bite Nkathazo's wrist. But Nkathazo drives him away with a blow from the handle of his spear and drags Moses back towards the hubbub of angry voices.

When the men are within sight, Nkathazo pulls Moses behind a tree and holds him with one hand over his mouth, while the other presses his spear against his throat. The men are jostling and shouting around Kazi and Dawid.

"Sawubona, Hoshumoya. Intoni nifunani? What is your business here?" A voice roars out. Gogo strides into the circle, transformed once more into that fierce woman with flashing eyes who had taught Moses his izithakazelo.

39

EYE BROTHER HORN BY BRIDGET PITT

The men fall silent. A tall, dark-skinned man is the first to speak.

"Ma Mvuleni....You are here?" he stammers. "We thought you were taken by a lion!"

"Well, I am alive, as you can see. I live here now. Why do you come here full of noise? Why don't you come respectfully and ask what you need to ask?"

"We've come for umthakathi, uNkathazo. We know he's hiding here."

The man towers over her and is made taller still by the white feathers standing up from the isicoco ring on his head. Twin scars forming two short parallel lines on each cheekbone add to his fierce appearance. But his eyes are lowered, as if he is afraid.

Gogo turns to Kazi.

"Let them take Nkathazo," she says in English. "If you let him go, they won't harm you."

"But they'll kill him...he came here for shelter..."

"Ma Mvuleni must come too," the tall man says, with more firmness but still avoiding Gogo's eyes. "You stole her from us for five years now. We need her at our homestead."

One of the men moves towards Gogo. Dawid steps in between them and the man raises his knobkerrie. Kazi grasps the knobkerrie and tries to wrest it from him. The man clings to it with gritted teeth.

"Leave it, Nkosikazi," Gogo says quietly. "I'll go with them. He's right, it's time."

Kazi drops the knobkerrie and the man retreats, glaring at her and holding his knobkerrie close.

"Agnes is a Christian now, let her stay," Kazi pleads with the tall man. He shakes his head.

"She's our mother. She belongs with us, not in the white man's house. Bring us uNkathazo, and we will leave you in peace."

At these words, Nkathazo tightens his grip on Moses' arm and drags him into the clearing, the cold blade of his *iklwa* spear still pressing against Moses' throat.

"I come freely for I'm innocent of witchcraft," he announces, his voice shrill with fear. "Here's the one who's been killing our people."

Moses stands staring ahead. His heart flutters within him, like a fledgling sparrow trying to fly. Kazi lurches towards him, but the men hold her back.

The sight of Moses seems to shock the tall man with the scars even more than the sight of Gogo. Moses feels the searing burn of his eyes on his face. The man's gaze flits to Gogo allowing some understanding to flash between them.

The other men are laughing now. "Unamanga manje! You're telling lies now, Nkathazo. That's a child, that's no witch!"

"He's a second twin! You recall that uHoshumoya had twins, in that drought six winters ago? Is this boy not the image of his living twin? We know that if a second twin is allowed to live, it brings death and misfortune to the homestead. But uHoshumoya didn't kill his child, he gave him to the missionaries. No wonder our people are dying now!"

"What nonsense!" Kazi interjects in English before breaking into a mixed muddle of the two languages. "This is Moses. His mother and father were from Natal, both deceased. We brought him from Natal in that wagon."

She gestures towards the black ribs of the wagon's high-hooped frame looming through the mist.

The tall man wrenches the spear from Nkathazo's grasp and knocks him down with a blow to his head. Moses creeps to Gogo and hides in the curtain of her skirt.

"You're full of rubbish. This child looks nothing like mine. Only someone bewitched by this man would believe this boy resembles my child."

He swings around to face the muttering group.

"Seize him!" Hoshumoya roars. "Seize this dog, uN-kathazo, for you know him truly to be umthakathi, smelled out by the most powerful sanusi in the King Mpande's court."

Nkathazo screams, scrambles to his feet and pushes Gogo down in his haste to escape. But the men are on him, pulling him roughly as they hustle him away.

Hoshumoya helps Gogo to her feet. "Come, Mama, we must go now."

Kazi puts out her hand to stop him, but Gogo shakes her head. "Hayi, 'Nkosikazi. He's right, I am needed at my home. Moses will be safe now."

Kazi's face is almost as white as the mist, with two spots of red blooming high on each cheek. She gives Gogo a quick, tight embrace and steps back.

"May God be with you, my dear friend..."

Moses realizes that some terrible bargain has been struck.

"No..." he screams, clinging to Gogo's skirt. "Please..."

Gogo bends to look into his face. "Be brave and strong, mfana wami, and remember all I've taught you."

Hoshumoya pulls Moses away, prying his fists open to release Gogo's skirts. He lifts him and puts him in Kazi's arms. Moses wriggles free and runs to the house. By the time he's come back with his wooden sword, the men have been swallowed by the mist. And Gogo is gone.

PART TWO
1871
THE PYTHON
AND THE GUN

The gun changes everything.

It comes to Daniel on their thirteenth birthday, a present from his father: a twelve-bore Westley Richards shotgun, given to the Reverend Whitaker by a trader who'd traveled through the district. Moses gets a Sheffield Bowie hunting knife with a staghorn handle and a sheath you can strap around your shoulder. It's a fine knife, but Daniel can tell by the way Moses looks at his gun that he thinks his brother has the better present. That's the first thing that changes. When Moses looks from his knife to Daniel's gun, Daniel hears the click of something recalibrating in their connection, like the cocking of the hammer before a trigger is pulled.

Moses knows all about guns from *The English Mechanic*— he and umfundisi have long discussions about percussion caps and gunpowder and caliber. Daniel has never cared for guns.

Their father takes them up to the hill to learn how to shoot. It's a cold cloudless day in early winter, the grass turning gold on the hills, the air so clear you can see a thin blue line of the sea in the east. uMfundisi* puts old tins in a white stinkwood tree for them to shoot at.

Daniel loads the gun clumsily, sabotaged by his father's eagerness and Moses' cool skepticism. As he pulls the trigger, the gun bucks hard against his shoulder, making his eyes water. His ears ring from the explosion, his nose burns from the gunpowder. At first his bullets go all over, but just as he's about to give up, something shifts, as if the gun's been fighting him but suddenly begins to trust him. It fires firm and smooth, the bullet following his eye straight into the middle of the tin. Moses narrows his gaze and turns away.

uMfundisi* laughs and slaps him on the back. "Well done, my boy! You're a born marksman, just like your mother! Now you can help us keep down the vermin and hunt for the pot."

Daniel feels his smile stiffening. When his father says vermin, he means the leopards, caracals and jackals that go for the chickens and goats. Or the porcupines, monkeys and bushpigs that raid the vegetables. And when he says hunt for the pot he means buck or guinea fowl. He looks down at the gun that is so heavy and beautiful in his hands and realizes that he's been given this gift so that he can kill animals.

"You have a go now," he says, passing the gun to Moses.

MOSES

Moses watches Daniel clean the gun, the candle light gleaming dully on the barrels as he pushes the rod up and down them to clear the powder, flushes them out, then dips the cleaning rag in oil.

"You have to dry it before oiling," Moses says. "Otherwise it rusts."

Daniel glances up at him. Usually he defers to his brother, but now something mulish sets in his mouth.

"I think I know how to clean a gun."

"Do you? When have you ever cleaned a gun? uMfundisi always asks me to do it. Because he knows I do a better job."

"You're just jealous."

"I'm not. I don't care about your gun."

"Then why do you care how I clean it?"

"I don't. Let it rust, for all I care. You'll never use it to kill anything, anyway. Remember how you cried when Kazi shot the leopard. You're just a baby."

Moses had wanted to cry too. He remembers the dead leopard with its tongue out and its black-spotted golden fur soaked in blood, Kazi bending over it, a lamp swinging in her hand. She'd straightened up, grinning. "I got him!" she'd declared, wiping the hair from her brow and leaving a bloody streak across her forehead. Her face was ghoulish in the lamplight, alien and repulsive to him.

But Moses hadn't cried. He hadn't cried since Gogo left.

Daniel drops the guns and lunges at him. They wrestle on the floor, until Moses gets the upper hand. He sits on top of

Daniel, twisting his arm behind his back until Daniel yelps in pain. They often wrestle playfully, but tonight there's a hard fury in Moses' grasp, and when he lets Daniel go, he's contrite to see a red bruise blooming on his brother's arm.

"Why shouldn't my father give me a gun?' Daniel demands. "He's *my* father. It's *my* birthright."

Birthright. The word erupts between them, like the sudden blast of a trumpet, like a call to arms. Moses flinches. My father. My birthright.

He pushes himself off of Daniel and walks out into the darkness outside. He walks a few feet away from the house and sits down under the umsinsi tree. He leans his back against it, pressing his skin into the hard thorny knobs on the trunk. He thinks of the stories that he's been told about his own parents, a mother who died in childbirth, a father who'd been killed in a wagon accident a few weeks before, both Christian converts on Bishop Colenso's mission in Pietermaritzburg. Kazi and uMfundisi* were always so vague about them, offering contradictory details or changing the subject whenever he asked about them. They offered only two Christian names, given by the missionaries: John and Mary. They claimed not to know their Zulu names or clan names. It made it hard to believe in them or any other family. Had they no relatives who wanted him? Zulu families were expansive and interwoven. How could his origins be so meagre? And why did he share a birthday with Daniel? His parents were vague about when he'd actually been born, sometimes saying it was while they were still in Pietermaritzburg, or on the way to Zululand, or soon after they'd arrived. Daniel was born one month after they reached uMzinyathi. So Moses had to be at least a few weeks older. If he pressed them for details, they changed the subject, and he'd given up trying. Joseph and Thuli just told him to ask Kazi and uMfundisi*.

Daniel didn't like talking about Moses' origins either.

"I bet we're both foundlings," Daniel would say after they'd read about these in fairy stories.

"Kazi prayed for two baby boys and one morning she found us in the sun flowers growing in her vegetable garden, like in Thumbelina. Or curled in the weaver's nests by the river. Maybe we hatched out of eggs."

They were silly stories, but Moses liked them. Now he sees how silly they were.

Birthright...the word explodes through his head, again and again. What birthright did he have? He looks up at the stars and loses himself in their constellations, in the dark boundless spaces beyond the range of any gun.

DANIEL

Daniel lies awake, waiting for the sound of the latch, but Moses doesn't come back. He thinks of Chief Nhlongolwana, whose gun exploded in his fingers, turning his hand into a jammy red mess with splintered bones protruding. He lost half his thumb and a forefinger. Kazi said it was because unscrupulous white traders had sold him a messed-up gun.

Daniel remembers firing the gun that afternoon, the power of the bullet rushing through the barrel and speeding into the heart of the target, as if drawn by an invisible cord.

This gun is the best thing his father's ever given him—
the only time, that he can recall, when his father has acknowledged him as a son and favored him over Moses.
Mostly he feels invisible to uMfundisi*, unable to compete
with his father's passion for gaining converts and grooming
Moses to be the perfect missionary.

But now it feels as if this gun has exploded in his hands,
like the gun of the Chief.

He falls asleep into restless dreams disturbed by the reverberating echoes of gunfire, and the soft, bloodied bodies
of animals dropping from the sky. He wakes up sweating,
despite the cold night air. Moses' bed is still empty. It's too
cold to be out. He's probably sleeping in the stable with the
horses. Daniel knows that he should get up and go and find
him, but he doesn't.

The gun lies on the shelf above his bed, watchful in the
dark.

The boys avoid each other the next day. After their classes,
Daniel goes out swimming with the other boys on the mission and only remembers at Evensong that he was supposed
to mend a hole made by a jackal in the chicken coop. His
punishment is to stay up guarding the coop. He'd wanted
to sit with the dogs, but uMfundisi* has shut them away.
He wants to make sure the jackal comes so that Daniel can
shoot it, and the dogs' barking might chase it away.

He sits, shivering despite uMfundisi's* thick woolen coat,
looking up at the frosty, star-pricked night, listening to the
high trill of the Scops owl. He mimics its call and is rewarded

with an answering trill.

"Is that you, Mkhulu?" he calls.

He thinks of the injured fledgling they found after a storm blew down the tree in which it was nesting, a ball of gray fluff small enough to fit in one hand, with enormous eyes. His mother showed Moses how to splint its wing. She said her father had taught her. They named it Mkhulu, for there was something grandfatherly about the way it peered up at them. They'd fed it with mashed mealworms from the animal grain, and later with minced raw chicken.

The owlet was adopted by one of the hens. It would flop along after her, flapping its wings in a comical dance. When it saw Moses or Daniel bringing its food, it would utter little mewing cries of delight.

As the owl grew, its fluffy gray plumage was replaced by silky ash-colored feathers with dark streaks. The white tail and wing feathers were barred with stripes the pale yellow of tallow candles. Its large round eyes, set in pale indented discs, were a penetrating lemon-yellow encircling a dense black pupil.

When it learned to fly, they released it in the thicket down the stream.

"Be happy that you helped a wild creature and are setting it free, " Kazi said.

But the next day the owl was back among the chickens.

"It doesn't want to be free," Daniel said, secretly pleased. "It wants to live with us."

Kazi said they must take it to the woods upstream, further this time. Two days later, the owl was back. On the following day, they released it again.

This time the owl didn't come back. Daniel scanned the skies for it. At night, if he heard a trill, he would run out to see if he could find it. Sometimes he thought he saw it in the trees. But it never came back to scratch among the chickens.

For weeks afterwards he felt diminished, as if the owl had made him more richly layered, and without it he was pale and attenuated.

Moses comes after midnight with a pocketful of dried peaches stolen from Kazi's pantry and tries to keep him awake by testing him on the names of constellations. Moses spends hours poring over his *Smith's Illustrated Astronomy* and is constantly astounded by the dimensions of the universe. Daniel finds the endless calculations of how far everything is from each other rather tiresome. But he doesn't mind listening, or Moses teasing him for getting the names of the constellations wrong. He knows that Moses is trying to dispel the chill that came between them with the gun.

"Can you imagine being up there..." Moses says, "...looking back at earth when it seems no bigger than the stars to us now?"

Daniel stares up at the distant specks of light and tries to comprehend the vast stretch of cold darkness that separates them from earth. A star detaches itself from the sky, arcing towards earth before disappearing into the blackness.

"Dawid says that in the daytime, the stars come down from the sky and crawl around the earth as beetles."

Dawid had been kidnapped from his Khoe clan as a child by a Boer trekker and forced into slavery. Later he was rescued by missionary travelers who brought him to Bishop Colenso's mission station. There he befriended Joseph, who also knew what it meant to lose a family. He'd joined Colenso's mission after most of his family was killed in a battle with Mpande's army when he was only thirteen, and he still has a dent in his skull from a soldier's knobkerrie. It was after that that he fled to Colenso's mission station. They'd both chosen to join the Whitakers when they came to uMzinyathi some years later. Dawid spoke little of his previous life, but sometimes he told them stories he could remember from his childhood.

Moses laughs. "They'd have to travel a long way. Alpha Centauri's the nearest one, and that's so far...a cannon ball going five hundred miles an hour would take four million years to reach it.

"One day they'll build machines to go into space, like ships that sail in the skies, instead of the sea. Starships. Not coal-fired—coal would make them too heavy. But I think you could power a starship if you could catch electricity from lightning."

"Remember when you tried to catch lightning with your kite?"

"I didn't have all the right things, like a Leyden jar or a silk string. But when I'm older, I'll go to England and learn how to capture lightning properly. Kazi says Uncle Robert might pay for my education."

Great Uncle Robert, (whose son, Roland, famously shot

five rhinos near uMzinyathi) is uMfundisi's* uncle—and a baronet. He inherited the family fortune, while his sister (uMfundisi* mother) just got a small stipend. He got even richer by buying sugar plantations around the world. He bought one near kwaDukuza in Natal, although he lives in England. So, while their parents struggle to get by on the modest wages of an Anglican missionary, Sir Robert is fabulously wealthy.

He's given us little enough, Kazi always says of Sir Robert. The least he could do is pay for the lads' education.

"Do you remember his son, Cousin Roland?" Moses asks.

"Not really. Do you?"

Daniel has a sudden memory of Cousin Roland's gnashing teeth threatening to bite his fingers off. Surely that never happened?

"A little. I didn't like him much. He shot all those rhinos and an elephant. You have to be quite mean to do that. But perhaps his father is nicer."

MOSES

In the early hours Moses is jerked awake by the noise of scratching. The moonlight gleams on the silver fur of the jackal's back as it digs at the rocks they placed in front of its hole from the night before. He nudges Daniel awake and points.

Daniel lifts the gun, but his hands are shaking so much he can hardly aim it.

"Pass it here," Moses whispers.

"No, I must do it."

The jackal pauses in its digging and looks at them, its neat face sharply delineated in the moonlight.

"Now!" Moses hisses, and Daniel fires.

The shot hits the jackal's spine, and it rolls in the dirt. Its high-pitched screams fill the air as it tries to run, but its back legs are dragging. Daniel is screaming too, clutching his stomach. Moses thinks the gun has misfired, but there's no blood on Daniel's shirt. He grabs the gun, approaches the jackal, and fires the other bullet into its head.

When he turns back, Daniel lies silent, huddled on the ground.

Moses kneels down and grasps his shoulder.

"Dan! Wake up...what's wrong? Are you hurt?"

Daniel's eyes flutter open. He sits up, rubbing his head. "What happened?"

"You fainted, I think. After you shot the jackal."

"I felt it," Daniel said. "I felt the jackal."

"What do you mean?"

"It was like...we swapped bodies, and I was looking at me, holding the gun, and I felt the bullet ripping through me, and this terrible pain in my guts as if I'd shot myself. Then everything went dark."

"Does it still hurt?"

"No...I just feel dizzy and sick."

"Should I get Kazi...?"

"No! No, don't tell them. Don't tell uMfundisi* or Kazi or anyone."

Daniel closes his eyes, shivering. "Is the jackal dead?"

Moses goes to the jackal and rolls it over. Its half-open

eyes gleam dully in the moonlight. He notices the swollen teats. The jackal has cubs.

He walks back and sits down.

"I shot it after you fainted. It died quickly...it didn't suffer." He doesn't mention the cubs or the jackal's screams. "I'll tell umfundisi you shot it. Then he'll leave you alone. He wants you to prove that you can do it."

Daniel picks up the gun and passes it to him.

"Take it. I don't want it."

Moses frowns, suppressing the eagerness that flares in his heart. "I can't...you can't give me a thing like this."

"I can...really."

"uMfundisi* will be angry."

"We won't tell him. He should have given it to you anyway. You like guns and understand them. I can't kill things, I see that now. I suppose I am a baby."

"I didn't mean...I don't think you're a baby."

"Was it easy for you? Killing the jackal?"

Moses thinks of the swollen teats, imagines the cubs waiting for the mother who will never return.

"No, it's horrible killing a wild creature like that. But if we didn't shoot that jackal, the hens would be killed."

"Solani enjoys killing things. He loves stoning birds and spearing frogs with sticks."

Solani is a swaggering, boastful boy, the son of Chief Nhlongolwana, whose hand was blown to pieces. The chief won't let him be baptized, but he has sent him to the mission station to learn to read and write.

"Listen, if you're giving me your gun, you should have

my knife," Moses says. He lifts the strap holding the sheath over his head and passes it to his brother.

"Are you sure?"

"Yes, otherwise I can't take the gun. It's not fair."

Daniel takes the knife out of the sheath and turns it to catch the light along the blade. He touches the blade with his thumb, flinching when it cuts his skin. He watches as a thin line of blood, black in the half-light, wells to the surface.

"Mosi, let's make a blood pact!"

"What's that?"

"You each cut your thumb, and you mix your blood. Then you can't ever break it, you'll be brothers forever. I read it in a story in *Boys of England*."

"All very well for you, you cut your thumb already."

"I'll cut the other one then."

He slashes his other thumb, sucking in his breath at the pain.

Moses runs the knife across his thumb, opening a thin seam. As Daniel presses their thumbs together with his other hand, he feels the slippery blood between their skins.

"I promise to be your true brother forever and may God strike me down if I break this promise. You say it too, Mosi."

Moses repeats the words. Daniel releases their thumbs.

"Now we'll always be true brothers, because now we're blood brothers."

"Brothers in blood," Moses adds, remembering how Daniel had said, *It's my birthright.* The gun rests on his lap, heavy and cold.

DANIEL

Daniel sleeps fitfully, waking often with the sensation of a bullet ripping through his flesh and shattering his spine, the sight of the jackal's face framed in the moonlight, the feeling of standing in its body looking at himself. When he sleeps, he falls again and again into the same dream. He's running under thorn trees that scratch his skin. The sharp scents of dry grass and crushed leaves rise up to his nostrils as his heavy legs pound the earth. His head is weighed down by something on his nose. From the corner of one eye he can see the tip of a long horn. There is tearing pain in his chest, and, behind him, a chorus of shouting and gunshots fired by his pursuers.

He wakes late and stumbles through morning prayers and the chores that follow with an aching head, his body filled with the dark awareness of what it is to die. After prayers, uMfundisi* congratulates him on killing the jackal, so pleased that he hardly seems to notice that Moses missed the service. Daniel squirms under his approval and escapes to the umkhiwane tree by the stream as soon as he is able. Climbing the tree always soothes him—the rough bark under his fingers, the leaves luminous against the sunlight, the busy traffic of its many inhabitants: beetles, ants, chameleons, bees, often vervet monkeys or baboons feasting on its abundant round fruits.

He grasps a lower branch, swings his feet up, and stands on the branch to reach the one above. But as he pulls himself up to the next branch, he finds himself staring into the unblinking black eye of an African rock python.

He starts violently and falls, knocking his head and scraping his elbow. He lies, dazed, on the grass below, scanning the branches above for the snake. The leaves are trembling in the windless air, releasing a faint twittering that shimmers through the air. The sound is something between the chirping of cicadas and high children's voices singing in the villages.

The snake is nowhere to be seen. He *knows* he saw it. He can still see it so clearly in his mind—the small nostrils, the overlapping scales of creamy pale yellow, the brown markings outlined with charcoal. But now there is no sign of it.

As he walks back to the house, his mind vibrates with some new clarity. The birdsong, the sunlight on the leaves pulse through his body with painful intensity, as though a layer has been stripped between his skin and the world. He pauses at the cattle kraal to look at the ox that is to be slaughtered later that day for Nomsa's wedding.

Nomsa was one of their first converts. She had come with Thuli to work at the mission in the early days, two sisters whose mother had died, and who were keen to escape their father's vindictive second wife. Kazi recruited them to help look after Daniel and Moses. Even after Nomsa had married by Zulu rites, she carried on helping in the kitchen, in between taking time off to have children. She'd been baptized and was an avowed Christian, but uMfundisi* had kept warning her that she was not married in the eyes of the Lord. Now her husband has at last agreed to convert, restrict himself to one wife, and sanctify their union in the church. It was the second wedding at the mission station— Thuli and Jospeh had been married there three years before.

It comes to him as something unbearable, the beauty of this ox—the sweep of its horns, the velvet softness of its muzzle, the mottled gray of its coat. Joseph calls the ox inkomo engamafu, because its coloring resembles clouds. Daniel pauses to stroke it, imagining the slash of the knife through its neck, bright red blood staining the pearl gray hide. This ox will not live to see the sun go down.

"I'm sorry," he murmurs. The ox stares back at him. He can see his own head mirrored in its dark liquid eyes and wonders if the ox can see itself in his eyes.

We are inside each other, he thinks.

But he's not inside the ox in the way that he'd been inside the jackal. Why had he felt the lead shot tearing through him like that? Was it because he held the gun? Was it because of his intention to kill? Whatever it was, he doesn't want it. He wants to go through life like others do, killing animals as necessary, without being crippled by their pain.

He kneels down by the ox and begs God to deliver him from this strange new way of being. But God, always elusive to him, seems even more distant than usual. As if allowing himself to fall into the body of another creature were a sin that even a merciful God cannot countenance. He sinks down and buries his face in his hands, despairing as he often does of his capacity to do what God wants of him. The ox bumps his shoulder with its nose.

MOSES

After coming back from shooting the jackal, Moses lies awake, disturbed by Daniel tossing and muttering, by the throb of the cut on his hand, by thoughts of the orphaned jackal cubs. When the gray dawn light fills the store room, he gets up and dresses quietly, carrying his boots outside so as not to disturb Daniel. He eats the last few dried peaches in his pocket, washed down with water from the spring, before heading to the chicken coop. They'd left the jackal's body in the kitchen outhouse for Joseph to skin—its pelt would be valued by local villagers for clothing. He picks up the jackal's tracks at the coop and follows them back. For some time, they are clear enough on a sandy path that winds down from the hill above the ironwood trees. But once the tracks leave the path, they are harder to follow. The earth has been baked hard by the winter drought, and the tracks are faint.

He doesn't know what he will do if he finds the cubs. Daisy has just birthed three pups in the stable. Moses has wild ideas of concealing the jackal cubs amongst the litter and raising them as pets. Daniel would help him hide them. But they couldn't hide them forever and uMfundisi* would drown them in an instant.

"They're born with a killer instinct," he'd say. "You can never tame it. Soon as that cub is grown, it will be after the hens. It's in their blood."

He'd tell that story he loves to tell, of the snake who rode on the fox's back across the river. But half way across, the snake bit the fox even though it knew that if the fox died they would both drown.

"The snake couldn't help it. It was in its blood. You can't fight that," uMfundisi* would say.

Daniel is in my blood, Moses thinks, remembering the blood pact they'd made in the night. Would God really strike them down if they broke it? And what would count as breaking the pact?

He loses the tracks, but spots a termite mound some way off. He knows that jackals sometimes dig burrows in mounds that have been broken by aardvarks and abandoned by the termites. When he draws close, he sees the jackal tracks leading away from the mound. But there are other tracks too, bigger tracks with no claw marks. Leopard tracks. When he reaches the mound, he sees the freshly dug earth and bright blood splashes on the soil.

The burrow is empty.

It's the way of the world, he tells himself. And better. What comfort could he have offered the cubs, after all?

He hears the bell for morning prayer. He should go down. But he is gripped by a sudden, stomach-churning despair he sometimes feels when he thinks of vulnerable motherless things, of his ephemeral parents. He turns and hurries up the hill, away from the bell, breaking into a run as he heads through the ironwoods, over the high hill and down through a thicket on the other side. The cloth of his shirt pulls against him, and he tugs it over his head and collapses onto the ground. He lies staring up into the branches above his head, closing his eyes against the shards of sunlight breaking through the leaves. He feels the earth beneath him, the sticks and grass and stones meeting his skin, and the mass of it beneath the grass with its hidden entanglements of tree roots and tunneling earthworms. And beneath that, the hard rocks in the earth's center. He pictures the earth spinning on its axis, its slow revolution around the sun, the planets in the solar system and the galaxies beyond, the patterns and mathematical formulae that hold them all in perpetual motion and eternal, constant relationship.

He feels the edge between his body and the earth blur and soften, until he can no longer tell where he begins and ends, what is boy skin and what is earth skin. He thinks of Dalton's theories, and images flash through his brains of the atoms of the earth meeting the atoms of his bone and blood and flesh. He feels the cool certainty of scientific knowledge and the laws of physics running through his veins, slowing his breathing and his heart to a regular rhythm.

Something is tickling his leg. He glances down to see a snake slithering onto his thigh. His heart beats faster, but he keeps his breathing steady, watching with one eye half-open as the snake moves slowly over his trousers onto the bare skin of his stomach, its scales smooth and warm against his flesh. It's pale green, with dark eyes the color of wet leaves. Its tongue flickers lightly over his skin, seeming to scan him for every thought and memory. He closes his eyes as the snake moves across his chest before slithering down past his ear, moving noiselessly away through the grass.

In the evening, Daniel tells Moses that he saw a python in the tree. Moses thinks about the green snake, but says nothing. He hasn't told Daniel about the jackal's cubs, about his search for them, and the snake seems to be part of the secret. He keeps it to himself, but the memory brings a tingling to his skin and some strange excitement.

MOSES

Some weeks after their birthday, uMfundisi* takes Moses onto the hill for one of his "little talks." Usually when they go up there, umfundisi points to the surrounding home-steads and reminds Moses of his sacred destiny to be a missionary and deliver the people from the "dark vale of heathenism." Or he wants Moses' views as to how Solani or the other boys are "progressing on the spiritual road to Christendom." Which means he wants Moses to snitch on any transgressions. Moses tries to keep his replies both vague and sincere.

But Moses can tell this is a different kind of discussion because uMfundisi* is reluctant to look at him while talk-ing. Usually he forces Moses to meet his eye and seems to be gazing deep into Moses' soul to detect any wavering from the path of righteousness. But now uMfundisi's* mild blue gaze falls on the distant hills, on a small hairy caterpillar that is progressing up a grass stalk, on his own hands...any-where but Moses' face.

"Moses, you are of an age now when you might have certain urges," uMfundisi* says, glowering now at the sky as if these urges were the fault of the clouds. "You might find your hands...er...straying to your...uh...manly parts. If you allow this to happen, you might experience...

a certain *eruption* in the night. It is particularly pressing that you resist any such inclinations. Touching yourself is a grievous sin and can invite the devil to lead you down a path of wickedness. Of course, you need to attend to bodily hygiene, but do not be tempted to linger when washing those parts of your body...cold water is advisable. I know that you may need to overcome certain...er...disadvantages due to your...parentage. This is not your fault of course, but you will need to strive extra hard to overcome these. Sincere prayer will help you...shall we pray now?"

Moses listens to this with growing bemusement and squirming discomfort. He can't imagine what kind of eruption his father is referring to. Shouting? Screaming? Breaking out into boils? And what does he mean by the disadvantages of his parentage? Had his parents, during their fleeting shadowy acquaintanceship with uMfundisi*, betrayed such "inclinations?"

In the coming days, he lies awake for hours, terrified to fall asleep lest he erupt. And now that he is trying so hard to keep his hands from his manly parts, they seem to want to stray there all the time. He longs to discuss it with Daniel, but wonders whether such troubles are only the provenance of boys with heathen origins.

Perhaps he could raise it with Peter. He and Solani are a little older than Moses and Daniel, and the only boys from the surrounding homesteads who stay at the mission station. There are also four girls around twelve, and Thuli and Joseph's son, Hlali. Other children come and go. Solani's father, Chief Nhlongolwana, encourages the villagers to send their children. He's not interested in Jesus, but says that their children are growing up in a world with white people and need to understand their ways. But the villagers need the children to help them with the cattle and planting and don't see any reason for them to learn about the white man's ways. uMfundisi* tries to get more scholars into Kazi's "school room" under the umsinsi tree by giving any family that sends a child a packet of strychnine. They use it to bait chicken carcasses to kill leopards or jackals.

He certainly can't talk to Solani. Solani never stops reminding Moses and Daniel that his father is a great inkosi and owner of over four hundred cattle and twenty-three wives. Whereas Daniel's father only has one wife and thirteen cows. And Moses is just the orphan of unknown "amakhafula," an insulting word, meaning someone who's been spat out.

Although it's often used to refer to the black people in the Natal colony, hearing Solani use this term to describe his parents cuts Moses to the quick. Moses prides himself on keeping cool in the face of provocation, but Solani's taunting seems to bypass his brain and go straight to his fists so that before he knows it, he is beating Solani with all the ferocity he can muster. He usually comes off the worst, but he almost welcomes Solani's retaliatory blows. The pain they inflict make the parents he is defending more tangible.

The only person Solani likes is Kazi. He hates it that he gets his sums wrong or that Moses helps Kazi teach him and Peter their daily lessons. Kazi imagines that seeing

Moses so accomplished will drive the boys to emulate him, but it just fills Solani with rage.

Moses doesn't mind filling Solani with rage. Solani's given him enough, he's happy to give some back.

Peter is much easier. He is Thuli and Nomsa's cousin, who used to be called Siya, but uMfundisi* gave him a new name when he was baptized. He's an amiable boy, always happy to show Moses and Daniel the best swimming places in the river or which trees grow the best wild fruits. But Moses has no idea how to broach the subject, even with Peter.

One evening, some weeks after uMfundisi's* chat, Peter asks him whether Christian boys also do the ukuthomba ceremony. Moses is milking the black cow with the bent over horn while Peter stands by her head and strokes her ears, the only way to stop her from kicking.

"What's ukuthomba?"

"When you get your first—that thing that happens to boys in the night—you get a good feeling and..." Peter gestures to his groin. "It's when you become insizwa, not a little boy any more. Then you can look after the cattle. But maybe you're still a small boy."

Is *this* the eruption? Moses has only the haziest idea of what Peter is referring to, but it seems to involve that shameful part of the body where eruptions take place.

"I'm not a small boy," he says, loftily. "Of course I know all about it. But I don't let it happen to me. I pray so it doesn't happen. uMfundisi* says Jesus doesn't like it."

Peter laughs so hard that he forgets to stroke the cow's

ears. Moses has to grab the bucket away before she kicks it over,

"Why doesn't Jesus like it?" Peter asks when he can stop laughing for long enough. "It's the best thing for a boy! My umkhulu says it shows you're on the way to becoming a man. We stayed up all night listening to uMkhulu. He told us everything we needed to know to be izinsizwa. Heh, your Jesus is a funny one, he doesn't like too many things."

Moses laughs too, hoping to suggest that he'd been joking. Peter will tell Solani now, he thinks. Give him something else to torment me with.

As he walks to the kitchen carrying the milk pail, he wonders what it would be like to have a grandfather who tells you everything you need to know to be a young man. To have a grandfather at all.

He thinks of Gogo, the feel of her hands stroking his head, the lift and fall of her voice as she explained the mysteries of the world through her labyrinthine stories. His hands stray to his throat, seeking the circle of white beads she had given him, the beads he had worn ever since she left. Until they were confirmed earlier that year. uMfundisi* gave him a silver cross on a chain, and told him to leave the beads. Christians don't wear beads, his father said.

He keeps them in his drawer and sometimes holds them in his hand at night. His neck still feels naked without them.

DANIEL

uMfundisi* has the talk about eruptions with Daniel too, although Daniel is far too mortified to ask Moses about it.

He is equally mystified by the nature of the eruption. He wonders whether his peculiar experience with the jackal might qualify. But some weeks later he experiences the "eruption" for himself. It wakes him from a dream in which he and Moses were wrestling, as they often do, but for some reason neither were wearing clothes. He wakes abruptly with a memory of a sweet warmth flowing through his groin and a sticky wetness staining his nightshirt.

"What is it, Dani?" Moses asks sleepily. "You called out. Did you have a bad dream? Shall I light the lamp?"

"No," he answers, ashamed to be seen in the light.

They lie silently. At length, Daniel brings himself to ask Moses if the Reverend also spoke to him about the eruption. He asks softly, half-hoping that Moses has fallen asleep and won't hear. But he replies.

"Yes...was that what woke you?"

"No," Daniel answers, too quickly. "Has it happened to you?"

"No...I hope it never does."

"It won't happen to me," Daniel says firmly, "because I pray so hard about it before bed."

Moses tells Daniel what Peter said about the ukuthomba ceremony. "He says it happens to all boys and his grandfather says there's nothing wrong with it, it's a good thing."

"Well, his grandfather also thinks there's nothing wrong with consulting witchdoctors or having many wives," Daniel retorts. "You should tell him it's wrong."

"He thinks it's the best thing that can happen to a boy. He just laughs when you tell him it's wrong."

Long after Moses has fallen asleep, Daniel lies awake, listening to the nightjars and crickets. The night is chilly, but he feels flushed and overheated. He moves his body, seeking a cooler part of the bed. His cheeks burn as he recalls the dream he'd been having about Moses. Imagine if his brother knew what he'd been dreaming! His body had been behaving so strangely recently—first body jumping, now this. Not to mention the way his voice sometimes shoots up, sounding like the squeaky wheel on the wagon. But at least the eruption also seemed to happen to other boys.

Why would God make your body able to erupt if it's so wrong?

It must be a test, he decides. Perhaps if he resists any more eruptions, he wouldn't have the problem of jumping into an animal's body if he needed to kill it.

He drifts into sleep and dreams again of being a rhino running through the thorn bushes, the light and shade flickering through his eyes, the shouts and gunshots pursuing him.

However hard he tries, he keeps falling into animals' bodies, whether awake or asleep. But at least this dream does not cause any more eruptions.

Mr. Struthers comes with the thunderstorms of early spring, when the earth softens with the rains and shiny millipedes as thick as your finger trundle over the damp soil like miniature trains. He arrives with two wagons buzzing with flies, pungent with the stench of the heaped dried skins, and salted meat hanging from the arched ribs of the canopies. Peering into one of the wagons, Daniel is startled when one of the pelts groans, and he realizes that he is looking at a man—filthy, emaciated and racked with fever, his red-rimmed blue eyes burning in a face infested with insect bites and blisters.

Mr. Struthers was the manager on Uncle Robert's sugar farm, but he left the estate and took up hunting instead. uMfundisi* is reluctant to put him up.

"He's persona non grata in the Fitchley family after he abandoned his post on the sugar plantation," he says. "It will hardly please Uncle Robert if we take him in. Besides, he's proved himself to be feckless, not a good influence at our mission."

But Kazi says he'll die if they don't take him in, and, feckless or not, Christians don't turn their backs on those in need.

For two weeks Kazi runs herself ragged restoring him to health—rubbing ointment into his infected scratches and bites, spooning calf's foot jelly and broth made from Liebig's extract of beef into his mouth, or emptying the chamber pot into the privy. Moses helps her. But Daniel is so sickened by the sight and smell of the patient, he can hardly bear to be in the same room.

Each day, he is drawn to the wagons. So many skins— plain, spotted, dappled, mottled, patched or striped—so many tails, so many horns of kudu and other antelope— spiraled and twisted or straight or curved—and hippo tusks and crocodile skins. Thirty massive elephant tusks piled in one wagon, which the bearers say will be going to King

Mpande to pay for the right to hunt in his kingdom.

"The king has two dwellings full of these tusks," one remarks. "Full, full full...from the floor to the top."

There are thirty-four rhino horns. When he rests his hands on them, he feels a tremor in his veins. *Bhejane*, he whispers, and remembers the rhino that he saw drinking from the stream one moonlit night. His mind fills with the slash of the horn in the sky above him, the burning coal of the red-rimmed eye.

MOSES

Kazi says Mr. Struthers is sick from malaria and tropical fever, but Daniel says he made himself sick from killing all those animals. It's true that the smell of blood seems to cling to his gray skin, underlying the other putrid odors of sweat and excrement and infection.

Moses' curiosity about how sickness shows itself in the human body overcomes his disgust. He is always Kazi's assistant when she tends to illnesses or injuries at the mission. Kazi says she used to do the same for her father. Her mother died when she was a baby, so, until her father married again many years later, it was just the two of them. She went everywhere with him, saw births and deaths, children mangled by the mechanized weaving looms in the factories, farmers who'd put pitchforks through their toes. Her father had been fascinated by the healing herbs that grew in their parish—elderberry and feverfew and marshmallow. When Kazi left for Africa, he gave her John Skelton's *Family Medical Advisor*, an imposing leather-bound tome which covered all manner of ailments, and a leather case filled with remedies. Kazi grows some medicinal plants, like the elderberries, in her garden, and she is also interested in local medicinal herbs. She says that she learnt about these from Gogo before she left and from other women and herbalists in the area.

"But let's not mention this to uMfundisi*," she says, with that smile which means she's pretending to be joking but is deadly serious.

uMfundisi* thinks that any doctoring practiced by the local people is "quackery at best and satanic witchcraft at worst."

Moses likes helping Kazi because she explains everything she is doing and asks his opinion and listens to his answers.

He doesn't like Mr. Struthers. He becomes ever more demanding as his condition improves and seems to think that Kazi's sole purpose in the world is to run about seeing to his needs.

When his fever subsides, Mr. Struthers sits on the veranda recounting hunting stories to anyone who'll listen—ignoring the Reverend Whitaker's dark looks whenever he walks past. His watery blue eyes glisten as he describes the bloody wounds caused by the bullets, his red hands fly about to convey the dramas of the chase. The bigger his audience, the more dangerous the animals become, the more daring his attacks on them.

Peter and Solani reward Mr. Struthers' accounts with admiring whistles, but they mock him behind his back.

"He looks like a goat," Peter says, "with that huge nose

and long nostrils and that pointy stringy beard."

"Yes," Solani agrees. "We should call him uBuso bembuzi, the goat-faced one."

Solani derides Moses for helping Kazi, for "doing women's work for that goat-faced thing." Moses ignores him. He knows that Solani is jealous because he's getting so much of Kazi's time and gratitude.

DANIEL

One sultry afternoon under lowering clouds and rumbling thunder, the boys walk up the river in search of a stray bullock. They've been arguing about whether it's better to find cattle by following the crested eagle or by holding the isiphungumangathi chrysalis. Peter says that if you hold the chrysalis in your hand, it'll point in the direction the cattle have gone, but Solani says the crested eagle is more reliable.

Daniel walks ahead through a thicket of bushwillows and acacia trees, the air hot and thick around him. He swats the flies hovering around his face and scrutinizes the ground for tracks. A strange spoor jumps at him, sharp in the red earth—three massive oval toe marks around the imprint of the central footpad. As he lays his hand on it, the memory of his own small foot laid on a spoor like this jolts his heart.

Bhejane...

He sits back on his haunches, looking for another footprint. Three more are faintly visible in the red soil, heading into the thicker bush. He strains his ears, but all he can hear is the insistent call of a barbet in the trees and the high shrill clicking of the cicadas.

"Have you found tracks?" Moses asks, coming from behind.

"Bhejane," he whispers, pointing at the print.

He hears the voices of the others coming through the trees and leaps up, kicking leaves over the spoor.

"The bullock's not here," he calls, hurrying away from the tracks before the boys can see them.

"What's that, moving through the trees?" Solani points past him.

Daniel turns. In the thick foliage some thirty yards off, are the tips of two pointed ears and the distinctive curves of the twin horns.

"It's nothing," he says. But the rhino is stepping out of the bushwillows towards them.

"Yo! Bhejane!" Solani hisses quietly, but not quietly enough.

The rhino lifts its head. It snorts and scuffs the dirt with its feet. Then lowers its head and charges. Moses, Solani and Peter swing themselves into a nearby mthombothi tree. Daniel jumps for the branch, but it's too high for him to grip. Moses reaches down, but Daniel's fingers slip through his grasp.

He ducks behind the tree as the rhino crashes up. He hears it squealing and grunting in fury. Its formidable horn swings into sight as it jabs at the boys in the branches.

The rhino smashes its horn against the tree, sending shockwaves through the bark. As it moves, Daniel moves to keep the trunk between them. Its body is a mountain of muscle and bone in a wrinkled hide, so close he can see the flakes of drying mud on its flanks. Its nostrils flare red beneath a horn as long as his arm. He pictures the horn gouging his body, his ribs splintering beneath its knees.

The sounds fade, but when he risks a glance, the rhino's still watching from a few feet off. When it sees his head move, it charges again.

At last, the animal moves away. Daniel leans, trembling, against the trunk. His ears ring with the crash of its horn against the bark.

The other boys drop from the branches.

"Hau, we thought you were finished, little brother." Peter puts his arm over Daniel's shoulders and gives him a friendly squeeze.

"Just wait till we tell uBuso bembuzi," Solani says. "I bet he'll give us a pocket knife each, at least, if we lead him to the rhino."

Daniel lowers his head and drives it hard into Solani's stomach. Solani staggers and bends double as Daniel rains blows on his back and head. Solani grasps Daniel's shirt and delivers stinging blows to his nose and face. Daniel retaliates with wild kicks and punches until Moses and Peter pull him off.

"Hey, wena, what's wrong with you?" Solani demands. "You think you can fight me? Don't you know that the other boys call me Mpisi'Kazimudli, the one whom even the hyenas fear?"

"You can't tell him about the rhino," Daniel roars. "If you tell I'll...I'll kill you."

"You'll *kill* me? You? How will you kill me? Pray your Jesus strikes me dead? Why do you care, anyway?"

"Because he'll shoot the rhino. He'll *kill* it."

"So? The rhino wanted to kill you, you soft-brained thing."

"The rhino's his idlozi," Moses interjects. "It's his grandfather."

Solani laughs. "White people don't have ancestors."

"Of course they do. Do you think they just grow out of the ground like amadumbe?"

"You're telling lies. Amadlozi don't come as rhinos, they come as snakes and lizards."

"It's different for white people. Their amadlozi come in different shapes. They call them ghosts."

"So why did the rhino chase him?"

Moses snorts. "Didn't you see? It wasn't *chasing*, it was *greeting* him."

Solani stares at Daniel narrowly. Daniel stares back, blood trickling from his nose, and feels the rhino flaring behind his eyes. He sees his own reflection in Solani's eyes morph and shift momentarily into a bloodshot eye and up-lifted horn. As if he has seen it too, Solani flinches and turns away.

"Hau, I don't care about your ancestor. I'll tell uBuso bembuzi if I feel like it."

But Daniel had seen the fear in his eyes, and he knows that he won't tell.

As they walk home, he knows that some splinter of himself was left in the rhino, is still running with the rhino through the light and shadow. Despite its terrifying ferocity, he doesn't believe that the rhino wanted to harm him. It came back to remind him, he thinks. To remind him that he is inkonyane likabhejane, the rhino's child.

Mr. Struthers leaves soon after. uMfundisi* finally manages to communicate that he's outstayed his welcome. The mission children run to the top of the high hill to watch his ox wagons wind down through the valley beyond and over the next rise, en route to King Mpande's umuzi. Daniel stands in the sunlight, listening to the crack of the whips and the calls of the drivers fading as they move across the valley. He sees ghostly herds of buffalos and zebras and elephants running after the wagons to take back their horns, take back their skins and their tails and their tusks, to take back the lives that they've lost.

Kazi should have let him die, he thinks.

MOSES

Soon after Struthers leaves, Reverend Whitaker embarks on an extended trip to meet the new bishop of Zululand at Eshowe and to ride with him to various mission stations. Kazi starts coughing a few days later. No one pays much attention until she crumples to the ground one morning by the chicken coop, her basket overturned and eggs broken and strewn around her.

Joseph carries her into the front room and lays her on the daybed. Thuli shakes her with alarming vigor (as she does everything), then loosens her clothing and fans her face with such vehemence that Moses is afraid she might acidentally strike her. Kazi opens her eyes to stare at them with confused indignation.

"What's all the fuss about?" she asks with a trace of her characteristic briskness. Moses tells her that she fainted while carrying the eggs to the house.

"Did I drop the eggs?"

"Yes..."

She sighs, closing her eyes as if the loss of eggs makes her infinitely tired.

"Thank you, I'll be fine now...just a chill..."

She breaks off in a paroxysm of coughing that raises red spots on her pale cheeks and leaves her sweating and trembling. She coughs until she vomits a yellow liquid onto her chest.

Moses grabs a cloth that is drying by the fire, wipes her face and dabs at the vomit. He looks at her chalk-white pallor, the beads of sweat on her forehead.

"It's not just a chill, is it?"

She shakes her head, grasping his wrist tightly, until the spasm has passed.

"Maybe not," she gasps at length. "I fear it may be pneumonia or pleurisy..."

She falls back against the pillows, her teeth chattering despite her burning skin. While Nomsa and Thuli undress and bathe her, Moses hauls the *Family Medical Advisor* off the shelf and rifles through the pages. He finds a recipe for cough medicine and sends Daniel to get elderflowers while he rummages through the jars in Kazi's medicine chest. They make a poultice—mashing oats with ginger and mustard in water heated on the fire—and a tea of cloves and cayenne and the elderflowers, sweetened with wild honey.

"What are you doing?" Thuli demands, emerging from Kazi's room.

"Mixing medicine for Kazi."

"You want to poison her?"

"It's not poison, Mama, it's medicine."

"Are you an English doctor now? You think you know everything about white people, Moses, but ubukhali nganx-anye njengommese—you're only sharp on one side, like a knife."

Moses suppresses a flash of irritation. Thuli has a fero-cious devotion to Kazi, who saved her from a troubled family life—Moses suspects that her professed faith in Christianity is more to please Kazi than God. He knows Thuli is terrified to see Kazi so ill, but her comment still stings.

"I don't think I know everything. I'm reading it in this book. An English doctor wrote down these things, so I'm just following what he says. Look."

Moses thrusts the book at her and points to the words. But Thuli can't read English well and this just infuriates her further.

"Hayi, wena, you think I'm stupid?" She knocks the book away. "Books are for God's word and Bible stories. Not medicine. You must get a real doctor."

"We can't get a doctor, Mama," Daniel says. "The near-est doctor is in Pietermaritzburg. They won't come up here, even if we could get a message to them. It's six days' riding at least."

"I mean a real doctor...our izinyanga in the homesteads treat these sicknesses better than any umlungu."

"Our izinyanga can't treat a Christian person," declares Nomsa. "uMfundisi says they do the devil's work because they consult the ancestors."

"Nomsa's right, you can't bring those people here," Daniel agrees.

"But izinyanga zokwelapha don't only work with the ancestors. They can treat her with amakhambi medicines," Thuli insists. "Those herbs work better than any English medicine."

This argument is conducted in furious whispers before the open door to Kazi's room. Kazi's faint voice calling Thuli interrupts them.

"Now you've disturbed her!" Thuli grumbles as she goes to Kazi's bedside. She comes out a few seconds later, looking aggrieved and clucking to herself.

"Just go on, then, with your...business," she says, waving her hands dismissively at their potions. "I'll ask Joseph to slaughter a chicken, and so I can make soup."

Moses lays the poultice on Kazi's ribs, puts a fire-warmed brick wrapped in a vinegar-soaked cloth at her feet, and spoons their concoction into her mouth. Now that she's clean and dry, her illness is at least not spilling out of her in frightening ways. She's pale and feverish, and her side seems to be hurting her fiercely, but her teeth are no longer chattering. Daniel kneels by the bed, patting his mother's hand vaguely.

She smiles weakly. "You're a born healer, Moses. And Dan—you too of course."

But Moses can see that Daniel doesn't want to be here, with Kazi's gray pallor and her hand burning beneath his fingers. He wants to be outside, with his mother normal and whole.

Kazi insists that there is no need to send word to uM-fundisi*. By the time he gets here, she says, she'll be quite well again, and this tour with the bishop is important. It's true that it will take several days to find him and several more for him to return. And he wouldn't be much help—Kazi is the doctor in the household.

At first she guides Moses. But as the days pass, she becomes less and less able to treat herself. Thuli gives up on getting an inyanga, but says they should at least use the local medicinal plants. She says the strongest medicine for this kind of sickness comes from the bark and leaves of the isibhaha tree, but she hasn't seen one nearby. She says the trunk is reddish, with white flecks as though the women have scattered corn on the red soil. The leaves are dark on one side and pale on the other. They send Daniel out to look for it since he's not much help around Kazi. He brings back the bark and leaves of many trees, but always Thuli shakes her head and says they are wrong.

There is a constant stream of people from the local homesteads, peering worriedly through the windows until Thuli and Nomsa chase them away. They bring sweet milk and corn, a white goat kid, and healing herbs, but Thuli says none are from the isibhaha tree. Moses adds them to the medicinal teas anyway. The Reverend Whitaker claims that izinyanga's remedies kill more than they cure, but Moses knows that Kazi has used remedies such as the isihaqa and umhlonyane leaves for sick children at the mission, and has often remarked on their efficacy.

Little Hlali, Thuli and Joseph's son, brings a picture he's drawn of his favorite cow, and the girls in Kazi's school sew her a small pillow with imphepho leaves inside. uNgqobiz-itha, a one-eyed white-haired soldier with a face rendered hideous by an old spear wound in his right cheek, walks three miles every day to bring a calabash of amasi. Moses won't let anyone into her room, but he puts the offerings beside her bed and passes on messages. Once Hlali crept in while Moses was dozing. He woke to find the child fast asleep, curled up on the end of the bed like a puppy.

Daniel tries to help Moses follow John Skelton's instructions, boiling up a scummy cough syrup of licorice root, honey and onion, heating poultices to ease the crippling pains in her chest, giving her inhalations of camphor. But he can hardly bear to sit with her when the others need a break. Moses doesn't blame him. He too is terrified by the bloody dark sputum that she coughs up, the alternating dry heat and clammy coldness of her skin, her continuous chest pain and headaches. But he fights his terror by trying to understand her symptoms, by methodically treating the illness as best he can.

DANIEL

As the days pass, their mother grows steadily weaker, and

Daniel and Moses agree to send Joseph to find uMfundisi*. At times she's agitated, calling out to her father or begging her attendants to make "those people" go away, pointing to the empty doorway. At other times she sinks into a stupor. Daniel places a mirror to her lips to check that she is breathing, or searches her wrist for the fluttering of her pulse.

Thuli's generous mouth tightens into a grim line as she watches her descent. Like Moses, she's reluctant to let Kazi out of her sight. But one morning she announces that she has to go to her homestead for urgent family business.

When Daniel comes in after evening milking, Thuli is still not back. He warms up some stew from the previous evening and chases Moses out of the room.

"Go eat and rest. I'll wait with her until Thuli comes," he says.

He sits in the flickering lamplight, watching the evening sky darken through the window, listening to the ticking of the clock in the front room dragging out the hours. He brushes the tangles from her long dark hair—she always loved him brushing her hair, but she doesn't respond. He reads her favorite psalms—*I lift mine eyes to the hills from whence cometh my help.* Then he sits alone with her labored breathing and his thoughts.

He finds himself walking up in the high hills with his mother, through nodding grass heads catching the light. Kazi laughs under her parasol. A cloud of yellow butterflies flutters up from the grass, swirling around his mother until he can't see her any more. When the butterflies flutter away, she has gone, and he stands alone calling for her, hearing nothing but the echoes of his own voice and the singing of the wind in the grass.

The singing wind becomes the rasp of his mother's breath. He lays his head on her bed, fighting back his tears. "Don't go," he whispers. "Please Mama...don't go."

He's never called her Mama. She's always been Kazi. But maybe when she's this sick, "Mama" is the only word she can understand. "Mama, Mama, Mama," he repeats until the word becomes a continuous murmur like the buzzing of bees in his ears, devoid of meaning.

Late in the night, he wakes from a doze to the sound of muttered words. The lamp has gone out, but in the firelight from the front room he sees a figure moving in the shadows, and hears the falling drops of liquid.

"Who's there?" he calls.

"It's just me, Thuli."

Daniel relights the candle on the small table by the bed. Thuli stands frozen in the candlelight, her expression both apprehensive and defiant, clutching a small calabash.

"What's that?" he asks, reaching for it. "Is it from the witchdoctor?"

Thuli pulls it away. "Look at her, Dani! Do you want her to die? Our izinyanga know how to treat these things... why do you think you know better? You, a mere child?"

Daniel lunges at her, trying to grab the calabash, but she darts across the room and pushes a chair between them.

"How can you bring witchcraft in here?" he demands. "Don't you know that God forbids anyone to practice witchcraft or communicate with ancestors?"

"Lalela, Daniel, she gets weaker every day. She needs these izintelezi to protect her from the evil ones."

"If you anger God, she'll never get well!" Daniel roars, causing his mother to wake and call out. Taking advantage of Thuli's distraction, Daniel leans over the chair, snatches the calabash, and runs outside. He flings the calabash away into the trees and falls on his knees.

"Lord, forgive Thuli! Forgive me too for my sins! Lord, please don't punish Kazi! Please let her live. Please Lord, punish me in whatever way you choose, but just let her live."

He lies with his face against the damp earth. The wind rustles in the dark trees, a baboon barks in warning. There are nightjars out there in the darkness, and crickets and jackals and moths fluttering towards the light.

But where in all of this is God?

That night Daniel dreams he is walking through the forest and sees a red duiker lying beneath a tree. As he kneels beside it, it becomes his mother, lying in a pool of blood. Her eyes stare up at him sightlessly. When he touches her, her body is leathery and desiccated, like the skins in Mr. Struthers' wagons.

You must make a sacrifice, a voice says from high in the tree, which has turned into the wooden Jesus. *Show me that you are pure of heart. Then she will live.*

He wakes with an ache in his throat, as though he'd been shouting, with the accusing voice ringing in his ears...*you must make a sacrifice...*

He gets out of bed—still dressed from the previous night—and puts on his shoes. The room is chilly and dark. He builds up the fire in the front room, blowing on it to rekindle the flame. The gray ash blows back into his face, its gritty flakes bitter on his tongue. He puts the water on for Kazi's tea and goes into her room. She is sleeping restlessly, tossing and muttering. Moses looks up wearily.

"I have to go somewhere," Daniel says. "Can you ask Nomsa to do my chores?"

"You're leaving? Dan, don't leave..."

"I'll make you tea before I go."

He goes back into the front room, followed by Moses. "How can you leave? She's dying. Don't you understand? Our mother is dying."

"Don't say that!"

"You have to face it. Stop running away! She's dying. If uMfundisi* doesn't get here soon, he'll not see her alive again."

Without responding, Daniel goes into the storeroom to get Moses' gun, powder and ammunition and pushes past him out the door.

"Daniel, have you gone mad? What are you doing? Who are you going to shoot?"

The morning is cool and misty, smudging the trees into a shadow world that maroons him in solitude. A steady drizzle falls, soaking his clothes and sending cool trickles running down his neck. The birds are silent, save for the mourn-ful call of the umgugwane bird. He feels an undercurrent of fear, a sense of small, tender creatures scuttling into the undergrowth, warning each other. For he is no longer a rhino's child, a boy who can dissolve himself into animals. He is a man with a gun, a man with a mission to claim his birthright and prove his faith...*and dread of thee will fall on all the beasts of the earth.*

Half a mile down the river, he picks up the spoor of a red duiker, each footprint imprinted on the damp soil like two teardrops. He follows it reluctantly, relieved when it disappears, sickened when it reveals itself again. The gun grows heavier with each step.

When he finally sees the buck, he is shocked by its physicality, as if he'd imagined that the spoor would lead not to a living creature, but to some ghostly apparition like the one in his dream. It is on the far side of a clearing with its back to him, rubbing itself against a tree, causing a small shower of leaves and raindrops. He moves noiselessly behind a bush, loads the gun, cocks it softly and raises it to his shoulder.

The buck swings to face him, ears twitching, dark eyes alert—a young male with small sharp horns tipped with black, as if they'd been scorched in a fire. Its wing-like ears are lined with droplets of water clinging to the silver fur. Two black strips run from its liquid dark eyes like the mark of tears.

The buck can't see him through the mist and the thick foliage. After a few seconds, it turns its back and carries on rubbing itself against the tree.

He squints along the barrel. He feels himself travel down

the gun into the buck's body. His ears twitch, his feet are hoofed and cloven, the bark of the tree is rough against his fur. He fights the trembling in his hands to hold the gun steady—he owes the buck that at least, to shoot true. He squeezes one trigger, then the other. The lead shot slams into his heart. His legs crumple, and all goes dark as his life is shocked out of him.

MOSES

Moses hears the gunshot and hurries towards the sound. He'd left soon after Daniel, as soon as Thuli came in to sit with Kazi, and had been tracking his brother's footsteps along the river. As he reaches the clearing, he sees his brother lying on the ground. He hurries forward, clenched with fear, but there's no blood on Daniel and he seems unhurt.

"Dani! Wake up...are you hurt?"

"Mosi...you are here? What...?"

Daniel pushes himself up, wincing, and looks around the clearing.

"The duiker...is it dead?"

Moses follows his eyes and sees the buck for the first time, lying beneath the tree, blood pooling on the ground.

"I'll check now...are *you* alright?"

"Yes...I just fainted, I think...why are you here?"

"I followed your tracks."

Moses walks to the buck and kneels beside it. It's lying still, its half-open eyes glazed.

"It is dead. You got it right in the heart."

Daniel walks over and crouches beside him.

"Why did you kill it?" Moses asks.

"I...had a dream...I think God wanted it. God wanted a sacrifice."

"It must've been hard for you. Is that why you fainted?"

"Yes, it was the same...like with the jackal. I felt everything. It is a terrible thing to die, Mosi. I wish I hadn't killed it. It was stupid. How could it even help Kazi?"

"It was brave of you. You thought it was what God wanted. You were trying..."

Moses brushes the leaves off the body of the buck. He pauses and looks sharply at the tree. Red trunk, speckled with white, the leaves dark green on one side, and pale gray on the other...

"Dan...look! I think it's the isibhaha tree..."

When they get back, they leave the buck with Dawid for butchering and skinning. Thuli is in the kitchen. They show her the leaves and bark.

"Yes! That's the right one! How did you find it?"

Daniel tells her about his dream, and about the buck leading them to the tree.

"The amadlozi sent that buck," she says.

She uses Kazi's pestle and mortar to grind the bark into a paste. They mix it with water.

Kazi is barely conscious. Her skin, stretched thin over her cheekbones, burns Moses' fingers as he holds her head, while Thuli spoons the tea into her mouth. It's too late, he thinks. She's beyond the isibhaha, beyond the sacrificial buck, the potions and poultices and broths and hours of prayer. She is on the far side of a deep ravine and nothing can bring her back now.

For the sixteen hours, they keep feeding her the tea from the isibhaha bark. Towards dawn, Moses drifts into dreams that he is walking through a forest with Gogo. Kazi is flitting through the dark trees ahead of them, her white night gown gleaming in the light. He runs to catch her, but each time he reaches her, she vanishes, only to appear again in a different place.

He wakes to sunlight and Thuli shaking him. He looks up blearily from the chair. His mother is lying awake, her eyes calm and clear.

"Moses!" she says, smiling—weak, pale-faced, but smiling! —and grasps his hand. Her skin is cool.

Daniel, Thuli and Nomsa are laughing and weeping, and Nomsa has broken into a boisterous rendition of *Praise my soul the king of Heaven*. Moses joins the hymn. But he finds himself wondering: was it God who saved her because of their prayers or Daniel's sacrifice? Or was it the isibhaha tree? Was it possible that the healing remedies of the amaZulu were stronger than English medicine, that their remedies were more powerful than prayer?

He thinks of Thuli's words...*the amadlozi sent that buck.*

"Siyabonga, Dani, Mosi. Thank you for trusting me. And for finding the tree."

"Thanks to you, Thuli. You saved her," Moses says.

"And the buck. The buck that I killed," Daniel adds.

"We all saved her," Thuli says.

PART THREE
1871 TO 1876
EVOLUTION

MOSES

The stealthy walker arrives in November, when the swallows are feeding chicks in their nests under the eaves of the stable, and Kazi has fully recovered from her illness. For weeks before his arrival, the mission is in a frenzy, as uMfundisi* exhorts everyone to get ready for Bishop Saunders, the new bishop of Zululand. A small house is built for him, its floor minted with fresh cow dung. The roughly built church is finished at last, although the congregants find it stuffy and less conducive to prayer than the shaded clearing that was used before. But uMfundisi* insists that the bishop can't perform his services under the trees "like some heathen voodoo dancer." The small wooden Jesus hangs in the dim light of the church, looking despondent about his new quarters.

The bishop arrives in time for a trip to pay respects to

King Mpande at Nodwengu. With his sharp, curved nose and hunched skinny shoulders, he reminds Moses of the glossy ibises that dig worms out of the soil with their beaks. The bishop digs out transgressions with matching fervor. He only spends a few days at the mission before their departure, but finds time to utter many opinions in a voice that makes itself heard from all corners of the mission station. Despite his penetrating voice, the bishop proves to be the master of quiet movement. His habit of sneaking up on people to check that they are working soon earns him the nickname of uMcathama—the stealthy walker.

The trip to Nodwengu provides a welcome distraction. They are visiting King Mpande's royal umuzi in honor of the Feast of the First Fruits, the umkhosi wokweshwama. uMfundisi* says it may be Mpande's last feast, as his health is declining—for some years, his son has been the real power in Zululand.

Moses' excitement is tempered because they're taking Daisy's pup, Maggie, to give to King Mpande. She's a long-legged black and tan bitch, with wise eyes and black-tipped ears. He and Daniel have trained her since she was weaned, and he feels sick at the thought of losing her.

They travel northwest by ox wagon over rolling hills, through high green grass capped with feathery crimson and white seed heads nodding in the wind. Vivid scarlet and black grasshoppers leap up from the grass at every step. They pass tracts of pink lilies and gladioli, and swathes of agapanthus glowing blue under darting sunbirds and humming bees. As the sun climbs, the breeze brings a welcome relief from the heat.

The boys run ahead to climb a rocky outcrop, and sit sharing the sour-sweet apricots that Kazi gave them, watched by blue-headed lizards basking on the sun-warmed rocks. Solani boasts that next year he'll be conscripted—uzobuthwa—and join his other age mates at a military umuzi to form a new regiment. He says it'll be the fiercest regiment ever and the soldiers will be desired by all the best girls, and when they go to battle, they'll wash their spears in blood.

"Me too," says Peter.

Solani laughs scornfully. "Christians don't join the impi. Imagine a soldier in trousers!"

Solani wears trousers himself—it's a condition of being at the mission. Kazi won him round by finding a pair of red braces for him in the missionary bundle. But he has refused to wear a shirt, even to attend church.

"uMfundisi said I can go if I want. He promised the Prince that even boys who've been baptized can join amabutho, and give allegiance to the king."

"Do you want to go?" Moses asks.

"Yes," Peter says. "It's a great honor to khonza to our king. If you were a true Zulu, you'd understand."

Moses flinches. "I give my allegiance to a higher king," he says stiffly.

"Yes, King Jesus," Solani says mockingly. "The king who was so great that his people nailed him to a tree."

Moses stands up and bunches his fists, his eyes flashing. "Take that back!"

Solani stands up too and pushes past Moses roughly.

"Come, Siya," he says. He never calls him Peter. "Let's leave these makholwa to their praying."

Moses watches them go, swallowing back his anger. Will they really become soldiers next year? Even Peter? He is so gentle with Hlali and the other small children, could he really stab his enemies and "wash his spear in blood?" He wonders what it is to have Solani's certainty and passion about his future. He knows that he is destined to preach the gospel to the amaZulu, but the thought sets no fire burning in his heart.

The White Imfolozi is a broad shallow river, with cloudy water the color of milky coffee. They cross at noon the next day and climb the steep bank into the long valley that has been home to generations of amaZulu kings. The air is much hotter than at uMzinyathi, without the highland breezes to disperse it. Giraffes glide past in the distance, their necks rising above the trees like the masts of ships at sea. The bush is so thick with flowering thorn trees that they have to stop every few minutes to hack the branches with pangas. Joseph tells them the isiZulu names of the trees—umlahlankosi, buffalo thorn, used by the amaZulu to bring the departed spirits home; umkhaya with long white flowers like wilting candles; flat topped umsasane. The bishop says they all look the same to him, and the sooner they're all chopped down to make way for sugar cane the better.

The thorns pluck at the bishop's shirt as if the trees are determined to tease him, and one especially mischievous branch steals his hat and glasses. The boys stifle giggles as they scrabble in the bushes to unearth his spectacles. Even Kazi struggles to hide her grin. But the bishop's thin smile grows thinner each time he's snagged. uMfundisi* keeps apologizing, as if he'd grown the thorn trees himself just to vex him.

As they draw nearer to Nodwengu, crowds of soldiers emerge from the valleys and over the hills—tall muscular men singing and running in formation. They're in full battle dress, with feathers in their headbands and silky ox tail hair fringing their legs. The sky is filled with circling vultures and yellow-billed kites drawn by the mass slaughter of oxen for meat. The air is thick with dust and a cacophony of shouts, drumbeats and singing.

The bishop glances about apprehensively. "How ferocious they look! Thank the Lord for the restraining influence of the missionaries. Without that, I am sure these savages would have made mincemeat of us."

Kazi laughs.

"You flatter us, Bishop, but I fear we have not been that influential. Luckily for us the Zulus have a rather more generous attitude to strangers than we do. Can you imagine what the English would do if the Zulu arrived at Dover wanting land and converts to their beliefs?"

"Really, my dear," uMfundisi* remonstrates, with a nervous chuckle. "What fanciful notions you have. But set your mind at rest, Bishop. We are the guests of the king and as long as we have his goodwill, we can go about without trepidation."

By the time they reach the king's umuzi, the sun is

casting long shadows from the interlaced branches of the stockade and the high lookout hut by the gate. They're met at the gate by an induna who introduces himself as Masiphula. He wears a necklace of lion claws and a string of many carved wooden beads.

"He's the king's advisor," Solani whispers to Moses as they follow the induna across the sprawling parade ground to the isigodlo, the quarters of the king. "He advises on who to send to KwaNtatha to 'marry the bewhiskered man.' Better read well, my boy, or he'll send you there too."

"That means you'll be killed," Peter puts in cheerily. "But not for bad reading. More for witchcraft."

"They take your head and twist it round on your neck, like a chicken," Solani explains with relish. "Then they feed you to the crocodiles."

Solani is furious because uMfundisi* chose Moses to read a psalm to the king, instead of him. "Imagine an ikhafula orphan reading to our king," he'd grumbled. "What an insult!"

Moses looks now at the broad back of the induna, who'd greeted them with great friendliness.

"He doesn't look very fierce."

"Look at his iziqu," Solani points to the wooden beads on his necklace. "Every piece is for someone he's killed."

Moses suppresses a shudder. Will the king be insulted if he reads to him? It's a simple enough task—uMfundisi* chose Psalm 23, which Moses had memorized before he was six so he'll only be pretending to read it. Even Solani could have done it, and Moses wonders why uMfundisi* chose him. He has the uneasy feeling that he is being presented to prove something to the king. That he is an empty vessel, filled only with uMfundisi's* intentions.

DANIEL

Daniel had always pictured Mpande as a dark-skinned King Henry VIII, whose portrait is in his *Kings and Queens of England* book. But King Mpande is quite different, although he rivals King Henry in girth. When they meet him the next morning, he's reclining on mats in an enclosure before his dwelling—an intricately constructed beehive structure about thirty feet high. Somehow, this makes him more commanding than if he had been sitting on a throne. He is wrapped in a crimson and black linen cloth, with a blue blanket draped over his generous stomach. His gray hair and fine wrinkles betray his age, but he has the eyes of a young man—lively and intelligent, with a humorous gleam. An induna sits beside him, holding up his shield to protect him from the sun. Other izinduna sit in a circle watching him solicitously. When a beetle crawls towards him, one creeps forward on all fours and delicately removes it without turning his back or taking his eyes off the king.

The visiting party crouch down in a respectful circle (even the bishop, although his expression shouts his objections) as it's forbidden to stand in the king's presence. The bishop's gift of a brace of pistols and four scarlet blankets is carried to the king by an induna, walking on his haunches.

With uMfundisi* translating, the bishop assures the king that he had the permission of the Lieutenant-Governor of

Natal to present him with the pistols. The king doesn't seem to care much about the governor's permission.

"We have many guns," he says, "but we need gunpowder and caps."

The bishop regrets that the British authorities have restricted the supply of caps and gunpowder to the natives.

The king laughs. "Maybe they are worried that we'll arm ourselves and go to war against them? Please tell your governor our soldiers can kill quite well with an assegai, and most would not choose to fight with a gun. They see that as the choice of a coward. But we need guns for hunting."

When Moses reads, the Psalter trembles in his hands and his voice is unusually husky. He reads each line in English, and repeats it in Zulu. *The lord is my shepherd I shall not want... uJehova ungumalusi wami, angiyikuswela.* The king listens with a broad smile, but Daniel thinks he looks more amused than impressed.

The king asks Moses about Queen Victoria's armies and ships and about steam engines. Moses draws a picture in the sand to show how a steam engine works and explains the mechanisms. He loves explaining machines. All his nervousness disappears, and the king now seems genuinely impressed.

"You must serve me here when you are older," he declares. "You can show my izinduna how to construct these machines. How is it that the English learned all these things?"

uMfundisi** launches into one of his favorite stories about how the English once lived as the amaZulu do now, but St. Augustine came from another land and taught them about the Lord Jesus Christ. King Mpande interrupts to ask if St. Augustine also taught the English how to make ships to cross the sea and guns to conquer other peoples.

"No, that knowledge came later, your Greatness..." uMfundisi** says. "God chose to reveal this knowledge to the British people when they became Christian."

"We'd like our young men to learn about machines and guns," King Mpande insists. "Such knowledge is more useful to us than to learn about your God."

uMfundisi** explains that God wants people to learn faith before other knowledge, and that the amaZulu must embrace Christianity if they wish to have all this knowledge.

King Mpande rolls his eyes upwards. "We cannot forgo the ways of our forefathers," he intones wearily, as if this conversation has happened many times before. It probably has. Daniel's heard uMfundisi* say it often enough to other Zulu people he's trying to convert.

"Send your sons to us, O magnificent one." uMfundisi* leans forward with eyes alight. "We'll teach them everything, like young Moses here, and they can still observe the old customs and serve in the regiments."

The bishop has been watching this discussion with growing suspicion. Now he snaps out in his high reedy voice, "Did you tell him that it's a sin to practice witchcraft and polygamy? Did you press on him that God will punish leaders who deny their people the opportunity to hear the Gospel, that he is damning his subjects to hell?"

"Ah, indeed, Bishop, I believe I...ah...have conveyed this quite well, without wanting to be too...ah...*hostile*, of course.

We're here on his sufferance, after all. He says he'll send boys to our mission station in due course."

uMfundisi* is fibbing! And to a bishop! Daniel looks down, trying to quell his grin. If he catches Moses' eye, he'll collapse.

When they leave, King Mpande calls his izinduna to bring a large elephant tusk to present to the bishop.

"I'm sorry it is only one...our elephants have all been killed by the English and amakhafula. We used to have so many, they were part of our landscape," he says.

Daniel wonders if it is one of the tusks that were delivered by Mr. Struthers. He asks Kazi later what the bishop will do with the tusk. She says he'll sell it to an ivory trader, and use the money to buy Bibles for the mission effort. She says that the traders get rich selling ivory in England to make piano keys or billiard balls or little caskets for ladies' rings.

He imagines these tusks, moving from hand to hand to hand, dripping money and blood. Elephant ghosts, buckling beneath the weight of all these people and the things they bought or made with the tusks—King Mpande and his guns, Bishop Saunders and his Bibles, the traders with more guns to shoot more elephants, the English gentry with their trinkets.

Later they are invited to see the king's snake charmer, Lwazi. He is a tall man, with the stalking gait of a cheetah. His right arm is paralyzed and hangs like a dead branch. His right forefinger is frozen in a hook as though he were constantly beckoning you to come closer.

6736398944229020603080

When they enter the hut—the bishop and uMfundisi* bending almost double to get through the low doorway—Lwazi tells them to sit against the wall and keep absolutely still. With a torrent of whistles and hisses, he calls forth one snake after another from the tightly woven spherical baskets lining the hut. A Gaboon viper, its geometric patterns mimicking the basket from which it had crawled; two puffadders as thick as a man's arm; a cobra, with a charcoal body and striped neck, rising in its basket and weaving from side to side. The last is a black mamba, the same dull silver as the barrel of a gun—a snake so deadly, uMfundisi* whispers to the bishop, its bite can kill a man in twenty minutes. The snake rears up at the visitors, while Lwazi casually rests his toe on its tail and watches their reactions with amusement. The bishop is rigid with terror; even Daniel feels a shiver, although he likes snakes.

Lwazi gets the snakes back in the baskets, then calls "Isithunywa." A huge golden python with brown markings uncoils itself from a rock in the shadows against the far wall and undulates smoothly across the floor. A boy goes out and comes back with a live chicken. For long moments the python watches the chicken, flickering its tongue inquiringly. The chicken stands rigid until the snake strikes in a blur of speed, grabbing the bird in its mouth and coiling itself around it in a single fluid movement. It suffocates its prey in a few seconds and swallows it whole.

Daniel and Moses linger after the others are gone. Moses asks Lwazi questions. Did he always know how to communicate with snakes? Is he ever afraid? Does he communicate with some more than others? Lwazi says he'd known from a young child, that it was a gift from the amadlozi, he's never afraid, it's different with each snake.

When he has secured all the other snakes in their baskets, he lifts the heavy python, and lets it settle around his neck. The chicken has completely vanished, save for a small bulge in the snake's midsection.

Lwazi smiles, his teeth gleaming in the dim light. The python coils languidly around his body, while regarding Daniel with a dark impenetrable eye. Its eye calls up the memory of the python he'd seen in the Umkiwane tree. The snake seems to swell as Daniel looks at it, its patterned coils shifting and merging with the shadows. He feels rather than hears the breath of its voice whispering to him. *Ngiyakwazi...Ngikulindele. I know you...I am waiting for you.* The voice fills the darkness and swirls around him. The hairs on the back of his neck rise up as a shudder passes through him. He stumbles out of the dark hut.

MOSES

The umkhosi wokweshwama ceremony begins before sunrise on the following day. Moses stands with the rest of the mission party on the parade ground, surrounded by the serried ranks of amabutho: uThulwana, uKhandempemvu, inKonkoni, isiBabule, iSangqu, and Ndabakawombe regiments, distinguished by shields of white, black, red or patterned ox skin. Tall white ostrich feathers and eagle feathers tremble in the breeze above their heads. Imishokobezi— white ox tail fringes—shiver on their legs. The regiments of isigodlo girls, with intricate hairstyles and decorative beads, stand in grass skirts, their oiled skin glowing in the dawn light.

The regiments are unmoving and silent. The only sound is the twittering of birds in the trees beyond the umuzi. As the sun's first rays touch the feathers on the soldiers' head-dresses, the king is wheeled out in a green wagon drawn by an induna. He has been transformed from the twinkly-eyed old man who asked Moses about steam engines into an imposing enigmatic figure, enshrouded in a cloak of grass fiber, with only his head visible. His face is painted in red, black and white. In his right hand is the crescent-shaped inhlendla, sacred staff of kings. As he appears, the regiments roar with one voice, "Bayete, nkosi!" The sound rolls out over the crowd and reverberates through the surrounding hills.

As the morning progresses, Moses is swept along by the power of the ceremony, by the sound of tens of thousands of voices, tens of thousands of feet stamping, and knobker-ries beating against shields in unison; by the ukugiya dances that mimic battles, with soldiers leaping high in the air and darting forwards with their spears, then retreating, forward and back, like waves crashing on a beach; by the dizzying synchronization of so many bodies moving in unison, be-coming one body with a multitude of limbs and feathered heads. What is it to be part of something like that? To dis-solve yourself into this great beautiful terrifying beast that is an army?

He remembers how he disappeared under Cousin Roland's gaze. Disappearing into this army would be a different kind of disappearing, one that made you more than yourself, not less, one that rolled yourself into a bigger self.

He remembers Peter's comment. *If you were a real Zulu, you'd understand.* To be part of this can never be his destiny. He would never have imagined that he would want it. But he is startled by the way his blood quickens to its rhythm, by the urge of his feet to join the dancing, by the sharp yearning for belonging in his heart.

DANIEL

In the heat of the afternoon, Daniel rests with Moses in the shade of a hut, his nostrils thick with the red dust and the smells of animal fat and human sweat and wood smoke, his ears ringing with the thud of shields against knobkerries and feet against soil. Peter runs up shouting, "It's my father's ibutho...they must kill the bull without assegais or knives, just with bare hands. Come, let's watch!"

Daniel doesn't want to watch, but the cluster of men is already moving towards them, carrying the bull. The creature is roaring and writhing, trying to release itself from the grip of its captors. But each time it wrenches a limb free, another five pairs of hands are ready to grasp it. Its gleaming black coat is covered with white flecks of foaming saliva and sweat. As they come past, he glimpses its rolling eyes, the red interior of its flaring nostrils. He feels its terror, the grasp of the men's hands on its limbs, its helplessness, its confusion at this tearing away of its strength.

The crowd surges past him towards the isibaya, with Peter and Moses running after them. He can't see what's happening, but he can hear the bellows of the animal and the howls of its tormentors. He falls again and again into the bull's body. He feels the thud of fists and feet against his back and stomach, feels hands pulling him this way and that, grasping his head, and twisting, the agony of bone and tendons tearing. He goes down, kicking and screaming, until he is lost in darkness...

He feels hands on him, not the rough hands of the men holding the bull, but gentle strong hands supporting his head. He opens his eyes to find a man bending over him.

"Drink this," the man says. He sips the bitter liquid from the calabash. It seems to drive away the fogginess as it flows through him. He sits up and passes the calabash back to the man.

"Thank you," he says. He looks briefly at the man's face and feels a jolt in his solar plexus. The twin scars on the cheeks, the burning eyes—it's him, he's sure of it. The man who stole Gogo.

"What happened to you, son? You were shouting as if you were being attacked."

He hangs his head, flooded with shame. "Angazi, baba. I don't know."

Moses runs up, his face furrowed with anxiety.

"Dan! Are you alright? I lost you in the crowd."

The man leaps up at the sight of him.

"I can't be seen with the child," he mutters, looking around nervously. He looks back at Moses.

"They shouldn't have brought you here...there are people who wish you harm."

Moses glances at Daniel and reads the alarm in his eyes. He looks back at the man, but keeps his eyes lowered, for he knows that it's not done for a child to look a Zulu adult in the eye.

"Who wishes me harm, baba?"

"Never mind, boy, just don't draw attention to yourself."

The man reaches out his hand and lifts the silver confirmation cross that Moses wears around his neck.

"What is this thing?"

"It's a cross, baba. It's a symbol for Christianity."

"Does it protect you from abathakathi?"

"Christians don't believe in abathakathi, baba."

"And you, boy? Do you believe in them?"

Moses hesitates. "No, baba."

The man pulls himself back, looking shocked. He glances around again, pulls a thong over his head, and places it around Moses' neck.

"This incweba will protect you from evildoers. Keep it with you, always. And don't walk around here on your own, nor with the other boys. Go back to your priest now and stay with him."

He turns his frightening gaze on Daniel.

"Look after him," he says. And he is gone.

MOSES

Daniel grabs the thong and pulls it over Moses' head. He drops it on the ground. They contemplate the object tied to it—a small pouch of animal hide sewn together around some substance.

"What is it?" Daniel whispers.

"I don't know..." Moses whispers too, although the man has gone. "He said it was an incweba...I think it's some kind of charm to protect you from ubuthakathi."

"What'll you do with it?"

"I don't know..."

"You can't keep it...imagine what uMfundisi* will say?"

"I know but...that man didn't want to hurt me...he said I should stay close to uMfundisi to be safe...if he wished evil on me, he wouldn't have said that, would he?"

Moses picks it up and strokes the fur of the pouch. It sits like a mouse in his hands, seeming to tremble with some secret life. Daniel stares at it with a fascinated horror.

"But it's to do with witchcraft..."

"I know, but...that man was wearing it because he believed it protected him. And he gave it up to me, to keep me safe. Can something given out of kindness be so evil?"

"But...he was the man who stole Gogo!"

Moses looks at him, frowning. "I don't think he was."

"Well, you can't keep it," Daniel says. "Imagine! It was right next to your cross. Maybe God is testing you...you know uMfundisi always says you should be extra careful because you were born a heathen."

Moses flinches. uMfundisi** does say that often enough, but he's never heard it from Daniel. He closes his fingers around the incweba, feeling a sudden fierce urge to keep it.

"Give it to me!" Daniel says sharply, holding out his hand.

Moses stares at him, bemused. "What's got into you, Dani?"

"Give it to me, I'll give it back to the man," he says, more calmly. "You know you can't keep it, Mosi."

"I could give it to him."

"No! Give it to me, otherwise I'll tell uMfundisi."

Moses opens his fingers slowly. Daniel snatches it before he can change his mind and slips it into his pocket.

"Don't worry, I'll give it to him."

But Moses is walking away, fighting the urge to punch his brother and take the incweba back.

He joins Peter and other boys in the kraal, where the men are cooking meat strips from the dead bull. The soldiers are throwing the strips into the air for others to catch. They suck the strips and spit them out.

"Why don't they eat it?" he asks Peter

"They suck it to make themselves brave. But if they eat it, it will make them too cruel."

The rest of the bull's carcass is carried to the fire. Now that it's dead, they carry it with reverence, as if afraid of hurting it. They lay the bull's remains on the fire and step back. As the flames rise up, the bull's face flickers in the glow, giving it the illusion of life. Moses imagines it rising from the flames—black, smoking and terrifying. Its ferocity mirrors the rage in his own heart. What gave Daniel the right to say that Moses could not keep the incweba? And how could he threaten to tell uMfundisi* about it? That was a grave breach of their code—they never told on each other.

The next morning Moses awakes to a gloomy atmosphere. Solani and Peter have not yet returned. After the man's warning, he'd gone straight back to their hut the previous evening, although he'd have liked to go with Peter to sit with the soldiers of his father's regiment, to drink the sour sweet utshwala and listen to stories of battles won and lost.

The mission party is preparing a Sunday service. Moses and Daniel spread grass mats on the earth for people to kneel on while uMfundisi* puts up the bishop's drawings on the side of the wagon. The drawings are supposed to depict Africans, but the men wear some sort of loin cloth, not proper Zulu clothes. The pictures show a fat man lazing under a tree while his wives work in the field; men beating others with knobkerries; a man consulting what Moses supposes is a sangoma or inyanga, although he has a bone through his nose which he's never seen on anyone. The next set of drawings show white missionaries reading the Bible to black people; a black man and woman getting married in a church; black people growing sugar cane and vegetables in front of little square houses. The people in these ones wear European clothes.

By half past ten, no one has arrived for the service. Bishop Saunders paces up and down—his black robe billowing like a thundercloud—and mutters about ignorant people, "just carrying on with their heathen rituals with no knowledge of the Sabbath."

"It's too bad," he declares, "but we shan't keep the Lord waiting a moment longer."

Moses endures the service with a feeling of remoteness. The familiar words and rituals seem to have nothing to do with him, as if he'd suddenly found himself amongst the few curious onlookers. The bishop is reading a lesson from Deuteronomy about witchcraft: "Let no one be found among you...who practices divination or sorcery, interprets omens, engages in witchcraft, or casts spells, or who is a medium or spiritist or who consults the dead. Anyone who does these things is detestable to the Lord, and because of these detestable practices the Lord your God will drive out those nations before you."

Detestable to the Lord. Moses catches Daniel's eye. Has he given the incweba back to the man yet? He supposes he should be grateful to his brother, but he feels only anger. He remembers the feel of the incweba in his hand, its strange life. The way that man had looked at him. As if he really cared about him.

He wants the incweba back. But even if Daniel still has it, if Moses takes it Daniel will tell uMfundisi*, and uMfundisi* will take it anyway. And drown him in shame for wanting to keep it.

By the time the service ends, the bishop is as red as a ripe amatungulu fruit and is mopping his face with a large purple handkerchief. A few of the king's wives and daughters have drifted over with their attendants. uMfundisi** asks Joseph to explain the pictures, but the women laugh so much that he finds it difficult. They think the black men are all sick because they're inked in with scratchy pen lines that make it look like they have rashes. They're perplexed by the medicine man, and feel sorry for the people with the square houses.

"Does the English queen live in a square house?" they ask

Joseph. "Surely they wouldn't make their queen live in an ugly square house?"

"That's why we amaZulu don't want to be Christian— we'd have to break down our round houses and build square ones. And how would our ancestors know themselves in a square house?"

Moses watches Joseph get more and more flustered. He grows hot with embarrassment in sympathy. Is this what it will be like to preach the Gospel to local people? Will he have to account for these stupid pictures? And endure such mockery?

uMfundisi* can't keep quiet any longer and assures them that God doesn't mind where you live. "Jesus, the son of the Christian God, was Himself born in a stable, a small house for cows and donkeys."

"A house for cows?" one asks. "Does he mean a cattle kraal?"

"Why wasn't this Son of God born in God's house? Did God send His wife out to give birth in a cattle kraal? What kind of husband does that?"

uMfundisi* gives up on the pictures and asks Joseph to lead in singing his favorite hymn about "warlike weapons" being "beaten into ploughshares." Joseph loves it because he hates war. He lost his whole family to Mpande's army twenty years ago. He truly believes that Christianity can bring peace to the amaZulu.

"This hymn was written by a Zulu person," uMfundisi* tells them. "You may remember him. William Ngidi. He visited Nodwengu with Bishop Colenso a few years ago."

They don't seem to remember William, but they sing along cheerily enough.

After the hymn, Masiphula arrives with his attendants to ask for sugar. uMfundisi** gives him a cup, which Masiphula hands to an attendant to take to his hut, but the others complain that he hasn't shared. He grudgingly thrusts a small spoonful into each mouth before sending the sugar off. uMfundisi** invites him to consider the missionary pictures. Masiphula glances at them dismissively and takes his leave before Joseph has a chance to explain them.

DANIEL

Daniel rises early the next day to take Maggie for her last run before their departure. The morning star is suspended between small high clouds thrown across the paling sky like a scattering of leaves on water. He walks out between the dark forms of the huts, their domes rising up against the mauve light, past the heavy stockade to the entrance to the umuzi. A dog barks, and Maggie barks back, prompting the induna on guard to come forward from the shadows. When he sees it is Daniel, he raises his hand in greeting and steps back.

They head down the rough track that winds steeply to the river. Maggie trots at his heels, looking up at him with her wide-mouthed grin as if to say, "At last we're doing what we should be doing."

As they near the river, the rising mist turns everything ghostly in the pale light. A few birds can be heard, along with the grunting barks of impala. The impala watch them pass, their horns black against the white cloud like burnt twigs in ash.

He sits on a rock midstream in the river, watching the mist turn golden with the first rays of the rising sun. Maggie looks towards the far bank with her ears pricked.

A tall man emerges from the mist between the bush willows. He wears a white blanket over his shoulders, an isinene skirt made of strips of white hide, and carries a short white stick with silky white cattle hair on the end. His dark body is framed by the whiteness of his clothes and the mist behind him.

He arrived so silently that Daniel almost thinks he's an apparition until Maggie runs across the river, barking. The man extends his hand when she reaches him. Maggie cowers and crawls towards him on her belly, smiling and whining. Daniel scrambles to his feet.

"Sawubona," the man calls, stepping across the boulders towards him. "Is this your dog?"

As he gets closer Daniel recognizes the twin scars and piercing eyes of the man who spoke to him after the killing of the bull. The mist drifts over the water, bringing memories of the day the men came to take Gogo.

"Sawubona, baba," he mumbles. "She is mine and my brother's, but will be presented to the king today."

"Ngubani igama lakho, mfana?"

"My name is Daniel, baba."

"And what do they call the boy who was with you yesterday?"

"His name is Moses, baba."

The man is quiet, staring across the river with a look of

uncertainty, as if unsure of what questions to ask to get the answers he needs.

"Is Moses happy, there at the mission? Do they treat him well?"

There is an urgency in his tone, as though he really wants to know.

"Yes, baba, my mother and father are very kind. I think he's happy."

He doesn't know whether Moses is happy. Or whether he himself is happy, for that matter. No one asks if you're happy at the mission. They just ask if you're good.

"Does he wear the incweba I gave him?"

Daniel hesitates, feeling it smoldering in his pocket. He remembers the strange fear he'd had when Moses closed his fingers around the incweba, that it might draw him into some unknown place where Daniel could never follow.

He promised to give it back to this man. He must give it back. But the incweba seems to be commanding his hands to be still.

"*Angazi, baba.* I don't know."

The man looks worried. He glances up the river and back at Daniel.

"And has he learnt well, your brother? Has he learnt about white man's things?"

"We learn together, sir. About history, geography, science, mathematics..." Are these white man's things? He has to use English words for the subjects, for if there are Zulu words he doesn't know them. "Moses is very clever. He is good at all of these things. Especially mathematics."

The man smiles and nods thoughtfully "Ah...kuhle uk-wazi lokho...that is good."

He looks out across the river again, lost in contemplation. Daniel follows his gaze but can see only reeds and mist. The man pulls himself out of his reverie, smiles again, and asks with a lighter tone, "Have you enjoyed the umkhosi, child?"

"Yes, baba, very much indeed, it was most interesting. Perhaps you can tell me what ibutho you are in?"

"I was once in the uDlambedlu Regiment, but I'm no longer a soldier. I was called to be a heaven herd, umalusi wezulu. Do you know what that is?"

"No, baba."

"I keep our people safe from lightning. I speak to the lightning and thunder and use medicine to turn away their anger."

Daniel remembers the night that the bell tower was struck at uMzinyathi. And Moses, kneeling at the window, whispering to the sky. His dark, awestruck eyes when he said, I have powers...

"My brother too—" He breaks off as the man's eyes blaze.

"Your brother speaks to lightning?" he asks sharply.

"Yes...he..." How can he explain, especially in Zulu? He remembers his brother aged ten standing on the hill grasping a kite with a wire trailing into a jam jar. He was trying to capture the lightning forking the black clouds above him, while Daniel watched mesmerized by terror. He recalls Moses' tears of frustration and his own relief when the wind snapped the string and whipped away the kite, and the wire fell harmlessly to earth.

121

"Tell him he must not do this," the man speaks fervently. "It's very dangerous if you're not trained and not protected by the amadlozi, by the correct rituals and medicines. You must tell him."

"Yebo, baba. I will tell him."

"And tell your father to keep Moses away from these gatherings. It's not safe for him. He must keep away from the iMfolozi district too."

Daniel wants to ask why he is not safe, but he's shaken by the man's intensity, the dark eyes drilling into him.

"Make sure he wears that incweba." His voice is low and urgent, as though he fears eavesdroppers. "If you love your brother, make sure he wears it."

Daniel raises his eyes but drops them abruptly at the burn of the man's gaze.

"Sala kahle, my boy. Don't linger here alone. Take your dog and go back to the priests."

He moves on toward the opposite bank. As he passes, he touches Daniel lightly on the chest with his whisk. Daniel feels a small electric shock, as if a tiny fork of lightning had flashed through his body. Then he's gone, moving across the stream and out of sight so quickly and quietly Daniel wonders if he'd imagined the whole encounter.

Whistling to Maggie, he wades back across the river and makes his way slowly up the hill, the incweba defying God in his pocket, his chest still tingling from where the whisk had touched it.

MOSES

After the Feast, the bishop disappears back to Pietermaritz-burg for three months, and everyone is relieved. But all too soon, he returns. Moses watches the approach of the wagons bearing the bishop and his wife with a sinking heart. The oxen strain up the hill, dragging their heavy loads of items deemed necessary for the bishop's comfort, such as a silver-backed shaving set and a blow-up India-rubber mattress (Nomsa, who helps them unpack their house, later provides a full inventory of these exotic artifacts). The bishop alights stiffly and assists his wife. She stands beside her beaky spouse, surveying her surroundings through a lorgnette. She raises her eyebrows and says, "Well, here we are," in a tone that suggests that this undeniable fact is a source of deep vexation.

She is a tall woman with a large bosom, which seems to sail before her like the prow of a ship, and an oddly prominent backside that sails behind. Nomsa, who has been given the luckless task of "lady's maid," later reports that she wears a device under her skirts to elevate the rear which she calls a "bustle." Mrs. Saunders raises her prominent eyebrows whenever something offends her. When Kazi explains that her parlor floor had been smoothed with cow dung—hoping to impress her with the ingenuity of indigenous home-making—the eyebrows bolt towards her hairline like scandalized mice. In the coming days, they are seldom at ease.

After a few days of her loud complaints about the

"slipshod indolence of the kitchen staff," Thuli and Nomsa insist that they can't understand her English and can therefore only be instructed by Kazi. Around Mrs. Saunders they are surly and withdrawn, but in her absence they come back to life and shriek with laughter when Nomsa mimics her gait and imperious declarations, and her attempts to convey her wishes through elaborate gestures in the belief that Nomsa can't understand her words.

Bishop Saunders also finds much to grieve him at uMzinyathi and finds Moses particularly displeasing. Soon after his return, uMfundisi* tries to impress the bishop by bragging that Moses has taught himself algebra and Euclidian geometry from books sent by Kazi's father.

The bishop pulls in the purse strings of his lips and settles his predatory eye on Moses' forehead, as if he would like to peck out any subversive hints of algebra.

"Algebra is all very well, my dear Reverend Whitaker, but I trust that Moses is learning a useful trade too. Let us not forget that the colonists' support of our work depends on our missions supplying *industrious* native Christians. They need education only to render them more able at their tasks than their heathen brothers."

Moses resolves to pursue as much useless knowledge as possible and to challenge the bishop with reason. When the bishop presents a lesson at Sunday School on Abraham and Isaac, Moses questions him about the slave woman Hagar, who bore Abraham the son Ishmael—apparently with the blessing of God. Moses had two wives, King David had at least eight. If God tolerated polygamy in these God-fearing men, why would he condemn it amongst the amaZulu?

He knows he's being provocative, although he has always asked questions of uMfundisi*, about the physics of burning bushes (sunlight through dewdrops?) and the mechanics of Noah's ark (just think how many animal species there are in Africa alone? How would they all have found their way to Noah's ark, and surely it would have sunk if they had all climbed aboard?). But these interactions with his father were usually quite amiable, always ending with uMfundisi* stating that a miracle by definition is a miracle, and Moses should have better faith.

However, the bishop is appalled that anyone should question the Lord's word. He tells Moses not to be blasphemous and refuses to entertain a single question.

A few days later, Moses returns to their room to discover that all his books have been removed. He eventually tracks uMfundisi* down in the church, where he is working with the bishop on the week's liturgy.

"Bishop Saunders thought you'd been overstimulated. He suggests you...ah...confine your reading to religious texts until your faith is more secure," uMfundisi** explains.

"The books are safely in a trunk in my house," the bishop says.

"How could you let him take my books?" Moses cries.

"Now, Moses, the bishop has only your best interests at heart. It will do you some good to focus on your faith. A missionary has no need for scientific pursuits."

"But you said you were proud of my algebra and geometry."

"Yes, indeed, you have a very quick mind which I am sure the Lord would like to see turned more to deepening your faith."

"Your insubordination and unseemly agitation underlines the wisdom of my actions," the Bishop says primly. A sunbeam shining through one of the small windows illuminates the pale dome of his balding pate. A scorpion scuttles along a rafter above. Moses wills the creature to fall on the bishop's head. It does not oblige.

He can see that this discussion will go nowhere and goes to find Kazi, who is working with Joseph tying the tomato vines to canes in her vegetable garden.

"Why would God have given me a good brain if He doesn't want me to use it? I can't live without my books."

It doesn't feel like an exaggeration. Ever since discovering that the books have gone, he has felt as if his chest were encircled in an iron cage and he cannot expand his ribs enough to draw breath,.

"I'm sorry, Mosi. I know it's unfair. I'm sure the bishop will relent in time."

"But why can't you get them back for me?"

"We depend on the bishop's good will. If he does not approve of the work we do, he may complain to the Missionary Society and uMfundisi will lose this posting."

As Moses walks away, his heart breaking with this betrayal, Joseph murmurs softly, "Come to my hut after evensong, I have something for you."

That afternoon dark clouds gather, heralding an unseasonal thunderstorm. As evensong begins, rumbling thunder all but drowns out the bishop's nasal voice as he exhorts the few souls in his care to follow the narrow path of righteousness or face damnation. Lightning flashes turn his bony nose blue, and the wind blows small white hailstones through the unglazed windows. The tumultuous weather mirrors the fury in Moses' heart. He too would like to rain down fire and ice on the bishop and is grateful to the weather for being more obliging than the scorpion. He recalls the lightning striking the bell tower when he was a child and imagines it striking the church. It would kill them all, but the thought sends a certain thrill through his body.

When the service is over, he goes down through the rain to the small hut that Joseph shares with Thuli and their son Hlali. Between the two narrow beds is an upended wooden tea crate that serves as a table. On top of the tea chest is a linen cloth that Thuli embroidered—despite her boisterous gestures, she embroiders the most delicate designs of flowers and birds whenever Kazi can get thread for her. And resting on top of that is a pile of books.

Moses falls to his knees, and goes through them. "Maxwell's Treatise on Electricity and Magnetism! And my *Smith's Astronomy*, and all my notebooks! Joseph, you have saved my life." He clasps them to his heart like long lost children.

"They asked me to help carry the books. I managed to keep these for you. I'm sorry I couldn't get all of them, this was all I could hide under my shirt. You can keep them here."

"You don't know what this means to me."

Joseph smiles. "I can't read a word of those books. But I do know how much they matter to you."

DANIEL

Daniel fares little better than Moses with the bishop, although at least he does not lose his few books. But the bishop has an uncanny knack of discovering him "wool gathering," as he calls Daniel's investigations into how dung beetles construct their balls or the passage of harvester ants carrying grains to their nests. The bishop's remedy for Daniel's "indolence" is to ban him from "gadding about with the local children" and from speaking Zulu, declaring that "babbling away in a heathen tongue at an early age has softened his brain."

Like Moses, Daniel discovers that neither parent will defend him against the bishop, and he and Moses become united in their resolution to defy him whenever possible. Daniel is grateful for this allegiance. It helps to rebuild the trust they lost because of the incweba.

He told Moses that he'd returned it to the scarred man. But he has hidden it—wrapped in oilcloth in an old gunpowder tin—inside a hollow trunk of a red ivory wood down by the stream. For weeks after he hid it, he felt strangely drawn to it, and, when he was sure that he was not being observed, he would run down to check that it was still there. One day, when he put his hand in the dark hollow, he touched scales instead of tin. He snatched his hand back, narrowly missing a strike from the green boomslang that was coiled there. After that, he avoided it. He had the uneasy notion that the boomslang was guarding the incweba from him.

Despite the bishop's exhortations, or perhaps because of them, Moses becomes ever more absorbed by science. He spends any spare minutes he has scribbling equations or drawing geometrical figures with pens tied to string nailed to a board. He mostly works at night to avoid the stealthy walker. Daniel gets used to falling asleep to the sound of his muttered calculations and scratching pen. Even Kazi starts to remonstrate because he is going through so many candles.

Daniel doesn't understand what electromagnetism is or why it's so valuable to measure it, and Moses' equations only obfuscate the matter further. But he's pleased that the bishop has failed to kill his passion for science. Moses insists that equations can explain everything in the universe, that equations hold the purest truth. The bishop claims that science is ungodly, says Moses, but nothing reveals God's power more profoundly than the elegant beauty of the laws of physics.

"Surely God would want us to discover the truth about this miraculous universe He created. To me, pursuing science is the highest form of worship."

"I don't think an equation can be more wondrous than a spider web, beaded with dew in the morning light," Daniel responds.

"But that is mathematics in practice. How do you think the spider creates its web? Through geometry. How does that light get there? Through electromagnetic waves. Why do the dewdrops gleam? Because of the reflection of those waves on a convex surface. Why does the water form a dewdrop? Because of surface tension. It's all science, Dan. The whole universe is science."

"Do spiders study geometry?"

"Yes, in their own ways. Their own God-given ways. All of nature conforms to formulas and proportions. That is why it's so satisfying, so perfect. Look at the fibonacci sequence of a spiral, found in a tiny snail shell or a boundless galaxy... the bishop says God hates geometry, but God is geometry. uMfundisi says that stories about manna falling from heaven and burning bushes are God's miracles, but to me a snail shell is miracle enough."

Daniel smiles. "That's where we meet each other then. Because to me a snail shell is miracle enough too."

MOSES

The bishop and his wife stay at uMzinyathi for two years before they finally give up converting the amaZulu and head off to try their powers of persuasion on the amaSwati. The Zulu are a lost cause while under King Cetshwayo, says the bishop. The sooner they are under British rule, the better. As if this were the natural order of things and it is only a matter of time.

Two years is not that long, but their stay will cast a long shadow, Moses thinks, as he watches the ox wagons wind down the valley and begin to climb the next hill. Before the bishop came, the mission had been regarded with affection by most of the Magwaza people around them. The children who attended loved Kazi's school and many had benefited from her doctoring skills. The Sunday services were jolly affairs, with much singing, dancing and hand clapping, and people were happy enough to attend them to secure trade with the mission even if they didn't embrace the teachings. But the bishop banned all such frivolity and used the sermons to dwell on what torments the Lord would inflict on those who persisted in living as they'd always lived—which is hardly cheering, even if his clumsy attempts at Zulu provoked some mirth. The bishop insisted that no child older than thirteen could attend the school without being baptized, and that if a man had more than one wife he had to somehow dispose of the extra ones before he could convert to Christianity. Within a few months he succeeded in scaring off almost all the converts that uMfundisi* had worked so hard to win over.

The British attack on Chief Langalibalele and the amaHlubi, on the flimsy pretext that the chief had failed to register guns he'd obtained from diamond traders, had made things worse. That wasn't the bishop's doing although you'd think it was by the way he boasted about it. After that, King Cetshwayo stopped allowing new baptisms and declared that all soldiers who converted would be put to death.

uMfundisi* has also changed, has become more fearful of dissent, preaches against polygamy with more zeal, and uses words like bloodthirsty and treacherous to describe King Cetshwayo, although he used to regard him as a worthy leader and a friend.

As the ox wagons finally crest the hill and disappear from

sight, the gathered group breaks into ululating, and Daniel performs three cartwheels in a row. Perhaps now that the bishop has gone, they can go back to the old ways of generating goodwill and being grateful for any small gains in spreading the word of God. But Moses suspects that things have changed at uMzinyathi forever.

DANIEL

Daniel has never grasped Moses' fascination with science. Until one afternoon, a few weeks after the bishop's departure, when Moses casually tosses him *The Annual Register* that had come with the missionary bundle a few days before.

"There's some science even you might like. Interesting theories on animals by a chap named Darwin."

Daniel takes it down to the spreading umdumezulu tree by the stream. He's not sure if he'll read it, but he wants to draw the monkeys, and the journal is a handy size to press on. He settles into a fork of the trunk, still relishing the novelty of an afternoon with no danger of the stealthy walker creeping up on him. The monkeys scold him from the upper branches, shielded from view by the leaves. He catches fleeting glimpses—a curious, wizened face peering through the foliage, a tail flicking after its owner—but never for long enough to make a decent sketch. At length he gives up, and glances over the Darwin review.

As the words slowly sink in, everything in his world changes.

He learns how Darwin's observations led to his conclusion that humans and animals had been created not from clay by God, but by centuries of incremental alteration into different life forms; that man is no more (or less) "than a more highly organized form or modification of a pre-existent mammal;" that the difference between the thinking powers of humans and animals is a matter of degree, rather than a difference in kind; that the emotions of animals "are plainly our own."

He reads the article over and over again. There is much he doesn't understand, but the words deliver a truth he'd somehow always known.

Humans were not created in the image of God. They were created by nature and time. Humans have *evolved* and animals have *evolved*. Our ancestors are apes, and before them small mammals, and before them creatures of the sea.

Animals are not his inferiors, but his brothers, relatives who traveled different paths to solve the challenge of sustaining life. He imagines evolution not so much as a transformation but a layering, so that within his human heart beats the heart of an ape, within that another, and another, going all the way back to some unimaginable life form, the shared ancestor of all breathing creatures on earth.

He lays the book down and sees that two of the monkeys have come and are now sitting on a nearby branch, watching him curiously. He watches them back, with new eyes, knowing now that his heart beats as theirs beat, his blood flows as theirs flow, his mind works as theirs work...

He had always known this in his skin. But religion taught him differently, taught him that humans were created in the image of God, that animals were inferior beings made by God to serve humans. He recalls his anguished prayers begging God to forgive him for experiencing the suffering of dying animals. Now body-jumping no longer seems so monstrous.

The Bible tells lies, he whispers to himself. The thought drops through him like a pebble in clear water.

He hears the bell for evensong and walks slowly back. It's so fundamental, this truth. He wonders that Moses had mentioned it so casually, as if it were just some interesting idea like a new design for a steam engine. He waits for Moses to ask about it, but he doesn't. After their evening chores, he just scratches away in his notebooks. Daniel lies listening to him, feeling this new knowledge swell inside him, filling him to his fingertips.

Moses raises it the following afternoon while they are helping their mother with the gooseberry jam. Moses is stirring the golden jam bubbling in a pot on the fire, when, with contrived nonchalance, he asks if she'd read about Darwin's theories in *The Annual Register*.

Kazi doesn't look up from the labels she's writing, but her body takes on a certain stillness.

"Yes, I did read it," she replies.

"Do you think they're valid?"

"Well, I haven't read Mr. Darwin's books. But scientific evidence supports the notion of evolution. My father was interested in the theories of Lammark. He felt that they made sense."

"So you knew about it before?"

"A little, yes."

"Well, Mother, why have you never told us about evolution?"

Moses' voice is even, but he only calls Kazi "Mother" when he's annoyed. Daniel realizes that Moses wasn't casual about it after all. That he too has been walking around incubating this knowledge—and honing some sharp outrage on it.

Kazi keeps inscribing the labels in her small spidery hand for so long that Daniel wonders if she's chosen not to answer. When she does, she spoons out her words cautiously as if each were as hot as the jam that Moses is stirring.

"uMfundisi believes that ideas of evolution are blasphemous and dangerous, particularly in places where Christianity has yet to gain a foothold. Keep stirring the jam, my boy," she adds, glancing up, "or otherwise we'll be left with taffy."

Moses stands frowning, with the ladle forgotten in his hand. Daniel leaves off spooning cooled jam from another pot into prepared jars and takes the ladle from Moses. Darwin is important no doubt, but burnt jam would be a tragedy for there is neither sugar nor gooseberries to make another batch.

"Do you think such ideas blasphemous and dangerous?"

"It's not for me to say, Moses. He is the theologian among us."

"uMfundisi always taught me that the Bible was the

truth." Moses' words escape in a sudden angry rush. "He said that by bringing the Bible to the amaZulu we were bringing the highest truth known to humans. But now it seems that we're bringing them fairy stories. Fables, with no more truth than the Zulu stories of uMvelinqangi and uNkulunkulu."

And still Kazi keeps writing, painstakingly inking each letter. When has jam ever been labeled with such attention?

"uMfundisi does hold those stories to be true. He has not deliberately lied to anyone."

"But *you* don't believe that the Bible is all true? Because you can't believe both in evolution and in Adam and Eve." With folded arms and a chin raised defiantly.

Kazi looks up at last from her labels. Her eyes hold a mixture of yearning and fear.

"I think perhaps there is a...blurring of stories and real events."

"But *evolution*, Mother...(one forearm unfolded, one hand chopping the air). Do you believe humans were created through evolution or formed from clay in the image of God in the Garden of Eden? It's a simple question."

Kazi puts down her pen. Her cheeks are flushed, and her eyes bright as though holding back tears. "For goodness sake, Moses! It doesn't matter what I believe! uMfundisi is in charge of your spiritual education."

Daniel turns the wooden spoon and stares down at the golden roiling of the bubbling jam. He wants to tell Moses to stop haranguing her because he can't bear the anguish in her voice. But who could ever stop Moses?

"But the *truth* matters!" Arms folded again, as if he

doesn't trust his hands with their liberty. "*You* always taught me that the truth matters more than anything. The amaZulu have as much right to scientific knowledge as any English person. You speak about bringing them the light. But if you hide the truth, isn't that keeping them in darkness?"

Kazi looks out across the yard at the chickens pecking in the sunlight. An olive-breasted thrush hops about under the gooseberry bushes, seeking worms.

"Your father feels that too much knowledge without the foundation of faith is dangerous," she says at length.

"But what do *you* feel?"

"This is *his* mission. He decides what gets taught to whom. When I chose to come here with him, I agreed to set aside my own views. He asked me not to discuss these views with you. He feels that your...inquiring nature...would be distracted, that it would weaken your faith."

Moses stares at her with hard bright eyes. "So why did you give me that *Register* to read? Or any other science book? If you want to keep lying to me, why don't you restrict my reading to religious tracts, like the bishop?"

She looks stricken. Literally, as if she'd been struck. Daniel feels his fingers curl into fists, unsure whether his anger is for Kazi or Moses.

"Perhaps I was wrong. But, in truth, I cannot bear to see a mind such as yours stifled. I thought I could trust you with that knowledge," she fires back. "I thought we could have a civilized discussion, without insulting each other. It seems I was mistaken."

EYE BROTHER HORN BY BRIDGET PITT

Her tear falls when he turns to walk away, just one, dropping onto a label and smudging it. She brushes it away angrily and carries on writing. Daniel is full of his own questions. But his mother feels too brittle for questions. He keeps his silence, stolidly spooning the cooling jam into the jars.

The subject is not raised again. Daniel puts *The Annual Register* in his drawer under his shirts, but when Moses asks for it a day or two later, it is gone.

"Looks like Kazi decided it was too dangerous for us after all," Moses says, his tone heavy with irony.

"You were hard on her."

"I trusted her to tell me the truth. I always knew uMfundisi* was blinded by his own beliefs, but I'd not have expected it of her. Aren't you angry that they've been lying to you too?"

"I don't know...not really. I'm just thinking about Darwin's ideas...I can't think of anything else. It's just... such a relief for me. It makes so much sense."

"Exactly. It makes so much sense. So much more sense than the story of Adam and Eve. But now it seems we are not allowed to hold sensible opinions."

"Will you say something to uMfundisi?"

"No...I'm disappointed in Kazi, but I don't want to hurt her by telling him. I suppose she did take a risk giving me that article."

Moses sticks to his word and says nothing to his father. But Daniel often catches him staring at uMfundisi* with

138

a new hardness in his gaze. Daniel feels little resentment towards uMfundisi*. He feels so relieved to be delivered of the God who had found him so wanting. He feels himself connected to some force bigger than the god he's always been presented with. Bigger than a capricious, jealous god who cares about sin and judges people who dance or have eruptions or marry more than one person. A force that runs through everything, through Moses' galaxies and constellations, through the tiny bright ladybirds that crowd the flowers in Kazi's garden, the spiral-horned kudu in the forest, the lappet-faced vultures that circle the skies. The chain of his evolved existences glows silently behind his eyes, like an infinite line of stars, stretching back to when time began.

PART FOUR
1877 TO 1878
THE SILENCE

MOSES

The letter arrives a few weeks after their nineteenth birthday. The Reverend Whitaker sends Nomsa to call them up from the cattle kraal, where they've been mending the split rail fence. Marigold—a black and white cow with a rolling eye and manic strength—had broken through it when her calf had been taken from her to increase her milk. All the other cows had followed, trampling the boards and leaving three sections of the fence flattened.

"Come quickly!" Nomsa cries, grabbing both their hands and tugging them towards the house. "There's a *letter*! From *Sir Roland*."

The last letter from Cousin Roland came some months before to say that his father had died. This news did little to alter the fortunes of the Whitaker household. Most of the estate went to Sir Roland, and the remainder was used to establish a trust fund for educating young men to serve as missionaries.

Kazi remarked that Uncle Robert might have given some thought to his nephew who was doing God's work in Africa, with hardly a penny to spare. uMfundisi* said one shouldn't speak ill of the dead, and Sir Robert, was a "God-fearing man" who gave unstintingly to the Church of England Missionary Society. However, he agreed—when pressed by Kazi—to write to his cousin to request whether Moses and Daniel might be considered as candidates for the Sir Robert Fitchley Trust Fund, and be given the opportunity to attend missionary college in England.

Now, at last, Sir Roland has replied.

"Ah, boys, wonderful news!" their father cries, when they enter the front room. "Cousin Roland writes that he had to return to Burma after his father's death, but will be traveling back to England next year. He plans to stop off in Southern Africa for a few months, to visit the sugar plantation in Natal and to go on a hunting safari. He needs assistants to help with translation and general chores. He proposes to employ you both, and, should you prove to be honest, devout and hard-working, he'll take you back to England with him and fund your attendance at missionary college! Isn't that a wonderful opportunity?"

Moses feels his chest swell with some wild hopefulness. He glances at his brother, but Daniel is looking more apprehensive than delighted.

"Does he still like hunting?" he asks.

"Very much! He so loved his first hunting trip here that

he's always wanted to come back. His duties have kept him in Burma, but I believe he's bagged quite a few elephants and tigers there. Luckily there's still plenty for him to hunt in this country."

uMfundisi** throws his hands together and raises his eyes to the ceiling, where he often locates God. "Does the Lord not work in such mysterious ways?" he exclaims. "You see, my lads, all you need is a little faith, and all good things shall come to you."

The boys return to the task of replacing two sets of uprights and hanging the fence rails, which Dawid stripped and sawed earlier that morning. Letter or no letter, the cattle must be kept in that night. On the way down, Moses erupts with a rare excitement, whooping and giving Daniel little rabbit punches.

"What do you think England will be like?" he asks, when he's calmed down enough to reapply himself to fence mending. He holds a post upright in the hole they'd dug while Daniel shovels earth back and packs it firm around the base.

"I don't know. Cold." Daniel laughs.

"Oh, just like you to think about that," Moses says impatiently. "I'm not talking about the weather! I mean, the steam engines and trains that go under the ground, right under your feet. And electrical telegraphs that send messages to places miles away through long wires attached to poles. And great telescopes to study the stars. And *ideas*, Dani! And James Clerk Maxwell, and Faraday, and discoveries about electromagnetic forces and light and astronomy... And Darwin, Dani, maybe you can meet Darwin."

The words trip over themselves as his tongue tries to keep pace with his galloping thoughts. It was too much, imagining it all. Imagining himself in the middle of it all.

"Do you think we'll learn about science in missionary college?" he asks, picking up the brace to drill holes through the upright post and rail while Daniel holds the rail in place. He tries to imagine Missionary College—he pictures a great drafty hall filled with desks and students inscribing texts from their Bibles, where you are served cold lumpy porridge and have to pray several times a day. Despite his excitement, it fills him with a certain dread. But if Daniel is there, it can't be too bad. He knows that it's unlikely that science will be high on the curriculum, but at least he'll be in the same country where all this learning and inquiry is happening. Surely he'll find some science somewhere?

"I don't know," Daniel replies. "But you shouldn't just go to missionary college, you should go to university to study mathematics and medicine and engineering..."

Moses laughs.

"How much money do you think Sir Roland has? I doubt he'd want to spend it sending a poor ikhafula orphan to university. Hold that rail still, Dani. I'll never get this hole straight through if you're jiggling like that."

"Oh, he has piles and piles of money," Daniel tries to keep the rail steady while Moses drives the bit through the outer posts and the rail between them. "Don't you remember Kazi's stories about his enormous house with all its galleries and ballrooms? And those staircases and passages just for the servants? I'm sure when he sees how clever you are, he'll want to send you to university...I don't love the idea of the hunting safari, though," he adds.

"Oh Dani, I know it will be hard for you. I don't want to go about killing things either. But it won't be for long. We'll help each other through it. And then, just imagine, we'll be on a ship sailing across the ocean..."

Daniel smiles bleakly. "Yes, it'll all be fine, I'm sure."

DANIEL

Arrangements are made for Daniel and Moses to travel with their parents to meet Sir Roland in Durban, and join his service from there. When the letter came, the weeks before their departure had seemed to stretch out infinitely. But the months go by quickly and suddenly it is only a few days away. Moses has grown increasingly excited. When he's with him, Daniel is infected with this excitement too. But when alone he feels a deep hollowing at the thought of leaving, as though all he knew and loved was being swallowed from beneath his feet.

In the days before their departure, a stream of visitors comes—everyone from the surrounding homesteads wants to say farewell to the boys, especially to Moses. Thuli and Nomsa are run off their feet feeding the steady track of well-wishers, deploying every pot in the household to cook up whatever food they can find. The days are filled with women ululating and praise singers flamboyantly extolling the boys' virtues. It is as well that the bishop and his wife have long departed as they would have been appalled by this display of "heathen hullabaloo." uMfundisi** is so thrilled by the prospects of his sons becoming missionaries that he is spotted clapping his hands and jiggling his feet along with the singing.

But on their last Sunday, uMfundisi* declares that he wishes to have their final dinner with just the four of them, to spend some time in quiet contemplation and prayer. Thuli prepares a special meal with roast fowl, potatoes and garden greens, followed by gooseberry pie and clotted cream. But Moses is not there when they sit down together.

"Where is he?" uMfundisi** peers fretfully out across the veranda as though he could conjure up his truant son with his eyes.

"He went off with Joseph after church," Daniel replies. "Joseph said he wanted to tell him something."

He shares his father's impatience. The roast fowl and potatoes on the table smell tantalizing, and it feels like many hours since the morning's oatmeal.

"Well, he knows the rules of the house. If he's late for dinner, he shall go hungry."

"Let's wait a little longer," Kazi pleads. "It's not like him to keep us waiting. Something must have happened to delay him."

But uMfundisi is adamant, although he draws the grace out longer than usual. They chew their way through the greens and potatoes and roast fowl, which Daniel eats with relish—in defiance of the glum air around the table. As Kazi is slicing the gooseberry pie, the doorway darkens. There stands Moses, staring at them with incredulous fury, as though he'd come home to find his house full of intruders.

"Moses, where have you been? You knew this was a special dinner—" their father says. But Moses cuts him off.

"Is it true?"

"What are you talking about, son?"

"What Joseph told me...about how I came to be at the mission. Is it true?"

uMfundisi** throws a horrified glance at his wife. But she has closed her eyes and is holding her head in her hands.

"Now, son, we can explain—"

"Mfundisi, please, don't...no more lies...I just want a simple answer. *Is it true?*"

"There is no simple answer—" his father begins, but Kazi breaks in.

"Yes, Moses," she says, looking at him steadily. "If Joseph told you that he found you as an infant on the banks of the iMfolozi River, it is the truth."

Moses nods. "So these so-called parents of mine, John and Mary, are all lies? This father, John, who died in a wagon accident? This mother, Mary, who died in childbirth, and with her dying breath asked that her son be raised a Christian? These parents, whose souls I've prayed for every night, never existed?"

uMfundisi** closes his eyes, presses his fingers together, and holds them against his mouth.

"We were *protecting* you, son. We had no idea where you'd come from, or who had left you. Zulu babies are usually treasured—it was strange to find one abandoned. Someone wanted you dead or gone. We had to conceal your origins, in case whoever wished you harm heard that you'd

149

been found and came after you. Joseph promised not to tell a soul, nor breathe a word to you..."

His father stands up, walks towards him, and grasps his shoulder.

"I know this must be a shock to you. I hoped to shield you from this knowledge. But if you know the truth, then you'll know too how miraculous it is that you came to be our child. That you were found in time by Joseph, that you came to us a few days after Daniel was born so your mother could nurse you...God kept you safe until Joseph found you, for He had great purpose for you..."

Moses remains stiff and unmoving until his father's words falter. uMfundisi* lets his hand fall and stands with his lower lip trembling, like an animal suddenly discovering itself exposed in the thicket of his beard.

Moses moves first. So abruptly, Daniel hardly sees him go. He just becomes aware of the space in the doorway, and his brother running past the window.

Daniel leaps to his feet, knocking over his chair and takes off after Moses. He pounds across the grass and down the path to the stream, but Moses has always been faster. It's all he can do to keep his back in sight through the trees. Moses doesn't even pause at the stream, just ploughs through the water in his shoes. Daniel loses his footing in the rapid current swollen by the summer rain. He goes down, striking his knee hard on a rock.

"Mosi...!"

Moses pauses and looks back at him.

"Stop following me. I don't want you around."

Daniel pushes himself up and sloshes through the water. "But I'm your brother."

"I have no brother...don't you see? I'm just a...a...*thing* that was thrown away. Everything you all told me about myself is a lie."

"I never told you anything! I never knew this any more about this than you."

He lurches towards him, trying to embrace him, but Moses pushes him roughly so that he staggers back.

"Leave me alone. I don't want to be with you. I need to be alone."

Daniel stands dripping on the riverbank, shocked more by the anger in his eyes than by the pressure of his hands. Moses turns and disappears into the thicket on the far side of the stream.

MOSES

Moses runs. He runs through the thicket beyond the stream, up the hill, and along the ridge, dodging termite mounds and mole hills and rocks. He runs through thorn trees, hardly noticing the rips in his shirt and skin. He runs past homesteads, ignoring the children who run after him, the women who call greetings or mockingly ask him to marry them. He runs into the forest beyond the hills, following old animal tracks under yellowwoods and red ivory woods and monkey rope creepers. A startled kudu charges out of the undergrowth, knocking him down as it hurtles past.

He lies, winded and gasping, his shoulder aching from

where the kudu knocked it. The tree canopies spin above his head.

"What am I?" he shouts to the forest. "What manner of being am I? Where on this earth do I belong?"

He pushes himself up and walks more calmly up the highest hill, the one they call intatshana lamatshe, the hill of stones. The day is warm, and he sheds his shirt, feeling the sun burning his skin. Swallows and bee eaters swoop and dive at the insects hovering over the meadow. The hill is crested by a rocky ridge created by a tumble of boulders and wooded by creepers and thorn trees. Dassies dart for cover at his approach, then creep back slowly, watching as he scrambles up one boulder after another to reach a series of rocky crags. Faintly inscribed on the smooth surface of one overhang are faded figures and animals, painted by ones who dwelt there perhaps centuries before. Elongated figures, rust-red elands, twisting snakes. The wind has carved the surrounding rocks into uncanny forms. Moses thinks of them as sentinels, guarding these painted testimonies of the long dead.

He found the paintings three years before. It's his secret. He never told Daniel, and the Magwaza boys never come up here, for the elders say that the rocks harbor evil spirits and that children who stray there will never return. Moses doesn't believe in such things and doesn't find the place sinister. But it holds a stillness that draws him, some sense that it exists outside of the boundaries of time and distance that govern the world, that it offers a sanctuary from the ongoing insistence of life.

He sits surveying his known world laid out before him, the dark blur of the great Nkandla Forests to the west, the hazy intimation of the sea to the east. The rock is warm and solid beneath his buttocks. Is he being watched? He catches a gleam in a nearby crevice. Concealed in its shadows are the dappled coils of a python, its dark eye fixed on his.

He is not afraid. He knows he is not the prey of a python, which, like the black eagles circling in the high clouds, feeds on the dassies and other small creatures of these rocks.

He tries to still the turmoil of his thoughts, to remember what Joseph had told him. Joseph seldom offers information without much parenthesis. This explosive revelation came with a typically circuitous introduction. He'd taken Moses up the river and shown him the nest of a scops owl in the hollow of an old umkhiwane tree. The female's head was just visible over the rim of the hollow. The male was perched on a nearby branch.

This was a beautiful discovery, but he was puzzled as to why Joseph had been so intense about it and why he had not invited Daniel.

"Do you remember your owl?" Joseph asked.

"Mkhulu? Yes, of course I remember."

"Do you remember how it would sleep under the hen's wing and scratch in the farmyard, like the other chicks? As if the hen was its mother?"

"Yes, I remember."

"But when you took it to the woods, it knew itself to be an owl, not a chicken. Not the first time, not the second time, but the third time, it knew itself for who it was."

Moses listened with some impatience because lunch was waiting, and he was hungry, but he knew not to hurry Joseph. Joseph kept talking—about the owl and then about how when they had first arrived at uMzinyathi, Kazi had been confined with giving birth to Daniel, and uMfundisi* had not wanted to leave her so he had sent Jospeh alone to take their offerings to the king. On the way back, he had passed the night at an umuzi near the iMfolozi. It was a time of great drought—the crops had failed, and people were surviving by eating the bulbs of arum lilies and porridge made from the fruits of the umkhiwane tree. They were suspicious of him, this stranger wearing the clothes of umlungu. They said he could shelter from wild animals within their stockade, but they had no food to give.

In the night he'd heard the cries of a woman in labor. He'd left early in the morning and glimpsed an old woman moving among the reeds by the river near the crossing place. When he reached that place, the woman had disappeared, but lying there was a newborn infant wrapped in an imbeleko.

"I lifted the infant," Joseph said, "and ran for sixteen hours to bring you to the mission station."

And only when he said *you* did Moses finally understand that he was the scops owl that had been raised by chickens.

"I gave uMfundisi my word I would not speak of this," Joseph said. "But this is not just uMfundisi's secret. It is mine, too, and most of all, it is your secret. You are not a child, you are a man now. And a man needs to know his own secrets. As your owl knows itself, so you need to know yourself."

Moses had left him then, his world turned inside out, feeling nauseous with shock. He had not doubted Joseph's account, but he needed to hear it from Kazi and uMfundisi before it could sink in. He had run to them, full of some wild hope that they would deny it, would finally produce some irrefutable evidence of the mythical Mary and John.

But they hadn't denied it. How could they?

Perhaps Joseph had not finished speaking, perhaps he had more to say. There is much, now, or perhaps in a day or two, that Moses would like to ask him. But he won't get that chance for they are leaving for Durban early in the morning.

The sun is beginning to dip over the mountains in the west. It's a long walk home. He won't get there before darkness falls. He should leave—he might lose his way in the darkness or be waylaid by a leopard. But still he sits. uMzinyathi is just over the hills, but it feels unreachable, as if he'd stepped out of any self that could find itself there.

He watches the sun's slow descent, imagines the spin of earth below him as it makes its eternal orbit around the sun, feels the force of gravity that holds him to its surface, feels his agitation quietening. It is his only redemption, his only rock in the shifting sands of human frailty and deceit.

The certainty of science.

DANIEL

Daniel limps slowly after Moses. With each painful spasm from his bruised knees, the words repeat themselves, throbbing through his body. *I have no brother...*

He follows the river for some time, wading through

streams or marshy patches of sticky black mud that coat his shoes before he walks up through the forest under stink-wood and red ivory wood trees. He's grateful for their shade against the harsh summer sun.

As the light on the hillside turns golden, he reaches an umuzi of the Magwaza clan, where he greets two pot-bellied old men sharing snuff in the sun outside the stockade, gap-toothed and gray-bearded, one with a neck cratered by a rash of scrofula scars. They inquire at length after the health of his family, the purpose of his journey, where he has been and where he is intending to go.

"We hear you will soon be crossing the seas to the land of the abelungu," one remarks.

"Yes, I will be going—and my brother uMosi too." Even as he says this, he suddenly doubts it. As if the day's events have thrown everything in jeopardy.

"Hawu! uMosi? Our son of the soil?"

"Be careful," says the other one. "They say there are water snakes in the sea that will swallow a man just as a frog swallows a fly."

"I will," he promises, although any fear he may have of crossing the sea is dwarfed by his fear of the safari that precedes it. "Did you see my brother?"

"uMosi? Yebo, he came running past here like he was being chased by a pack of hyenas. He didn't even greet us. He went up there."

As he climbs the hill above the small umuzi with its en-circling necklace of beehive huts, a group of herd boys leave their cattle to run after him shouting *umlungu, umlungu,*

Give us some sugar. He roars and mock charges, causing them to shriek with laughter and scatter.

At the top of the hill, he scans the landscape for Moses, but there is no sign of him. He could be anywhere. Feeling defeated, he winds his way back down to the river, now far upstream. In the slick black leaf mold under an old misshapen umsinsi tree, he sees a round white stone. Bright red lucky bean seeds lie scattered about, like drops of blood. He kneels down and lifts the stone, dropping it as he recognizes it to be a human skull, minus jawbone and teeth. Its dirt-encrusted eye sockets contemplate him with inscrutable malice. Ants from the skull are crawling on his hand. He shakes them off in horror. The shrill chirping of the cicadas swells around him; air fills with faintly audible voices.

He recalls the dark eye of the python at Nodwenga, the whispering voice *Ngiyakwazi...ngikulindele. I know you...I am waiting for you.*

He recalls the man with the scars, his penetrating gaze, the electric shock as his whisk touched Daniel's chest.

He recalls the incweba.

How the man had said, "If you love your brother, make sure he wears it."

Moses must have it. Of course he must. Why had he kept it away from him? He feels sickened by his own actions.

He hurries away from the umsinsi tree and heads back along the stream, moving urgently now, worried that something might have happened to it, for it is over two years since he last looked at it. He reaches the red ivory wood tree at last. As he puts his hand in, his fingers touch scales again, and he snatches them back. Surely the snake was not still there? He peers in cautiously, and makes out in the dim light something lacy and pale beside the old gunpowder tin. He pulls it out—not a snake, but a snakeskin, over four feet long, the memory of scales perfectly imprinted, even the eyes and nostrils clearly delineated. He drapes the skin around his neck and pulls out the gunpowder tin.

It has almost rusted shut, but he loosens it by banging it with the stone. He pries it open, unwraps the oilcloth and drops the incweba into his hand. The pale fur gleams softly in the dusk. His fingers, lacerated from opening the tin, smell of rust and blood. He no longer believes in the evil of witchcraft so strongly, but the incweba still possesses a strange power—whether malignant or benign he can't say.

He walks back under the darkening sky. Clouds of twittering bats are silhouetted against the lemon band on the horizon as they erupt from the forests on their nightly forage for insects. In the distance he hears the mission bell calling congregants to the evensong.

He skirts the house and heads for the barn. He breathes in the sweet grassy smell of the horses and leans against the old bay, Captain. Firefly, Kazi's jittery chestnut mare, tosses her head and pushes him with her nose. The horses snicker softly and nuzzle his pockets, looking for treats.

He sits by the barn door listening to the twittering of the swallows in the eaves and the murmur of voices as people head back to their quarters from evensong. Some are laughing, some still humming the hymns, some calling for their children. Long after all has fallen silent, Moses walks past, hunched against the cool air rising with a mist from the river.

"Mosi," he calls softly, getting to his feet.

Moses hesitates, then turns.

"What are you doing here?"

"I was waiting for you."

"uMfundisi and Kazi must be worried. You should've gone in."

"I didn't want to until you came."

Moses stands, shivering, although the night is quite warm. Daniel takes his cold hands, and rubs them between his to warm them. Moses looks down at his hands, and pulls them from Daniel's grasp.

"We should go inside," Daniel says. "You're freezing."

MOSES

They walk past the buildings, the mud brick walls threaded with the dreams of their sleeping occupants. When they reach the main house, Moses pauses at the window. Kazi is sitting by the fire. On her lap she is holding what seems to be an animal skin, stroking it while staring into the flames. She looks up, alerted by the whining of the dogs, Lily and Shadow, descendants of the now deceased Daisy and Trigger. He feels a lurch of longing for the person he'd been that morning, whose love for Kazi, while never simple, seems so much simpler than it is now. He moves away from the window, and opens the door.

She puts aside the animal skin and leaps to her feet as

they enter. She calls through the door to their bedroom to tell uMfundisi* that they're back. He doesn't come out, but Moses can hear him praying.

"You must be hungry," she says. "There's some leftover potato and cold guinea fowl and a slice of gooseberry pie. I'll brew some nice hot tea. Whatever do you have around your neck, Dan?"

"I think it's a boomslang skin. I found it in a tree hollow. I kept it for you, Mosi." He takes it off and holds it out.

Moses looks at it blankly but makes no move to take it. Daniel lays it on the table, looking hurt.

They sit in silence at the table where the food is waiting, while Kazi fusses around, stoking the fire, taking the simmering kettle from the hearth, and pouring water into the brown earthenware pot. She brings the pot to the table and fills their blue enamel mugs.

"I'm sorry, Mosi," she says.

"What for?" he asks.

"I'm sorry that you were abandoned, sorry that we lied to you. But also not sorry. Because if you weren't abandoned, you'd never have come to us. And if we hadn't lied, you might have been taken away."

"It doesn't matter," Moses says tonelessly. He wants to respond to her, but everything inside is dead.

They eat in silence. The food should be delicious, but he chews and swallows mechanically without tasting anything.

Kazi clears the plates, then fetches the skin she'd been holding and lays it on the table.

"You should have this. You were wrapped in it when

Joseph found you," she says.

Moses sees now that it is an imbeleko—the softened buckskin used to carry an infant on its mother's back. He touches the smooth red-brown hide, wondering about the hands that wrapped the imbeleko around him nineteen years before.

"Do you remember Gogo's story of the snakeskin boy?" Daniel says, looking at the boomslang skin besides the imbeleko

"Yes."

"I think...whoever wrapped you in that imbeleko wasn't trying to kill you, but to hide you."

Gogo. Was it Gogo?

"What happened to Gogo?" he asks Kazi.

"I don't know. We were too afraid to ask too many questions, in case we endangered you."

"When did she come to uMzinyathi?"

"About a year after we found you. She said that she'd been converted by Mr. Grout, that she wanted to live as a Christian and had permission from her family. She could speak some English and knew something of the Bible so we had no reason to doubt her story. She never told us her Zulu name or clan or where she was from."

"Do you think it would be possible to find her?"

"Perhaps. But doing so may risk your life and hers, and you may not get the answers you want."

"What answers do you think I want?"

"You want to know why, I guess. Why would anyone want an infant dead?"

Moses shrugs. Kazi stares at the imbeleko, as though seeking its permission to speak.

"Do you remember when those men came for Nkathazo?" she says at length.

"The one they called the witch?"

"Yes. When the men came for him, Nkathazo said that you were a twin who should not have survived."

"A twin?"

"Yes...there was an old custom, I don't think it happens any more, but some of our converts have spoken about a superstition amongst the amaZulu about twins...sometimes, when twins were born, the second-born was left to die or was killed by having earth put in its throat. You were born in a time of great drought when there may have been more pressure on parents to follow this custom. Nkathazo said that your father didn't kill you, as he should have, but brought you to the mission. The men said that you looked nothing like the surviving twin, and Nkathazo was just making mischief. But maybe there was some truth to it."

A twin? A hot flash stabs through him, like a bolt of lightning. Is there some split off version of himself somewhere, living a parallel life? A brother? A *biological* brother?

Kazi reaches across the table and grasps his hand.

"Moses, I can't answer your question. But I'm sure of one thing. Daniel is right—whoever left you by the river wasn't trying to kill you, but to save you. If you go looking for Gogo, you may endanger not only yourself but whoever it was who put you there for Joseph to find."

DANIEL

Moses doesn't pray that night. He just climbs into bed, blows out his candle, and lies on his back, staring into the darkness. Daniel sits on his bed, fiddling with the wax on his own candle.

"Do you remember that man?" Moses asks. "The one we saw at Nodwengu. You said you thought he was the one who came to take Gogo."

"Yes...but I don't know if it was the same man."

"He gave me that incweba...to protect me from abathakathi."

Daniel feels the back of his neck tingle. The incweba smolders in his pocket.

"Yes...I remember."

"What happened to it? Did you give it back to him?"

Daniel closes his fist around it and wills himself to bring it out. He imagines Moses taking it from him, using it to find his family, his *real* family, his *real* brother....His hand stays in his pocket, held fast by an entanglement of emotion he can barely comprehend.

"I can't recall. I must have, yes, I'm sure I did. I saw him on the last morning by the river."

"You never told me about meeting him."

"I'm sorry...I forgot until now...he asked me about you, if you were happy."

"Did he say anything else?"

"He said...he was a heaven herd. He protected home-steads from lightning."

"I wish I had kept it," Moses says, in a low voice. "You had no right to take it from me."

"I...was trying to protect you."

"From what?" Moses asks bitterly. He rolls over to face the wall and pulls the blanket over his head.

Daniel sits, waving his finger through the candle flame, holding it just long enough to make it hurt. But that's not what's bringing tears to his eyes. It's the knowledge of the incweba, how impossible it is to explain, even to himself, why he kept it, why he is still keeping it. The only thing that feels more impossible than keeping it is giving it to Moses.

MOSES

Sir Roland arrives on a sultry February morning, the sky overcast with clouds that intensify rather than dissipate the heat. Moses stands with Daniel at the edge of the break-water, looking out across the shallows at the *Kashgar*—a small ship, low-slung, with two rigged masts and a single funnel. This ship brought Sir Roland from Bombay. It's smaller than the four other ships in the harbor. He is disappointed that the engines are not working, so the funnel is not belching steam or smoke—the ship had docked the evening before and spent the night in the port.

He and Daniel are both wearing suits—the first new garments either has owned—which were ordered from the Royal Welsh Warehouse and sent over on a ship. Moses' suit is a light gray with a pale vest. Daniel's has dark gray pants with a light stripe, a short single-breasted charcoal wool coat and a matching button-up vest. In addition, they'd each received two white shirts, collars and cuffs, two black bow ties, and a dark gray bowler hat. A big investment, stretching their father's paltry stipend and drawing on their mother's savings from her small inheritance. uMfundisi** hopes that the suits will so dazzle Sir Roland that he forgives whatever failings they might demonstrate in the coming months.

They'd unpacked the suits that morning, giddy with the excitement of receiving new clothes, of meeting the great Sir Roland. Moses had slid the silky shirt over his head, drawn up the flannel trousers and pulled on the waistcoat and jacket with reverence, hardly daring to breathe. But as soon as the suit was on, he found it unbearably constraining and wanted to rip it off.

He and Daniel slathered each other's hair with oil to persuade it to part down the middle. They'd stood contemplating their unrecognizable new selves in the looking glass. About all that was familiar was Daniel's row of three freckles running diagonally across his nose, which Moses calls his "Orion's belt."

"Pleased to make your acquaintance, Sir Roland," Daniel said, doffing his hat and bowing to Moses' reflection. "I don't believe I've had the privilege of meeting someone quite so distinguished."

"Indeed, for none so distinguished has ever there been." Moses raised his eyebrows loftily and flicked imaginary dust off his collar. "And wealthy, don't forget. I'm quite astonishingly wealthy. You shall have to do a great deal of bowing if you wish to partake of my astonishing wealth."

"I shall bow you all the way to England and beyond,"

Daniel said, grinning. "You shall grow quite weary of my excessive bowing."

"Oh, that won't do! Verily, I am weary already. Perhaps you shall vary your bowing with some curtseying."

"Why the very thing!" exclaimed Daniel, curtseying with a flourish. "I shall bow and curtsey most prolifically."

Kazi stuck her head around the door.

"If you lads are quite finished with your tomfoolery, we'd best be going."

Her smiling eyes belied her severe tone. "Well, you two certainly look like fine gentlemen. Just try to retain your dignity, and you'll do very well."

The suit grows more stifling by the minute as the humid air of Durban wraps itself around him like damp lamb's wool. His shirt clings to his skin, and sweat trickles down under his armpits. He distracts himself by imagining the suit's journey across the sea from England, how it would travel back one day with him inside. As if it had come to fetch him.

The bustle of the waterfront provides a further distraction, along with a welcome salty breeze. The cries of the seagulls mingle with the calls of the people gathered on the dock. His nose quivers with a pungent array of smells—rotting fish, tar, wood smoke, coal dust, horse piss, ox dung, tobacco smoke, all wrapped in the salty mystery of the ocean. The water stretches out before him towards the bluff. A stone tower rises imposingly from the headland—built by the British in 1867, uMfundisi* said, and the only lighthouse on the eastern coast of Africa. He spoke with that particular air of satisfaction that Moses has noticed when he recounts the achievements of fellow Englishmen, as if anything done by another English person affirms his own excellence. *Here we are*, the tower says. *We the British. Making our mark on the world.*

He and Daniel wander among the crowds along the point. They pause to consider a chain of bare-chested men in ragged trousers heaving sacks of sugar off waiting wagons and passing them to the rowing boats. They sing in chorus, creating a rhythm to lighten their load. The workers eye Moses' suit with derision and some break their song to throw mocking comments after him. They are distracted by a passing woman selling roasted mealies from a wide basket balanced on her head. They call to her suggestively, provoking a flurry of indignant clucking and scolding.

They walk on, passing the open doors of a wooden shed. A mountain of ivory gleams faintly in the dark interior. Daniel steps in, Moses waits at the doorway, deterred by the dust and a lingering stench of decay. The tusks are heaped up on the floor or leaning against the wall, many taller than his brother.

"Look how many there are," Daniel calls to him. "Can you imagine...so many dead elephants."

"Eyeing the merchandise, are you, boy?" A voice barks out behind him.

Moses turns to see a potato-faced man in a dirty coat and stained bowler, with a pistol holstered at his side. His jaws are working a wad of tobacco. He follows his question with a spray of dark saliva that spatters Moses' shoe.

"Get along with you then," the man says, jerking his chin over his shoulder. "That lot's worth a small fortune, and the guv'nor won't be pleased to have some filthy darkie fingering it."

"I imagine many 'darkies' have fingered it," Moses replies coolly. "It's hardly likely to have gotten here without black men carrying it along the way."

"Oh, you *imagine*, do you, you cheeky bugger? Well, you'd better do your imagining somewhere else if you don't fancy a flogging."

"Is there a problem?" Daniel asks, coming out of the shed.

The man whips off his battered hat, and stands, twisting it in his hands.

"Begging your pardon, sir, just sending this black-a-moor on his way," he says.

"Are you referring to my brother?"

The man looks around in confusion.

"Begging your pardon, sir, I don't know what you mean?"

"This man here is my brother and a gentleman. He certainly does not deserve to be sent on his way like a common thief."

The man shoots Moses an evil glance.

"Begging pardon, sir, I did not appreciate the situation."

"No, clearly not," Daniel says, waving his hand at him loftily.

"What an idiot," Daniel snorts, as they walk away. "*Beggin' pardon sir, I did not happreciate the situ-hation.* I'll say he did not."

But Moses doesn't laugh.

"He shouldn't have spoken to anyone like that. And why should I need you to vouch for me?"

DANIEL

A piercing whistle announces the arrival of the train from Market Square. The sugar loaders abandon their task and cluster around the black clanking engine, jumping back when it lets off a noisy eruption of steam. Daniel surges forward with them, but Moses hangs back as if he sees such things every day, although Daniel knows he must be itching to examine it. The station workers push back the laborers with wooden batons, making way for the white people climbing down from the carriages—the men in suits and hats, the women in bonnets and tight-waisted long dresses. The children run shrieking between them or cling to their skirts. Daniel has never seen so many white people in his life.

There are calls of *the boats are coming*, and the crowd hurries to the water's edge. He looks out across the water and sees the long boats heading towards them, flanked with oars and white crested waves created by their bows. As the first boat comes into the shallows, it is greeted by a large crowd of workers who have waded out to meet it. Some are carrying chairs. The women from the boat are loaded onto the chairs and carried suspended between two men— the older ones try to maintain a dignified air, but many clutch the sides of their chairs and their hats and utter squeals of alarm as they are borne through the shallows. Some men wade ashore, but others are carried on the backs of the workers—their red faces beneath the hats struggling for appropriate expressions of jovial or stern imperiousness.

One man strikes him for he has none of the bluster of his fellows. He sits astride his human bearer with bored nonchalance, as though riding a horse, and seems indifferent to the waves splashing his boots. His beard is notable too, for its density and blackness, the squareness of its cut reinforcing the thrust of his jaw.

It's him, Daniel thinks, suddenly remembering that big loud man who filled their house, the rough assault of his fingers when he tickled him. How strange that he used to carry Daniel on his shoulders, and here he meets him again being carried on another man's back.

The man meets Daniel's gaze, nods and lightly tips his brown bowler hat. There is something mocking in his salute, some irony. But whether it's directed at himself or at Daniel is hard to tell. Daniel feels himself flushing and turns away.

MOSES

Moses stands watching the arrivals. His gaze has shifted from the English on the shoulders of the stevedores to a boatload of Indian men and women. Kazi said that Indians were traveling on the ship with Sir Roland, part of a group of indentured laborers sent to work on the sugar cane plantations. They're not carried, but leap over the sides of the boats and wade through the shallows. The women's colorful saris billow and swirl in the water around their knees like tropical jellyfish.

"So many white people, eh?" someone says in Zulu behind

him. "You wonder if there are any left in their own country, they come in such numbers."

He turns to find a tall man in traditional dress, carrying a spear and shield.

"Sawubona, my friend,"

"Where are you from?" the man asks.

"A mission station in Zululand, in the KwaMagwaza district."

"Are you of the Magwaza clan?"

"I was raised by the Christians and have no clan. My name is Moses."

"No clan? You Christians are strange. I am from the Sisonke district, Dlamini clan. My friends and I like to come here in military dress to alarm the newcomers. The English police find it amusing so they don't fine us for not wearing trousers. There's a living to be made like this, now that they've stolen our land and imposed a hut tax. My cousin has gone to London with a dancing troupe."

He waves towards the cluster of people and baggage. "It's a pity King Shaka didn't meet the English with a real army when they first came, to chase them back into their boats. There are too many now—and more every month. They'll take all our land and cattle before my children are grown. And yet we carry them ashore as though they were precious cargo."

"They won't take Zululand," Moses says. "The army of King Cetshwayo is too strong."

The man laughs harshly. "Oh, they'll take Zululand. Didn't you hear what they did to Chief Langalibalele?"

"Moses! Daniel!"

Their father is waving them over. Beside him stands a man with dark eyes, the nose of a Roman general, and a full black beard cut square. His deep-set eyes hold a gleam of amusement that seems more mocking than kind.

"Ah!" uMfundisi* exclaims. "There you are. Cousin, this is our son, Daniel, and our protégé, Moses. Lads, do you remember Cousin Roland?"

"Pleased to meet you, Sir Roland," Moses says, stepping forward with his hand outstretched. "Welcome to Natal."

Sir Roland ignores his hand and turns to uMfundisi* with a short burst of incredulous laughter. "Good heavens, Cousin, is this the boy you wrote about in your letter?"

uMfundisi** peers at Moses anxiously, as if he might have suddenly transformed himself into something else.

"Well, yes, this is Moses," he replies.

"Forgive me, I suppose I have become used to the coolies. I've rather forgotten how very...uh...dusky the African negro is. Underneath all that finery, he's as black as tar!"

Moses looks down at his raised hand, drops it, and brushes it against his trouser leg as though wiping off something offensive.

"But you met Moses when you came in '62," uMfundisi* stutters. "I thought you'd remember..."

"Ah, yes, of course, now I do recall a little pickaninny crawling about the place...well, never mind, eh...ah...Moses, is it? Handsome is as handsome does, as they say. And this is your boy then? Why, he's the very spit of you, isn't he, Charlie? Just like the scrawny little bird you used to be, I see."

He gives a bark of laughter, which uMfundisi* rewards with a tepid smile. Sir Roland squeezes Daniel's shoulder briefly, as if to assess the ripeness of an orange.

"Never mind, son, you'll bulk up in time, I'm sure."

He turns back to uMfundisi* / the Reverend Whittaker.

"Well, Cousin, where is your carriage? Can't wait to get my nose in the manger—we've had the most wretched provisions on ship, fit only for coolies and dogs."

They can't all fit on the wagonette, which is to take Sir Roland to the household of Judge Langford, where he'll be staying. So it's agreed that Daniel and Moses return to the Reverend Baker's house on foot.

Despite the cloying heat and steep climb up to Berea, Moses strides ahead, his suit tugging at his legs and arms as though resolved to detain him. But no matter how fast he walks, Sir Roland's remarks snap at his heels, like hyenas waiting for their prey to tire.

Over dinner that evening, there is talk of the lighthouse, the steam train, the complications of building the new harbor. No reference is made to Sir Roland's comments. But afterwards, Kazi says to Moses, "You don't have to go through with this, you know."

"What do you mean?"

"Cousin Roland...he suffers certain prejudices. Like many Englishmen, I regret to say. Once he knows you better, he cannot fail to see the good, intelligent man under the skin. But if you don't want to tolerate his rudeness, you can decline his offer."

"Are they all like that, in England?"

"I can't deny there is a lot of foolish prejudice, Moses. But attitudes are harder in the colonies. I believe you will find plenty of sympathetic good souls in England."

"Very well, then. We're not children, Mother," Moses says coolly. "I can keep my temper, and I'm sure Dan can too."

Kazi drops her eyes to her hands. She's been twisting them together as she often does when she is saying things she doesn't like saying.

"You'll be meeting him tomorrow to discuss the venture. Let's see how that goes. No doubt your father would be disappointed if this doesn't work out, but if you feel that too much is being asked of you, I'm sure he'll understand."

Moses thinks of the frenzy that has gripped the Reverend Whitaker ever since Sir Roland's letter came, the way he fussed about them that morning, exhorting them again and again to make a good impression. He smiles bleakly.

"I don't think uMfundisi will understand, Mother. Do you?"

DANIEL

They meet with Sir Roland and their father in the Reverend Baker's parlor. It's another stultifying afternoon, and the heavy drapes drawn half across the window keep the heat in as much as they keep the sun out. The boys are again in their suits—Daniel assumes that they won't have to serve out their time with Sir Roland trussed up in these suffocating garments, but uMfundisi* seems resolved to have the boys keep them on as long as possible.

Sir Roland asks them about their intentions should they be given the opportunity to study in England, and they both aver their desire to return to Africa to further the cause of Christendom. uMfundisi** assures his cousin that they are hardworking young fellows, equal to any challenges that missionary work presents, be it making bricks or ministering to lost souls.

"Well, we'll see how they get on....However, this brings me to a rather delicate matter. Moses, I gather you've been raised to be an equal in the household?"

"Yes sir, the Reverend and Mrs. Whitaker have been kind enough to raise me as their own son."

"Indeed...although whether it is a kindness may be disputed. I fear you've been living in circumstances that do not reflect the greater reality of our world. You've expressed your desire to serve the colony, but I'm sure that you can appreciate that the colony is best served by those who know their place."

He sits forward on the Reverend Baker's blue velour and mahogany armchair, elbows resting on spread and sturdy thighs, and pins Moses against the brocaded sofa with his hooded gaze.

"I believe I know my place, Sir Roland." Moses' tone is opaque, but something flashes in his eyes. Daniel notices it. He sees that Sir Roland notices it too.

"I am pleased to hear that. I am a liberal man, unlike many of my counterparts. I see the value in training native subjects to hold positions beyond menial labor. It benefits a colony to have native people with some skill to help govern

EYE BROTHER HORN BY BRIDGET PITT

their more primitive countrymen. But I'm sure we can all agree that it benefits no one to have aspirations well beyond their position in society."

How his beard bobs about, Daniel thinks. As if it can't wait to escape his chin and go and live its own life somewhere else.

"My aspirations are only to serve God and to deliver my people from the dark vale of heathenism, sir," Moses says, parroting one of umfundisi's favorite phrases that he has never been able to say without irony. But now his tone is wooden.

"Splendid!" Sir Roland declares, slapping his meaty thigh as if a great bargain has been struck. "Of course, your position on my estate may be somewhat different from what you have been used to. Daniel is an Englishman and my relation, and it is his birthright to be treated as one of my own class. But I will find you a suitable position, perhaps as a supervisor with a status above the common laborer."

Daniel stares at Sir Roland, trying to make sense of this statement. Whatever is the man saying? He speaks in a voice somehow both soothing and bullying, suggesting that only the most foolish could possibly disagree...but there was that word he used, *birthright*. That word that came with the gun—and left when Daniel gave the gun away. Or so he'd believed. But here it is again, with its smell of gunpowder and blood.

He flings a panicked look at Moses—who has turned into a statue, eyes fixed into the middle distance, face immobile—then at his father. But uMfundisi* has apparently lost his mind among the bric-a-brac in the small glass-fronted cupboard, for he is staring at a porcelain shepherdess as though she holds the key to all mysteries.

"But...Moses is one of us! He's my brother!" Daniel blurts out.

Sir Roland slides his hooded eyes to Daniel and smiles again. Such square white teeth he has...

"Well, that's very touching, my boy, and I'm sure you were good pals scampering about as youngsters. But we're not children now, are we? And the real world is a little different from a mission station."

Daniel stares out of the half-draped window to the sweeping view of the bay of Durban in the distance, the tall masts of the ships rising above the fringe of dense forest lying between the sandy flats of the town and the shoreline. The lighthouse on the bluff beyond points up like a cautionary finger. Why is their father saying nothing? Why is Moses so still, and what is this new voice of his, so planed of rough edges and sharpness? Why is he himself not grabbing Moses by the hand and running out of that stuffy room, away down the hill to the sea, to anywhere but here? Sir Roland is still speaking—he talks and talks about arrangements and things to be purchased and lists to be drawn. His voice sucks all the life out of the other three so that they sit like sacks of straw and nod at everything he says.

At last Sir Roland takes his leave. After he has gone, uMfundisi** beams at some invisible being behind the two of them and declares that everything is working out splendidly.

Daniel stares at him incredulously.

"I don't understand what he was saying. What does he mean Moses will be treated differently? Moses is my brother. How can I treat him differently...?"

"I'm sure he will accommodate Moses quite suitably... it may seem strange at first, perhaps, but you'll settle into it quickly enough. The Lord gives us no challenge we can't meet with a stout heart and good faith."

"But...are we not all equal in the eyes of God?"

"In the eyes of God, indeed we are, but society is another matter. And if we are to go about in society, we have to follow its laws and customs too."

"Even if they go against God's word?"

"Well, now, son, I have no fear that Sir Roland will go against God's word."

Moses watches uMfundisi*/ his father with a weary resignation.

"Dan, don't fuss," he says, brusquely. "This is what Sir Roland wants. If I can do it, I'm sure you can."

"There we are, Moses understands perfectly! That attitude will take you far, my son. Already you are learning to temper your pride. Daniel, follow your brother's wisdom in this and you'll both get on splendidly. And boys..."

uMfundisi* hesitates. He fiddles with his waistcoat buttons and glances swiftly out of the window as if checking for eavesdroppers.

"Perhaps it's best if we say nothing of this arrangement to your mother. Just between us men, eh? Women tend to overcomplicate matters."

So, his father is ashamed after all, Daniel thinks, as uMfundisi* hurriedly takes his leave before anyone can catch his eye.

"Mosi, we can't do it," Daniel declares, as they walk outside, the sunshine brutal after the dim light in the parlor. "There must be another way to send you to England."

"What other way? We have no choice, Dan. uMfundisi will be furious if we refuse. Besides, I don't want Sir Roland to win."

"Win what? Whatever do you mean? Won't he win if you go along and let him treat you whatever way he thinks you should be treated?"

"No, he won't. He can't change how I feel inside. That's what matters. I *have* to go to England, Dani...if I go there to get educated, I can prove that I'm the equal of any man... I can do it if you help me."

Moses looks frantic suddenly—and afraid.

Daniel bends down to pick up a pebble and flings it as hard as he can. He turns to Moses with a sigh.

"Well, if that's really what you want...if it's insufferable we can just ride away, can't we?"

Although he knows that Moses is not the sort to ride away from anything. When Sir Roland spurned Moses' hand, some gauntlet was thrown. If anyone will fight a mortal battle for honor, it is Moses.

The days pass in a whirl of arrangements. Nothing more is said about their interview with Sir Roland. Daniel and Moses see little of him as they go about organizing his various supplies as instructed. Kazi watches them uneasily. Daniel wishes she'd ask him about their meeting, for he's never been able to lie to her, but she doesn't—she's probably afraid to know. The silence about what is happening lies thickly over them, like the humidity and heat that beats down on the sandy streets of Durban. Its oppressive presence seems to grow with each passing hour.

Two days before they leave, a dinner party is held at the home of Judge Langford where Sir Roland has been staying. uMfundisi* insists that Daniel and Moses attend, declaring it "bad form" to decline the Judge's invitation.

Daniel is placed between Kazi and Mr. John Harris, the wealthy owner of a trading company, whose florid face is framed by abundant whiskers which guard each cheek like small angry dogs.

Also seated around the large oak table are Mrs. John Harris; Judge Langford and his wife; the Reverend Baker and wife; Sir Roland, and the Reverend Whitaker. The men wear black suits with bow ties, their wives richly colored satin dresses, trimmed with a cacophony of ruffs and twirls, lace and feathers. Kazi is in her one good unadorned blue gown. Mrs. Harris sports a quantity of ringlets which spring about her head like agitated snakes. Her protuberant blue eyes are fixed on Moses in fascinated disbelief.

Pea soup arrives, served by two black men in white uniforms and white gloves. There is a bewildering array of silver to choose from to eat it. Daniel is grateful for Kazi's murmured guidance on which utensil to choose.

Judge Langford's chinless face perches on his skinny

neck like a wizened grape. After the soup has been served, he fixes his pale eyes on the Reverend Whitaker accusingly and inquires about the missionary effort in Zululand.

"A little difficult right now, your honor," uMfundisi*/ he replies. "King Cetshwayo used to be quite amenable to the missionaries, but I believe he is under pressure from the amakhosi, who think his father was too soft. I fear that Christianity won't take hold in Zululand as long as the kings hold sway."

"I've been saying for years that we must curb the power of the Zulu king and chiefs." Mr. Harris barks. "From the day of his coronation, Cetshwayo has shown arrogance and disrespect."

"Too true," uMfundisi*/ the Reverend Whitaker agrees. "Apparently, he sees no reason to hold allegiance to the British. He claims his army is a match for ours any day."

"It will be a dark day for us all if the British were to go to war against our Zulu neighbors," Kazi says.

Sir Roland laughs. "Oh, women are always squeamish about war. Sometimes it's just the thing to settle unruly fiefdoms. If Cetshwayo wants to avoid it, he should be more cooperative, but it may be too late—I've heard that Sir Bartle Frere is set on that course."

Mrs. Langford, whose billowing curves in contrast to her husband's scrawny frame suggest that she has spent her married life eating on his behalf, implores the Reverend Whitaker to assure her that the missionary effort in Zululand has not been in vain.

"Oh, no, my good lady, not at all. We have planted seeds

in many hearts which will bear fruit when the time is right. I believe that the most effective carriers of the Word will be Christianized Zulus themselves."

Sir Roland relieves his moustache of wayward soup with his napkin, takes a generous swallow of wine, and gestures with his glass towards Moses.

"My cousin hopes that the solution to the missionary woes lies in this native boy we find at our table. He wishes to send him to England to theological college, to train him as a missionary."

Several pairs of eyes swivel towards Moses. He nods in acknowledgement and allows his own eyes to briefly cross the mocking gaze of Sir Roland before fixing them on the salt cellar in front of him.

"What a fascinating project!" cries Mrs. Langford. "And doesn't he look quite the young gentleman in all that finery?"

She tilts her head while peering at him quizzically, as if trying to identify a troublesome insect.

There is much talk about whether it is possible or advisable to "take the native from his kraal." Mrs. Harris recounts the case of Miss Barter, who took a Zulu child back to England to get educated. "She made a point of ensuring that the child never speak Zulu. It's said that children who speak it are at risk of impurity of mind."

"Our Dan learnt Zulu along with his mother tongue," Kazi says. "But I'm sure his mind is quite as pure as any English boy of his age, don't you agree, Reverend Whitaker?"

This revelation causes all the eyes to turn from Moses to Daniel. He smiles, and says in Zulu, "Yes, I've always spoken isiZulu and would rather be speaking it now with members of the Magwaza clan than speaking English around this dinner table with people who have such foolish attitudes."

Mrs. Harris utters a small shriek, setting her ringlets trembling. "Why, I never heard the like! He jabbers away just like a native. Whatever were you saying, boy?"

uMfundisi** clears his throat sharply. "He was saying how...er...*delighted* he is to be in such charming company."

Daniel takes a generous swallow of wine. He's never drunk alcohol before and it's making him rather reckless. He's tempted to repeat the remark in English, but Kazi pinches his wrist in warning.

Mr. Harris lets out a mirthless bark of laughter. "Good gracious, Mrs. Whitaker, what a liberal household you run! I hope you're not following Bishop Colenso with his baptizing of polygamists and defense of Langalibalele? He's quite done for himself in the colony with those radical views."

The Reverend Whitaker insists that Moses has been raised with the highest English morals, is quick with his lessons, and will make a fine missionary with the right guidance. Judge Langford gloomily suggests that too much education will only confuse the natives as they lack the necessary moral foundation to cope with it.

Sir Roland lays down his spoon in his soup bowl and leans back with the air of man well-padded against misfortune. One of the serving men swoops down and whisks the empty plate away.

"With respect, your Honor, I disagree. Educated colonial subjects can be a boon if they have the right attitude. In

Burma and India they've proved very useful in keeping order among the locals. Admittedly, the Asian native may be better suited to clerical work, but I'm willing to give the boy a fair chance."

"Well, Moses, you are indeed a fortunate young man to have been given such opportunities," Mr. Harris declares, fixing Moses with a stern eye. "I trust you'll make the most of them."

"I certainly intend to, sir," Moses intones in his new voice, which makes everything he says sound as if he were reading lines written for someone else. "I'm well aware of my good fortune to have been raised by Reverend Whitaker and his wife—and to now be considered for sponsorship by Sir Roland."

The evening drags on. Daniel tries to catch Moses' eye, but his gaze remains steadfastly averted. Soup plates are collected; dishes of cold fowl, hot beef, tongue, boiled squash and potatoes are dispensed, dirty crockery is removed. How they talk, despite all the food to occupy them, and what a great quantity of opinions they have, each one sillier than the next, in Daniel's view. The only topic of any interest to him was gossip about a trader's wife, so deranged by her last confinement that she slit her throat from ear to ear with her husband's razor, leaving him with six motherless babes.

The conversation turns to the ivory trade, which was one of the interests financing Mrs. Harris' ribbons and lace. But Mr. Harris reports that it is no longer so lucrative.

"Ten years ago, we were exporting close to a hundred tons annually—around thirteen thousand tusks. When we arrived in '55, there were still elephants in Berea. But now we're running out of them. Last year we only exported around eleven tons. Same with the rhino horn—about two and a half thousand a few years back, now almost nothing. No animals left. Luckily the sugar trade is picking up."

Daniel thinks of the tusks piled up in the shed at the waterfront and conjures up a herd of angry elephants to trample Mr. Harris and his wife.

"Well, I hope they left a few tuskers for me," Sir Roland responds, narrowing his eyes against the plume of smoke from the cigar smoldering between his fingers. "I have a hunting trip planned for March."

MOSES

Moses endures the evening by blocking out most of what is being said. Even the words coming out of his own mouth seem to be meaningless noises conjured by umfundisi's expectations. He watches the other mouths open and close, distorts the voices in his mind, until they become as mindless as a flock of geese, honking in the farmyard.

He thinks about their Scops owl which was raised by the chickens. How its mother hen had cosseted it, but the others often pecked it. How it had called after Moses and Daniel plaintively, the first two times they tried to release it. And how, on the third time, it had flown off as soon as he opened his hands.

He remembers another story that Joseph told him, after heavy rainfall had caused the stream to burst its banks. They were walking along the flooded areas, looking at the uprooted trees and bushes.

"Do you see," Joseph said, "how the trees break when the flood waters come because they cannot bend? Even though they have good roots, they are washed away. But the reeds remain. They don't get washed away. They have good roots, but they also bend with the water."

He thinks about what it is to bend with the water. How much a reed can endure before it is washed away.

He and Daniel are given permission to leave at last, and to walk home rather than wait for the others. It's a moonless night. Despite their lantern, they almost crash into a herd of oxen lying spread out across the broad sandy street.

Daniel is making jokes about the evening, about Mrs. Harris' ringlets, mimicking their voices and phrases, until he starts to sound like a honking goose too.

"It's all a game to you, isn't it?" Moses snaps as they turn up the long avenue to the Bakers' house.

"What do you mean?"

"This whole thing...Sir Roland...those people...it's all a big joke."

"You're the one who wants to go along with Sir Roland. He's insufferable. I don't know how you could sit there and listen to them all insulting you."

"While you so bravely insulted them in a language they couldn't understand."

"That was funny."

"No, it wasn't funny. None of this is funny for me. I had no choice but to suffer it. If I'm not on my best behavior with Sir Roland, uMfundisi will turn his back on me. I was there tonight, as his...performing dog. I was on show. See how well we're doing at the mission—we have our very own soon-to-be-missionary native boy."

"uMfundisi would never turn his back on us."

"There's no us, Daniel. You're his son. I'm not. You're a white man. I'm not. There's no us."

The words hang in the silence that falls between them. Moses has never called Daniel a white man before. But how white he'd looked in that dining room. How white they had all looked.

"I'm sorry, Mosi. I'm just fooling around, perhaps because...I'm afraid."

"Of what? Sir Roland?"

"Of what will be asked of us, I suppose. Sir Roland seems like a hard man."

"He's just an Englishman. Like any other."

"Like me, you mean?"

"If the cap fits..."

"Well, damn you, anyhow," Daniel growls.

He pushes Moses, and Moses pushes him back, and then something breaks in both of them, and they are fighting in earnest, grimly trading blows, until Moses knocks him down and runs off into the black night.

DANIEL

Their lantern has gone out. Daniel lies in the darkness listening to his brother's fading footsteps, feeling a bruise swelling on his cheek. He remembers the last time they fought as if they really wanted to hurt each other, the day uMfundisi* gave him the gun. He stares up at the shadowy tree branches that meet above his head, at the heavily scented white moonflowers, gleaming above him in the faint starlight.

He gets up at length and walks slowly up the road. As he approaches the small fire that Dawid made by the ox wagon outside the Bakers' house, he hears singing, punctuated with whistles and clicks. He pauses in the shadows. There are two figures clapping and dancing in the firelight—it takes him a few moments to realize it is Dawid and Moses. Moses never dances, not since that afternoon by the pigsty wall—not even the jigs and polkas that their father taught the missionary children as an alternative to what he calls "heathen high jinks." But here he is—he has discarded his jacket and shirt, his shoes. His body flickers with the flickering flames, he has become a thing of spirit and light and wind. Dawid too is transformed from a stiff, grave man curled around some deep private grief into a joyful presence, darting birdlike with quick movements, uttering shrill grunts and clicks in a language Daniel's never heard. The oxen lie quietly on the edge of the firelight, looking on with dark eyes.

Daniel stands in the shadows watching them, longing to join. He's known both of them his whole life, but they suddenly seem beyond his knowing.

His suit lies heavy on his skin, seeming to grow into him, strangling him with its Englishness. Moses' words echo in his mind...*there is no us...if the cap fits...*

He turns and walks softly away.

MOSES

Packing an ox wagon is an intricate business, especially under the supervision of Aaron, Sir Roland's driver. He's a small nut of a man with a permanent scowl on his face. It's disfigured by a burn scar scouring his left check with a swath of puckered shiny skin. Baba Mbanda, who was sent down from the Fitchley estate to guide their trip, said he heard it was from a former master who threw boiling water at him for not preparing supper to his liking.

For the entire afternoon before their departure, Aaron barks at them in a language of his own creation, mixing imprecations in Dutch, English, Zulu and his mother tongue, Nama, as they stow the items Sir Roland deems necessary for his journey—most of which Daniel and Moses have collected in the past few days. These include: a leather trunk containing his clothing and shaving set; mattresses and bedding; provisions of coffee, tea, sugar, flour, salt, exotic spices, salted and fresh meat; cooking pots and kettles; a wickerwork basket packed with cutlery, china cups and plates; saddles, bridles, and grooming brushes; hunting knives, twelve rifles, four double-barreled guns and a large elephant gun; powder, buck-shot, slugs and bullets of lead hardened with tin; a chest of tools; a medicine-chest; tent, a folding-table and folding chairs; a carved rosewood box of tobacco and pipes; a Bible and two hunting journals; blankets, pots and extra knives for trading. When all has finally been neatly stowed, Aaron permits himself a grudging smile, letting the company know that the job has been done to his satisfaction but with no thanks to anyone else.

Early the next morning, they stand, transformed by the golden dawn into mythical beings in a legend with an unknown ending. Cloudy vapor rises from the nostrils of the twelve matching red oxen yoked to the traces, Sir Roland's black stallion, Midnight, the other two horses and three milk cows that will accompany them.

uMfundisi* / the Reverend Whitaker presents them each with a new Psalter, with the inscription *Fear thou not; for I am with thee: be not dismayed; for I am thy God: I will strengthen thee; yea, I will help thee; yea, I will uphold thee with the right hand of my righteousness.* Isaiah 41.10.

Tucked into each Psalter is a print of the photograph that the Reverend Baker had taken for them—the photographer was coming to do the Baker family and offered to do the Whitakers for the cost of the prints. From their mother, they each receive a parcel wrapped in a brown paper. "Open it later," she says.

They ride out into the morning, led by Sir Roland on Midnight. Alongside him is Baba Mbanda, mounted on a stiff-necked brown pony called Jabula whose only gait seems to be a rapid triple. He rides with a rope halter and blanket, but no saddle. Daniel rides behind the wagon on Peppercorn, a flea-bitten gray gelding with a fondness for walking crabwise and turning his head to nip Daniel's ankles. Mr. Khumar, Sir Roland's cook, rides in the wagon. Sir Roland brought him from Burma, as he had "developed a taste for oriental cuisine." Mr. Khumar wears a white turban and an expression of bewildered sorrow, as if unable to fathom how he came to be so far from his original home in Madras and his adopted home in Rangoon.

Moses walks behind Daniel, coaxing their three milch cows. As the road turns the bend, he looks back at the house. Their parents still stand waving: Kazi in her familiar gray shawl, uMfundisi* in his old houndstooth jacket. They look diminished and insubstantial—shadows from a life that already seems unattainable.

DANIEL

That evening, when Aaron and Jakob, the voorloper who walks at the head of the span, have been ushered into sleep by the tots of brandy that form part of their payment; and Sir Roland's baritone commands have yielded to guttural snores; and Baba Mbanda has arranged his elaborately styled head for sleep on the small wooden cradle that he carries with him, Daniel and Moses build up the fire and open their parcels together. Daniel peels back the brown paper to reveal a note, five pencils, and two books: Kazi's *Collected Works of William Wordsworth*, and a blank notebook. He holds the note to the firelight, and reads:

Dearest Dan:

I am giving you these books to inspire and comfort you, for I know how much joy you derive from nature. The Wordsworth was a gift from my father when I departed for Africa, and his wise and beautiful words have kept me good company. This part of your life's journey will tax you, my dear Dan, but you have more strength than you know. Remember that the bond you share with Moses has been forged from the purest metal of love, loyalty and brotherhood. If you are resolute, no man on earth can tarnish it.

Moses passes his books to Daniel without speaking. One is also a blank notebook. The other is *The Annual Register* with the Darwin review. Inscribed on the front page are the words:

Dearest Moses:
The truth can be painful, but you have never lacked courage. Don't let anyone stop you from seeking it.

Daniel runs his fingers over the gold embossed letters on *The Annual Review*.

"So she has given you evolution after all..."

Moses nods.

"You were right, I was hard on her..." His voice is tight. "And now I can't apologize."

"She'll understand. She knows you love her."

Daniel rolls onto his back, hugging his books and staring up at the great dense swath of stars above him.

"We can do this, Mosi," he says. If he sends the words out there, they'll grow and become manifest.

Moses stretches out, resting his head on Daniel's stomach.

"Of course we can. We're the brothers of the great uTika

clan. We can do anything."

"Your head is mighty heavy," Daniel complains, flicking his ear lightly. But he's pleased to feel its weight—since Sir Roland's arrival, these moments of spontaneous affection from Moses are rare.

"Too many brains, dear brother! What a stupendous sky...shall we do the naming of the stars?"

The stars wheel above them, the earth tilts below. And everything is momentarily possible.

MOSES

The journey to Sir Roland's sugar estate near KwaDukuza takes two weeks, traveling in the evening and early morning. Sir Roland sleeps in his tent, an awkward contraption of canvas, poles and ropes, which they never manage to erect to his satisfaction. Mr. Khumar sleeps in the wagon and the rest sleep in the open, except on the two rainy nights when they sleep beneath the wagon.

Sir Roland often rides ahead with Baba Mbanda and sometimes ventures inland to visit various homesteads while the others camp with the wagon. When Sir Roland vanishes over the horizon, a lightness falls on the group, as though relieved of reins held too tight. Daniel is supposed to be "in charge" in his absence, but no one takes that seriously, Daniel least of all. Aaron makes the decisions about which road to take and where to camp. Moses gets them going in the morning and encourages them up the steep slopes. Mr. Khumar reads books in the wagon, climbing out to walk only when they need to relieve the oxen on the hills.

Daniel helps wherever needed and plods along dreamily beside the wagon on foot or on Peppercorn.

The brothers find ways to neutralize Sir Roland. They call him Sir Bugaboo, after a monster in a book they'd read as children. Moses exorcises his rage at him through savage mockery.

The oxen are called Colesberg, Human, Wildeman, Plaatberg, Vryman, Sausman, Leerman, Botman, Oortman, Kleinveld, Engeland and Koopman, all the red color of the mud they churn up. Sir Roland likes his oxen to match. Aaron holds a gruff tenderness for them, and is constantly fussing with the brakes on the wheels to ensure no oxen is injured when they go downhill. He makes a show of whipping and yelling when Sir Roland's around, but the whip cracks above their backs. Moses has seen him secretly stroking their ears and crooning to them when no one is looking. When hauling the heavy wagon uphill, they sometimes stagger and bellow or fall to their knees, but they keep going for Aaron. If anyone else tries to drive them, they stand still and won't move.

The passing days bring rolling hills covered in crops of coffee, cotton, and sugar cane. The high green cane waves and ripples in the wind, turning the hills into restless living animals. Moses remembers the Reverend Whitaker giving Masiphula sugar at King Mpande's umuzi, the way Masiphula had spooned it into the izinduna's mouths. You can almost hear the march of the sugarcane as it consumes ever widening tracts of grassland and forest to grow more sugar, to buy more favor from the amaZulu, to get more land for the British, to grow more sugar.

They cross broad meandering rivers, or encounter deep ravines which force them off their route to find a crossing place. They skirt the steep granite walls draped with ferns and creepers. Swallows swoop below them to nests plastered under rocky overhangs.

Patches of wildness endure in between the encroaching cane fields—dense forests hugging the rivers and coastline, or shrinking slopes of wild grasslands dotted with spreading thorn trees and euphorbia bushes reaching green fleshy fingers towards the blue sky.

Here and there they find an umuzi with its rising mounds of beehive huts surrounded by small fields of corn and vegetables. Baba Mbanda stops at each one for long exchanges of family gossip. The men complain of the hut tax, the low wages for farm work, the pressing of the English farmers around them. *Soon there will be no more place to graze our cattle,* they say. *Truly, these English people eat the land.*

DANIEL

Sir Roland takes Daniel to view an estate he is interested in purchasing. The owner is abroad, but his overseer, Mr. Grainger, shows them around the land riding a sturdy bay cob. Mr. Grainger is a large-boned man with straw-colored hair and a face reddened by the sun. His hair rises in tufts on the side of his head. His small beaky nose and side-whiskers make him resemble an eagle owl, except that his eyes are a watery hazel rather than a hypnotizing gold. He treats Sir Roland with great deference, which seems to extend to Daniel—as if Sir Roland's "sirness" had somehow rubbed off on him, despite Daniel's patent unsuitability as an overlord.

Mr. Grainger unveils the estate eagerly: the teams of Indian workers wielding picks to construct a road; the black men slashing and burning bushes to create more fields; a sugar mill waiting for the season's harvest. When Daniel asks the men in Zulu how it is to work for this umlungu, they look at him dubiously and answer that it is very nice, thank you, the umlungu treats them well, they have no complaints, and he realizes that the *sirness* has rubbed off on him in the eyes of these workers too.

When they ride away the next morning, Sir Roland asks him if he thinks the asking sum of seven hundred pounds is a fair price for this estate.

"I wouldn't know, sir."

"Come on, son. Do the arithmetic. You were at dinner last night when Mr. Grainger was giving us the numbers. Or were you too busy making eyes at his daughter, eh?"

Daniel feels himself redden. He had noticed the way the light fell on her hair, the swell of her breasts under her bodice and the particular blue of her eyes, which she had occasionally fixed on him with a sardonic contempt.

"It seems like a very pretty farm, sir."

"Very pretty? For heaven's sake, what has prettiness got to do with it? How many acres of raw land, how many under sugar, under coffee? What is the annual yield of each? How much sugar does the mill produce and what does it cost to run it? How many workers, and what do they cost?"

"I'm afraid I don't recall those details, sir."

"One thousand acres under cane and a hundred and fifty acres under coffee...one hundred and twenty-two coolies and one hundred natives, employed at thirteen shillings and nine shillings per month respectively...these are not mere details, my boy. This is wealth. You want to be educated in England? Do you think the money for this falls from the sky? This is where it comes from. There are plenty of landed gentry pilfering away their family fortunes on crumbling country mansions, but that is not the Fitchley way. My grandfather and father invested in sugar estates in the Americas and built our wealth by paying attention to such details. Thanks to their foresight and good management, boys like you may be sent to Mission school."

"I understand, sir. I apologize for my inattention."

"It's all in your attitude, my boy. If you can look at a piece of land and see ahead to the wealth that can be turned from it, if you can put in the hard work to see that wealth created, you'll go far in life. This is what distinguishes the British from the African native. The natives are content to grow enough merely to feed themselves. A true Englishman wants more. If you don't want more, my dear boy, you'll get nowhere in the world."

Sir Roland leaves him and canters ahead. Daniel follows slowly on the reluctant Peppercorn. He wonders how you turn yourself into someone who can stand on a golden hillside and look out at the snaking rivers and the antelope grazing in the high grass and say, This is not enough, I want more...you'd need to have some weightiness, he thinks.

Some ballast that sinks you into the ground instead of floating over it like a dandelion seed. He tries to imagine himself in Mr. Grainger's muddy boots, under Mr. Grainger's broad-brimmed leather hat, riding the bay cob about the farm, instructing other men to fell trees and till soil and hack out roads. He feels the shiver of the land under the boots of this man, the weight of his footsteps on the earth.

That evening after supper, Moses is hungry for details too, especially about the sugar mill. How this cog fitted into that drive shaft, its gears and ball bearings and daily capacity. Daniel can't provide these details either. He can recall only the cloying smell of old sugar, the way the light fell through the slatted door in stripes on the dusty floor, and a particularly pleasing spider web strung between two rafters.

"I wish I could have seen it for myself," Moses grumbles. "How could you not have noticed these things, Dan?"

"I'll ask Sir Roland if you can go in my place, if he asks me again, although I doubt he will. I was not very satisfactory."

Moses frowns. "You should try harder. This whole thing will be a waste if we don't impress him."

"I am trying."

"Well, try more. I'm working myself to the bone just to please that man."

"I know, I'm also working hard."

"It's not enough, though. He wants you to take charge."

"It's not in my nature. Besides, I don't think you'd appreciate me bossing you about, would you?"

Moses laughs. "Not much...who'd want to be bossed by a

nincompoop who can't even understand a sugar mill?"

"Nincompoop yourself!"

Then there's a push and a shove and they end up wrestling in the grass. Moses gets the upper hand, pushing Daniel's face down into the dirt so that he struggles to breathe while he twists his arm behind his back. Daniel thumps the ground, but Moses gives a harder twist before he lets go. Daniel rolls over and looks up at him, disconcerted by the blaze of fury in his eyes.

"What the hell, Mosi?"

But Moses avoids his gaze. "Going to get some sleep," he mumbles, turning to walk away to the wagon where their bedrolls are waiting.

One stifling afternoon, they discover a burnt-out stock farmer's homestead in a desolate valley strewn with rocks. Blackened thatch and half-burnt timbers are collapsed into the small room, its mud-brick walls cracked and scorched. The ground outside is strewn with scattered animal bones, broken crockery, and a faded framed print of Jesus. His white robes are spotted with mold. His eyes stare through cracked glass at a hazy white sky.

"What do you think caused the fire?" Daniel asks Moses.

"Lightning, maybe. They probably died when it struck so the place burnt to the ground."

Besides the house are three graves, marked with heaped stones but no headstones, one the size of a small child. Lying beside the smallest one, a dog—washboard ribs under a dull, tick-infested coat the color of the red earth. It watches them with wary boot-button-black eyes. As Daniel kneels beside it, a shadow falls across the dog's face.

"That creature needs to be put out of its misery. Get out of the way, son."

Sir Roland is standing over them with his gun raised. The dog half-raises itself and snarls. It flicks a glance at Daniel, not so much in appeal, but as if to say, Stop him if you will. I don't much care.

"Don't...please...don't shoot it!"

"It's the kindest thing to do."

"He could make a good ratter," Moses remarks. "With a bit of feeding...useful for the cane rats on your estate."

Sir Roland lowers the gun and stares at the dog. The dog lifts its lip, growling softly.

"It's got pluck, I'll grant you. But infested with vermin."

"I'll care for it," Daniel insists. "I'll detick it and feed it."

"You're not carrying it. If it can't walk, it's staying here, and it won't thank you for sparing its life."

Sir Roland shakes his head and mounts his horse. He watches as Daniel tries to coax it away, but the dog doesn't move.

"Leave it," Sir Roland says, turning his horse.

Daniel walks away, looking back every few paces to call it. When he can no longer hear the crack of the whip and Aaron and Jakob calling the oxen, he hurries after the departing group, feeling the dog's eyes on his retreating back. That evening he lies awake, wondering about the bodies beneath the graves and why the dog had chosen to maintain his lonely vigil.

In the early pre-dawn light, he sees a movement in the bushes near his feet.

"Is that you, my little ghost?" he calls. It comes out, slinking on its belly, polite but not obsequious, and lies at his feet. Nose between paws, legs so short its nose extends beyond them; its bat-like pointed ears flick towards him and away, antennae to a world that has so far proved unpredictable and cruel. Its black eyes, gleaming in the half-light, are fixed on his face. Daniel smiles.

"Good dog," he says.

PART FIVE
1878
MY BROTHER
EVERYWHERE

MOSES

The red ivory wood stump grips the earth with grim tenacity. Even though it is no longer a tree, it grips the soil with the desperation of a drowning man clinging to a boulder in a fast-flowing river. Moses hacks the fibrous roots with his machete, both awed and enraged by its intransigence. The tree was cut some months before, but the sap is still rising, giving the roots a moist fleshy quality as though he were hacking at human limbs. When they have finally chopped through the last strands, they heave the picks together to lever the stump out of the soil. It yields with a wrenching groan and topples onto the hard baked ground. Its roots clutch debris from the earth—pebbles, snail shells, the jawbone of a small antelope. Scorpions, woodlice and centipedes scuttle back into the furrows.

Moses straightens, takes a gulp of water from his

calabash and wipes the sweat off his face, leaving a gritty trail of dirt. The sun spins above him, white-hot behind a thin blanket of cloud. He unties the cloth from around his neck, pours a few precious drops of water on it and uses it to soothe his smarting hands. At least he doesn't get blisters anymore. After two weeks of hard labor on Sir Roland's estate, the skin has hardened over the scars, forming callouses.

When Bucket, Sir Roland's foreman, at last strikes the iron pipe hanging from a branch to announce the midday break, he trudges with the other workers to the edge of the clearing and collapses onto the grass bank under the trees. Daniel is waiting with his dog—three weeks of devoted care have filled out his ribs and shined his coat. But he's still an odd-looking creature with his short legs and over-sized ears. He keeps his eyes buttoned on his master, watching his every move.

Daniel offers them bread and bacon to go with their meager portions of grisly meat and lumpy dry umbhaqanga porridge.

"That stumping looks like hard work," he says. "I'll help you in the fields this afternoon. I've finished my other work for today."

Phumlani says that stumping is not as bad as harvesting cane, when you work from sunrise to sunset and the sharp leaves shred your fingers. He says that last year one of the women was bitten by a black mamba. She was dead in two hours.

"Watch out, white boy," he says, grinning. "I think the

mamba likes new flesh to taste. Especially umlungu flesh."

He laughs heartily but not kindly, nudging Moses, who laughs too. He's a watchful young man, with little friendliness in his narrow gaze

"We'll be gone before harvest time," Moses says.

Phumlani shrugs. "Everyone believes that," he says.

"Why do you stay?" Daniel asks. "Aren't you free to go?"

Phumlani laughs bitterly. "Free? That word means many things, my friend. Our izinduna make deals with the white man so that they can keep their grazing lands and fields. If we break our contracts, they fine the headman, who fines us. Then we have to work double to pay the fines."

Bucket's unlovely silhouette looms against the sky, his angular legs in black stovepipe trousers, the tatty ostrich feathers on his stained fedora trembling in the hot windless air. The long greasy strands of hair hanging beneath his hat resemble tails of the giant cane rats that Baba Mbanda likes to trap and roast to supplement his rations—and have given Bucket his nickname among the workers of uGundane.

"Gerrup you lazy bastards, back to work—" he yells, stopping short when he sees Daniel.

"Begging your pardon, sir, I didn't see you there."

Daniel ignores him and follows the others to the field. When Daniel is out of earshot, Moses hears Bucket mutter, "It's a fine day when the gentry lounges about with natives like they was kin."

"Daniel is my kin," he retorts, without turning around.

Bucket flicks his whip to sting the back of his legs.

"He's soft on you, all right, but don't think that gives you privileges, boy. A native is a native on this farm."

Moses walks after the others, thinking back to the day that they arrived. Sir Roland had taken him down to the worker's compound, a leaky shed crowded with neatly rolled sleeping mats.

"I've instructed Mr. Wyeth to clear out a storeroom to provide you with better accommodation. It should be ready by Friday," he'd said. "You will meet with Mr. Wyeth and Mr. Bucket tomorrow to discuss your tasks in supervising the labor in the fields. These quarters are spartan but no doubt you can tolerate them for a few days. And staying here will help you get to know the workers."

Moses had looked at the men sitting around the yard in front of the shed, eating their evening meal. They stared back at him with mingled curiosity and suspicion. He saw himself through their eyes, an oddity who looked like them but dressed and spoke like a white man. Many of them had the isicoco rings sewn to the hair, indicating their status as married men. Many were old enough to be his father, some even a grandfather.

He suddenly understood that what was being asked of him was utterly impossible.

"I'm sorry sir, I don't believe it's appropriate for me to supervise these men. I'm younger than most of them, and they don't know me. I think it's better if I just live among them and do the same work they do."

Sir Roland regarded him coldly, his nostrils flaring slightly. "Are you questioning my judgement, Moses?"

"No, sir. But the status of age is very important in Zulu

culture. Grown men would not willingly listen to someone my age."

"Are you afraid of them?"

"No, sir. But I don't wish to disrespect them. I'm sure there is an elder here who could serve that function quite well."

"No doubt. But I chose you. I'm disappointed in you, Moses. This is a test of your character. I wanted to see if you could put your education and advantages to good use."

"I'm sorry to disappoint you, sir. I can assure you I will work as hard as any man in the fields."

"Oh, you will. Mr. Bucket will make sure of that. You will."

He'd strode off, abruptly, as if he could not wait to be done with him. Moses had watched him go, then approached the oldest of the workers to introduce himself and ask where he should put his bed roll.

A reed must bend with the water. But it must also hold fast to the bank. Otherwise, it will be swept away in the flood.

DANIEL

"Take my pick," Phumlani says to Daniel when they reach the next stump. "Let's see how the umlungu does. I'll do the hacking."

He watches Daniel, perhaps hoping that he will drive the pick into his own foot. But Daniel and Moses have had enough practice clearing stumps at the mission station. After a while, the three fall into a natural rhythm. But it's some months since they did such heavy work, and within two hours, Daniel's hands are red and blistering. Moses offers him some liniment made from the leaves of the intshungu plant, given to him by Baba Mbanda. He applies the paste to his palms, wincing at the sharp sting.

Daniel looks across the wide field to the stumps and brush that must still be cleared. Acrid smoke rises from the smoldering piles of cleared bush, casting cobweb drifts over the rubble. The air above the sunbaked earth shimmers in the heat as the cicadas' shrill incessancy fills his ears. The scene blurs before him, coming into momentary focus to reveal an elephant towering above him, lifting its trunk to pull leaves off the large red ivory wood tree that has blossomed from the mutilated stump. He staggers back, blinking, and the elephant is gone. His ears are filled with the muffled sounds of birds and monkeys, barking kudu, squealing elephants...all the life once sustained by this piece of earth.

The landscape spins and steadies. He recorks the calabash of intshungu paste and sets it down. He steels himself against the ache in his muscles and the burn in his hands and grasps the pick. Ten more stumps to go. Then the stumps and brush will be burned, the land will be ploughed and all traces of that chattering web of former lives will sink beneath the sugarcane. Does this stump remember being a tree, he wonders, watching his pick bite into the roots again and again. Does the earth remember the feel of the elephants' feet?

That night, as on every other, Daniel returns from the fields, scrubs off the day's dirt, forces himself into his suit and presents himself for dinner with Sir Roland. While Moses is sleeping in a leaky barn with fifty other workers, Daniel occupies a spacious bedroom in a large brick and stone house built fifteen years earlier for Sir Roland's father, Sir Robert, when he planned to spend some years on the estate. Sir Robert had furnished it with all comforts so that his wife should feel at home, Sir Roland said, hauling everything through rivers and over hills by ox wagon. Even an upright piano, for she was fond of music. But she'd died of typhus before they left. Sir Robert lost heart in the project and left the management of the estate to the feckless Mr. Struthers, later replaced by Mr. Wyeth. Since then the house has stood empty, the piano and Chesterfields and Bentwood rockers moldering under dustsheets, the skirting boards nibbled by white ants.

Dinner is prepared and served by Mr. Khumar. The food is peculiar to Daniel. The spices make his eyes water and the rice sticks in his throat, not least because he can't stop thinking of the lumpy maize porridge and watery cabbage that Moses is fed. He slips as much as he can into his handkerchief to take to Moses later, but little escapes Sir Roland, and he can usually only manage to smuggle a few mouthfuls.

Tonight, Sir Roland is watching him with particular hawkishness.

"Working hard, I take it?" he remarks, eyebrows raised at Daniel's blistered hands.

Daniel thrusts his hands under the table.

"Yes sir, but we've finished the stumping in the top field today."

"Wyeth informs me that you were working alongside the laborers today."

Wyeth's a little fox of a man, red-haired, with a dense coating of freckles—as if he'd been spattered with mud by a passing ox wagon—and the pugilistic stance of a small terrier. Daniel hadn't seen him in the fields, but no doubt Bucket had reported his presence.

"I was just helping my brother, sir—we've always shared our chores."

"Moses is not your brother here, Daniel. You do him no favors by treating him differently. It'll only make him a target of resentment. The men here are primitive, but they understand authority. Their chiefs do not work by their sides, and we must be as their chiefs are to them. It unsettles them to see a white man doing native work—they'll never respect a man who declares himself their equal."

Moses is my brother everywhere! Daniel wants to shout, but he just stares miserably across the table at a row of dingy oil paintings featuring the bloodied corpses of hares and pheasants. It's hard to imagine that these were chosen to charm the late Lady Fitchley, but perhaps she shared her husband's bloodlust. He thinks of the five rhinos at uMzinyathi, of the elephant tail in the store room, and wonders how many other animals have died at the hands of Sir Roland and his father.

Sir Roland is watching him narrowly from across the table.

"I think it may be a misuse of your talents to help Mr. Bucket supervise the workers. Mr. Wyeth's young lads are running wild and could greatly benefit from some schooling. You can teach them the three Rs, I'm sure?"

"Yes, sir. Moses and I taught the children on the mission station."

"Very good, then this will be no trouble for you."

"Moses is a far better teacher than I, Sir Roland," he throws out, hopefully. "Especially mathematics."

"For heavens' sake, son, they need the mere rudiments of writing and arithmetic. I'm sure you can manage. Besides, it would confuse everybody to have a native teaching white children mathematics."

For the rest of dinner, Sir Roland holds forth on the profitability of sugar cane over coffee. Daniel spots something moving beneath the sagging dust-caked curtains. The small whiskered snout of a mouse appears, retreats, appears, retreats, then its owner makes a mad dash across the floor to a hole in the skirting board. He glances up and sees that Mr. Khumar, who was standing by the door waiting to remove the plates, has spotted the mouse too. He catches Daniel's eye and winks.

By the time the sago pudding arrives, Sir Roland has exhausted all efforts at conversation. They chew their way through it in a silence as stolid as its gelatinous beads. When the grandfather clock chimes, the noise is so sudden that Daniel drops his spoon with a clatter. The clock metes out eight strokes with sonorous melancholy, as if announcing that everyone's best days are over.

"Eight o'clock," Sir Roland exclaims with relief. He wipes his mouth with his napkin, lays it down, and pushes back his chair. "Well then, young Daniel. You'll busy yourself with the Wyeth boys in the morning, and you can come with me to inspect the sugar mill in the afternoon. No need to bother Moses at his work, eh?"

"No sir."

MOSES

Moses sits on a tree stump by a low fire outside the bunkhouse, writing in his notebook. He looks up as Ghost runs into the clearing, followed by Daniel with his sleeping roll under his arm.

"I thought you weren't coming."

"Oh, he took forever to go to sleep."

"You don't have to come."

"Yes, I do. It's insufferable there. And I can't sleep if I'm not near you."

"Well, it's kind of you, but there's no shortage of fine company here...bedbugs, cockroaches, rats.... Frankly, I'd give anything for a night in your feather bed, and I think you're an idiot to relinquish it."

"You could always sleep there. If you climbed in the window and left before dawn, he wouldn't notice."

"No thanks. I won't be reduced to sneaking around. I wouldn't give him that satisfaction."

Daniel pokes at the fire with a stick, sending sparks shooting into the dark sky. He squats on the ground beside Moses.

"Wyeth told Sir Roland I was working on the stumping today. He says I shouldn't do that because it's bad for the workers to see white people doing manual labor. Can you imagine such nonsense?" He laughs.

"They're afraid," Moses says. "Wyeth, Bucket. Old Bugaboo. Living out here, surrounded by black people. They have to convince themselves that they're untouchable."

"He says I have to teach those awful Wyeth boys. I'm sure he cares nothing for their education. He just wants to keep me away from you."

"If I'm to be honest, Dani, it makes it harder to have you around. Phumlani and the others are suspicious enough of me as it is. They think Sir Roland told you to work with us so that you can spy on us. They mistrust me because I'm close to you. And that awful Bhungezi resents me because he's always trying to curry favor with Bucket and Wyeth, and he thinks my English ways will make me more popular with them. Seeing you with me just makes him worse."

"But...I *must* see you, Mosi. Surely they understand I'm not a spy?"

"It's hard to explain to them. I hardly fit in, as it is. Having you around just makes them more suspicious of me. It's not unreasonable of them. Old Bugaboo *has* been doing his best to get me to spy on them.

"Anyway, I think it best if you just do his bidding, Dani. It won't take much for him to send us back to uMzinyathi. At least don't let me break my back working for no reason."

"Would it be so bad, to go back to uMzinyathi?"

Moses jumps up and stands with his back to the fire,

staring down at him.

"*You* go back if you want. But I'm never going back. I *must* go to England! If Bugaboo doesn't sponsor us, I'll walk to Durban and work my passage on a ship. My life is meaningless at uMzinyathi. Every day the same, just doing chores to keep alive...trying to win over a few reluctant souls to Jesus. If you question anything, uMfundisi thinks you're the Devil. I might as well be dead there!"

Daniel looks startled by his outburst. Moses is startled himself. He suddenly realizes how imprisoned he had felt by his prospects at uMzinyathi, how it was only the hope of going away that had made the last few months bearable.

He leans down and blows on the fire to coax more life from the embers, but he just produces a billowing cloud of smoke. He stands up and waves it away from his face.

"Mosi, maybe you should be the supervisor, like Sir Roland wanted. You don't have to be a bully, you can treat the workers decently...but at least it would free you from that awful Bucket..."

"How can you even suggest that?" Moses snaps. "I've got little enough dignity left. It seems that I'm obliged to be Sir Roland's servant, but at least I can refuse to be his lackey. And it wouldn't free me from Bucket because I'd have to work with him, aping his toxic notion of supervising.

"Anyway, Bucket can't touch me. He's just a wasp, flying around. He can crack his stupid whip, but he'll always be a misshapen drunk lowlife in the backwaters of a colony, whereas I will cross the sea one day and learn all the secrets of the universe."

It's true. It *has* to be true.

"It's so much easier for you." Moses moves to his tree stump and sits down. He squints through the smoke at Daniel. "You don't have kill yourself working while Bucket flicks you with a whip. If I can endure it, surely you can?"

"I'd rather do the hard labor with you."

Moses snorts. "Really? Even if you stand beside me with a pick, you're not really beside me. Bucket would never push you. I'd rather you do what they want and don't annoy Sir Bugaboo."

"But aren't you annoying Bugaboo by refusing to be his supervisor?"

Moses winces. "No doubt, but at least you can please him without selling your soul."

"There are different ways to sell your soul, Mosi. Neither of us will walk out of this unsullied. I just can't believe uMfundisi / our father agreed to this. He couldn't have known how bad it would be."

"He must have had some idea," Moses says. "But he'd never stand up to Cousin Roland. Too dependent on his generosity...and Bugaboo has a lot of influence on the missionary society because of his father's bequests. uMfundisi is terrified of offending him."

"We should've told Kazi. She'd be sick to know what was happening."

"I'd have told her if she asked. But she didn't."

It was her betrayal that hurt worst, Moses thinks. The more you imagine someone loves you, the more it sears your soul when you learn their love has limits. Your only defense, he supposes, is to ensure that your love has limits too. And life on Hanbury Estate has already been an effective teacher in the art of limiting love.

DANIEL

"Is your bed quite comfortable?" Sir Roland asks when Daniel reports for instructions the following morning.

"Yes, sir," he replies. "My room is very comfortable, thank you."

"I'm glad to hear it, because I could swear I've heard you wandering about at night."

"I like to take the air at night, sir."

"Wyeth tells me he saw you down by the workers' compound last night. Not a good idea to fraternize with the staff, my boy."

Wyeth again! Does the man have nothing better to do than spy on him?

"I was just walking past, sir."

"Still, I think it's best not to go strolling about at night, eh? Your father would scarce forgive me if you were eaten by a leopard, I'm sure."

The teeth are flashed to signal a joke. Daniel offers a sickly smile in return. He looks at the dead hare in the painting opposite, strung up by its hind leg, and feels the tug of a tether around his own ankle.

The Wyeth boys are presented to him later that morning, three ginger-headed clones of their father in descending order, their reluctance to further their education writ large in their scowls. They have been shepherded there by

Mrs. Wyeth, a small woman with skin pitted like oatmeal, and red-rimmed darting eyes under pale lashes. A baby is balanced on her hip. Her skirts are being tugged by two small girls as she thrusts the boys at him, exhorts them to behave, and hurries off with undisguised relief to be rid of them.

So begins his new routine—mornings spent in Sir Roland's dining room dodging flicked gobs of chewed paper and being told, "You can't make me," each time he suggests multiplication or spelling. When, through bribery or threats, he finally induces the boys to scratch on their slates, he stares out the window and worries about Moses digging irrigation ditches or scything grass under Bucket's baleful eye. Bucket has it in for Moses, perhaps because Moses speaks better English or because of Daniel's loyalty to him. But he's also a craven coward, which Daniel hopes will stop him from doing more than flicking Moses with his whip from a safe distance.

In the afternoons he is expected to ride with Sir Roland to visit other estates, but if he finds any unoccupied hours he walks into sun-drenched hills, wandering "lonely as a cloud" with Ghost and William Wordsworth. The hills rise from a skirt of dense coastal forest. Some are grassy knolls dotted with thorn trees, but most are covered in sugar cane over six feet tall. South is Durban; north, beyond the steep twisted valley of Umvoti, are the Imfolozi Rivers, White and Black, where one day he and Moses will go to help Sir Roland kill animals. Northwest is his old home and the uKhahlamba mountains beyond. East, beyond the dark milkwood forest, lies the ocean.

He reads Wordsworth aloud to Ghost, who listens with his ears cocked and quizzical amusement in his eyes.

And hark! how blithe the throstle sings!
He, too, is no mean preacher:
Come forth into the light of things,
Let Nature be your teacher.

The nature that Wordsworth describes seems milder than the wilderness he knows. He doesn't know what a throstle is, but he's sure it's not as disconcertingly wild as the crocodiles that were occasionally seen sunning themselves on the river banks. He grows impatient with the words, and thinks enviously of *The Annual Register.* The story of evolution tells a truer narrative for him—of how wildness is not in our surroundings but stitched into our bones; of how other creatures are not merely to be marveled at, but acknowledged as other versions of ourselves. He could ask Moses to lend it to him, but that would just highlight the time he has to read while Moses labors long hours in the fields and collapses from exhaustion at night.

More often than reading, he sits quietly, dissolving into the landscape until the animals relax enough to reveal themselves. Then he sketches them, using his pencil to channel their bodies through his, bringing sensations of scratchiness or scaliness, the protective rigidity of an exoskeleton, the air-borne warmth of feathers, the expansion of a compound eye.

These precious hours are darkened by the persistent undertow of dread of what is happening to Moses. He recalls Kazi telling him that on the ship from England they were told that if anyone went overboard, they had to keep watching and pointing at them until they were saved. If you lose them for a second, you won't find them again, and they'll drown. The very least he can do for Moses (and how little it is!) is to keep him, if not in his sights, then, in his mind.

Dinner brings the torment of trying to conjure up winning responses to Sir Roland's queries about his day under the dejected gaze of the dead pheasants. When Sir Roland tires of his poor replies, he fills the silences with discourses on topics that he deems instructional—hunting tigers in the Burma grasslands, the difficulties of moving teak from the jungles to the port, how to achieve mastery over a horse. Daniel tracks the movement of his beard with his eyes and wonders how weavers learn to build their nests, whether dung beetles ever tire of pushing their balls of dung.

Whether Moses is hungry or hurting or sad.

"I'm sure you agree, Daniel," Sir Roland says.

"Absolutely, Sir Roland," Daniel replies, with no idea of what he is agreeing to.

One evening Sir Roland bemoans the state of Hanbury Estate. "It's most regrettable that my father did not pursue with his plan to come here. This place would have been far more profitable had he got it onto a good footing. It was a complete mess under Struthers. Mr. Wyeth is reliable enough, but no good at taking initiative, and the staff seem extremely demotivated."

He fixes Daniel with a speculative gaze. "Perhaps, after a few years' education, you could oversee this farm yourself? It's good to keep these things in the family, and I have no son of my own."

Daniel nearly chokes on his mouthful. He takes a gulp of water to sooth his outraged tongue. It had been negotiating a chicken curry in tiny mouthfuls with plenty of rice.

"That's very kind, sir, but I'm not sure..."

"Oh, kindness doesn't come into it, my boy," Sir Roland assures him. "It would be a profitable arrangement for both of us, but you'd have to demonstrate that you have what it takes. You're young and have been misdirected. But you could perhaps still make something of yourself. Unless you're too committed to the missionary effort, eh?"

Daniel blushes. He is a poor liar, and on even his most godly days he can make no claim to being overly committed to the missionary effort.

"It is my father's wish that I follow in his footsteps, sir."

"But what do you want, Daniel?" Sir Roland leans forward and fixes him with his dark eye. "A man must have his own ambitions beyond filial duty, after all."

Daniel casts about vainly for something to say that might impress him.

"I'm happy to follow the course my father has chosen for me."

Sir Roland sits back and conveys with a wave of his hand how inconsequential Daniel has once again proved himself.

"Indeed, indeed...well, we shall see how it all turns out."

MOSES

Sunday is Moses' only free day. On their first two Sundays, Daniel went to church in Glendale with the Wyeths, Sir Roland and Bucket. But today he hurries into the yard in front of the worker's compound, announcing that he has persuaded Sir Roland to allow him to stay behind and preach to the workers on the farm.

Moses is not convinced that he wants to spend his precious day off preaching. Most of the workers melt away when Daniel invites them to gather under the stinkwood tree. But a few hang around out of boredom or curiosity. Daniel stands before them, manfully reciting the Lord's Prayer. His voice gets quieter and croakier until it is barely more than a mumble. Aaron and Jakob lean against the hitching posts, watching him through derisive eyes. The women from the kitchen giggle and gossip loudly in Zulu. Baba Mbanda sits on an upturned wooden pail and dozes.

Moses steps in to rescue him. He was supposed to read a lesson, but he puts down his Bible.

"You're wondering what can this missionary boy tell us about our hard lives, about our sorrow?" he says. He knows this, because he has been wondering himself.

"And you are right to wonder, for I myself am nothing. But I would like to tell you a story..."

The story jumps into his head, the one about how God looked past the shiny and the precious vessels and chose the broken clay one, for that vessel asked only that it may pour out to others what God has poured into it. He finds himself talking with conviction, the words coming easily, flowing into him.

"And so, my beloved brothers and sisters, God chooses always the most humble among us. The vessels of God are those who are whipped, broken, starving...for it is only these souls who truly understand God's grace. It is said that it is easier for a camel—an animal much larger than a cow—to pass through the eye of a needle than for a rich man to pass into the kingdom of heaven. The rich are too often corrupted by their power and their wealth. It turns them hard-hearted and cruel. The poor have open hearts, a willingness to share what little they have with their brother. Is it not these small acts of kindness that enable us to endure great suffering?

"Many who call themselves Christians treat their fellows with cruelty and disdain. Don't be fooled, my brothers and sisters. They're not true vessels of God. Listen only to those who humble themselves, to those who are willing to wash your feet after a day's work, as Jesus himself was willing to do..."

As he speaks, he feels something shift in the gathering. Their eyes become more alert, the gossiping women fall silent, even Aaron looks as if he is listening, his customary scowl replaced by an expression of indefinable longing. Moses feels something alive and crackling within him, feels his power to move, to comfort, to inspire. It doesn't matter what I say, he realizes. It's how I convey that I care, that I truly care what happens to them.

"You gave a strong sermon this morning," Daniel remarks

that afternoon. They are walking beside the stream running through the dense forest bordering the beach—they'd set out to follow the muffled roar of the waves to find the sea.

"You really could be a missionary. I never quite imagined it, you never spoke like that at home."

"I don't want to be a missionary, Dani."

Moses hears himself saying the words, the words he has been carrying for so long, hidden even from himself. Letting them out fills him with an unsettling mixture of elation and dread.

Daniel stares back at him, eyes wide with shock. "What do you mean?"

"I don't think the amaZulu need Christianity. They need knowledge. They need to understand the English so that they can negotiate with them as equals and not be fooled into making bad bargains. They need technology to make their lives easier and medicine to cure their ailments. How can Christian beliefs help them?"

Daniel shakes his head slightly, like Ghost trying to dislodge a flea in his ear.

"How long have you known?"

"For months—years, perhaps. Or maybe I just knew it now. I didn't want to admit it, even to myself. But it feels so good to say it. I don't want to be a missionary."

"But your preaching...you sounded so passionate..."

"The people on this farm are suffering. They've been pushed from their homes, forced into labor, insulted and assaulted by Bucket every day. If I can bring any hope or comfort by preaching, I'm happy to do it. But the words ring hollow for me. We didn't know what was happening beyond our valley when we were at uMzinyathi. But the more I see of how English Christians conduct themselves, the less I believe in the God they worship. As a missionary, I'd be forced to preach church doctrine and be answerable to the likes of Bishop Saunders. I'd have to ignore science, preach fables as truth. Worst of all, I'd be bound to counsel the locals to despise their black skins and beliefs and to bow to the yoke of British rule because it is 'God's will.'"

"But do you still want to go to England?"

"Yes, of course. I said I didn't want to be a missionary. I didn't say I wouldn't be one. I know I have no option. My destiny was sealed the moment Joseph handed me over to uMfundisi. I don't have your choices, Dani. At least if I go to England, I might also get a chance to study science."

"I have no more choices than you—uMfundisi also expects me to be a missionary."

"Oh, Dani. We both know that's not true. You're his child. I'm his...what was the word that Mrs. Langford used at the party? His *project*. No Christian father will abandon his child, but he'd be foolish *not* to abandon a project that has failed. We've never been equal, much as you might wish it."

They follow the stream past low spreading milkwoods and silver oaks and giant wild bananas with flowers like the heads of crested cranes. The trees are alive with chattering monkeys and birds, warning each other of this invasion. Momentarily, on a rock across the stream, Moses spots a caracal—smoke-colored eyes outlined in black beneath high tufted ears.

"Look, Dan!" he whispers, but already it has gone.

The roar of the sea grows louder and the forest ends abruptly, as if shorn by giant shears. They step from the dim coolness into a world of glittering light and sound. White sand stretches out to a distant headland on their right, a tumble of rocks rises to their left on the far side of the stream that is meandering into the sea. The waves are far bigger than the ones at Durban harbor, great white foaming beasts flinging themselves into the shallows, then pulling back for another onslaught. Gulls keen overhead, their cries faint against the crashing of the surf.

They unlace their boots and run down to the shore whooping, sending a crowd of sand pipers skittering away on spindly legs. Moses stops in the shallows and stands, cupped by the roar of the waves, contemplating the immensity of the ocean. He is small, such a small thing. No bigger, it seems, than the tiny crabs dodging the seagulls, as they scrabble after the sanctuary of the retreating waves, like children left behind by their mother.

He pulls off his shirt and trousers and charges into the waves. Daniel strips and runs after him. Moses dives into the water and grabs his legs, pulling him down. He comes up sputtering and laughing and lunges at him. But Moses ducks away, and wades out further relishing the pound of the surf against his body. Such power...he imagines the tug and release of the moon's gravitational pull on the tides, the ocean currents circling the globe, himself a small speck in this great swirling interaction of matter and force and energy.

He lets the water take him out, fighting momentary

panic when his feet no longer touch the sand beneath them. When he is beyond the breakers, he lies back in the water and looks up at the sun, feeling the lift and buoyancy of the waves beneath his body. He could just float, he thinks. Let the sea take him where it would, away from Sir Roland and Bucket and uMfundisi, away from the dragging weights of their expectations, the hard edges of their fears, the ever-narrowing confines of the colonial order.

He hears splashing and rolls over to see a sleek-finned body diving through the waves not twenty yards away from him—and another and another, leaping and swooping into the water and out. Dolphins, he thinks, or porpoises. For a few moments he is immersed in them as they leap and flash past, filling the air with strange chirps and clicks. Imagine being so free, so unbounded...*take me with you*, he shouts, but already they are past him, disappearing from sight.

A faint cry reaches him. He looks back to shore and sees Daniel waving frantically before a wave crashes over him. Moses paddles towards him, conserving his energy between the waves, swimming hard as each one approaches until he is beside his brother.

"Don't panic." Moses tells him. "Just keep calm and keep afloat."

"The sea's pulling us out!"

"It'll take us back to shore. Don't fight it."

But the sea is pulling them back, and Daniel is fighting it, kicking and splashing. A massive wave towers above them—a glassy green, impossibly high wall of water, with a band of white foam fringing its crest.

"Swim now!" Moses yells.

They swim hard together, momentarily not moving. Then they surge forward as the wave lifts them and propels them towards the shore. The water barrels them down in a turbulence of white surf and sand. Daniel comes up choking, but the sand is once more beneath their feet.

As they stagger out through the shallows, Ghost runs up, barking and nipping Daniel's ankles, scolding him for leaving him. Daniel walks to the warm dry sand and flings himself down, fending off the dog's attentions. Moses flops down next to him. Daniel turns and delivers a volley of hard rabbit punches to his shoulder.

"What the devil were you thinking? Why did you swim out like that?"

"I was just swimming. What are you so fussed up about?"

"I thought you were dead...you could've drowned."

"Don't be a nincompoop, I was fine. Anyway, it didn't help coming after me. You just nearly drowned yourself."

Daniel sits up and hugs his knees, angrily brushing away the tears that have sprung to his eyes. Moses sits up too.

"Sorry, Dani. I didn't mean to scare you. I wasn't trying to drown myself, if that's what you were worried about. Although—"

"Although what?"

"Well, there was a moment in those waves when it seemed somehow...simpler...just to let myself be carried out to sea."

Daniel stares at him in horror. "It wouldn't be simple at all...why would you even think that?"

Moses cuffs him on the shoulder. "Silly! I wasn't being serious. But don't you sometimes feel that dying might be quite peaceful compared to living?"

"Stop it! I don't want to hear you say such terrible things."

Moses smiles at him with a sudden sadness. "I should be dead already, Dani. I should have died when my family left me by the river. Sometimes I think I'm just a ghost."

Daniel punches him again, on his arm.

"Ouch, stop doing that!"

"There, you see, you're not a ghost. Ghosts don't hurt."

"Why're you so angry?"

"Because of all your foolish prattle about dying and ghosts."

"Don't take it so hard. Did you see the dolphins? Or perhaps they were porpoises. But, oh Dani, they were so beautiful."

"I didn't see them, I was too busy looking out for you."

Moses stands up and brushes off the pale grains of sand clinging to his thighs and chest and pulls on his clothes. He knows that Daniel is watching him although he is pretending to keep his eyes closed.

"Don't be huffy," he says, nudging Daniel with his foot. "Anyway, we should go. Sir Bugaboo will be back soon."

"I'll catch up."

At the forest Moses turns to look back at his brother on the shore. How small he looks. Like a lost, broken thing washed up by the sea. Moses waves him over and calls him, feeling bad about frightening him in the waves. Daniel scrambles into his clothes and walks towards him, carefully placing his foot into each of Moses' footprints.

DANIEL

After five nights of not seeing Moses, Daniel waits until all is quiet from Sir Roland's room, climbs out of the window and walks down to the men's quarters. Moses is sleeping outside near a small fire under the stinkwood tree, as he often does on warm dry nights. Daniel sits beside him, looking at his face in the faint red light from the glowing embers, at the rise and fall of his chest. He looks so young when he sleeps—his thick dark eyelashes resting on the curve of his cheeks, his face smooth and soft, empty of shame, of betrayal.

Moses opens his eyes.

"Dan? Is something wrong?"

"No, it's nothing...I just couldn't sleep."

Moses sits up yawning.

"You shouldn't be here...what if Bugaboo notices?"

"I'll only stay a little while. How was work today?"

"It was so hot...we're clearing a road up on the hill above the cattle kraal. It's brutal work, but my hands have toughened up and I'm getting stronger. My back does ache tonight though."

"I'll get some liniment from the stables and rub it on."

He finds the jar of oily liniment on the shelf of the tack room and hurries back. As he rubs it on Moses' back and shoulders, the pungent camphor fills his nostrils and makes his eyes water.

"Thanks, that feels better. I don't mind the work so much. But Bucket goes at me all the time...calling me filthy and idle. It's all I can do not to smash his face."

Daniel feels his own fists curling. "Should I say something to Sir Roland?"

Moses rolls onto his side and props himself up on his elbow.

"Oh Dani, you really don't get it...Sir Roland came past the stumping field to talk to me yesterday."

"What did he say?"

"He said that both Bucket and Wyeth have reported insolence. I told him I always followed their instructions. He said that I should temper the way I looked at them, that I had an 'arrogance of bearing.' He said that Bucket told him that I made jokes in Zulu about him to the workers, bringing him disrespect. He said for my own good I needed to learn to humble myself and acknowledge the authority of the Englishman."

"Do you make jokes about him?"

"Yes, of course. We all do. How else could we endure him? But Sir Roland will never chide Bucket on my account, you can be sure of that. Bugaboo is punishing me because I wouldn't let myself be co-opted. I made a choice, and he's resolved that I should suffer the consequences."

Moses shoots Daniel a fierce look.

"And don't start on about how we can give up. If this farm has taught me anything, it's that there's no place in this colony for me. The amaZulu think I'm a peculiar black umlungu, and the abelungu think I'm an impudent over-educated native. If Sir Roland won't sponsor me, I shall work my passage myself. Anywhere else has to be better."

"I get so frightened for you..."

Moses utters the steel-tipped laugh he has lately acquired.

"Oh don't worry about *me*, dear brother. You just concentrate on charming old Bugaboo into sponsoring our education. If you keep up your side of the bargain, I'll do my work like a good native and keep my temper with Bucket."

"If he dares touch you with that whip, I'll kill him, I swear."

Moses laughs again. "Really? You'll *kill* him? I doubt it, Dan. Let's forget about Bucket—look at this sky! Baba Mbanda is teaching me more Zulu names of the stars—he's a star gazer too. Orion's belt is iMpambano, and the sword is ondwenjana—it's a kind of long stemmed flower, I think, and Venus is called isiCelankobe, or 'asking for food' because it comes at supper time..."

Daniel listens to Moses naming the stars in Zulu and English, feeling the sting of his dismissive *I doubt it Dan...* How poor his regard for me, he thinks. But hardly surprising. For he just wanders about reading poetry, and there's little evidence that he is "charming" Sir Roland into anything.

He stares up at the great arcing wheel of the stars above him and remembers how Gogo told them that the Milky Way was the entrance to Mvelinqangi's cattle kraal, how Dawid said that the stars turned to insects during the day and crept on the earth. Moses is telling him how sailors navigate ships with the stars, using sextants and chronometers to find out latitudes and longitudes.

"Imagine, Dani, we'll be following the stars to find our

way to England," Moses says. "Just like the three wise men." When Daniel walks back to the house, he's alarmed to see a light glowing in the dining room window. He creeps up to the window and peeps through a broken slat in the shutters. Sir Roland is sitting at the table staring right at the window. He pulls back hastily, anticipating Sir Roland's roar of outrage. But the night is silent save for the incessant songs of the crickets. He creeps up again and puts his eye to the glass. Sir Roland is still sitting there, with an empty glass and a bottle of brandy before him, his eyes unfocused, turned inward. Daniel treads softly through the garden to his own room, climbs through the open window, and lowers it. He could have sworn he saw the gleam of tears on Sir Roland's cheek.

A trick of the candle light, he decides. Sir Roland was not a man to weep.

In the night he lies awake, worrying about Moses, holding the incweba in his hand. He still plans to give it to back, but he can't bear to part with it now. The more he feels his brother slipping away, the more he needs this talisman to somehow keep him close. The chorus of crickets and frogs rises to a crescendo, the clock in the dining room whirrs angrily and begins to chime. *Something is going to happen,* the clock seems to say. *Something terrible. And there is nothing you can do to stop it.*

DANIEL

On the following Saturday, when Daniel comes back for breakfast after feeding the horses, he finds Bucket hovering outside. His misshapen face has been further disfigured by a swollen split lip and a purple bruise blooming on his unshaven jaw. He reeks of the raw crude rum that Mr. Wyeth gets made by a local distillery from the sugar crop and gives to Bucket every Friday as part of his pay.

"What do you want?" Daniel asks sharply.

"Begging your pardon, Mr. Whitaker. I got matters to discuss with the guv."

"He won't take kindly to being disturbed. Why don't you talk to Mr. Wyeth?"

"'Twas Mr. Wyeth as sent me here."

"Well, let me know what it's about and I'll tell him."

Bucket flicks a sideways glance into the dense bush behind the house, and licks his lips. "Begging your pardon, Sir, but I'd as soon tell him myself. 'Tis a rather delicate matter."

Sir Roland doesn't take kindly to the news that Bucket is on his doorstep, but he agrees to see him after breakfast. All through their oatmeal, sausages, bread and tea, Daniel can see Bucket's unlovely face hovering in the window. When Sir Roland is finished, he dispatches Daniel to bring up the horses—he and Mr. Wyeth are visiting the sugar mill in Glendale. He calls Bucket into the dining room and shuts the door. Daniel lingers outside the window, but it's closed against invading insects, and he can't make out their conversation.

Daniel goes reluctantly down to the stables to saddle up. As he's fixing the girth on Midnight, he sees Sir Roland and Bucket walking towards the workers' compound. He finishes tightening the girth and tethers the horses to the rail before hurrying after them.

He runs down to the long low building that houses the black workers. In front of their quarters is a wide yard of beaten earth, with a white stinkwood tree growing in the middle. Sir Roland, Bucket and Moses are standing under the tree, watched by a few of the other workers hovering near the doorway of their bunkhouse.

Bucket's whining voice is rising as he gesticulates lavishly towards Moses. Moses stands motionless and stony faced. Daniel can't see Sir Roland's face, but his stance is one of immovable insistence—arms akimbo, boots planted firmly, legs slightly spread. As if in anticipation of a high wind.

"...'twas this very savage, Sir Roland, what struck me unprovoked and inflicted this injury upon my person...," Bucket is saying, stabbing one blackened fingernail at his swollen lip, while the forefinger of his other hand jabs at Moses' face.

"Well, Moses, you stand accused of a grave offense. What do you have to say?" Sir Roland asks.

"I did not assault Mr. Bucket, sir."

"And yet, he has clearly suffered injury."

"It was not by my hand, sir. He fell."

"He fell?"

"Yes, sir. Last night he came down here, somewhat... under the weather. He stumbled and fell against the doorpost."

"He's lying, Guv, as the Lord's my witness, I never touched a drop..."

"Thank you, Mr. Bucket. Moses, are you telling me that my foreman is a liar and a drunk?"

Moses says nothing, but his eyes are eloquent enough.

"Well?"

"I believe Mr. Bucket's memory of the events of last night may be impaired, sir. The others will bear me out..."

"Will they indeed? But who's to say you haven't counseled them what to say? Mr. Bucket is your superior, Moses...must I take the word of a few disgruntled native skivvies over that of a white man in charge of their discipline?"

"It is not for me to say whom you should believe, sir. But if you want to know the truth it might be helpful to hear the testimony of those who witnessed what happened."

Daniel has sidled round so that he can see Sir Roland's face. He has a particularly dangerous look, the heavy lids of his eyes half lowered, his nostrils flaring, his mouth a tight red line in his dark beard.

"You'd do well to spare me your sarcasm, boy," he snaps. "This is not the first complaint Mr. Bucket has laid against you. I've spoken to you more than once, but it seems that words have little effect. Mr. Bucket's authority over the workers on this farm is absolute. I will not have it tested like this."

"I have no wish to test his authority, sir."

"I am glad to hear it, Moses. In that case, you will not object to succumbing to his punishment of you."

Moses flinches. "I would not object, sir, had I done something wrong. But I haven't."

Sir Roland sighs and dissolves his menacing face into a mask of studied regret. "Moses, you place me in an impossible position. If you are reluctant to concede the authority of the white man, I simply cannot foresee any useful future for you in my service or indeed in the colony.

237

Were you any other worker on this farm, I'd hand you over to the authorities to punish you as they see fit. But I'll give you a choice, out of charity to my cousin: Succumb to Mr. Bucket's punishment or relinquish my patronage and leave this farm."

Daniel feels a treacherous flaring of hope. Moses will never agree, he thinks. They can leave, at last they can go! But his brother's face is riven with such despair that guilt quickly quells his elation.

Moses looks away from Sir Roland, catching Daniel's eye. His eyes are frantic, pleading for some deliverance from this toxic "choice." *Leave,* Daniel mouths. Moses flinches and looks away.

"Very well," Sir Roland says. "I want you out by this evening. You may take such provisions as necessary to sustain you for the journey back to the mission station. I'll write to my cousin explaining the situation—I doubt he'll be pleased by your conduct."

He turns on his heel and walks away. Moses looks after him, his face contorted by some inner violent struggle. At last he says in a low voice, "I will succumb."

Sir Roland keeps walking—for a moment Daniel wonders if he's heard. Then he pauses, and says without looking back. "I beg your pardon?"

"I said I will succumb. I'm not conceding my guilt. But I will succumb to the punishment, unjust as it may be."

Sir Roland turns and looks at him narrowly for long seconds. It seems he might ask for more, but perhaps something in the set of Moses' jaw tells him that this is as far as

Moses will go. He nods curtly, and says, "Mr. Bucket, you may administer six lashes."

"No!" Daniel shouts, lurching forward. "Sir Roland, you can't..."

Sir Roland drills into him with his coal-black eyes. "Hold your tongue, boy!" He snaps. "Any more from you and you'll both be going back to the mission station today. Go ahead, Mr. Bucket."

Daniel throws a desperate glance at Moses, but Moses shakes his head. Daniel stands, his stomach lurching with nausea as Moses leans against the tree, and Bucket raises the whip. Ghost runs at him snarling, but his charge is deflected by a kick from Sir Roland. He yelps and slinks back to Daniel.

Six lashes. Six times, Bucket raises his arm for another blow. His misshapen nose is scarlet and quivering, his bloodshot eyes bulge beneath a knotted forehead, his upper lip is curled up from his blackened teeth. Moses' body shudders with each stroke, but he makes no sound. How long does it take to administer six blows? Forever, it seems to Daniel. As if he has been doomed to spend eternity watching his brother being whipped. A small whirlwind scurries through the yard, stirring up dead leaves and dust. The singing of the cicadas crescendos in his ears, drowning out the sickening whine of the whip through the air and its dull collision with flesh. Daniel senses the dark expansion of the python's eye in his solar plexus, the shiver of high voices carried by the whirlwind. Spots flare before his eyes, and he feels himself swaying. He grips the incweba in his pocket, and forces himself to stay present, to bear witness to the jerk of Moses' body, the beads of blood appearing through his shirt. Sir Roland's face is impassive. All the ugliness of his actions are channeled through Bucket, this grotesque, twisted creature with his infinite well of spite.

We're all drenched in shame, Daniel thinks. It will stain us forever, blight the lives of our children, haunt us far beyond the grave.

When Bucket has given his last stroke, Sir Roland takes the sjambok.

"Why are you still dithering here, Daniel? I told you to bring the horses to the house," he barks, before walking off. Most of the workers have drifted off, but Baba Mbanda and Phumlani and a few others crowd round Moses, sucking their teeth and clucking to show their anger. Moses stands stiffly, his eyes bloodshot, his face twisted with pain and distress. When Daniel approaches, he waves him away.

"I'm fine, Daniel. Go see to the horses, Sir Roland is waiting."

Phumlani looks at Daniel accusingly, as if he were somehow complicit in this odious charade. Baba's face is more sympathetic. He calls after Daniel to bring some intshungu leaves from the kraal when he returns.

Daniel walks away, cursing Sir Roland. The horses are already saddled in the stable yard, it would've been perfectly easy to get them himself on the way back to the house, but no, he must prove some point by getting Daniel to do it for him. He leads them up to the house where Sir Roland and Mr. Wyeth are waiting. Sir Roland mounts his horse without acknowledging him. Daniel stares up at him as he adjusts his stirrups, momentarily distracted by the view up his nostrils. How large they are, he thinks, and so forested with hair! How strange that on his horse a nostril is a tender, rather glorious thing, yet on Sir Roland it is quite repellent.

The moment they have clattered down the track, he hurries back to Moses, pausing to pull out some of the pungent leaves of the intshungu creeper growing on the kraal post. Moses is sitting on an upturned bucket under the stinkwood tree, with Baba pouring water over his back. Phumlani leans against the tree trunk and watches. Baba takes the leaves and crushes them between his hands, then lays them on the welts crisscrossing the skin and binds them with Moses' shirt.

"How did Bucket get injured?" Daniel asks.

"He came into our hut late last night, as drunk as a lord, and accused Aaron of stealing his hat—why he thinks anyone would want that lice-infested thing I can't imagine," Moses replies. "He just picked on Aaron because he's small. He came in with a lantern and started kicking Aaron. The lantern was swinging around—he looked sure to drop it and set the whole place up in flames. I tried to calm him down, and he swung his fist at me. When I ducked, he lost his balance and his face hit the doorpost. He passed out, more inebriated than injured. We carried him back to his quarters and left him there."

Daniel shakes his head. "I don't understand it...why would Sir Roland take his word over yours? He must know that Bucket's a drunk."

Phumlani laughs sardonically. "Didn't you know that abelungu can't lie in this place, white boy?"

"You know he's right, Dan," Moses says. "Sir Roland would never take the word of a black man over that of a white man."

"That uGundane is rubbish," Baba Mbanda puts in, shaking his head. "Nalapho kungekho qhude liyasa—he's like the rooster who thinks his voice makes the sun rise, but what's he got? Nothing! At home I have cattle, three wives to cook and plant and bear children for me, seven fine sons. But he talks to me like I'm his serving boy."

"Sometimes men like uGundane have accidents," Phumlani muses. "A cobra finds its way into their boots. Or their lamp falls over and sets their bed on fire. Especially a man who drinks like that."

"Don't do anything crazy, Phumlani. Not on my account."

"Oh there are many accounts, umhlobo wami. Many accounts. You're not the first to be whipped for no just cause, and you won't be the last. That uGundane likes his whip too much."

Later, the others go about their tasks, and Daniel offers to read to Moses to distract him from the pain. But Moses asks for a story—that one Gogo used to tell them, about Sithungusobendle and the amajuba, the rock pigeons.

Daniel tells the story as well as he can remember it, how Sithungusobendle was taken across the seas by the amajuba and parted the seas to return, only to find that her village had been eaten by the isiququmadevu monster—

all the men and women and children, the huts and the cooking pots, the cattle and the chickens and the dogs, the grain stores and the stripy field mice that fed on them—and how she'd slit open its belly to release all the animals and people inside.

Daniel thinks back to the farmyard at uMzinyathi, the dung heap they turned into the isiququmadevu monster, the dogs dozing in the sun, Gogo sitting against the wall weaving her baskets, teasing him when he took himself too seriously. About that day he told his father about Gogo dancing at the pigsty, and Moses broke the animals.

He looks up at the sky through the branches of the stinkwood tree and remembers saying he'd kill Bucket if he touched Moses with his whip. How Moses had said, *I doubt it*.

"We should get you inside, Mosi. Looks like the rain is coming."

He speaks gruffly, for he's trying not to cry.

He goes to dinner with a prepared speech laced with words such as *outrageous, egregious, travesty of justice*. But only Mr. Khumar is there, who tells him in his stilted English that Sir Roland is "fatigued" and will not be dining.

An hour later, Daniel hurries down to the workers' compound with his bedroll and a covered enamel bowl containing Sir Roland's uneaten dinner. Although the worst of the earlier storm has passed, it's still raining softly. He and Moses sit inside the doorway of the hut by the guttering rush light, with its pungent scent of animal fat, talking softly so as not to disturb the others.

"How is your back?" Daniel asks, watching Moses break off pieces of roti and use them to scoop up mouthfuls of lamb curry.

"The pain is nothing against the humiliation. But at least the whipping has helped my popularity with the other workers—they seem to have accepted that I'm not Sir Roland's spy now."

"Yes, even Phumlani, I see."

Moses winces. "I feel like such an imposter. They don't understand that I chose this, Dani...they couldn't follow everything that was happening...they think I agreed because otherwise Sir Roland would have me arrested. But by agreeing to allow Bucket to whip me, it's like I conceded that he had the right."

"You didn't concede that he had the right."

"Effectively. Sir Roland made me complicit in my own humiliation."

"He gave you no real choice, Mosi."

"Ah choice...what is more poisonous than a choice which is no choice at all?"

Moses' falls silent, staring into the flames, lost in the darkness of his thoughts. At length he asks, "Did he say anything at dinner?"

"He wasn't at dinner. I'll speak to him tomorrow."

Moses gives a snort of impatience.

"For what? Do you think you'll somehow make him see things differently? Make him apologize? Just leave it, Daniel. There's nothing you can do. From the moment I refused to work with Bucket in supervising the men, he's been looking for an excuse to do something like this."

Daniel presses his face into his hands, pushing against his eyes with his fists until he sees stars.

"Mosi, please let's leave this place."

Moses is quiet for a few moments, staring into the flickering flame. But his eyes are not quiet. Daniel can sense the rage pent up in his body, the electricity crackling under his skin.

"Now? Really? You want me to leave now, after what I endured today? No, I will not," he says. "I *will* not. He took a piece of me today, I won't deny that. He diminished me, and I feel it bitterly. But I'll not give him the satisfaction of walking away. I'll do everything that is expected of me. And if, at the end of it, he still refuses to send me to England, let it be on his conscience. uMfundisi always told us how an Englishman's honor burns so brightly. Let's see how brightly Sir Roland's honor burns."

"Is this what this is about? Proving that Sir Roland has no honor? Because if so, I think your work here is done."

"It's not that. It's...showing him that I'm not just a native, an orphan, a nobody. I'm a human being. If I give in, I'm giving him what's left of my soul. My integrity. My isithunzi, as the amaZulu call it. Without that I'm nothing, I really am just the ghost of a baby who should have died."

He turns his eyes from the flame and fixes them on Daniel.

"It's all I have, Dani. I don't have wealth or power. I don't have ancestry or community or lineage. My family members are all borrowed. The only thing truly mine is this—this kernel, this inner worth. It's all I have, and it's the thing Sir Roland most wants to break. Because he knows you can't subjugate a man who won't collaborate in his own enslavement. He could've just told Bucket to whip me. But he made me ask for it—that cut deeper than any whip."

Daniel keeps silent, staring at the soft-bodied moths. They fly around and around the candle flame until their wings are singed, until they fall into the pooled candle grease and die. What it is that impels them to circle the light, despite their certain doom?

MOSES

Moses wakes in the night, his back stiff and throbbing. The rain has stopped. He takes *The Annual Register* outside with a candle, hoping that reading might take his mind off the pain—in his back and in his heart. As he opens the book, the photograph that uMfundisi gave him falls out.

There they are, all outside the Baker's house. uMfundisi and Kazi sit on chairs in front, Daniel behind them in the center, himself on the side, half-behind Kazi. Both boys are in their suits. Kazi is staring straight ahead and smiling with a kind of grim unfounded optimism. The other three are looking slightly to the left with apprehension as if they can see an approaching danger.

They knew, Moses thinks. They knew where this could go.

He thinks of the day that uMfundisi spoke to him after finding him dancing with Gogo, when he was six years old. How he'd warned him that God could not love a child who was given the teachings of Jesus and yet still chose heathen ways. How only he, uMfundisi, could show Moses the path of righteousness, the way to God's love. Only he could save Moses from hell.

He made me so needy of his love, Moses thinks. Then he turned me over to his cousin to be whipped like a dog.

He holds the photograph above the flame of the candle. Imagines the flame consuming it, consuming this family of chickens that had taken him in and tried to make him one of them, but also not one of them. He pictures uMfundisi's face burning, then Kazi's, then Daniel's, then his own. He could destroy this, just as he'd broken Gogo's animals to show God that he was done with her world, knowing as only a child can know that uMfundisi offered a more secure sanctuary. Not knowing, as only a child cannot know, what that sanctuary would cost him.

The flame licks the corner of the card holding the photograph, and begins to creep towards the image. He watches it for a second until it reaches uMfundisi's* arm, then drops the photo on the ground and pushes it into the damp earth to extinguish the flame.

"Don't hate," he whispers to himself. They're trying to make you hate. Sir Roland used Bucket to carve hatred into your flesh. Don't let them do that to you. Be strong, but don't hate.

He lies with his back against the cool rain-soaked earth. The Milky Way wheels above him, with all the constellations in their place: Scorpio, the Coal sack, Pleides, Orion's belt and sword, the Southern Cross and its pointers, Alpha

Centauri and Beta Centauri...he knows that stars are born and die, yet their lifespans bring them as close to eternity as anything imaginable. He has little faith in the God uMfundisi tried to bring to him, but he trusts the universe. It has no fickleness, no cruelty, no pride. It is itself—magnificent, austere, its relations are governed by laws of time and motion and energy, not invented by some capricious and power-hungry colonial authority. The gravitational force between two objects is always a function of the gravitational constant, the masses of the objects and the distance between them. It doesn't depend on the faith or race or class of the person doing the calculation. No imperial ruler can outlaw gravity, nor decree that it exert a different pressure, nor send its armies to conquer it, nor condemn it to death for its arrogance.

As the lode star guides sailors across the sea, so would the constancy of the universe guide him through the quagmire of human inconsistency and self-interest.

DANIEL

When Daniel returns to the house in the morning after seeing to the horses, Sir Roland has finished breakfast and is sitting at the oak table and smoking his pipe. The sun streaming through the window catches the upper rim of his right ear, rendering it a delicate pink.

"Ah, there you are, Daniel. Mr. Khumar has removed the breakfast dishes. However, I daresay you can find some food in the kitchen."

"Thank you, but I'm not hungry, sir. I am concerned that

a grave travesty of justice has been perpetrated—"

Sir Roland averts his face slightly. He holds up his hand as though dodging an annoying insect.

"Before we get into that, Daniel, I need to point out that you put me in a most invidious position yesterday. How dare you challenge my authority in front of Mr. Bucket?"

"I was very distressed, sir."

"That's no excuse to lose your manners."

"Moses is not a liar, sir. Nor is he inclined to violence. He's never struck anyone in his life. I'm sure if you knew the circumstances, you'd concede that he was punished unfairly."

He addresses the words to Sir Roland's glowing right ear—he can't trust himself to keep going if he meets the full glare of his gaze. His mouth is dry and his heart is pounding. He holds the incweba in his pocket, squeezing what courage he can from its soft body.

Sir Roland strikes a match, relights his pipe, and sits back puffing, eyeing Daniel through the smoke. He speaks at last with the weary air of a schoolmaster explaining simple arithmetic to the classroom dunce.

"It's not for you to question my judgement, boy. But I can see that you are upset and in the interests of your education, I'll indulge you.

"As Englishmen in authority, we're often called on to make hard choices. Yesterday was one such time. Moses said this, Bucket said that. Whose word do we put above the other? Bucket had been assaulted, that much was evident, and the workers were keenly waiting to see what punishment would follow. I needed a swift, firm response. I'm not happy about it, but he gave me no choice.

"When Moses came here, I gave him the opportunity to be set above the men, to help me with their supervision. But he chose to be treated as any other worker on this farm— and I would've disciplined any other worker in the same way. He succumbed to the punishment of his own volition, no doubt because he knew he was in the wrong."

"He succumbed, sir, because he knew he has no prospects without your patronage! An innocent man has been whipped. Surely this is of concern to you?"

Sir Roland sighs and taps his pipe on the ashtray.

"Wake up, son! Look at our situation here. How many white men live on this farm? Four right now. When you and I leave on safari, it will be two. And how many black men? Over fifty, never mind the hordes who live nearby. It's simple mathematics!"

Sir Roland smacks the table with his hand as though trying to drum his point through its surface. Outside a turtle-dove is calling in the trees—*stop talking, stop talking,* it seems to implore. But Sir Roland is not a man to heed a dove.

"I rely on Bucket to maintain authority. It's regrettable if he gets drunk and uses his authority unwisely. But the workers on this farm have to understand that the white man is always right, no matter what.

"Whether he assaulted Bucket or not, Moses is the most dangerous man on the estate. His conduct sends a message to the other workers that a black man can be equal or superior to a white man. And that message is the gravest threat we face."

"Yet Moses clearly *is* Bucket's superior."

"You test my patience, boy! If we let ourselves imagine that black men are equal to white, this colony is doomed. We're not brutes, like the Boers. We've conquered the Zulu not with massacres but with our innate superiority—and natural authority. But even a benevolent father knows better than to spare the rod when needed, and the Zulu man understands that.

"The only reason your mission station is tolerated by the Zulus is because of our authority in the colony. Fear of English authority has kept the Zulus from your door. Were it not for that, you, your father, your mother, and the man you call your brother would have been slain in your beds long ago."

Daniel wonders what this authority is, who gave it to the English, if they carry it on their shoulders or on the tops of their balding heads or sitting heavily in their stomachs. And what kind of benevolence compels you to whip an innocent man? He stares out of the window at the dense forest a few short paces from the house. The forest stares back hungrily, as though it can't wait to devour the house and all its inhabitants. *That's the sort of man he is,* the forest whispers. *We know him well. For we feel the nails of his boots on the fingers of our children.* He feels something shifting in the pit of his stomach, something deeper and quieter and deadlier than anything he has felt before. It coils itself about itself and lowers its head. *Ngikulindele...*it whispers.

"You know he didn't hit Bucket. You punished him for having aspirations."

He is alarmed to realize he'd spoken this thought aloud. Something cold and hard swims through Sir Roland's eyes. He pushes his chair back and rises from the table.

"Ask yourself, Daniel, who's done Moses the greatest cruelty here? The moment your father took him into his household as an equal he doomed him to such punishment—or worse. Moses has no future in this colony—or indeed the civilized world—if he cannot appreciate the superiority of the white man. His aspirations, as you call them, are not becoming in a black man. He should aspire to serve the Englishman, not to be one. And now, my boy, the carriage awaits to convey us to church in Glendale, and I should not like us to miss the service."

Daniel stands too, blocking Sir Roland's passage to the door.

"Sir, may I ask—if you truly believe Moses' aspirations to be so dangerous, are you still considering sponsoring his education?"

"I'd counsel you to pay more attention to your own advancement. You'll not go far in life if you persist in promoting Moses' cause. You are perilously close to losing my favor. If I send you away, your brother goes too. I beg you now to detain me no longer from my service to God. My life is far from blameless, and Heaven knows I could do with His blessing."

He squeezes Daniel's shoulder painfully and smiles his terrible smile, the white teeth leaping from the black moustache like a mamba striking from the sugar cane. Daniel stands to one side to let him pass, clenching his fists in his pockets. *Not yet,* the thing inside him whispers. *Not yet.*

MOSES

Moses looks at the crowd gathered for his "sermon" by the stinkwood tree. It's considerably more than the workers on the farm. It seems that word of his whipping has got out, and many have come—from curiosity or in solidarity. He still feels like a fraud for agreeing to Sir Roland's punishment—what can he possibly say to them? He takes a deep breath and lets the words come from somewhere deep inside.

"Some of you saw what happened yesterday. These farmers whip their workers because they want to strike fear in their hearts, to prove their strength. But whipping proves only the weakness of the man holding the whip.

"Never mistake cruelty and bullying for strength, my brothers and sisters. The Lord's hand guides not the whip hand. The Lord holds the hand of the man who is being whipped, giving him comfort and the strength to endure. The power of God lies in the heart, not in the fist. And when the powerful strike us with their fists, we don't strike back with our fists. For violence is a flame that burns not only the enemy's house, but turns with the wind to destroy your house also. We strike back not with our fists, but with our hearts. We strike back with our refusal to be rendered less than human. We strike back with unity, with compassion for our fellow sufferer.

"Yesterday, Bucket rent my flesh. But his whip could not reach my heart. It could not weaken my spirit. Resist all efforts to diminish your humanity, your compassion, your kindness to each other. Resist all efforts to say that one is better than the other, that the amaZulu are superior to the amaHlubi or the amaPondo or any other tribe, that white men are superior to all others. We are all children of God, equal in value and equally loved. Alone we are weak, together unbreakable. Resist."

The workers and the others from neighboring farms start to sing, clapping their hands and stamping, raising clouds of dust. Bucket's nickname, uGundane, is woven into the songs—they sing of him falling down, of cane rats being beaten by knobkierries. Moses dances and sings with them, mocking Bucket and his whip. He dances the dance that he learned from Gogo, and as he dances he remembers the praise song that she created for him.

Nina, bantu bomfula—You, people of the river with the power of the great rivers, you who know the secrets of the wizards from across the seas, you who were carried by the waters of the great iMfolozi to walk in two worlds.

The words of his own praise song intermingle with these phrases—*You who called the lightning to strike the bell tower, you who are a reed that moves with the water yet holds fast to the bank, you who are an owl raised by chickens that still knows itself to be an owl...*

The words and the stamping and clapping ignite his feet and banish the pain in his back. He dances as he has never danced before, as though all the currents of the oceans and the cosmos were running through his veins, as though he was beyond all bondage and disgrace.

Later, he sits with Daniel in the shade of the stinkwood tree, sharing a tin beaker of utshwala beer which had been brought for him in a tightly woven basket by one of the visitors from a local homestead. The rest of the beer had been shared amongst the others, as well as the other gifts: the roasted mealies to Phumlani, the indignant white pullet in a basket to Aaron and Jakob, a snuff box made from the horn of a cow to Baba Mbanda.

As they savor the cool beer, Daniel recounts the conversation with Sir Roland.

"He said you were the most dangerous man on the estate."

"I'm glad he recognizes this."

"Jokes aside, Mosi, urging the workers to resist will hardly temper Sir Roland's hand against you...I saw uBhungezi hanging around, I'm sure he'd be quick to suck up to Sir R. by reporting to him about your sermons."

Moses shrugs. "I'm just telling the truth. uMfundisi loves that quote from Matthew about turning the other cheek, but the Bible does not only preach meekness. Didn't Moses himself kill the Egyptian who was whipping the slave?"

"Truth it may be, but Sir Roland won't like it. And I doubt you'll ever appreciate the Englishman's superiority sufficiently to satisfy old Bugaboo. You think I'm a nincompoop, for starters."

Moses smiles. "Well, you are—half the time at least."

The smile fades as a shadow crosses his face. "Do you think I was weak to agree to the punishment, to play Sir Roland's game...?"

"Weak! Mosi, you are the strongest person I know. He gave you no choice."

"I could have just walked away."

"And then what? You're right. You don't have any life here. I've struggled to see that. But I understand it now. The weak choice would've been to cling to your pride and leave. The strong choice was to take the whipping and stay, because it's your best, maybe only, chance at a better life."

Moses looks at him with a new eagerness. "Really, Dan? I never imagined I'd hear you say that."

"Yes, I do understand. But I'm afraid of what it will ask of you, of both of us..." He offers a strained smile but his eyes are bleak.

"You're wearing Gogo's beads," Daniel remarks, reaching out a finger to touch them. "I'm glad you kept them."

"Yes. I have taken off my confirmation cross. I hold no more allegiance to the white man's church."

"Yet you preach like a man possessed of the Holy Spirit."

"And who is to say that the Holy Spirit dwells in that church?"

DANIEL

By the Monday morning, fifteen men have left the farm, stealing out during the night. Sir Roland comes down to the bunkhouse to address the others, warning that this is a "breach of contract," and if any dare follow suit, he will come to their kraals and whip them himself.

"Did Moses put them up to it?" he demands of Daniel. "Is

256

this his idea of revenge?"

"I am sure Moses never suggested any such thing, sir. Perhaps they left for fear of Bucket's whip?"

"Don't take me for a fool, boy. Will you deny that he was inciting the workers yesterday with talk of equality in his so-called sermon? Along with half the workers from neighboring farms—who were trespassing, I might add."

Daniel feels a treacherous blush creeping up his cheeks.

"He led a prayer, sir, with a good Christian message. He made a particular point to counsel against violence."

"That's not what I heard. And why's he addressing them at all? I thought you were doing the preaching?"

"I believe it is inspiring for the workers to see a black man preach the gospel, sir."

"Not that kind of gospel! You're either a gullible fool or as devious as he is. Anyway, that's the end of the church services. In future, you'll accompany us to Glendale. And if I hear that Moses has been preaching again, I'll send you both back to your father in disgrace."

Moses is not impressed with the injunction that he may not preach again. Daniel dreads leaving him on the upcoming Sunday, in case his sermon is even wilder. But before Sunday comes, Sir Roland declares that they'll depart for the safari within the fortnight. Moses concedes that it's not worth risking another sermon when they're so close to leaving. He solves this dilemma by leaving the estate and preaching in a nearby umuzi. Daniel doubts that Sir Roland will accept this. But nothing is said so perhaps his informant did not alert him.

DANIEL

A few days later, Daniel accompanies Sir Roland and Baba Mbanda to Groutville to interview aspirant hunting assistants. Sir Roland is particularly keen to find a tracker called Khanyiso, whom he'd heard about from other hunters in Durban.

Groutville was set up by the American missionary, Reverend Grout, known by the locals as uGiluti. It reminds Daniel of the bishop's drawings illustrating the benefits of Christianity—around sixty thatched brick cottages interspersed with a few beehive huts, surrounded by fields of vegetable gardens and groves of fruit trees, tended by men and women in European clothes. The plain on the far side of the broad, shallow Umvoti River is covered with waving fields of sugarcane.

The hunter hopefuls from surrounding homesteads are waiting by the small stone church. Sir Roland peers into their mouths and prods the muscles on their arms, tests their shooting and loading speed on his muzzle loader and breechloader. At length six hunters are found, and the terms negotiated and settled: food for the duration, a shotgun and 4s per week to be paid if Sir Roland arrives back uninjured. This contract is achieved with indignant eye rolls and throwing up of hands by the incumbents, and arm-folding and jaw-thrusting by Sir Roland to convey his implacability. Despite Daniel's faithful translation of their words, both parties find it necessary to amplify their meaning with forceful gestures.

Sir Roland warns that he'll reward any breach of this agreement with a whip woven from sea cow hide, renowned for its capacity to inflict pain.

"uMahlekehlathini is very hard," Daniel overhears one recruit complain. Sir Roland's ready smile and big beard have earned him this nickname, which means he who laughs in the bush.

"He is hard indeed," Daniel interjects. "And won't hesitate to punish you if don't follow his orders. Why do you want to hunt for him?"

"It pays better than working for white farmers. Also we get a gun, which we need to shoot bush pigs and leopards."

Daniel tells them that umlungu hunters like Sir Roland are killing all the wild animals, that soon there will be no antelope to eat when the cattle are sick, no leopards for the king's head dress, no genets and monkeys for the regiments. But the men just laugh at him for imagining that anyone could kill all the wild animals.

"There are too many wild animals," they say. "The leopards take our calves and the hippos smash our crops. Wait till you're chased by a buffalo at iMfolozi—you'll shoot it."

The men also laugh when Daniel asks where Khanyiso can be found.

"Tell this umlungu that uKhanyiso is the tracker. He is the one who finds. If he wants to be uMahlekehlathini's tracker, he will find uMahlekehlathini."

"Where is his umuzi?"

The men point vaguely to the west.

"Two days' walk from here, but he's seldom there. Don't

worry, word's gone out. If he wants to come, he'll come. But he'll ask for more than four shillings a week and a gun."

Sir Roland is not impressed. "He'll find me, eh? Insolent fellow. Who does he think he is?"

They visit the general store on the outskirts of the village: a tiny whitewashed stone building presided over by a diminutive man with an amply bosomed, highly decorated wife. Daniel wonders if she'd anticipated their arrival or if she made a daily habit of adorning herself with all the ribbons and buttons and bits of lace that were for sale. Their shelves are crammed with goods which had presumably been deemed desirable to the good citizens of Groutville and passing travelers: jars of preserve; folded bolts of cloth; a windup musical box which plays the first few bars of Rule Britannia; guns and ammunition; harnesses and whips; five florally inscribed china plates; brass bedsteads; sacks of flour, rice, tea and coffee; a shiny French horn coiled like an exotic snake on a pile of blankets, and—most useful of all in the tropics—a pair of ice skates.

Sir Roland picks out trinkets for the Wyeth children— spinning tops for the older boys, a tin monkey with a moveable tail for the younger, and ribbons for the two little girls. Daniel has noticed Sir Roland's clumsy fondness for them, expressed by mock charging the boys and giving barley sweets to the girls.

As they ride back, storm clouds are amassing, casting dark shadows interspersed with a hard metallic glare when the sun breaks through. Lightning flashes on the distant hills are followed by low rumbles of thunder. Sir Roland rides besides Daniel, extolling praise for Groutville for so convincingly demonstrating the benefits of colonialism when compared to the "wretched kraals" they'd passed on the way. He's particularly pleased with the trading store.

"The African works only until he has earned his hut tax, then returns to his life of idleness. The traders help to foster a longing for the finer things in life. Once this is awoken, they'll be reluctant to settle for the poor comforts of their native villages and will serve their masters faithfully. That shop will recruit more labor for the colony than any priest."

Daniel wonders how "civilized" someone has to be before the desire for a musical box or a lace bonnet can drive them from their homes and families to toil for a foreign master. Guns are another matter. The hunters seemed quite willing to toil for guns.

They come on a lone kudu bull atop a ridge, its great, spiraled horns outlined against the storm clouds. Its nose is lifted and twitching, trying to get the scent of them— their outlines resemble no animal it has known. Sir Roland reins in his horse and pulls his gun from its cover. The kudu, hardly thirty paces away, stands still as he takes aim. Daniel rides up behind Sir Roland's horse and Peppercorn obligingly nips his haunches. Midnight kicks back and bucks as Sir Roland fires, sending his bullet wide. The kudu leaps six feet into the air and bounds away.

"What the devil are you doing, boy?" Sir Roland roars. "Hold your horse, can't you?"

Sir Roland takes off after his quarry, reloading his breechloader without slackening his pace. As they crest the ridge, they see the antelope running down the slope away from them, head lifted to flatten its horns against its back. Sir Roland fires again. He snatches the double-barreled muzzle-loader from Daniel and shoves the breech-loader at him for reloading.

"We'll run it down," he yells. "Reload but don't waste your shots until we're closer."

The kudu runs ahead dodging stones and bushes and clearing anthills, but Sir Roland's horse keeps pace with it. Daniel reloads the breech-loader and gallops after them. Sensations of the kudu break through his consciousness, the growing fatigue in its legs, the breath burning its chest. Why is he feeling this? He did not fire the shot.

They mount another ridge and gallop along it before it descends a long slope down to the river, aiming for the thick bush on the far side of the river where it can find cover. As it approaches the river, its leg catches in a warthog burrow. Daniel feels an agonizing crack through his own shin as the antelope goes down. It struggles to its feet and hobbles on, one leg dangling. Sir Roland fires one barrel and catches it in the shoulder. He rides closer and fires again, now barely ten paces away. The final shot reverberates through Daniel's body. His cells recoil as he feels the bullet ripping through skin, muscle and bone. He collapses against Peppercorn's neck, overcome by a wave of nausea.

"For pity's sake, boy, what's come over you?"

Sir Roland's voice rouses him. He half falls off his horse and follows Sir Roland's instructions to cut off the antelope's head with his hunting knife. Baba Mbanda dismounts and holds the head steady as Daniel saws grimly through the cartilage, muscle and bone under the first heavy drops of rain.

Sir Roland leaves them to it, hoping to get home before the storm. They hack through the kudu's neck at last and strap the dripping head onto Jabula behind the saddle, with Baba Mbanda mounted in front. The storm breaks as they walk up the hill—squalls of rain and small hail stones sting his face and hands, washing the kudu's blood in red rivulets from Jabula's coat. The going underfoot is a slippery morass of churned up mud as the deluge turns the path into a stream. Forked lightning stabs at them from the towering black and purple clouds, thunder roars at their heels. Moses will be out to feel it, he thinks. He pictures his brother, his eyes alight with that wildness he gets in lightning storms, laughing to the sky, the rain on his face.

The shot that killed the kudu rips through his chest again and again, trailing searing pain and nausea. *It's still there,* he thinks. *I'm still body jumping, worse than ever, even if I didn't kill the animal myself.* He plods on through the rain behind Jabula, drawn by the sightless eyes of the kudu staring back at him, pulling him along.

In the days that follow, the kudu's suffering swells within him. It chokes him when he tries to eat and fills his limbs with a lethargy that makes it almost impossible to carry the water pails for the horses. With each passing hour he grows weaker. He vomits up almost everything he eats, his skin feels clammy, there is a continuous burning in his chest.

His nights are plagued with terrors. At times the air fills up with shrill voices, too indistinct for him to make out their words.

At dinner he can barely force down food—the kudu's severed head keeps imposing itself on Sir Roland's shoulders.

"Are you quite well, Daniel?" the kudu asks, blood dripping from its mouth.

Daniel blinks, and Sir Roland's face swims back, his dark eyes beaming concern.

"Yes, sir. Quite well, thank you."

His nights are tormented by dreams—old dreams of the eye and the horn, the rhino running through the thorn trees, the black steam train from the Point ploughing through grasslands towards him as he stands paralyzed, waiting to be crushed. He goes back to sleeping down at the compound— he cannot bear to lie under Sir Roland's roof, listening to the malevolent counting of the hours by the grandfather clock. But sleeping next to Moses doesn't dispel his nightmares.

One night he hears the sound of a whip cracking through the air and landing on flesh. He runs through trees trying to find it, then realizes that the whip is in his hand. Moses is tied to a tree, and his own arm is lifting again and again to strike the whip against his bleeding back.

Stop, he screams to himself, STOP!

"Dan...yo, Dani. Vuka!"

He opens his eyes to see Moses bending over him, shaking his shoulder.

"You're shouting in your sleep, Dani. Are you ill?"

"Nothing, it's just a dream. I'm sorry if I woke you."

Around them are grumpy mutters and calls of "thula wena" from the men disturbed by noise.

"He is sick, that one," Baba Mbanda puts in, sitting up on his sleeping mat.

"I'm not sick, Baba."

"You're sick, I'm telling you. You walk round shaking your head like you have wasps in your ears. Vomiting in the night, shouting in your sleep. Even your dog is worried."

Daniel glances down at Ghost—who is indeed sitting looking at him with quizzical concern—and laughs uncomfortably.

"Someone has bewitched you," Baba says. "Maybe it's that Indian man. He's got that picture of umthakathi in there with four arms and a blue face."

"Mr. Khumar?" Daniel asks. "That's not umthakathi, Baba, that's Shiva, the Hindu god."

"Well, it looks like umthakathi—and didn't I see umhlangwe snake in the tree near his sleeping place? Everyone knows that snake is the familiar of a witch. You must go to isangoma, Dani. They'll tell you who is bewitching you and what you must do."

Moses says Daniel's sickness has nothing to do with witchcraft. He says witchcraft only has power over those who believe in it, and Daniel doesn't, do you Dan? Baba Mbanda says he's seen people die from this kind of sickness, and izangoma are the only ones who can help. Daniel says he's fine, it was just a bad dream.

"I'll just have a little walk to clear my mind."

"I'll come with you," says Moses.

They walk outside, into a night filled with frogs and crickets and the twittering of foraging bats.

"Do you think Baba Mbanda is right?" Daniel asks. "Do you think a sangoma could help?"

"No, how could it help? They only work—if they do work—if you believe in them. You have to be part of that culture, believe in ancestral power, in witchcraft. Otherwise, you're just playing."

"I'm getting desperate, Mosi. I don't know how I will cope with the safari if being with Sir Roland when he killed the kudu is making me so ill...maybe isangoma will help.... We used the isibhaha leaves for Kazi...that was a Zulu remedy, and it cured her...why is this so different?"

"You *know* it's different, Dan. iZangoma deal with witchcraft, they ask the ancestors to intercede for you.... Do you actually believe that you're the victim of witchcraft or that your ancestors can help you?"

"No, of course not...but what harm could it do, really? Do you think it would anger God?"

Moses gestures impatiently.

"That's between you and your God. But you shouldn't encourage Baba Mbanda to believe in the power of the izangoma. I don't think those beliefs serve the amaZulu well, and they can be harmful. I was cast out from my family because of those beliefs. The amaZulu don't need magic charms to ward off English bullets, they need their own bullets and an army trained to use them. They need to be able to read and to understand English laws and treaties, so that they're not tricked into giving away their homeland.

"If English people go to izangoma, it makes the amaZulu believe that their ways have power," Moses continues, his voice hardening. "But you English just do it to amuse yourselves, to have funny stories to tell at your dinner parties."

"*You English?* Really, Mosi? Is that what I am to you now?"

They're walking past the cane fields, heavy with the sweet scent of rotting leaves. A jackal slinks across their path ahead, its silver back catching the half-moon light. Daniel watches as it disappears into the shadows, thinking of the night he shot the jackal. The first time he body-jumped. The night of their blood pact.

From blood brother to *you English*...

"I'm sorry, Dani," Moses says. The anger has left his voice, leaving a dragging despair that hits Daniel in the solar plexus. "I wish I knew how to help you. I'm barely keeping myself together as it is. We just have to be strong for a little while longer."

"I'm sorry too. I know you have been burdened beyond endurance. I don't want to add to your troubles. I'll try to be strong. I won't go to the sangoma if you think I shouldn't."

But what *will* I do? he wonders as they walk back down the track to their sleeping quarters. He feels the sickness rising in him to grip his throat, squeezing his chest so that it hurts to breathe.

Three days later, Sir Roland instructs Daniel to travel with Baba Mbanda to the homestead of the elusive Khanyiso to secure the tracker's services—despite the hunters' assertion that Khanyiso would find Sir Roland, he has not yet presented himself. With the promise of a full moon, they set off after the evening milking as the sun is setting. As they ride out, Baba says that he knows of a powerful sangoma whom they could visit on the way.

"She's very old," he says. "She might even have died. But if she's still living, she is the best one. You know you need help, Dani. This is your chance."

And Daniel finds himself agreeing, scarcely knowing what he is agreeing to.

They ride through Hanbury Estate, then through a neighboring farm. The cane fields roll out silently in the dim light, dreaming of wealth. In their fetid depths, cane rats scuttle, dodging the black mambas that lie in wait.

"These lands are much changed," Baba Mbanda sighs. "I no longer know myself in this place. The grasslands where my forefathers' cattle grazed have gone, and gone too are the buffalos and antelope that once passed over these hills."

They leave the cane fields at last and follow old animal tracks winding between the black shadows of giant boulders and rocky outcrops on the higher hills. They join the Umvoti River beyond Groutville and follow its course through a steep winding valley. The night is warm and still, heavy with the sweetness of jasmine and bush lilies. Nightjars call on the good Lord to deliver them, crickets celebrate the rain with a shrill cacophony. Hyenas mock them from a distance and baboons shout across the hills. Sometime after the moon has begun its descent to the horizon, a mist rises from the river, softening and erasing the dark bulk of the ridge.

"Hawu, you are making me ride far in my old age," Baba Mbanda grumbles as they push through a patch of thick scratchy bushes to clearer ground.

"You're not ikehla yet, Baba!" Daniel laughs. "Just last week you were talking about taking a new wife when you go back to your umuzi after harvest. But I am sorry to make you ride so far. We can leave the sangoma and go straight to uKhanyiso."

"No, you need this, Dani, and at least we have inyanga egcwele—a good moon to light our path. This sangoma is special, truly she has eaten imphepho. She is igqirha lemilozi—a doctor who enables the ancestral spirits to speak to you with the whistling voices of the birds. If anyone can divine what is troubling you, she'll be the one.

"They call her Ma Ndlovu. No one knows where her family is or where she's from, but she's been living alone in the Umvoti district for as long as anyone can remember."

"Have you consulted her?"

"Not me, but when I was young my little sister got lost. She was with the older girls going to fetch water when she wandered off. All the people in the village went out, calling and calling, but we couldn't find her. Everyone said a lion or a leopard had eaten her, but my mother kept hearing my sister calling and wouldn't believe she was dead. When she was gone two nights, my mother consulted Ma Ndlovu. The imilozi of Ma Ndlovu said she must bring my sister's ubendle skirt and the calabash that she drank from. So my mother brought these things. Then the imilozi said, 'Bury these things under that anthill and return this afternoon.

When you return, there'll be a honey guide waiting to show you your child.'

"So, my mother returned with her sister, and there was the honey guide. They followed it until they came to a cliff above the river. There were the bees in a hive in a tree. My mother's sister said, 'This honey guide just led us to the bees. Let's go home.'

"But my mother said, 'Wait, I hear something.' And my mother's sister heard it too, very faint: *mwaa, mwaa*. It was coming from a small crack in the rock behind the tree. *Mwaa mwaa*...just like that."

Baba Mbanda pauses. Daniel shivers, either from the damp mist or from the eerie voice in the rock.

"My aunt ran to tell us abathakathi had stolen my sister's body and were keeping it prisoner in the cliff. But my mother struck the rock with her bare hand. She struck it so hard, that ever after her fingers were crooked and would not straighten. She cried, *Open the rock and release my child*. And the rock opened and my sister crawled out. Since that time, I remember the name of Ma Ndlovu—she saved my sister."

Daniel wonders if the child was truly swallowed by a rock or perhaps had fallen into a cave and got stuck. Although he's been raised to be skeptical of such stories, it's easy to believe as they travel through the dark, secretive landscape. A small wind has come up, and the black rustling trees seem to be alive with ancient spirits, the crevices in the rocky cliffs dark enough to house all manner of strangeness. What is he doing here on this road to Ma Ndlovu? He promised Moses that he wouldn't do this. He should tell Baba Mbanda that he has changed his mind. But the moonlight keeps pulling them along, and he remains silent.

They skirt the reeds beside the river, guided by the chorus of the frogs and the gurgle of water. A porcupine shuffles across their path, rattling its quills warningly. An owl calls from a tall dead tree, the silhouette of its tufted ears framed by the black ribs of the branches against the pale clouds. *It's warning us,* Baba Mbanda whispers. *It's telling us abathakathi are near.* Just after the rising of a star that Baba Mbanda calls inqonqoli (because it is knocking on the door of night to warn it of the coming morning), they begin to climb again, following the course of a small tributary. At last, on the crest of the hill, he sees the shadowy outline of two beehive huts.

"That's her dwelling," Baba Mbanda says. "We can rest here until daylight."

They unsaddle and tether the horses after letting them drink in the stream. They share salted meat and dry biscuits, drink from their calabashes, and stretch out their mats. Daniel lies awake listening to Baba Mbanda's snores before falling into troubling dreams of whips falling on flesh and the mission bell ringing on a far distant hill.

He wakes a few hours later to the sound of an eerie singing drifting through the misty dawn. Baba Mbanda is sitting up on his sleeping mat.

"Ma Ndlovu is singing her praises to the spirits," he whispers softly. "We'll approach her when the sun is risen."

Daniel lies listening to the singing, willing himself to leap on his horse and ride far away. But he remains rigid as a corpse, staring at the lightening sky.

When the sun rises, Ma Ndlovu falls silent. Another younger woman appears, stokes the embers with fresh kindling and stirs porridge in an earthenware pot. After Ma Ndlovu has eaten, Baba Mbanda walks towards her and squats on the stone. They speak for some minutes, then he waves Daniel over. Daniel takes the incweba from his pocket and places it around his neck, feeling its secret life throbbing against his chest. He takes the chain holding his silver cross off over his head and lays it on the rock where he'd been sitting. Perhaps the cross would be better protection against whatever witchcraft might present itself, but the incweba feels more powerful. *I can see what you're doing,* God's voice sings in anger from the rock. *You are dabbling in witchcraft which you know to be a grievous sin.*

I prayed, Daniel replies. *I've been praying about this since I was thirteen. You never helped me.*

Ma Ndlovu sits by the fire with her legs outstretched under a calf-hide skirt: a tiny, ancient person with the upright spine of a child. Her face is so inscribed by creases that it resembles the skin of the matriarchal elephant after which she is named. Her eyes gleam with the playful shrewdness of a robin. The inflated bladders of sacrificial animals are tied around her head, which, save for a sparse sprinkling of tight gray curls around her ears, has the shiny baldness of a well-worn saddle. She has several heavy brass rings around her ankles, a row of small rings piercing the outer curve of each ear, and strings of beads dangling between long withered breasts. But she has none of the many pouches and skins he has seen on other izangoma he has encountered. His upbringing tells him that such people are emissaries of the devil, but it is hard to believe of this twinkly-eyed grandmother. She calls to Ghost and laughs uproariously when he puts his paws on her lap and tries to lick her face.

Daniel takes her hand in both of his and bows briefly, before laying down his red blanket, a folding pocket-knife, and a pouch of snuff donated by Baba Mbanda. She nods at her assistant, who takes the bundle into the hut. Then she rises and withdraws into her hut, so short that she barely has to bend to pass through the low entrance.

"I have told her nothing about you," Baba Mbanda says quietly. "You must tell her nothing too. Let the spirits divine who you are and why you have come."

For a long time, they sit without speaking. He can hear the murmurs of Ma Ndlovu and her assistant in her hut, the faint crackling of the fire, the busy interchange of songbirds, the musical clicking of a passing beetle.

After some time, the assistant emerges from the hut and motions to Daniel to go in. He crawls through the low entrance on his hands and knees. The hut is dimly lit by the opening and cracks of light coming through the woven roof and sides. A bundle of imphepho smolders on a potsherd in the umsamo, filling the air with smoke. The hut wall and roof rafters are hung with bundles of medicinal roots, sticks and leaves; calabashes; pouches and animal skins. Ma Ndlovu sits wrapped in a white calfskin and wreathed in the smoke, with the skin of a python draped around her neck. Her face is daubed with white paste. Her eyes are closed and she is humming and rocking rhythmically.

He sits before her, breathing in the smoky sharp scent of the imphepho, the earthy herbal smells of the various remedies, and the musty odors of dried animal parts. His stomach is churning in fear—he hardly dares look around. Does the devil himself lie concealed in these calabashes or in the dark recesses of the hut, waiting to spring out? Would Daniel recognize him if he did? He can hear the bishop intoning, *"Anyone who consults the dead...is detestable to the Lord..."*

He closes his eyes and focuses on Ma Ndlovu's voice, which is low and gravely and holds him to the earth. The scent of the burning imphepho dissipates his terror—or at least dispatches it to some outer reaches of his consciousness. He slips in and out of a dream, a sensation of floating down a slow-moving river.

A high childlike voice pierces his drowsiness: "This child has come to consult us."

He opens his eyes, startled, and peers into the darkness. But there is no child present. Only Ma Ndlovu, still rocking and humming, eyes and mouth closed.

"Ingane yezulu intshontshiwe...kumele ibuyiselwe...." another voice says. "The child of the sky has been stolen... he must be returned..." The voice, momentarily clear and sharp, is drowned by a chorus of high voices coming from the roof above. He looks up, but all he can see in the dim light are the interior latticework of woven branches and the small bundles of herbs and sticks tied to it. The reedy whistling voices clamor together, filling his skull with whispering echoes until he becomes a small speck of light sinking into darkness.

As the hut grows dim, Ma Ndlovu seems to expand until she towers over him. Her edges blur and fragment until she disappears into the shadows. Above the chorus of voices, he hears the squeal of an elephant, glimpses a waving trunk, a flapping ear, the gleam of a tusk in the darkness. The python skin around her neck dissolves into a living snake, which glides towards him, its eye a dark glowing orb. *I know you,* the eye says. *Ngikulindele...I am waiting for you.* He closes his eyes in terror.

Drifting on the tide of the whistling voices, his body seems to rise and leave the hut. He finds himself pressed against a warm back being carried through trees and bushes, light and shadows flickering over his eyes. The bare-skinned shoulder, neck and ear of the woman who is carrying him blurs and comes into focus as his head jolts against her with the rhythm of her running. He feels a high-pitched wailing vibrating through her body, smells the sharp scent of her fear. He hears an angry squeal and thunderous footsteps pounding the earth behind him, reverberating through the woman's back and his own chest.

He feels himself being pitched forward and falling. He lies against a warm body, his head turned sideways to look up to the sky. The sky fills with darkness, and in the darkness all he can see are the eye and the horn above him, the red-rimmed eye and the raking dark horn, trailing sparks of fire as it sweeps over him.

Then he is running through thorn trees again, the dark

curve of the horn rising before his eyes, the light and shadow falling on his face, light and shadow. He can hear shouts and distant gunfire. The smell of gunpowder and fear is thick in his nostrils, but whether he is being pursued or is pursuing he cannot tell. Curving beside him, around him, and through him is the python. Its patterned coils fade in and out of the dappled shadows of the trees, its eye is a well of darkness sucking out all light inside him, its sibilant voice rustles through the leaves. *Ngiyakwazi...Ngikulindele.*

Then the darkness closes in and all is silent.

He wakes to the trickle of drops on his face. Ma Ndlovu is bending over him, sprinkling liquid over him from a small calabash. His limbs are leaden. His head, when he tries to lift it, feels like a great, heavy melon.

"Lie still," she says. "You have traveled far. Did you hear the words of the imilozi?"

"I heard something...I could not understand it well though."

"These imilozi are in distress about their child who was stolen. They call him the sky child. They say that the child must be returned....This is what is causing your sickness, it is not abathakathi."

He finds that he is weeping and turns from Ma Ndlovu, embarrassed.

"I don't understand," he says. "What stolen child? Do they mean Moses? But he was saved, not stolen? He would have died if my father had not taken him in."

"Death is not stealing. Death is the passing from the land of the living to the land of the amadlozi. Your brother is still their child if he dies. But if he does not know the amadlozi, if he has not been introduced to them in the right way, if he does not know how to feed them or listen to their counsel... that child is lost to them."

"What can I do? He was taken twenty years ago..."

"This is not a simple problem. You must open your heart to them, to hear what must be done. You must stay here for some days, I can help you to find out how they may be appeased."

"But I must leave soon...we must reach the homestead of Khanyiso before nightfall. And I cannot come back."

Ma Ndlovu looks at him shrewdly for long minutes, then gives a small nod, as if she is acknowledging a message.

"We can try ukuvala idlozi—to bar the way of those ancestors who are entering your dreams. This might work."

She goes out of the hut. He hears her murmuring instructions to her assistant. She returns and tells him to lie back and open his shirt. She touches the incweba on the thong around his neck.

"You have good protection from the evil ones," she said. "Was it isangoma who gave you this?"

"It was a Heaven Herd. I don't know his name."

"He must have cared for you."

"It's not mine," Daniel says. "I wear it for my brother."

She takes small knife from a basket on the side of the hut and makes several light incisions on his chest. She helps him to sit up and catches the beads of blood trickling from these incisions in a shallow bowl formed from half a calabash. She draws various medicines from the containers around the room and grinds them into a paste in a potsherd before adding them to the blood.

The assistant returns with a frog held carefully in both hands. Ma Ndlovu gently eases the mouth of the frog open—the creature blinks bemusedly but otherwise seems unbothered—and dips the calabash to pour the blood and medicine into the open mouth. She helps Daniel to his feet and passes the frog to him.

"Hold it gently, for it must not be hurt. Carry it to the stream, release it into the water with your eyes closed so that you see not where it lands. Turn your back on the stream and return here without looking back."

He walks to the stream on trembling legs, cradling the frog in both hands. Its throat pulses gently against his fingers. He releases it with his eyes closed, resisting a powerful urge to watch it swim away, and walks off without looking back. His legs have grown unaccountably heavy. As he nears the hut, he finds he can lift them no longer. He collapses where he stands, and falls into a deep dreamless sleep.

They leave at midday. Daniel has recovered some strength after sharing a stewed hare that Baba Mbanda trapped. During their meal, Ma Ndlovu sheds her solemnity and reverts to a merry old woman, chuckling delightedly at Baba Mbanda's accounts of the curious habits of white people. But as they prepare to go, she calls Daniel out of hearing of the others. She tells him that there is something else he can try to bar the way to the ancestors if the remedy with the frog fails.

"What is it?"

"You must kill a black rhinoceros with your own hand and scrape some shavings off its horn. You must mix this with the blood of the rhinoceros, make cuts on your chest as I have done, and rub this mixture into the cuts. The blood and horn will enter your skin and make you as hard and impenetrable as the rhino horn. But I warn you, it will harden you in other ways too, harden you not only to the suffering of animals but also to the suffering of other humans."

She reaches out a finger to touch the incweba.

"Return this to your brother, my child. He needs it more."

His cheeks flush with shame. He bows his head in acknowledgement and turns to follow Baba Mbanda down the hill. At the bottom of the slope, he looks back. The tiny figure of Ma Ndlovu is silhouetted against the pale afternoon sun, the bladders tied to her head glow in the golden light. She is clapping her hands and singing while performing a curious, happy little dance.

"Hambani kahle," she calls, merrily. "Go well, my friends."

He waves and calls, "Salani kahle! Ngiyabonga kakhulu." Then he turns and hurries after Baba Mbanda.

They ride swiftly to reach Khanyiso's umuzi before nightfall. Soon Ma Ndlovu is far behind them, but the whistling of the spirits stays in his head, tangling with confused thoughts. The dark eyes of the python follow him, its voice whispering in his ear. He doesn't know what to make of his visit to Ma Ndlovu, but it's clear that it has brought no simple remedies for his distress. Even if he accepted that his illness was caused by angry ancestral spirits, how can he return the child who was "stolen" twenty years ago?

PART SIX
1878
THE BLACK
IMFOLOZI

DANIEL

The alarm call of the rhinoceros birds alerts them to the buffalo—an old solitary bull, helmeted by wide curving horns that form a solid plate across its forehead. Its slate-colored coat is almost hairless, save for a ridge along its spine. Its massive head is dwarfed by the heft of its neck and shoulders. A dozen red-beaked rhinoceros birds are perched on it searching for ticks and other parasites.

They skirt the clearing and creep towards it, taking cover behind a clump of water berries. Sir Roland raises his gun and fires. Daniel feels no pain and knows that the shot missed, even before the head of the enraged buffalo thrusts through the foliage. The branches crack and splinter as it slams against the trees, but the trunks hold, giving them time to run back and scramble up into the bushwillows behind them. The buffalo gives a few blind charges and gallops off, followed high in the air by its feathered attendants.

"Wawu, you miss him!" Khanyiso remarks cheerfully.

They'd arrived at the hunter's camp the previous evening, after two weeks of traveling from Hanbury Estate. First by ox wagon, then four days on foot carrying the supplies—predators, difficult terrain and tsetse flies prevented them from taking oxen and horses any further. Moses and the rest of the hunting team were busy setting up camp. But Sir Roland was impatient to start "bagging" animals, and had gone out at dawn with Daniel, the tracker—Khanyiso—and two bearers to carry the meat back.

Khanyiso had not been at his homestead when Daniel and Baba Mbanda reached it after seeing Ma Ndlovu. But they'd left a message, and the tracker had strolled into their camp a day before they'd crossed the uThukela River and announced his availability and his terms. When Sir Roland said his terms were absurd, Khanyiso picked up his gun and bedroll and walked off. Ten minutes later, Sir Roland sent Daniel after him to say that his terms were, on reconsideration, acceptable.

Whatever his terms, Sir Roland could not have secured a better tracker. In the few hours that they've been hunting, Daniel has been mesmerized by the way he moves through the landscape, scouring for tiny details like a scholar perusing ancient scrolls. He can spy out a single hair left in the crevice of a rubbing tree, spot the difference between leaves incised by a black rhino and those nibbled by a kudu, tell from flattened grass what animal has lain there and how long ago. He knows the behavior of every species and seems able to read an individual animal's character from its tracks, to deduce its reasoning and anticipate its choices. He can tell whether a bird's alarm call signals a snake, a stalking predator or a bird of prey, whether a baboon's bark is in response to a leopard or a cobra. But he seems to communicate with the animals in some invisible way too. When they were tracking a waterbuck earlier, Daniel noticed him moving his lips as if talking to the antelope and observed his particular stillness, as if listening to its response.

His torso is scarred by two deep furrows—one beneath his shoulder blades, the other near his navel—legacies of a buffalo, which thrust its horn right through his body. Khanyiso told him that the hunter he was working for pushed back the innards hanging from his wound and sewed him closed with white acacia thorns. "I was lucky— some abelungu just leave you to die. It taught me a good lesson. Never be arrogant towards wild animals. They're clever, they're brave, they're strong, and they'll die to defend their herds or their young ones. If you wish to kill them, be humble when you approach."

Khanyiso rarely speaks and more rarely smiles. But watching Sir Roland bungle a shot fills him with glee, and it pleases him to comment on it.

"Yes, yes," Sir Roland concedes now, knowing that the only way to end his taunting is to admit error. "I made a right mess of that. But can we please go after the wretched brute before it gets too far away?"

Khanyiso permits himself a dry chuckle, like the barking of a gnu, then turns to the business of tracking. Through the long hot afternoon, they share the buffalo's journey: here it rested in a gloomy cavern formed by tangled creepers and prickly euphorbia trees; here it wallowed in a mud bath and rubbed itself against a giant umkhiwane tree—leaving damp mud, black hairs and three red ticks; here it lay down under a fever tree, crushing the grass and small plants beneath.

Up and down they go, tormented by soft-bodied midges that fly into their nostrils and ears. They stop briefly to allow Khanyiso his afternoon snuff. Hungry and thirsty, their water long gone, they plod on under the unforgiving sun, grateful for the small relief offered by the dappled shade of intermittent trees. The drag of Sir Roland's guns and lead slugs on Daniel's shoulders grows heavier by the hour, its weight as much to do, he thinks, with their morbid energy as with their mass.

As the sun lowers, the tracks lead into a thick reed bed extending some hundred yards into the flat plains flanking the river. The reeds tower several feet above them, penetrable only on the paths made by larger animals.

A rhinoceros bird draws their attention with its harsh call. It flutters high above the reeds, then dives down abruptly.

"There's our quarry!" Sir Roland exclaims. "Let's go on in."

"Hayi, angizohamba. I won't go in there. Too easy for the buffalo to ambush us," Khanyiso says firmly. He catches the pleading gaze of the Tsonga bearers and adds: "The bearers too must stay with me. Too much noise if you all go."

Sir Roland will bully any of the other hunters. But no one bullies Khanyiso.

"Very well. You wait here, " he says loftily, as if it had been his plan all along. "Daniel, you come with me."

Daniel drags himself after Sir Roland into the dark tunnel, thick with the cloying scent of mud and rotting vegetation. They tread softly—if they alert the buffalo by brushing a reed, it will be ready to charge the moment they're within sight.

After creeping forward for several minutes, they hear the twittering of rhinoceros birds.

Sir Roland prizes the reeds apart with his gun barrel. Daniel can see the dark outline of the massive head just a few feet away. He feels the buffalo's blood thrumming through its veins, the worrying of the rhinoceros birds on its back, the cool crush of reeds beneath its belly. The crack of the rifle thunders in his ears and blazes with a searing white flash through his head. He bites down hard, clenching his jaw and squeezing his eyes to stop himself falling. The buffalo thrashes frantically as it tries to gain purchase in the slippery reeds and get to its feet. After several agonizing minutes, it succumbs with a low, wrenching bellow, releasing Daniel back into his own body.

He stands fighting waves of nausea while Sir Roland examines the buffalo and exclaims how he nailed it with one bullet right between the eyes, how he'd never seen horns so broad and so thick.

Day one of killing. How many more to go?

MOSES

Back at the camp, Moses is digging a latrine ditch with the remaining Tsonga bearers. It's an old hunters' camp on level ground beside the river, bordered by a jagged cliff on one side, and a rough stockade of thorn branches on the other three. They'd spent the morning dragging dead branches to reinforce the remnants of the old stockade, although the hunters tell him that it is fear of the humans and their guns that keep the animals at bay, more than the fence.

The head hunter, Shibela, is a rangy refugee from the amaNgwane tribe. On their first day of traveling, Sir Roland put Moses under Shibela's authority—he's apparently abandoned any effort to give Moses some kind of superior status. Shibela is a jovial fellow, but his ready laughter—usually at someone else's expense—masks a steely ambition and self-interest. Moses sometimes feels his eyes watching him suspiciously. But as soon as Moses catches his eye, he just laughs as if the mere existence of Moses is a source of amusement. On the first day he gave Moses the name iKholwa, a derogatory term for black men who wear trousers and espouse Christianity and English ways. He enjoys ordering him to do unpopular tasks, such as digging the privies and drainage ditches. But Moses doesn't mind hard work, and there is far less of it than there was on Hanbury Estate. The other hunters follow Shibela in mocking him, but without much malice. The Tsonga bearers keep to themselves, but are kindly towards him.

The days spent traveling to this place have been a timely

respite. He did not think he could have borne a single hour longer on Hanbury, with the toxic Bucket and insidious Wyeth. Sir Roland is also less oppressive away from the estate, and seems content to ignore Moses and leave his supervision to Shibela. Despite the grandeur of his life in England, Sir Roland seems happiest when he is roughing it, and has a boyish excitement about the prospect of hunting. He almost skipped out of the camp this morning, with poor Daniel trailing after him in a cloud of misery. The sight of his brother's distress diminished the delight Moses was feeling at being away from Hanbury, but he put aside his misgivings and lost himself in the steady rhythm of manual work.

By the end of the day, they have reinforced the stockade, dug the ditches, and erected three rough A-frame shelters, bound with monkey rope and creepers and thatched with reeds and grass. One is for Sir Roland to sleep in (his tent was left with the oxen and wagons since no bearer would agree to carrying it), the others store their supplies. The shelters are waterproof with a drain cut around to stop water running in, although rains come seldom now that they are heading for the dry winter season. All the rest of the party will sleep out in the open.

When Daniel comes back that evening, Moses realizes how hard it will be to get his brother through the coming weeks. His eyes have a bruised, vacant look, his face is pale, cheeks hollow with fatigue. In the days that follow, he sinks ever deeper into some somnambulistic underworld. Moses often hears him crying out in the night—when he rouses him, Daniel jerks up, staring wild-eyed as if he hardly recognizes his brother. *Such dreams,* he mutters, *so much blood....* Sometimes Moses wakes to find Daniel sitting beside him, holding a candle and peering down at his face.

"What's wrong, Dani? Tell me how I can help you?" he asks.

But Daniel just shakes his head and walks away.

Moses knows that the days must be torture for him— and there's no escaping the ongoing slaughter, even in the evenings. As the kills mount up, the camp begins to resemble a charnel house. Skinned animal carcasses hang dripping from a stand of large umkhiwane trees in the center; the fence is ringed with discarded bones and hides not deemed worth keeping. A dead tree near the settlement is the permanent roost of vultures waiting for the next carcass. The nights are punctuated with the growls and scuffles of scavenging animals, the gnawing of tooth on bone. Under one A-frame shelter grows a pile of skins, horns and skulls to be taken back. The stench of blood and decaying flesh permeates the air along with the heavy drone of blowflies in the drowsy afternoons.

The banter around the evening campfire is rough, full of stories of the day's killing, how many bullets in how many bodies, how many tails cut off and horns harvested and pelts skinned. Moses finds it sickening, but tries to go along with it to lessen his estrangement from the other hunters. In the first few days, Daniel would join the group. But he is clearly appalled by the discussions and glares at Moses reproachfully if he laughs or participates in the banter. Moses can't help feeling relief when Daniel starts to avoid the hunters' gatherings, eating his evening meal with Sir Roland and retiring as soon as it is finished. And he can't help feeling some impatience. They are so close to the end now—can't Daniel just toughen himself a little and do what Sir Roland expects of him?

The only time Daniel seems easier is when he is with Khanyiso. Khanyiso doesn't brag about kills. He speaks little, and the stories he tells are respectful, as though animals were members of another tribe with much to teach. He treats everyone the same, from Sir Roland to the humblest of the bearers, and Moses also feels at ease in his company. Sometimes Daniel will join him and Khanyiso after the others have gone to their sleeping mats, and will be more like his old self, eagerly asking questions and absorbing Khanyiso's prodigious knowledge of the wildlife around them. At these times, Moses can pretend that there is nothing seriously wrong, that Daniel will be fine, that he may suffer through the hunts but together they will get through the days.

But on the nights that he wakes to find his brother staring at him, he looks into those wild eyes and knows that Daniel is drifting into some foreign country where he cannot follow.

DANIEL

One night, as Daniel approaches Sir Roland's shelter with his evening coffee, he hears a rapping, as though Sir Roland were drumming on a wooden table with his fingernails. He finds him gripped by a violent shivering, clutching blankets pulled up to his chin. His chattering teeth, the source of the tapping noise, have set his spade beard shaking.

"M...m...malaria," he gets out, through a clenched jaw. "Caught the blasted thing in Burma...comes back some times."

He reaches for the coffee, but his hand is shaking violently. If he tries to hold it, he will splash it all over himself. Daniel puts the mug down on the little folding stool by his sleeping mat, eases his hands under Sir Roland's shoulders and lifts his heavy head. He holds the coffee to his mouth for him to sip. As Daniel lowers him back down onto his mat, Sir Roland grasps his hand.

"Don't leave me, boy..."

"Just building up your fire, sir."

Daniel fetches a buffalo hide to throw over Sir Roland, builds up the fire outside his shelter, and goes to consult Moses. Khanyiso follows them back and sticks his head into the shelter to contemplate the patient.

"Not much you can do," he says. "I've seen abelungu with this before. Sometimes they live, sometimes they die. Keep this one alive, Dani, or we'll be in trouble when we get back and we need him for our wages. I'll get some inkunzi bark or inkuphulana roots tomorrow if I can find any growing here."

Daniel tries to make Sir Roland comfortable, while Moses investigates the medicine box in the other shelter. A big man at the best of times, Sir Roland seems even bigger in this small enclosure, his shadow thrown huge against the reed walls by the storm lamp beside the sleeping mat. The space is filled with the sound of his chattering teeth and the rustling of his mat under his shaking limbs.

Through the long night, Sir Roland alternates between violent shivering and flinging off his covers as sweat pours from his body. At one point he vomits all over his sleeping mat, vest and continuations. Daniel runs out of the shelter to vomit himself, then comes back to help Moses roll him off his bottom sheet and replace it with the top one. He fetches cold water from the bucket outside and finds clean under-wear in his trunk while Moses wipes him down with a rag.

When gripped by delirium, he tosses about, raving and weeping, and begs for mercy from invisible demons.

"Don't take me," he implores. "Let me be, for the love of God, let me be." Sometime in the night he grasps Moses' hand with the ferocity of a drowning man and cries pite-ously, "I never did, I swear I never did."

Daniel sits beside Moses, thinking of Khanyiso's words. *Don't let this one die.* It seems unimaginable that Sir Roland would allow malaria or anything else to vanquish him. He looks at Sir Roland's pale, square-tipped fingers, gripping Moses' hand as though it was all that stopped him from sinking into an abyss.

"How can you be so good to him after all he's done to you?" he asks.

Moses shrugs. "If we let him die the hunters won't get paid. And we won't get to England."

If he dies, the killing will stop, Daniel thinks. He imagines the cool silence that might inhabit the world once Sir Roland has left it. He is filled with gratitude for this illness. His flesh feels toxic to the bone with the residue of animal suffering, he can hardly bring himself to eat. He'd begun to dwell on what Ma Ndlovu told him, that he could harden himself by killing a rhino, and rubbing shavings from its horn into cuts in his flesh. It is unimaginable, but is becoming less unimaginable than enduring the days and nights until Sir Roland has decided that he has killed enough and they can leave.

He resolves to keep vigil with Moses, but he must have dozed off. He dreams that he is standing on the veranda at uMzinyathi with his mother, watching the seasonal grass fires set by local tribes to renew the grass. The orange ribbons of flame snake down the black hillside towards them, drawing ever nearer. The air is thick with bush smoke and the agitated rustling of small things fleeing for their lives.

What will happen if it burns the mission? he asks.

Then we will all become fireflies, she says, and laughs. Her eyes glitter strangely in the light of the flames, and he is afraid.

The roar of the flames mingles with Sir Roland's breathing. He wakes with a start to the violet light of dawn heralded by a resounding chorus of birds. A cool breeze brings the muddy scent of the river, dispelling some of the fug of Sir Roland's sweat and vomit. Moses has gone.

Daniel sits up, stretches to ease his stiff shoulders, and stares down at Sir Roland's face. A pale green caterpillar is making its way steadily down Sir Roland's left sideburns, extending its body then bringing its back legs to its front legs to create an inverted U before stretching out its front legs again. Sometimes it raises itself on its back legs and casts about, as though seeking a more rewarding destination. He watches it for a few seconds, wondering what the caterpillar's understanding is of what it is walking on, before leaning over and gently removing it.

MOSES

Sir Roland languishes for several days. Between chills and fevers, he is lucid but greatly enfeebled, so that Daniel and Moses have to help him wash and bring a basin for his ablutions. He seems resigned to the intimacy of these operations, but won't let anyone other than the two of them perform them—and of the two he seems to prefer Moses. Moses does not flatter himself on this account. He knows it is most likely because he is calmer, more methodical, less disgusted by the whole process.

Moses looks after him by disconnecting the body from the man. Sir Roland has become a set of symptoms, a medical conundrum. He administers the medicine he found in Sir Roland's medicine box according to the instructions on the bottles: a few grains of quinine, a few drops of Warburg's tincture, so many times per day. Cooling lavender compresses and a little laudanum to soothe the headaches and fevers. The laudanum bottle warns him that it is a poison in excessive doses. When measuring the drops out, he can't help reflecting on how easy it would be to add a few more drops, to sit beside Sir Roland and watch him slip away. It was this temptation that made him realize the necessity of separating the disease from the man. He cares little for the life of this man who, so far, has brought him only misery. But he is fascinated by the course of the disease through Sir Roland's body and is resolved not to let it defeat his medical skills.

He has put himself in charge of administering the medicine. He doesn't trust Daniel to get it right, in his current state of distress and distraction.

One night, as Moses is straightening his bed, he finds a folding leather photograph frame. Inside is a photograph of a young Asian woman, with a little round hat and spray of jasmine in her hair, wearing an ornate embroidered skirt. She is holding a small child in the dress of a young infant.

Sir Roland stirs and begins to mutter and scrabble among the bedclothes as though looking for something.

"Did you want this?" Moses asks, offering him the photo.

He grasps it and stares at it, tears leaking from his eyes and running into his beard.

"My boy," he murmurs. "My beautiful boy. And Mi San."

"Is this your child?"

"Oh, remember them, remember them well...both dead... brain fever...first the boy then his mother two days later... she died of grief as much as..."

He looks at Moses with his feverish wild eyes and grasps his hand.

"You'll remember them, won't you? Mark well, the boy's name was Robert Fitchely. I gave him my father's name. I wanted to...I would have...you will remember, if I die? Little Robert, not two years on this earth..."

He gets more agitated. At one point, he tries to rise, crying, "I must get help...for pity's sake, get the doctor, the child is burning with fever."

Moses calms him eventually with more drops of the opiate. He sits watching the rise and fall of his chest, the stirring of his beard with each exhalation. Outside the shelter the bushbabies are calling, their cries eerily reminiscent of an infant in distress.

Moses shows the photograph to Daniel the following evening, while Sir Roland is sleeping.

"It's his child."

"His *child*?"

"He showed it to me last night when I was sitting with him. He said they both died of brain fever, within hours of each other. He was weeping."

"I can't believe he told you."

"He was very feverish. He scarcely knew who he was talking to, I think. He kept telling me to remember them."

"I saw him sitting and weeping in the dining room one night at Hanbury. Perhaps it was over this. Surprising that he'd have a Burmese wife."

Moses laughs. "I don't think they were *married*, Dani. I just hope he never remembers that he told me," he adds. "It'll make him hate me all the more."

"Why would he though? Surely it would make him appreciate you?"

"My dear brother, you really understand animals a lot better than you understand people, don't you?"

"Well, I certainly don't understand Sir Roland most of the time. But I must say, I find him a lot more bearable since he's been sick. Do you think he will recover?"

"Yes, I wasn't sure if he would make it at first. He had a bad night, but I think he is getting stronger."

Daniel sighs. "I dread him getting well, Mosi. To be honest, I was...well...I would not grieve if he died. I know he's my cousin, but sometimes I feel more kinship with the crocodiles in the river—at least they only kill to eat. I don't know how I will get through the days once the slaughter starts again."

"The hunters are still going out shooting every day."

"Yes, but it only affects me when I'm there. And Sir Roland insists that I go with him on every hunt. He says he's determined to make a man out of me. Sometimes I think he's just dragging me along to torment me."

"So the sangoma didn't help?"

Daniel looks at him sharply and turns crimson. "How... how did you know?"

"I saw the cuts on your chest. And Baba Mbanda let something slip. You promised you wouldn't go."

"I'm sorry, Mosi. I know I promised, but I was desperate. Why didn't you say something?"

"You chose to keep it a secret. It wasn't for me to say anything. But it hurts me that that you lied about it. Anyway, it's done now...did it help you at least?"

He tries to keep the anger from his voice, but his tone is cold and Daniel flinches.

"What do you care?" he asks sharply. "If it's going to

England you're worried about, I'm doing my best."

"That's not fair, Dan. If this is really making you sick, we can walk out tomorrow."

He has to say that. He knows he has to say that.

Tears spring to Daniel's eyes, but he wipes them away angrily.

"We can't...you'd never forgive me. I wouldn't want to live with your resentment."

They'd been whispering, but now Daniel raises his voice. Sir Roland stirs and mutters, flings out one heavy arm, groans and opens his eyes. "Water..."

Moses helps him raise his head, and holds a beaker of water to his lips. Daniel walks outside.

When Sir Roland has settled, Moses walks out to join his brother, who is sitting against a nearby tree. Daniel smiles at him bleakly as he sits beside him. "I'm sorry, Mosi. I was being unfair. But, don't worry, I will get through it one way or another."

"I know. We'll get through it together," Moses says, because something has to be said.

He looks up at the star-studded sky and laughs. "Do you know what day it is?"

"No, I've completely lost count of the days."

"It's our birthday! I've been marking off the days and noticed yesterday, but I forgot it again."

"Really? It seems a lifetime ago since our last one. Not our best birthday, but at least Sir Bugaboo obliged us by being sick and giving us a break from his ghastly orders."

"May I present you with Scorpio as a birthday gift?" Moses asks, pointed up at the stars—Scorpio's tail had just cleared the horizon. "Such a lovely constellation, don't you think?"

"Thank you. And in return you may have that call of a Scops owl on a starry night," Daniel replies, as the shrill sounds float to them through the darkness.

Moses laughs. "A fair exchange. Do you remember Mkhulu?"

"Of course. I was so sad on the day he flew away."

"I wasn't sad," Moses says, recalling the feel of the owl leaving his hands, the way his own heart had lifted with its flight. "It was one of the happiest days of my life."

Two days later, Moses returns from washing in the river to find Sir Roland standing outside his shelter in his underclothes. His face is sallow with dark rings beneath the eyes, but there is a trace of the old imperiousness in his bearing. He takes a step and staggers—Moses hurries up to help him, but Sir Roland waves him away.

"Fetch Daniel," he says gruffly. "I won't be needing you anymore."

Moses resists the urge to push him over. He'd not expected gratitude but had hoped for some civility. He walks away without saying anything. The reprieve is over, he thinks. The killing will begin again. And what will happen to his brother then?

Khanyiso and the other hunters have gone out most days

during Sir Roland's illness to keep the camps supplied with meat. That evening, Moses hears the triumphant hunting song of the returning men and knows that they've killed something unusual. The men come into sight walking past their own camp and up to Sir Roland's shelter. Moses joins the other hunters and bearers as they follow the hunters in excitement. A hunter deposits his burden at Sir Roland's feet—the freshly skinned pelt of a large male lion. The crowd perform the dances of a successful lion hunt, and sing praises for Khanyiso. Sir Roland orders Daniel to prime the double-barrel shotgun with gunpowder but no shot. He aims it into the sky and pulls both triggers. The hunters follow suit, setting off repeated volleys that send the vultures in the dead tree flying up, their pale wings drifting against the darkening sky like flecks of ash floating above a bushfire.

Later that night, Moses sits with Khanyiso by the fire, hearing his account of the day's events. "The first lion I saw was when I was too small even to herd the cattle," Khanyiso says. "Small as I was, it was my job to look after my younger brother. One day we were sitting on the edge of a donga near our homestead, with our legs hanging over the edge. I saw the back of a lion creeping towards us along the bottom of the donga. I jumped up and reached for my brother's hand to pull him away. But my brother was gone. Then I saw the lion running off, dragging my brother."

Khanyiso shakes his head, still staring into the flames.

"I didn't hear him cry. This worries me, even today. Why didn't I hear my brother cry?"

Khanyiso gets up to throw another branch on the fire, sending a bright shower of sparks into the dark air. He stands before the flames, warming his hands.

"So now, I have killed lions with spears for the King, I have killed lions with guns for abelungu hunters. But truly, every lion I kill is for my brother."

"Will you wear the claws of this lion?" Moses asks.

"Perhaps, if uMahlekehlathini agrees that I can have them."

"Aren't you afraid to wear the claws of the King?"

"Abelungu are our kings now, Mosi. If umlungu says Khanyiso can wear the claws, then Khanyiso can wear the claws."

"King Cetshwayo is still king in Zululand."

Khanyiso shakes his head. "The old ways are changing, my friend. The king asked uSomtsewu to crown him. What king asks the messenger of a foreign queen to crown him? The British queen rules us now."

Moses frowns. "I don't understand, Khanyiso. You killed the lion. Surely, if the claws don't belong to King Cetshwayo, they belong to you?"

"Those are the terms. Everything we kill belongs to Sir Roland."

"But how can he set these terms? We're not even in British territory?"

"Lalela, brother. Open your ears. The British are the new rulers here. As we speak, the British are gathering their soldiers to take the amaZulu kingdom. When the dry season comes again, the British queen will own everything here. Every lion, every elephant, every umkhiwane tree, every umsinsi tree, every grass stalk, every last ant, and truly every man. You and me. Our wives, our children, our cattle."

On the way back to his sleeping mat, Moses passes the lion's pelt hanging over a branch, the fur glinting pale silver in the starlight. He thinks of the pictures he has seen of Queen Victoria—a squat, dumpy woman with a great complexity of clothing about her. How can this queen own these things—every lion, every stalk of grass? A queen who's never even stepped on African soil? Surely a lion belongs only to itself. He runs his hand through the thick dark mane.

"The Queen doesn't own us, my friend," he whispers into the lion's ear.

Somewhere in the dark, a hyena laughs.

Shibela is furious that Moses looked after Sir Roland through his illness. He is convinced that Moses was currying favor with Sir Roland, with a view to being appointed head hunter. He takes to calling him Impisi, the hyena, because he says he steals meat from the lion instead of hunting for himself. He tells the other hunters that Moses has been spying on them and telling their secrets to Sir Roland. He tells Moses to watch out, he too can speak English, and whisper secrets in uMahlekehlathini's ear—it's true that his English is better than the others.

And no doubt he is whispering secrets, for Moses has again become visible to Sir Roland. He feels his dark gaze following him—sharp and accusatory—dispelling any lingering delusions that his kindness during Sir Roland's illness may change the man's attitude to him.

I saw him at his most vulnerable, he thinks. He clutched my hand and wept and begged me not to leave him.

He won't ever forgive me for that.

The only relief is that Sir Roland has given instructions that Moses must be confined to camp and not go out with the hunters. He assumes this is intended as some kind of punishment (for what?), but he is happy enough to escape his tormentors during the day.

But it also means that he seldom sees Daniel alone. When he does see his brother, he can see the familiar signs of distress returning—the shadows under the eyes, the wild looks, the grimacing in pain, the silent brooding.

Am I my brother's keeper, Cain asked. The cruelest words in the Bible. Moses knows that he is Daniel's keeper, and he trusts Daniel to be his. But as he suffers through the days of goading from Shibela, barked commands from Sir Roland, and mistrustful stares from the other hunters, he feels as if all his strength is sapped just by keeping himself. The weight of his brother's illness drags on his shoulders.

Can it be so difficult for him to take command of himself?

When the hunting parties leave, taking the complicated burden of Daniel with them, he feels a sense of release, mixed with guilt because he knows it comes at the price of Daniel's suffering. He does his chores with the Tsonga bearers, cleaning privies and chopping firewood, maintaining ditches and the stockade, skinning animals and preparing meat for cooking. If he finds any empty moments, he fills them with algebraic problems, allowing the elegance of the equations to take him away from the mess of life. Or he wanders beyond the stockade to observe some small drama in the natural world: a scorpion fighting a lizard; a standoff between a boomslang and a mongoose; a guinea fowl hiding her chicks from a sparrowhawk flying overhead. He observes the precise architecture of a weaver's nest or a termite mound and feels comforted by their order and constancy.

He counts the days—a few more weeks of hunting, some weeks of traveling down to Durban with a stopover at uMzinyathi, then leaving at last for England. This is the journey he has mapped out in his own head. Sir Roland has said only that they will leave the hunting grounds before the rainy season in August, but he has said nothing of what happens beyond that. When they set off from Durban, the understanding was that, all being good, they would leave for England in early September. There has been no further talk of this. But Moses has to believe it. The promise of going to England is the only glimmer of light in the long dark night of their service to Sir Roland. The thought that it might not happen sometimes waylays him, like a crevasse appearing abruptly before a mountain climber. He quickly suppresses it—if he lets himself fall into that thought, he will never stop falling.

DANIEL

Daniel wriggles into a more comfortable position in the fork of a cabbage tree, prompting a hiss to be quiet from Sir Roland, who is on a branch below him. All he can see of his master is one boot protruding from the thick foliage.

The tree is by a waterhole near the new camp further up the Black Imfolozi. Sir Roland has grown tired of shooting buffalos. He wants to "bag some rhinos," and the rhinos around the old camp have been driven out or slaughtered by successive waves of hunters. Only a few of the hunters and bearers have come—the rest stayed behind to guard the pelts and horns. Moses is helping the others set up, but Sir Roland can't wait until morning to go after the rhino, so he's taken Daniel out with him. Sir Roland is holding his Snider Enfield breechloader, his favored all-purpose gun. Daniel has the muzzleloader shotgun and a large-bored elephant gun, as well as extra slugs, cartridges and gunpowder.

They sit in the tree in silence, leaving Daniel free to watch the evening parade of animals venturing down to the waterhole. It's a long strip of deep clear water open on one side and fringed by tree ferns, wild dates, mthombothi and cabbage trees on the other. He focuses on a lone bushbuck kneeling to drink, the pattern of white spots on its red coat gleaming in the evening light. If only he could revel in the wonder of watching it, without the constant fear that it and every other animal may fall prey to Sir Roland's bullets.

A flurry of birds alerts him to the approach of bigger animals. Framed on the top of the bank is a herd of kudu, scanning the waterhole for any sign of danger. An elderly doe steps forward with her great ears twitching and is followed by the whole herd. A bull pushes its way through and stands in the deeper water below their tree—so close that Daniel can see the scratches on its long-spiraled horns from fighting and the thick lashes over its large dark eyes. He tenses, waiting for any signs of body jumping, but the kudu stays in its own skin.

Sunset is followed by the rapid onset of darkness and a cool breeze rustling through the leaves. Daniel pulls his wool jacket closer, envying Sir Roland's leather trousers and sheepskin coat. He drapes his blanket over his knees, but the wind seems determined to penetrate it.

He looks up through the leaves to the black sky dazzled with countless stars. How long ago it seems that he lay down with his brother on moonless nights at uMzinyathi, naming the stars. How he wishes they were still those boys—that the old Moses was here, beside him, with the light of the stars in his eyes, free from the dark stain of betrayal.

The stars are bright enough to cast black shadows, dappling the pale ground beneath the trees. Bats skim the water's surface in search of insects. Time drifts on the night sounds, the faint rustles and chirps, the persistent chorus of the frogs. The peace of the night is broken briefly by an altercation between a marauding leopard and an outraged baboon on the ridge behind them. Not that there is ever peace in the bush at night. Night is the time of the predators (human and animal), and many creatures will be dead by morning.

Shortly after moonrise, he wakes to the rumbling of some heavy creature issuing from the direction of an open clearing some sixty yards off. *Go away, go away*...if only he could fly up like the rhinoceros bird to warn it.

For long minutes he listens to the animal moving

through the bushes, to the crunch of its teeth on the twigs. He feels something tugging his toe—Sir Roland's pale face is staring up from his branch below, his beard black as coal in the darkness. Sir Roland jerks his head to indicate that he must follow, and descends the tree. Daniel takes up his guns and bandolier pouch and climbs down after him. The heavy guns catch the branches and knock against his back.

He follows Sir Roland on stiff legs beneath the rising yellow moon. They reach the thicket at the far end of the waterhole and creep through, walking with painstaking slowness to avoid crackling twigs underfoot. Beyond the thicket is a silvered glade, at the far end of which can be seen the dark outline of a rhino browsing on small bushes.

Motioning for him to stay back, Sir Roland crawls forward on his stomach, moving out of sight in the darkness. Daniel keeps his eyes on the animal, feeling the first tingles of a body jump. The sensation of heaviness in his head, the bittersweet crunch of leaves between his teeth. Some protective awareness of a smaller presence beside him. *She has a calf.* He can see it now, just visible behind her hind quarters.

The moonlight glints on something across the clearing: Sir Roland's gun barrel, barely fifteen paces in front of the rhino. Daniel loads and primes the elephant gun, ready to drop the rhino if it spots Sir Roland and charges. He could shoot it now, he thinks. Sir Roland would be furious if he stole a shot from him. But if he shot it, he could take scrapings from its horn, and cure himself forever. A clammy sweat breaks out on the back of his neck. His whole body shudders as his finger presses against the trigger. He thinks of the calf, the rhino's child, and his finger freezes.

Who is he fooling? He could never bring himself to pull the trigger.

After several minutes, the rhino turns away from Sir Roland, presenting a better shot. Daniel can see the calf clearly now. It's wandered a little way off, but its mother stands between it and Sir Roland so he probably can't see it. It wouldn't stop him from killing the mother anyway—the only animals that escape Sir Roland's gun are those he deems not interesting enough to shoot.

There's a flash of fire and a shot reverberates through the clearing. As the ball hits the thick skin with a thwack, a burning pain erupts in Daniel's shoulder. The animal staggers and charges at the smoke, but Sir Roland has rolled out of the bush and is concealed in the long grass, reloading. The calf is keening high-pitched wails of terror. The rhino turns and bolts into the thicket, followed by its terrified calf. Sir Roland sends a bullet after them, but the crashing noise continues until it fades into the distance.

As Sir Roland walks back across the clearing, Daniel crawls out of the bush and stands to greet him.

"What happened to you, Daniel? We could have brought it down."

"I was afraid of hitting you, sir. I couldn't clearly see where you were."

"Don't be a ninny, son. I was miles from the brute, and I've seen you hit a target at fifty paces. Anyway, we've lost it for now. Pretty sure I wounded it, though. We'll track it tomorrow. Didn't realize it had a youngster till after I'd shot it. Might've been a bit more cautious. They're vicious at the best of times, those black rhino, but more so when they have young."

They walk back to the pool and climb back up the cabbage tree. Now that he knows that rhino are around, Sir Roland keeps the loaded elephant gun to hand as well as his breechloader.

Daniel settles back into his tree fork and pulls the blanket up to his shoulders. The wind has dropped. Although the air is crisp, the chill is not as penetrating. He's still trembling from the earlier encounter and can't imagine sleeping. But he finds himself drifting into a dream of a running rhino, not running through sunlight and shade now, but running through moonlight, with a growing coldness in his shoulder seeping ever closer to his heart.

He starts awake at the gurgle of mud. A rhino is wallowing in the shallows, its short legs flailing above its ungainly body, clear in the moonlight. Its bigger companion stands on the high bank, its horn outlined against the sky. Perhaps a young male with its mother? Khanyiso says rhinos are "Mommy's boys" and hang around their mothers for some years.

He hears a slight rustle in the tree, then the soft click as Sir Roland pulls back the hammer. A thundering crack rips through the tree with a yellow flash, releasing a plume of pale smoke. The rhino on the bank utters snorts of alarm and canters over the ridge. The rhino in the water rolls onto its feet in a shower of mud and charges out. It pauses on the bank to sniff the air, trying to trace the source of this threat. The gun roars again. Daniel feels the bullet slamming into its shoulder, knocking it down. The rhino scrabbles back on its feet and charges towards the gun flash. As it comes beneath the tree, Sir Roland fires again, striking the hump above its shoulder blades. The rhino swerves and falls into the water. It founders for some seconds, giving Sir Roland time to reload both barrels. He releases the balls one after the other into its flailing body. The rhino thrashes in the water and again manages to rise to its feet. It flees out of the pool, scattering drops of silver water as it ascends the far bank and disappears in the wake of its companion.

"What the devil are you doing, boy?"

He is curled up, clutching the tree branch, his body wracked with pain. A high-pitched wailing is tearing through his head and vibrating in his chest. Is he making this noise? No, it's coming from outside, across the water. The rhino is dying a slow and agonizing death, and he can feel every spasm.

Sir Roland tugs his leg.

"What's the matter? Are you ill?"

Daniel shakes his head and tries to answer, but his teeth are chattering and lips are numb.

"Well, get down, find the brute and finish it off. Nothing else will come near with that racket going on, and it might bring the lions around."

Daniel climbs down after Sir Roland. Sir Roland squats at the foot of the tree and takes out his tobacco pouch and pipe.

"Go on," he says, passing him the elephant gun. "You can do this yourself. If you'd done your job properly and fired, that animal would be dead at our feet instead of screaming in the bush. Just watch out for the other one."

He loads the gun and sets off on trembling legs. He skirts the edge of the waterhole and climbs the bank. He doesn't look into the dark shadows as he passes. Being attacked by the other rhino is a real danger, but he hardly cares. He follows the sound over the bank and along the ridge, past a series of dark hollows created by the creepers in the trees.

The squealing has faded to whimpering breaths. They guide him to the dying rhino in the last of the hollows. Its eye rolls towards him, but it makes no move at his approach. He kneels down and embraces it, resting his hands and cheek on its great bulk. Its tortuous breaths shudder through it. The skin is soft, like old suede leather, still damp from the water but burning, its life flaring with a last glow before death.

A young male.

A rhino's child, like him.

"Thula, thula mfowethu," he murmurs into its thick, leathery ear. "Be still, my brother. Soon your pain will be over. Soon you will be wallowing in cool mud under the moon again, with all your friends beside you."

He pushes himself to his knees, lifts the loaded gun, lays the muzzle behind its ear, draws a deep breath and pulls the trigger. He feels a white-hot flash through his brain as the gun kicks back, wrenching his shoulder, then darkness. He falls onto the rhino's thick, folded neck, clutching it as the animal jerks. When the world stops spinning, the rhino is still.

He pushes himself up, and stares down at the animal.

I've killed a rhino, he thinks. I raised my gun and pulled the trigger and killed this rhino.

He could do it now. Use the remedy. If it works, he could be free of the suffering of animals. Free of the suffocating weight of their death. He could watch Sir Roland shoot animal after animal, even shoot them himself, without feeling a thing.

He takes out his hunting knife—the knife that Moses gave him years before—rips off his jacket and shirt and slashes his chest in six places, as Ma Ndlovu had done. He thrills to the purity of a pain that is his own and not that of another creature. He remembers the last time he cut himself with this knife at uMzinyathi, when he was thirteen and made a blood pact with Moses.

That was a pact to join him to his brother.

This pact will separate him.

Separate him from animals, separate him from humans, even from Moses. Put him beyond the reach of the ancestral spirits, free him from this pointless distress.

All he has to do is rub a mixture of shavings from the horn and rhino blood into his cuts. He presses down on the tip of the horn with one hand and scrapes the knife lightly against it. A shudder goes through him as the point of the horn digs into his palm. The black horn and red-rimmed eye of his old dreams swing above him, the eye of the python gazes unblinking from inside.

The blood and horn will enter your skin, Ma Ndlovu said, *and make you as hard as the rhino horn. But it will harden you not only to the suffering of animals but also to the suffering of other humans.*

What does he care about hardness? Hardness is the way of humans, it seems. The only way to be human. He grips the knife handle and scrapes the blade harder against the horn. He struggles to keep it steady, for his hand is shaking as though resisting a massive force. He closes his eyes. He can smell Gogo's scent of soap and cotton and wood smoke and see the rhino she showed them drinking from its moonlit reflection. The eye and the horn swing in the sky above him.

A wave of high twittering voices swirls around him, the voices in Ma Ndlovu's hut *Ingane yezulu intshontshiwe... kumele ibuyiselwe.... The child of the sky has been stolen.... He must be returned...*

Was Moses stolen? uMfundisi/ His father would say he was saved...but was he? *If the child does not know the amadlozi...that child is lost to them,* Ma Ndlovo said. Hadn't his father made it his mission to turn Moses away from his Zulu origins? To mold him into a vessel to spread the Gospel and eradicate Zulu beliefs, to turn other children from their ancestors too? And perhaps he was not just lost to the amadlozi, but also lost to himself. He remembers Moses' words, *I should have died when my family left me by the river. Sometimes I think I'm just a ghost...*

But if Moses was stolen, how can he, Daniel return him? How can anyone return him?

The knife falls from his hand, clattering against the

rhino's face and onto the ground. He collapses onto the rhino's shoulder.

He can't do it.

He can't harden himself to the suffering of others. He's been chosen to carry it, this awkward, sorrowful legacy. Chosen when Joseph picked up Moses. Or when the rhino spared him—or wherever it came from. He doesn't know what the ancestors are asking of him. But feeling the suffering of animals is part of it, for that is how they are making their own distress felt. And he knows this is *his* thing, and carry it he must.

Akukho ndlovu yasindwa ngumboko wayo—No elephant is burdened by its own trunk.

He lies with his cheek against the rhino's hot, velvet skin. His own heart pulses against its chest, bringing the illusion that its heart is still beating, that his heart is beating for both of them.

He feels it cool beneath him as its life ebbs out into the earth.

The calf is still with its mother when they track her the next day. They reach it in the early afternoon, after a long morning following the spoor. Despite her injury, the rhino walked several miles, circling back frequently, trying to protect her calf from whatever attacked her. She collapsed eventually in a thicket of bushwillow trees.

Sir Roland has been taken by the notion of capturing the calf, getting it back to Durban and shipping it to a zoo in London. All the men in the camp have come, with strong reims—strips of buffalo hide—to help them secure it.

The spoor leads to a thicket. There is the still gray bulk of the mother's body, with the young one resting its head on hers in the space between her horns. As they approach, the calf scrambles up and charges, then stands again by its mother. It is still without horns, no taller than a large dog although much more solid. It charges any who approach, but the hunters surround it and eventually slip a noose around one back leg and then the other. With several men holding each hind leg, the party tries to drive it from the thicket. It resists with everything it has, charging back, puffing and snorting or squealing with terror or rage.

Sometimes it is jerked off its feet by the thongs, and lies down, kicking out.

Khanyiso proposes that someone stand in front of it and run towards camp as soon as it charges. Sir Roland directs Daniel to be the "carrot" to induce the rhino to go forwards. They reach camp eventually, with Daniel jogging in front, the exhausted, terrified calf running behind, both urged on by the laughing men.

Daniel can't think or feel beyond a blur of rage and a visceral revulsion at the cruelty being meted out to this calf. His body is weighed down by the deaths of the two rhinos, his arms and legs move with stiff reluctance.

The calf is tethered within the stockade by a patch of sweet grass near the river. Khanyiso names her Nolaka, for her fierceness. Khanyiso brings branches for her to sample and pours water over her to cool her down through the hot afternoon. By the second day, Nolaka runs up to

Khanyiso when he brings the leaves and tolerates some of the hunters close by. But when Sir Roland approaches, she makes a snorting sound by clamping her lips together and forcibly expelling air through them. If he comes closer, she charges.

Daniel avoids her on the first day. He can't bear the men's laughter at her clumsy charges, the bewilderment in her eyes as she tries to distinguish friend from foe in this brutal new reality that has claimed her. Had she any chance of surviving he'd release her and face the consequences. But she'd be killed by lions or hyenas within the hour.

That night he brings his sleeping mat down to sleep near her. Khanyiso and Moses are already there, sitting beside a small fire.

"You're here too?" Daniel says to Moses in surprise.

"I was watching her for you till you came," Moses says.

Nolaka stands a little way off, watching them. Her skin is the soft gray-brown of weathered wood, smoother than an adult rhino but already crisscrossed with folds and wrinkles. Her huge feet with their three hoof–like toes splay out beneath stumpy legs, like too-big shoes on a toddler. Donkey ears, fringed with hair, flicker in different directions. Halfway down her boot-shaped face, a dark round eye regards them from under long lashes with doleful apprehension.

"She's missing her mama," Khanyiso says.

"Sir Roland shouldn't have killed her," Moses says.

"Yes, it's cruel to kill one with such a young calf. That's not our way."

"Will she survive the trip to Durban?" Daniel asks.

Khanyiso shrugs. "I don't think so. She's too little. But she is eating. She likes especially the leaves of the uMlahlankosi and the leaves from the marula tree.

For three days Daniel and Moses care for her, with Khanyiso's help at night. On the fourth day, when Daniel wakes at dawn, her eyes are dull, her ears floppy, her breathing rapid and shallow. He and Moses try to induce her to eat, but she won't.

"She needs milk," Moses says. "But where can we get it?"

As the day wears on, Nolaka grows steadily weaker. Khanyisa joins them in the evening and the three stay beside her through the night, trying to keep her warm with blankets and building up the fire. They are driven by an urgency to keep her alive, but all the time Daniel is wondering why they're trying to save her. What life is it for a rhino to travel in captivity to Durban, to go across the sea in a ship, to stand in a cage in a zoo?

Shortly after the Southern Cross has dipped to the horizon, with her head resting on Daniel's leg, she stops breathing.

"She has her wish," Khanyiso says softly. "She is home now. Hamba kahle, sisi wami omncane. Go well, my little sister."

Daniel pictures her lying in the thicket with her mother, resting her head on her mother's face between the two horns. He sits for a long time with his leg going numb under the calf's heavy head, watching the sun rise through the white mist that hovers over the river. It is heralded by a chorus of weaverbirds with no time to mourn.

MOSES

Moses trudges along the path behind Shibela, the heavy ammunition pouches for the elephant guns dragging on his shoulders. The winter sun is punishing, the air dry and crackling with static. Small flies hover about his face, biting whenever they can settle. But these vexations are overshadowed by his concern for Daniel. Some last tether of wellness had snapped in his brother that morning. He'd felt like a shattered thing, splintered and jagged, his eyes turned inward to some alien fury and despair. After hearing about the rhino calf's death, Sir Roland had said there should now be nothing keeping Daniel from joining the hunt for a black rhino that has been lurking near the camp. But perhaps even he could see that Daniel was in no state to go out, as he'd agreed that Moses might take his place.

They track the rhino for long hours through the day. Its spoor is evident, but Khanyiso keeps losing it. They trail it along the river, over ridges, through reed beds, through one thicket after another, going in circles as the trail doubles back on itself again and again. The afternoon brings bruise-colored clouds amassing on the horizon with a low surly rumbling of thunder and glowering flashes of lightning. The clouds spit out a few angry spatters of hard rain, then withdraw, leaving the parched earth still dry.

Shortly after the rain stops, they track the rhino to a particularly thorny thicket. Moses longs for the hunt to end, but he has no wish to see the rhino killed. The beaters fight their way into the bush. Sir Roland waits in position, half kneeling, with his favorite breechloader, cocked and aimed. Shibela and Moses provide cover with the elephant guns. The rhino charges out abruptly in a cloud of dust and flies. He's coming from an unexpected angle, to the side and much closer than anticipated. Sir Roland fires but misses, followed by shots from the other two. But the rhino somehow dodges them and keeps charging, forcing Sir Roland to scatter with the other hunters and beat an ignominious retreat through the thorn trees.

When they regroup, Sir Roland is in an evil mood. His shirt is ripped, his face and hands covered in scratches. He lambasts them all for being "bloody useless": Khanyiso for being so slow to track, the beaters for driving the animal out from the wrong angle, Shibela and Moses (especially Moses), for missing the shots. It's not unjustified—Moses had deliberately aimed wide. Once Sir Roland finally tires of his remonstrations, Shibela lays into Moses with his own grievances.

At last Sir Roland declares it a day, resolving to redouble his efforts to kill the rhino with more men and guns on the following day.

"No vicious dumb brute is going to get the better of me," he declares.

DANIEL

Daniel endures the day in the grip of an agitation that stirs up his lethargy like wind on a stagnant pond. He helps the others who have stayed behind to skin and prepare Nolaka's carcass—not for a sacred ritual, as she deserves, but to provide supper. He forces himself to do what is required, but a pressure is building up in his skull until he feels he must smash himself, or someone else. The python writhes in his gut.

The hunting party returns after nightfall. He is weak with relief to hear that they missed the rhino. But Sir Roland is imbued with that particular kind of splenetic outrage that holds everyone accountable for his ill temper. In this smaller camp, there is only one fire, so the hunters can't escape but must sit with Sir Roland, waiting for the meat to roast. The flames flicker over their weary faces, over Sir Roland's scowl, over the upraised barrels of the guns resting against the trunk of a dead tree. When the first portion is ready, Daniel carries the succulent, dripping meat on a stick to his master.

As Sir Roland begins eating, they hear snorting and puffing, as if a train were steaming up its engine before departing. There is a cracking of branches in the stockade, and a thundering of heavy footfalls. The men leap to their feet as a black rhino bursts into the firelight. The hunters fall over each other trying to get to their firearms or to scale any handy trees. The rhino charges to the fire and stamps on it, scattering the meat and burning branches in all directions. It came so fast that no one had time to grab a gun—they are still under the tree by the fire and some have slipped down and been trampled into the mud under the rhino's feet.

The rhino leaves as abruptly as it came, a trail of devastation in its wake. A burning log has rolled onto Sir Roland's sleeping mat and set his blankets smoldering. Water calabashes have been smashed, two guns ruined—one shotgun and Sir Roland's prized .577 Snider Enfield breech-loader. Sir Roland's tin coffee mug is flattened, his topee cracked like a boiled egg with a teaspoon. The meat has been stamped into the ground or tossed into the bushes.

Sir Roland is infuriated by the loss of his supper, the trampling of his gun and the crushing of his helmet. He is all for going after the rhino immediately, but the hunters are hungry and exhausted from long hours in the field.

And there is a deeper uneasiness.

"There is something strange about that bhejane," one of the hunters murmurs. "It's not a normal animal."

"Yes, and how did it know to trample Mahlekehlathini's special gun?"

"It's that one we tried to shoot today, but none of our bullets could touch it."

"Even Khanyiso could not track it, as if it can fly without leaving footprints. There is some witchcraft going on here."

Some of the hunters scoff at this, but none has the appetite to pursue an angry rhino at night. Daniel doesn't translate these misgivings to Sir Roland. He knows that such "heathen fiddle faddle" will annoy him and might push him to force the hunters to go out at once. He explains that the men are tired and hungry, and it'll be impossible to track the animal as the moon had not yet risen. Besides, the men are needed to repair the stockade where the rhino burst through it.

"We leave at dawn, then," Sir Roland says. "I always heard that these animals had a vicious disposition, but this beats everything. I'll happily dispose of any black rhinos we come across—their horns are worthless and this country will be better off without them. Daniel, make sure the guns are clean and ready and get ready yourself. We need all hands tomorrow."

By the time Daniel has finished making up a new bed for Sir Roland and getting the guns and equipment ready for the hunt in the morning, the others have finished repairing the stockade and are asleep. Sir Roland is sitting on the folding canvas stool beside the rekindled fire, smoking his pipe and drinking whisky. He calls Daniel over and offers him a drink.

Daniel perches on a tree stump.

"Thank you, sir, but I don't drink."

"Have a drink, boy! What are you, a maiden aunt at a church fair?"

He sloshes some whisky into a tin mug and passes it over.

"That'll put some hair on your chest. Cheers!"

Daniel obediently sips from the mug, grimacing as the burning liquor slides down his throat. Sir Roland usually tamps his anger down under a mask of bland imperturbability. But tonight, he is in a strange unpredictable temper.

"A right mess of things that wretched brute made this evening."

"Yes, sir."

"Bet you're eager to sink some lead into its cursed hide tomorrow, eh?"

"Yes, sir."

He laughs harshly. "Don't lie, boy. You hate killing things.

I've seen you out there. You go green about the gills and start swooning like a vicar's daughter. I just don't understand it. The sight of a slug downing a wild beast would fire the blood of any half–decent young fellow."

"I suppose hunting is not in my nature, sir."

"And what exactly is in your nature? Frankly, I've seen little to inspire me. I had hopes for you, Daniel. I was willing to embrace you as my son, but you've been a grave disappointment. You have no authority with the men, no ambition I can see beyond what your father wants for you..."

Daniel takes another sip of his whisky and stares woodenly at the fire. Sir Roland downs his own whisky, pours more into both mugs and fixes him with a calculating stare, as if assessing whether a lamb is grown enough to be worth slaughtering.

"This may come as a shock, Daniel, but in many respects, Moses is a far worthier candidate than you."

This is not so much a shock as quite unhinging. Is this the same Moses that Sir Roland considered dangerous? Has this hunting trip somehow opened Sir Roland's eyes to Moses' qualities? Does this mean that Moses will be going to England? And that he, Daniel, can pick up his bedroll and go home at last? But Sir Roland has not finished speaking.

"Moses may be a far worthier candidate than you," he says again, "but only you will be going to England."

Daniel stares at him blankly.

"I don't understand..."

"You are my cousin's child. I am duty-bound to support you, however poor your performance. But you'll have to apply yourself diligently to your studies. And, should you fail to meet the requirements of your masters, I won't continue to sponsor you."

Sir Roland stares at him expectantly. Clearly some thanks are anticipated, but Daniel is too bewildered to be grateful.

"But...why not Moses? He too is your cousin's child, and you said yourself he's a worthier candidate."

"He's not my cousin's child in any way I recognize. And, thanks to my cousin's misguided experiment, he is infected with an unshakeable conviction that the white man is no better than the black. I can see it in his eyes every time he looks at me. He could have been a real boon to the colonial cause, but your father has ruined him. His qualities might go far in an Englishman, but they're disastrous in a native. He is already a danger to the colony. Educating him further would make him deadly."

"But, Sir Roland...he's always done what you asked and more...he never raised a hand against his masters, even after being whipped for something he didn't do. He works harder than any of the others."

"He's sly, Daniel. And you too, if you deny that his so-called preaching was but an incitement to rebellion. He has been biding his time, pretending to be meek until he has an opportunity to strike. Even now, I've been told he continues to stir up the hunters against me.

"Moses has deceived you all—you, your mother, my poor foolish cousin Charles. I have written to tell him as much. You'd do well to turn your back on him. He's a bad influence on you."

Daniel shakes his head as if to dislodge Sir Roland's words.

"I beg your pardon, sir, but you have sorely misjudged him."

"You have all misjudged him. I know a man's character. My experience in Burma sharpened my eye for insubordination."

"He tended you...when you were sick. He stayed up all night...cleaned up after you..."

Sir Roland flinches.

"Of course, he did. It was in his interests to keep me alive. No, Daniel, your concern for him is misplaced. Look how he ingratiated himself in your father's esteem. Were you never angry that he stole the love and regard that was your birthright? When I read your father's letter, I was shocked at the glowing terms in which he described Moses, while finding so little to say about you."

Sir Roland reaches forward to grasp his shoulder. How large and sincere his eyes, how urgent his voice, how white his teeth in his dark beard.... Daniel stares back, bemused. His head is spinning from the whisky which he has drained without thinking—not helped by three days of no sleep and little food.

"Leave this so-called brotherhood behind you, Daniel," Sir Roland urges. "You're a soft-hearted, weak boy, susceptible to manipulation, and you can be sure that Moses will continue to exploit that. Leave him behind and go to England. Make something of yourself."

Daniel stands up, pulling away from Sir Roland's grasp.

"I can't go..."

"I beg your pardon?"

"I can't go to England. If Moses can't go—" he falters, as Sir Roland's eyes blaze. He forces himself to meet their searing gaze.

"Moses is my true brother, my best brother, and the only brother I have. If he can't go, then I can't go..."

Sir Roland stares at him silently for several seconds, then sits back on his canvas stool.

"Then you're a bigger fool than I took you for, and that's saying something. Sit down, my boy. There's something you need to understand about your brotherhood."

Daniel sits, because Sir Roland's eyes are so glittery and his voice is so cold. Sir Roland pours more whisky into both their mugs and raises one foot to rest across his other knee.

"Your father, and his father before him, were very holy, very full of principles about the brotherhood of man. Both of their careers in holiness were sponsored by my grandfather. And do you know where he got his money?"

Daniel shrugs. This conversation is so exhausting and there is barely any part of him that has not been consumed by the multiple deaths he has experienced, by the whipping of his brother, by the whole catastrophe. He can offer Sir Roland a mere sliver of himself—a fingernail perhaps, or an eyelash.

"From sugar plantations, sir," he intones wearily.

"From sugar, indeed. The new gold of the British empire. My grandfather had huge sugar estates in the Caribbean.

And who do you suppose toiled in the cane fields to make my grandfather so wealthy?"

"I don't know, sir."

"But you do know, Daniel—or you would if you'd been paying attention. Slaves! Slaves who were taken from Africa by force. Men, women and children, taken across the seas in slave ships and sold in markets. The slaves naturally did not want to work, but they were induced by the threat of whipping, of hanging or shooting if they ran away. It was a cruel system, no doubt, but this is how empires are built.

"My grandfather saw slavery as an evil necessity and made peace with God by paying for his son-in-law to be a priest and for his grandson and many other young boys to be missionaries. His generosity to the Mission Society granted Cousin Charles his posting. Were it not for slavery, you'd have never been born—your mother would never have settled for Charles without the lure of travel to Africa. And your so-called brother would've been left to die.

"You imagine that you live a blameless life, don't you, Daniel? But your life—and Moses' life—was only made possible by slavery."

The teeth come out again and leer at him from their dark cave. Sir Roland takes a gulp of whisky and leans back with the air of a man who has proved yet again the unassailable superiority of his perspective.

"So you see, my boy, a blameless life is quite impossible. Everywhere humans by their nature are tainted. We are at heart savage creatures, and if you think the Zulu are any more gentle than the English, speak to those tribes who've been vanquished by their impi. Charles himself, for all his preaching, is whining at the gates of the hard men now, begging that the power of the Zulu king may be broken so that he can have more kneelers in his pews. He knows that innocent people will die. No war sheds only the blood of soldiers.

"Many faults can be laid at my door, but I value honesty and will not cast a veil of prettiness over the affairs of men. The world is divided into the conquerors and the conquered, and you are fortunate to have been born a conqueror. We conquer with civility, we conquer with restraint. But, if need be, we conquer with cruelty too."

Something strange is happening to Sir Roland's face. His beard is growing and growing, it has spread itself all over him and is creeping along the ground towards Daniel's feet. His voice booms and fades, certain words leap out— *conquerors...savages...cruelty*—others disappear. His teeth, those square white teeth, gleam in the firelight as they snip and snap. Biting off lives, chewing up Moses and his dreams, chewing up Daniel, chewing up the campsite and Khanyiso and the hunters and the mat-bearers and camp skivvies and the trees and the rhinos and the vultures and the hyenas and everything that prowls around the fence and the baboons on the cliff and the frogs down by the river and even the crocodiles that sleep on the sandy banks...until at last, Daniel sees him for what he is:

"*Isiququmadevu*," he whispers.

He throws back the remaining whisky in his mug. His body is leaden, his lips numb, his head a wasps' nest. He

329

drags himself to his feet and stumbles away, even though Sir Roland roars, *"Sit down!"* and burns holes in his back with the flames of his eyes.

He longs to find Moses, to lie beside him and listen to his breathing until his vision clears and his mind steadies. But Sir Roland has eaten up his brotherhood and even now is sucking on its bones. All he can do is get away—away from Sir Roland; from the toxic version of himself that Sir Roland portrayed; from his own unwilling complicity in Sir Roland's monstrous intentions.

At the entrance of the camp, he falls to his knees and vomits. His confirmation cross swings free from his shirt and dangles below his face. *A mission supported by slavery....* He grasps it and rips it from his neck, snapping the chain.

He staggers to his feet, closes his eyes and breathes deeply, trying to steady the whirling in his head. His nostrils fill with a medley of odors—the sickly smell of the whisky he just threw up; the sharp scent of crushed imphepho and ufuthana leaves from the rhino's rampage through the bush; river water; mud. He opens his ears to the night sounds—the chorus of frogs and insects, wild dogs yipping on a distant hunt, the hyenas squabbling over the bones of Nolaka.

He becomes aware of high-pitched whistling voices close by, and the faint rustling of grass. He opens his eyes to see a small whirlwind stirring up the leaves a few feet beyond the stockade. *Ngilandele! Ngilandele!* the whirlwind sings. *Follow me.* He pushes open the makeshift gate and stumbles out of the camp into the shadowy night.

As he moves towards it, the whirlwind moves away. When he pauses, it pauses. He keeps on following it, dragging stiff reluctant limbs. His mind is a dense fog filled only with the whistling voices—and the conviction that if he yields to this numbing drowsiness and lies down, he will never rise again. He plods after his ephemeral companion, with no sense of how far or how long he is walking. Sometimes he loses it and stops, listening for a rustle, a tremor of vegetation. Then he spots the shiver of leaves in a nearby tree, as if the wind has come back for him.

The wind leads him to the great reed beds stretching out in a horseshoe bend of the Black Imfolozi. He hesitates at the edge of the dark tunnel, remembering Khanyiso's warning about the dangers of reed beds. The whirlwind seems to be waiting for him—he can see a flickering tremble in the reeds a few feet ahead. The high singing is all around him urging him on.

He steps into the reeds, and the whirlwind moves ahead. He winds through narrow channels under stars just visible in the narrow strip of sky above the pathway. The cloying pungency of rotting reeds is thick in his nostrils. Sometimes the reeds close over him, and he moves in utter darkness, guided only by the rustle ahead of him. He comes across black pools, gleaming in the half-light, and hears the soft splash of iguanas and crocodiles retreating into the dark water—he nearly trips over one he'd taken for a log. He begins to think he may be walking forever through these dank passages with their eerie stillness, the only sound the susurration of the whirlwind.

The gurgle of running water penetrates the stillness, growing louder until he finally emerges from the reeds onto the banks of the river. Besides the river is the python—no longer inside him but coiled in the mud and grown immense. It seems to fill the world, as the patterns on its coils bloom and fade in the dappled shadows of the trees. Its eyes are as dark as the back of the moon. "Kade ngikulindile," it whispers. *I have been waiting for you.*

He takes the incweba out of his trouser pocket and places the thong over his head. He removes his trousers, boots, and shirt, and lays them down. He is naked, as he was when he entered the world, before they molded him and made him their weapon. When his hand moves to the harness holding his hunting knife, he remembers the night that Moses gave it to him, as they waited for the jackal. The night of the blood pact.

His hand drops. The knife lies against his chest, cool in its sheath.

He approaches the python, and thrusts his hands into the earth beneath its coils. He takes out handfuls of dark, sticky mud and rubs it over his body.

He becomes alive in a way that he has never been alive. Beneath the coat of drying mud, his skin is a landscape of infinite sensation. His ears seem to swivel and twitch, capturing every sound—the twittering of the weavers, the soft whirring of their wings as they emerge from their roosts and nests; the sorrowful dirge of a woodland dove; a hippo family munching grass downriver. The high singing of the reed voices is gone. He has no thoughts. Only awareness.

The suffering of the animals that has clogged his veins over the past weeks drains into the earth. For the first time in years his mind is free from self-loathing and confusion, leaving only a clarity of purpose as crisp as a morning frost.

A thin band of light above the trees tells him that dawn is coming. He sniffs the air and sets off, jogging alongside the river. His feet have been softened by months of wearing boots, but a childhood spent barefoot has toughened his soles enough to withstand the sticks and stones underfoot. He runs for some time as the sun unpeels itself from the horizon into a red disc glowing through the tangled branches of the thickets, casting a roseate light on the rocky cliffs to his left. As he lopes along, he meets his dreams of the rhino running through light and shade. He feels the steady beat of its heart, the soft thud of its feet, and he knows that the rhino is in him.

MOSES

Moses lies dreaming, not for the first time, of the man with twin scars. They are out together, looking for something called the lightning bird. The man grasps his shoulders and shakes him, crying, *Why did you lose your incweba? Now we will never find it...*

He begins to punch Moses in the ribs. Please stop, Moses begs, and the man disappears, but the punching continues. Moses opens his eyes and looks up into the reddened face of Sir Roland. He is kicking him in the ribs.

"Wake up, you lazy laggard. Where is Daniel?"

Moses scrambles to his feet.

"I don't know, sir. I haven't seen him...is he not with you?"

"Obviously not. He's run off, somewhere, sulking. I had to get my own coffee...my guns are not ready...anyway, there's no more time to waste on that. We have to get after that rhino before it moves too far."

Icy dread runs down Moses' spine. He remembers Daniel's agitation on the day before, his brokenness.... *Oh Dani, what have you done?*

"But we have to look for him...he might be in trouble...or injured. We can't..."

"He'll come home soon enough. He's skulking out of sight because he didn't want to join the hunt today. Very well, we shall go without him. Jump to it, boy, we're leaving in five minutes."

As Sir Roland stalks off, Moses pulls on his boots and shirt. He grasps his gun, the gun that Daniel gave him seven years before. It's no match for a lion or a rhino and he doesn't have many slugs, but he has no intention of getting caught up with Shibela and the others. He moves hurriedly, skirting the knot of hunters handing out the guns and ammunition.

"Where are you going?" Khanyiso calls as Moses runs past.

"Daniel is missing. I'm going to find him."

"How will you track him?"

"I don't know."

Khanyiso picks up his gun and jogs after Moses.

"Khanyiso, you'll lose your wages, you can't—"

"Thula, Moses. I know what it is to lose a brother. You need me, you'll never be able to track him."

At the entrance to the stockade, Moses sees something glinting in the sun. He picks up Daniel's confirmation cross. So he did leave the camp. Did he break the chain?

He follows Khanyiso as he picks up Daniel's trail through footprints, flattened grass, disturbed ant nests, broken twigs. As they enter the dark reed tunnels, he is consumed by foreboding.

He knows that this is the end of his dream to go to England. He knew, in some deep part of him, that that dream was dead on that very first morning when Sir Roland had ignored his outstretched hand. He's always thought that a life where that dream was not manifest would be un-endurable. But to lose Daniel...to go through life without the brother who has been beside him from almost his first day of life...that was truly unbearable.

They move quickly through the reeds, calling as they go. The footprints are clear in the mud. It's unlikely that he'd have veered off the path into the dense growth. But as they pass a deep pool, they see the tail of a crocodile sliding into the water...could it have dragged Daniel down there, deep in the murk...?

But Khanyisa picks up a boot tread, and they carry on.

They pass through the reeds on the other side at last and follow the tracks down to the river. There, neatly folded, are Daniel's clothes beside a mud patch where some animal has clawed the mud.

A human animal, Khanyiso says. "I think it was Daniel."

"But why would he do that?

"Angazi, I don't know, my friend. But he has taken off his boots. Even I will find it hard to track him now."

"Daniel!" Moses screams again, his voice hoarse from shouting, from the lump in his throat, from fear. But the only response is a volley of alarm calls from gray lories in a nearby tree. Then silence.

DANIEL

Daniel sniffs the rubbing stump. He recognizes the scent of the black rhino that had come into camp the previous night. He runs on, following the scent and occasional spoor, easy to spot now as the sun climbs higher. He pauses to sniff its urine and later comes across a midden, the dung heaps left by rhinos to mark their territory.

The mud, cracking as it dries on his skin, protects him from the sun as it ascends and floods the landscape with dry winter heat. He leaves the river to follow the rhino's trail as it climbs a slope onto a ridge. He pauses to look out from the ridge, down at the horseshoe bends of the Black Imfolozi—white sand and dark water intertwined—snaking through grassland and thorn scrub. A massive herd of buffalo is crossing the river upstream; wildebeest and zebra graze together on an open grassy plain to the north east. The great reed beds stretch out in the distance, a waving sea of green from which rise the white skeletons of dead trees.

He sees new spoor in the red earth—boot tread and foot prints. He smells Sir Roland—sweat-stained cotton, pomade, gun oil and pipe tobacco—and the sweat and animal grease of the hunters.

He picks up their trail, which is like a high road of scents and markers, compared to the subtle path of the rhino. The trail takes him down the slope, through dense thickets that he negotiates by wriggling on his stomach. He passes two gunbearers unnoticed, screened by the bushes. As he comes through a stand of buffalo thorn, he hears Shibela's soft low whistle along the cadence of the words, Woza, nang' umkhondo—Come, here's the spoor. He creeps noiselessly forward, and looks through the tangled branches. Shibela, Sir Roland, and five hunters are standing together.

From behind, Sir Roland looks less like a monster. He looks almost human, someone who might weep for a child. Daniel's resolve flickers. But a high-pitched squeal of terror from the thicket drives out any thoughts.

The rhino is calling him for help.

The men spread out into the thicket that lies across the clearing. Sir Roland moves quickly from tree to tree, pausing to scan the thicket and surrounding bushes. The rhino is snuffling the air to get their scent. Sir Roland freezes. Daniel follows his eyes to the gray blur of the rhino visible through the branches—about fifty yards away. Too far for a good shot. Sir Roland might have tried with the Snider Enfield, but that was crushed by the rhino. The smooth-bore elephant gun, though more powerful at close range, is inaccurate beyond twenty paces.

Sir Roland takes cover behind the sturdy trunk of an umsinsi tree with a low branch and goes down on one knee. He rests the barrels of the gun on the branch, aimed at the rhino's shadowy bulk.

Shots are fired on the other side of the thicket—the other hunters are trying to flush the rhino out into the clearing.

The rhino throws up his head, confused by the scent before him and the sounds behind him. He charges a short distance into the clearing. He stands facing them, head lifted, trying to catch the wind. Sir Roland lowers his head to sight along the barrels and cocks the hammer.

The rhino calls to Daniel again, its voice shrill with terror...*inkonyane likabhejane!*

Energy floods Daniel's body, eliminating thought, eliminating hesitation. He pulls the knife from its sheath and charges out of the thicket. Sir Roland doesn't turn, so focused is he on the quarry before him. Daniel crashes into his back, knocking him off his feet, and drives the knife into his flesh between his shoulder blade and ribs. The gun fires wide as it falls.

As the knife grates against muscle and bone, Daniel is thrown back into his human body. He pulls out the knife and flings it away from him. His ferocity drains out, leaving him confused and enfeebled. His mind is a single howl of *What have I done?*

Sir Roland rolls over, throwing him off. Daniel tries to scramble away, but Sir Roland grasps him around his neck from behind and pounds his head with his fist. He tightens his grip, clamping Daniel's windpipe. He claws at Sir Roland's arm, but the grip is tightening, and the blood is roaring in his ear. A dark mist rises over his eyes as his body screams for oxygen.

How strange to be feeling his own death, after feeling the death of so many animals.

The earth shudders with pounding feet. A high-pitched squeal rips through the grass. Something slams Sir Roland's body hard against his, knocking the remaining air from Daniel's chest. He feels a sharp point pressing into his back as Sir Roland's grip is torn from his throat. He rolls away and kneels on the grass, sucking air into his winded lungs.

A scream makes him look back. Sir Roland is lifted on the rhino horn, his body hoisted on its snout as though he weighed no more than a bird. The rhino flings him onto his back. Sir Roland tries to roll away. But the rhino charges again and tramples his chest, huffing and blowing in rage. It runs straight over Sir Roland towards Daniel. Daniel falls back as the bloodied black horn blots out the sky above him, above the single red-rimmed eye. He waits to feel horn rake his flesh, the knees grind him into the earth.

But the rhino has gone. Its pounding feet fade in a volley of gunfire from the other hunters.

He pulls himself up onto his knees. Sir Roland is lying a few feet away, his chest a mess of blood and bone, his black beard trembling in the breeze. His eyes are wide open with disbelief. His mouth is moving, blood spilling into his beard, as he tries to form words. Daniel crawls to him, and bends to hear him speak. Sir Roland grasps his hair, as if to pull him towards his face.

"Glichhehhh...arrrgh...ur..." he says, releasing a string of unintelligible utterances, his breath bubbling through the blood of his shattered lungs. He is dying slowly and hard, protesting with everything he has left against this final indignity, and Daniel feels pity for him.

The other hunters run up and push him away. They kneel over Sir Roland, exclaiming and gesticulating. They shout at Daniel, and Shibela kicks him. It comes to him that the men will kill him for causing their umlungu hunter to die, for bringing trouble and depriving them of their wages. He doesn't much care. Dying seems more peaceful and simpler than anything else that might happen. But the others pull Shibela away.

Daniel gazes up at the trees spinning above him. The voices of the men are muffled and distant, as though he were flying high above—like the three vultures he can see circling in the depthless blue sky, drawn by the scent of blood and death. He thinks of the rhino running through light and shade. He hopes that none of the bullets touched him—that long after they have left this place, and Daniel has faced whatever retribution or regret he will have to face, the rhino will be here, rolling in cool mud and dreaming under fever trees, that the buffalo will be lying together in late afternoon glades, the sunlight glinting on their horns.

PART SEVEN
JULY 1979
EYE BROTHER
HORN

Moses stands looking out across the bluff, watching the dog trying to catch the flat-footed whelks before they dig themselves into the sand. The tide is out and a broad expanse of pale sand stretches out before him, transversed by the undulating tracks of waves. He wonders if you could calculate the gravitational force exerted on the tides by measuring their movement and then use that figure to calculate the weight of the moon. You'd have to find a way to isolate the gravitational pull of the sun, but perhaps you could calculate a total and allocate the weight, taking into account their relative size and distance from the earth. Not a simple calculation, but he's sure an equation might exist for it. If it doesn't, he's confident that he could develop it.

Moses is intrigued by the multitude of invisible forces governing our world, but he has never counted ghosts among them. Yet, when he turns back to the shore, there is Sir Roland with his sinister geniality, his terrible British benevolence, standing on the very spot he stood some eighteen months before and pronounced Moses "as black as tar." You can almost see the bristles of his beard, almost smell his pipe tobacco and pomade. It's not only Sir Roland's ghost, of course. They're all there, the ghosts of their former selves, Daniel and uMfundisi and Kazi and Moses, all washed and brushed for the occasion, glowing with eager expectation as they behold this man—who will indeed change their fortunes, but not in any way that they imagined.

The last time Moses saw Sir Roland, he was being sewn into a buffalo skin, his bloodied face a mask of incredulous outrage. They'd carried his corpse for ten days to the border authority at Nonoti, first on the shoulders of the bearers, then in the ox wagon—the men hadn't wanted to bury him, in case they were blamed for his demise. Moses can remember little of what he thought or felt as he walked along behind the wagon with that shameful reek of death growing stronger by the hour. Did he talk to Daniel? He must have, he supposes. Yet all he can recall is Daniel's silence, his face wrapped around some private catastrophe. And his own almost visceral aversion to his brother, so disbelieving and appalled by what he'd done.

He will never forget that morning with Khanyiso, calling and calling, his growing despair. In those frantic hours he'd imagined many terrible fates for his brother—being killed by a crocodile, dying by his own hand...

In no life could he have imagined him sinking a knife into Sir Roland.

Khanyiso had surmised that Daniel was following the

rhino from the faint signs of his barefoot trail, and they'd tracked it themselves and then picked up the trail of the hunters who were also tracking the rhino. Soon after midday they'd met the hunting party, carrying the corpse of Sir Roland. Daniel naked, caked with mud and blood, yet alive and walking tall with a strange wild light in his eye, emerging from the trees like an apparition. When he saw Moses, a sweet tenderness had flooded his face.

"My brother..." he cried. He'd raised his tethered hands to his chest, lifted off the object that was hanging around his neck and thrust it out to Moses.

"I have been keeping this for you," he said. "But you need it now."

Moses stared at the object in his hands, taking some seconds in his bewilderment to realize what it was.

His father's incweba.

On their last night together, they'd sat on the hill above the camp, looking down at the pale blur of the covered wagon. It was eerie in the moonlight, even if you didn't know what it contained. Moses needed words—words that could package the mess in the wagon into a sensible account that he could present to uMfundisi and Kazi. But Daniel had no such words. He said only that Sir Roland was an isiququmadevu monster who laughed in his beard while eating up the land and all that lived on it, human and non-human.

"The same might be said of most Englishmen in this country. Will you take your knife to all?" Moses replied. "Sir Roland's death will do nothing to deter the rest and will bring much trouble to the hunters, to all of us."

"He was destroying everything...you, me, the rhinos...
Everything. I had to stop him," Daniel said. "I didn't know
how else to do it. I'm sorry about any difficulties it may
bring. But he had to be stopped."

"A man lost his life, Dani. Was that truly your intention?"

"He had to be stopped."

What had happened to his brother that day? To the brother
so averse to violence he lamented the ants he inadvertently
crushed underfoot? Had Sir Roland's cruelty pushed him
beyond the bounds of sanity, beyond reason and restraint?
Certainly, in those last days at iMfolozi, Daniel had not
been well. Yet on their last night, he had shown no signs
of madness. His eyes were clear, his voice steady. He spoke
about his actions calmly, as if their logic was too obvious
to warrant explanation. But he expressed no remorse or
regret. He'd seemed unable to see that, whatever the provocation, it was an egregious act that would solve nothing
and bring only a deluge of troubles. Perhaps this unnatural
composure was a form of madness itself, evidence that he
had wandered into an unknown realm, governed by laws far
beyond Moses' comprehension.

Would he ever come back?

Moses left for uMzinyathi three days later—after Sir Roland
had at last been buried and the party interrogated by the
border agent at Nonoti. The agent seemed inclined to in-
carcerate them all but finally accepted Daniel's insistence

that he was exclusively responsible. Daniel would leave for Pietermaritzburg the next day, under police escort. When they said goodbye, Moses shook his brother's hand—how odd that was, as if they were merely acquaintances—and wished him a safe journey. Daniel thanked him and asked for his fondest regards to be conveyed to his parents. Their eyes had crossed briefly, full of horrified disbelief at this transaction. Then Moses mounted Sir Roland's horse and rode away.

It was the last time he'd touched his brother. Why didn't he embrace him? How he wishes he could erase that handshake by embracing him now. But the authorities have denied him visitation rights and the handshake is still with him, as if branded on his palm.

Moses rode to uMzinyathi, with no good account of what had happened or why, and with a letter addressed to uMfundisi/ the Reverend Whitaker that had been found amongst Sir Roland's possessions. *Don't give it to uMfundisi,* Daniel had said when it was found. *It contains only lies about you.* But Moses had carried that letter over hills and through rivers, stubbornly pursuing his course of honor in defiance of all Sir Roland's attempts to beat it out of him. He watched umfundisi read the letter, watched Sir Roland reach from the grave and sweep away any vestige of good regard his adopted father held for him.

uMfundisi lowered the letter and said, "You and Daniel have betrayed everything I taught you. I cannot recognize the children I raised. May God forgive you."

As uMfundisi** walked away, Moses said, "I knew what

347

that letter might contain. I brought it to you anyway. Will you not at least hear my case, Father?"

The Reverend Whitaker stopped. "What could you possibly say to redeem yourself? I gave you every opportunity and you squandered it. Worse still, it seems you corrupted my son. I believed in the purity of your soul; I believed that if I raised you in the light of the Lord Jesus you could not fail to reflect that light back. But clearly the stain of your birth is not so easily erased. Just as the snake bit the fox that carried it across the river, so have you bitten the hand the nurtured and fed you. I will pray for you, Moses, but it is for God to forgive you, not me."

Later, uMfundisi said that as the sole surviving male heir, he would inherit the Fitchley estate and could now afford to pay for Moses' education himself. But he did not feel it right that Moses should profit from Sir Roland's death. And, without Sir Roland's endorsement, Moses would not be accepted by the missionary society anyway. The Reverend Whitaker would shortly be returning to England to wind up the estate, but he'd make inquiries to help Moses find a position on another mission where he could "make a fresh start." If you truly humble yourself, he said, you may yet find your way back to the path of righteousness.

Sir Roland's letter was his last test of uMfundisi's loyalty. At least now Moses was left in no doubt. As he watched his father walk away after reading it, his legs almost buckled. He felt himself drowning in a wave of mingled terror and fury. It was all he could do not to run after him and fling himself at his feet. But the wave passed, and the thought it left behind was, *I am free.*

He would have been indebted to the Reverend Whitaker forever for giving him a life, obliged to be whatever he wanted him to be. But uMfundisi himself had now severed this bond.

He was free. Fatherless, penniless, with few prospects. But—from this bond at least—he was free. And free of the fear of uMfundisii's rejection, which had haunted him all his life.

He'd expected it for himself, yet he'd never imagined that uMfundisi would turn his back on Daniel too. But the Reverend Whitaker told Kazi that he felt it best that he cut off all contact with Daniel for the foreseeable future, although he would continue to pray for his soul. Much as it pained him, he said, his first duty was to God. He had to protect the reputation of the mission and retain the good will of the Church of England. He would write Daniel a letter explaining this and urging him to pray for forgiveness for his heinous crimes and for "bringing shame and disrepute to the missionary cause in Southern Africa." He said that while he understood that Kazi's womanly sentiment may make it difficult for her to be as resolute, it was his wish that she temper her support for Daniel, particularly in public, and that she return to England as soon as possible to avoid being tainted by association.

"I always believed that a wife should stand by her husband," Kazi said, when she recounted this to Moses. "I was willing to stand by him through fire, flood and disease, to follow him to the ends of the earth. But to close the door on your own sons when they need you most...that I cannot countenance."

Perhaps it was not that surprising. The Reverend Whitaker had always been an Old Testament man and had grown more rigid over the years. His God was the God who instructed Abraham to sacrifice Isaac. The God who was willing to force a man to choose between his faith and his children.

Moses knew he'd always be the loser in that contest. He hadn't realized that Daniel would be the loser too.

He and Kazi left for Pietermaritzburg soon afterwards. uMfundisi** arranged for them to stay with Bishop Macrorie. But as they rode away from uMzinyathi, Kazi announced that she'd made her own arrangements for them to stay at Bishop Colenso's mission, Ekukhanyeni.

"I'd rather reside with a so-called heretic than endure Macrorie's po-faced disapproval, no matter what the Pietermaritzburg biddies have to say about it," she declared.

No doubt the biddies have had plenty to say about it, and even more to say about the lurid details of the trial. Moses could almost hear the tongues wagging at a hundred dinner parties each night. Particular entertainment was provided by the testimony of Shibela, who described Daniel "flying out of the bush, naked and blackened by mud." He told the court that Daniel was a shape-shifting witch who'd conspired with the black rhino to kill Sir Roland.

Newspaper sales soared with the scandalous story of a missionary's son dabbling in witchcraft and stabbing his wealthy benefactor while in a state of indecency. Most commentators blamed the Whitakers' misjudgment in harboring and raising a Zulu child alongside their own. Dr. Galsworthy wrote to the *Natal Witness* that he'd warned the Reverend Whitaker of these dangers when he visited the mission thirteen years before. Moses imagines that the story also rippled through the imizi far and wide, but with a different cast of heroes and villains.

Moses and Khanyiso did their best to testify in Daniel's defense, but the jury found him guilty of the lesser charge of attempted murder (since it was the rhino that actually killed Sir Roland, and, as the judge helpfully explained to the court, a rhino could not be tried). Judge Langford gave him ten year's hard labor. A lenient sentence, the newspapers declared, but the judge explained that he took Daniel's youth and good breeding into account.

Also taken into account was the "likelihood" that he acted under the "pernicious" influence of Moses. Sir Roland's journal, which was presented as evidence to establish Daniel's motive, described Moses as "devious," "of violent disposition," and vengeful toward Sir Roland who'd "disciplined him for assaulting a manager." It also described his "unhealthy power" over his weak-willed brother. The journal revealed that Moses would not be offered sponsorship because further education would only increase his capacity to threaten the colony—this, the defense proposed, was what drove Daniel, under the influence of Moses, to take revenge. No doubt they'd have had Moses in the dock alongside Daniel, but even they could find not a shred of evidence to justify this. However, the white citizens of Pietermaritzburg did not let that deter them from cursing, spitting at, or jostling Moses on the courtroom steps or wherever else they found him.

Enough of these ghosts! Moses whistles to the dog and walks away from the place where he'd first met Sir Roland. He tries to distract himself by the goings on at the port. The Union RMS Durban will be leaving for Southampton in the morning, and there is much activity to get it loaded up for the journey. Despite the war in the north, it seems that trade is continuing unabated. Wagons bearing crates of sugar, ivory, coffee, tea, horns and pelts are crowding the beachfront, and workers are off-loading cargo and carrying it out to the boats to be rowed to the ship. An endless outpouring of the riches of Africa flowing into British coffers. And bringing in return more British overseers to squeeze the land and its people even harder. The whole colonial enterprise is an isiququmadevu monster, he thinks. But who will ever slay that beast?

A ragged knot of British soldiers has gathered by the customs shed. They look young, no older than him, and all are wounded—a bloodied bandage around a crown, an arm in a sling, one on crutches with his lower leg gone. Sliced and diced for queen and country. Their red jackets are torn and battle-worn, their boots scuffed. As he passes, one says something to the other, and they all laugh—loud, defiant guffaws. Mutilated as they are, they count themselves his victor, but their laughter betrays a brittle edge to their bravado, their eyes are shuttered against their memories.

He supposes they are the lucky ones. He hasn't heard reliable numbers, but several hundred of their countrymen fell to Zulu spears—and even greater numbers of black men from Natal, amakhafula who marched with the British, and died at Isandlwana and on the other battlefields. Not least, he has heard, because the British officers were reluctant to furnish them with ammunition. He wonders what made them go to war against their fellow Africans—fear of defying the British? Or a desire to settle old scores? Many of their families had suffered defeat at the hands of Mpande and Dingane's izimpi. They must have been bitter defeats indeed to make them fight alongside their colonial masters. But perhaps they had little choice.

Yet these casualties are dwarfed by the thousands of amaZulu killed or dispossessed, their homesteads burnt, the women violated, their cattle lost or stolen. What became of the boys he grew up with, Peter and Solani and the others from the mission? Or his twin brother? His shadow half, who'd lived the life that Moses might have lived? Had he fought the British soldiers at Inyezane or Isandlwana, at Rorke's Drift or Kambula, at Gingindlovu or Ulundi or Eshowe? Had he survived or had he bled out under darkening skies, watching the stars coming out over Zululand?

He thinks so often of that brother now. Of the life he might have led, the life that Moses had been denied. How, as an infant, he'd have been held in the smoke of burning protective charms such as leopard whiskers, lion claw and powdered meteorite—and introduced to his ancestors through the *imbeleko* ceremony and into manhood through the *ukuthomba* ritual. How he'd have known nothing of Lord Jesus or steam engines, but would've been able to recite his ancestral heritage going back several generations, how he'd have joined a regiment at sixteen, would have been trained to fight and to kill, to serve the king.

He thinks of the fierce love and loyalty that the children at the mission showed towards their families. How his grandmother risked her own life to keep him safe, gave up her family and community to watch over him at the mission, how his father had tried to protect him with the incweba. He never had the opportunity to choose his twin brother's life, he doesn't know how to weigh it against his own. *A life lived in darkness,* the Reverend Whitaker used to say of Zulu lives. *Born in a hard cradle and destined for a cruel grave.* Perhaps. But he'd have grown up without feeling he had to spend his life overcoming the shadow of his birth.

Moses touches the incweba that he now wears around his neck. It has taken him some time to forgive his brother for keeping it from him. Still, at least Daniel did keep it and now he has this tenuous link to his biological father and family. Both his fathers sacrificed him for their beliefs, but he has grown more forgiving of his Zulu one.

He recalls how Joseph described his night in that homestead, how they'd been so ravaged by the drought that they had no food to spare, how they were eking out an existence on the bulbs of arum lilies and porridge made from wild figs. The custom to kill the second twin seemed so cruel, but in such pressing times it would have been hard to nourish one infant, let alone two. Perhaps there was a tough economy underlying the practice. How grateful his grandmother must have been when Joseph offered an alternative to that terrible course of action.

Joseph is with them at Ekukhanyeni, along with Thuli, Hlali and Dawid. He has offered to go back to that district to try to find out more. But it would be dangerous for Joseph to go now—this is not the time for amakholwa to go about the devastation of Zululand in their trousers and shoes, asking strange questions about a boy who should never have been allowed to live. One day, when the time is right, Moses knows he will make that journey himself.

UMzinyathi has gone, burnt to the ground, because the Reverend Whitaker allowed a British garrison to commandeer it. Everyone had left by then, fleeing in terror from the British and from Cetshwayo's armies that would follow. Images of the burning mission haunt him—he pictures the wooden Jesus looking out over the flames, ash falling like snow on His crown of thorns, the mission bell ringing in the wind for a congregation that will never come. He remembers the night that he "called" the lightning to strike the bell tower and the fire that followed—the terror of his own thrilling power to destroy. He feels little regret for the place, but is sad for this betrayal of the Magwaza clan who treated the missionaries with such kindness and respect, even if few were converted.

A strong salt breeze is blowing off the sea, dispelling the images of the burning mission station, of blood-drenched battlefields and booming canons. He has walked some distance, and the cries of the wagon loaders have been drowned out by the crashing of the waves. He stands watching the sandpipers skittering on the shoreline, smiling at the dog's frantic and futile efforts to catch them. Before coming to Pietermaritzburg, he'd gone to Hanbury Estate to pay the hunters and to fetch the dog—he couldn't leave Daniel's beloved companion to the mercy of the Wyeths. He's a somewhat absurd creature, with those short legs and huge ears. But he makes Moses laugh and helps him to imagine that Daniel is around somewhere, just out of sight. Moses often walks the dog up and down outside the Burger Street jail, calling him loudly and playing with him to make him bark, in the hope that Daniel might hear.

He can hardly bear to think of Daniel locked up behind those walls for ten years. How strange to be going on with his life without his brother beside him—he feels constantly diminished, as if missing a limb. He worries about him—about his mental composure and whether he is bullied by the other prisoners. But Kazi says that Daniel has acquired a certain steeliness, which enables him to endure. She says the rumors about him being a murderous shape-shifter who consorts with witches have made him somewhat fearsome. The others mostly keep their distance. The chief warden has taken a liking to him and allows him to spend most of his days working in the governor's garden, rather than building roads with the rest of the prisoners.

She says he's never explained his actions to her, but he seems at peace with what he did and insists that he does not regret it. He says he did what he had to do and would do it again in the same circumstances.

How absurd and cruel that Moses is not allowed to visit or even to send letters. How he wishes he could see Daniel now, to erase that handshake with a hug. To see for himself how his brother is looking.

And to tell him that he is going to England.

He is going to England. It still feels so unreal, after all these years of longing, after all the pain he and Daniel suffered for it. But now it really is happening.

At first, Sobantu, as Bishop Colenso is affectionately known, tried to discourage him. Moses has been teaching at the school and helping with letters to the queen protesting the war mongering of Sir Bartle Frere and Lord Chelmsford. Sobantu said that Moses was needed here, for he could do so much good work teaching science and mathematics at the mission station and promoting justice for the indigenous people. He said that it wasn't easy to be a black man in England—and was growing harder, thanks to the pernicious views on racial inferiority perpetrated by the likes of Thomas Huxley and Sir Francis Dalton.

But when he saw that Moses was resolved to pursue his ambitions, he agreed to help him. He told him that some black people had succeeded in England against the odds— in the last century, a Jamaican of African descent named Francis Williams studied at Cambridge University. Charles Darwin himself learnt taxidermy from a freed slave called John Edmonstone, who was employed by the University of Edinburgh. He said if anyone could succeed, it would be

Moses. He threw himself into the project to seek sponsorship, and at length found a benefactor to pay his passage, and a doctor in Oxford who was willing to take Moses on as an apprentice. Perhaps once there he could attend lectures at the university.

A hard road, no doubt, and relying much on good will. Well, Sir Roland had warned him against having ideas above his station. Moses knew better than to imagine it might be easy. And some days he finds himself holding his incweba, feeling its mysterious potency, and knowing deep inside that this is what holds the key to his salvation. That the incweba will lead him back to his origins. That he will cross the sea, only to discover that his elusive sense of self lies not in the London streets but in the homestead where he was born, near the banks of the Imfolozi. His fingers reach for the incweba again now. As he touches it, it suddenly comes to him why his father gave it to him. Not to keep him safe from the witchcraft of Zulu abathakati, as he had always assumed. But to protect him from the more insidious and dangerous witchcraft of the abelungu, the white wizards from across the sea.

To enable him to be an owl raised by chickens, that yet knows itself to be an owl.

He knows all too well how much he needs that protection. But he knows too that there is a hungry, striving part of himself that will never be satisfied if he doesn't cross the seas and learn everything he can learn.

Sir Roland was right about one thing. Educating him is dangerous for the colony, and Moses is resolved to make himself as dangerous as possible. To learn what he can, not only about chemistry and physics but also about the subtle and not so subtle science of resistance. And to come back and share this knowledge with any who are suffering under the British yoke.

Whatever hardships England might bring, the hardest part now is leaving his brother here in jail. Kazi has reassured him that Daniel will be fine, that she will stay at least for the duration of his prison sentence and keep him in good spirits. She says that when she told him that Moses was going to England at last, his face had lit up, and he laughed freely for the first time that she'd seen since Sir Roland's death.

Kazi has never asked Moses about what happened at Hanbury Estate and on their hunting expedition; about his theories on why Daniel might have attacked Sir Roland. He is relieved. So much has exploded beneath their feet, it seems wise to tread softly. Still, the questions hover, and he supposes that someday the conversation will happen. Truly, though he could not have told her what was going on in Daniel's mind that day. He doesn't know and perhaps he never will.

Astral bodies are governed by the laws of physics, yet human behavior follows its own erratic course. Moses believes that all mysteries of life can be captured in the right equation, but he has yet to formulate one for his relationship with Daniel. It's a complex thing, an impossible thing, hovering between opposing forces, countering them with some powerful force of its own. A force that has endured, despite Sir Roland's best efforts to destroy it, despite the weight of history, despite the fury of the colonial powers.

A force that he knows will endure.

He turns back towards the harbor and contemplates the Union RMS Durban, a low-slung twin-masted craft that will be his home for the next three weeks—time enough, he hopes, to get the chance to see the engine room and learn something of the mechanics of the ship. Other passengers are gathering on the shore, bringing their trunks and boxes to be loaded ahead of their departure. But he is traveling only with a small valise, which he'll carry with him when he embarks tomorrow.

He doesn't need much—a few clothes, a few books, notebooks and pens. And five things from the people he values most: the incweba from his father, the imbeleko his mother wrapped him in; the string of beads that Gogo gave him; the Annual Register that Kazi gave him when he went to KwaDuduza. And, folded into this, Daniel's first drawing of the eye and the horn and the spider that Daniel once assured him is a portrait of Moses. He found it among their things at uMzinyathi.

He doesn't think that Daniel will begrudge him this drawing, which seems to offer a formula to capture something essential about his brother. Eye brother horn. An eye to recognize his brothers, be they human, plant or beast, and a horn to defend them against the monsters of the world.

He has left Daniel a gift in exchange for the drawing—Kazi says she'll find a way to get it to him. It's the clay rhino that Gogo gave Moses for his sixth birthday. Daniel always coveted that rhino, even after it was broken, and Kazi carefully glued the horn back in its place...

Moses pauses to whistle to the dog—which reluctantly leaves its pursuit of the sandpipers—then turns and quickens his pace back to the port. He is leaving in the morning, and there is much to be done.

ACKNOWLEDGEMENTS

A novel is never the work of one author. So many people, alive and dead, played a role in the creation of this story, some through just a chance remark, others through hours of invested engagement. Space does not allow for thanking them all, but some deserve particular mention.

Massive thanks are due to the team at Catalyst Press, for believing in this book and investing so much expertise and dedication to making it the best it can be. In particular Jessica Powers, Lee Byrd, SarahBelle Selig and Ashawnta Jackson, and Karen Vermeulen for a great cover.

A special thanks to, my dear friends Therese Boulle and Sicelo Mbatha. Therese's infinite wisdom guided me through the agonies of multiple drafts, difficult feedback, and my manifold insecurities. Sicelo has been a constant source of inspiration, helping to set up interviews, accommodating me at his home in rural Zululand, opening my eyes to the intricacies of the iMofolozi wilderness and answering my queries about Zulu history, beliefs and cultural practices with tireless patience.

Thanks to Sandile Ngidi and Professor Adrian Koopman for help with translation, insights into Zulu knowledge and belief systems, and guidance on cultural sensitivity issues. Any missteps are entirely my own doing.

Thanks to all the other readers who ploughed through clumsy early drafts and provided the insights and feedback I needed to help me hone the story. In particular, Joanna, Luca, Gavin and Michael Evans, Jenifer Shute, and Margot Lawrence.

For helping me to understand that the poaching of rhinos is a manifestation of a long history of dispossession, I thank particularly Baba Gumede, but also Richard Mchunu, Baba Mangethe, Siphesihle Ncgobo, Sabelo Msweli, Bonangiphiwe Mbanjwa, and Sabelo Mdlalose,

For insights into the Anglo-Zulu wars and the British occupation of Zululand, thanks to Thulani Khuzwayo.

Thanks to Canon Cyprian Mncwango of the KwaNzimele mission for so generously sharing his knowledge of the mission's history and insights into its relationship with the local communities, as well as making the library available for my research.

Finally, heartfelt love and gratitude to my life partner Michael, who stands by me through my rashest under-takings and makes everything possible.

A NOTE ON SOURCES

The Umzinyathi mission in the novel is based very loosely on the KwaNzimele mission in KwaMagwaza, but the story is entirely fictitious and the characters unrelated to anyone associated with the mission. However, I drew heavily on the diaries of the nineteenth century missionaries and their wives who lived there to provide an understanding of the context. I am grateful for these and other diarists who recorded their experiences—in particular those missionaries who made the effort to learn isiZulu, to record its vocabulary and grammar, and to document the medicinal knowledge, and religious and cultural beliefs and practices of the Zulu people during the colonial era. These records provide a rich resource, notwithstanding the bias of the missionaries' perspective and the limits this bias might have imposed on their comprehension. A special thanks also to those who have spent hours digitizing these historical texts and making them available through websites such as Internet Archives.

It would take pages to list all the texts I consulted, but a highly selective bibliography is included below for interested readers. Some key modern texts are included.

Selective Bibliography

1. Axel-Ivar Berglund *Zulu Thought-Patterns and Symbolism*, Publisher : Indiana University Press; Indiana University Press edition (October 22, 1989).

2. Barter, C. *Alone among the Zulu: account of Catherine Barter's travels to Zululand in 1855.* Reprinted by Killie Campbell Africana Library Publications, 1995

3. Barter, Charles. *The Drop and the Veld or Six Months in Natal*, William S. Orr and Co., London, 1852 [Wonderful detail about daily life in the colony, hunting, farming, ox wagons, social mores, clothing etc..]

4. Bryant, A.T *Zulu Medicine and Medicine-men* Reprinted from 'Annals of the Natal Government Museum', Vol. II, Part 1, July, 1909 (Internet Archive).

5. Bryant, A. T. *The Zulu Cult of the Dead. Man,* Vol. 17 (Sep., 1917), pp. 140-145 Published by: Royal Anthropological Institute of Great Britain and Ireland.

6. Callaway, H.
   1. *Nursery tales, traditions and history of the Zulus in their own words with translations into English*, 1870, Trubner & Co, London 1868.
   2. *The Religious System of the amaZulu in their own*

words with translations into English, 1870, Trubner & Co, London.

7. Bishop John Colenso

1. *First steps of the Zulu Mission*, London, Society for the propagation of the gospel, 1860.

2. *Three Native Accounts of the visit of the Bishop of Natal in September and October 1859 to Umpande (Sic) King of the Zulus; with explanatory notes and literal translation and a glossary of all the Zulu words employed in the same.* Third Edition. Printed by Magema, Mubiand co. Published by Vause, Slatter, & Co, Pietermaritzburg and Durban, 1901.

3. *Ten weeks in Natal first tour of visitation among the colonists and Zulu of Natal*, Cambridge, Macmillan & co 1855.

8. Dlamini, Paulina. *Servant of Two Kings*, Killie Campbell Africana Library Publications/ UKZN 1986. [Nomguqo Dlamini served King Cetshwayo, later becoming a Christian and changing her name to Paulina.]

9. Drummond, W.H. *The Large Game and Natural History of South and South-East Africa.* From the journals of the Hon. W. Drummond. Edmonston and Douglas, Edinburgh 1875. [Drummond provides beautiful details of the landscape and animals, and particularly vivid accounts of how he shot most of the animals he encountered.]

10. James Stuart; Colin de B Webb; John B Wright, *The James Stuart archive of recorded oral evidence relating to the history of the Zulu and neighbouring peoples*, Pietermaritzburg : University of Natal Press, 1976 [a comprehensive record of oral testimony provided by Zulu individuals during the late 19th and early 20th century].

11. Koopman, Adrian. *Zulu Names* University of Natal Press, Pietermaritzburg, 2002.

12. Krige, E.J. *The Social System of the Zulus* Shuter & Shooter, Pietermaritzburg 1981 [originally published in Great Britain 1936].

13. Masondo, Sibusiso. *Indigenous conceptions of conversion among African Christians in South Africa* J. Study Relig. Vol.28 n.2 Pretoria 2015.

14. *Mission Life among the Zulu - a memoir of Henrietta, wife of Rev. R. Robertson*, Published by Bemrose & Sons, London, 1875. [Recorded life on the mission in KwaMagwaza.]

15. Samuelson, L.H. *Some Zulu Customs and Folk-Lore* London, the Church Printing Company, Burleigh Street, Strand, WC, 1912.

16. Tyler, J. *Forty years among the Zulus*, 1891, by Rev Josiah Tyler, a missionary based in Zululand. Congregational Sunday-School and Publishing Society, Boston and Chicago, 1891.

17. Wilkinson, A,M *A Lady's Life in Zululand and the*

Transvaal During Cetewayo's Reign: The Experiences of a Missionary in 19th Century South Africa by Annie Margaret Wilkinson. Originally published in 1882, Published by Leonaur 2012 [Recorded life on the mission in KwaMagwaza.]

18. Zulu, Prince Bongani Kashelemba. *From the Lüneburger Heide to Northern Zululand A history of the encounter between the settlers, the Hermannsburg missionaries, the amaKhosi and their people, with special reference to four mission stations in Northern Zululand (1860 - 1913)* Masters Thesis, University of KwaZulu-Natal, 2002.

CPSIA information can be obtained
at www.ICGtesting.com
Printed in the USA
JSHW080155121222
34699JS00002B/2